D0199326

"*Lost Gods* is fresh, fierce, and lush with
lands and mythology of ancient Africa a̶n̶d̶ ̶t̶h̶e̶ ̶M̶i̶d̶d̶l̶e̶ ̶E̶a̶s̶t̶.
Cameron Johnston, author of The Traitor God

"*Lost Gods* is a fully immersive experience which made me
a fan again. It made me seriously take my time, soak in its
prose, get lost in this fully realized, rich and vital world, and
get whisked along in its adventure. Micah Yongo pays respect
to his elders, like Charles Saunders, while defining a space
for himself in the pantheon of great sword & sorcery (sword
& soul!). He is a griot, a true storyteller, coming into his own."
*Maurice Broaddus, author of the Knights of Breton Court
trilogy and* The Usual Suspects

"Fast-paced and intriguing... with an African inspired setting
that makes a refreshing change."
Anna Smith Spark, author of The Court of Broken Knives

"Micah Yongo invigorates the epic fantasy genre with
his original and accomplished voice in the striking and
throroughly enjoyable *Lost Gods*."
Adrian Tchaikovsky, Arthur C Clarke Award-winning author of
Children of Time

"*Lost Gods* is a tense, complex fantasy thriller that keeps the
reader guessing until the very end."
Mike Brooks, author of the Keiko series

"There's a lot of lore here, beneath the skin, and for lore junkies
like me, that's pretty much irresistible. So a big thumbs up
from me, and I'm going to keep an eye on Micah's career."
This is My World

MICAH YONGO

Lost Gods

WITHDRAWN

ANGRY
ROBOT

ANGRY ROBOT
An imprint of Watkins Media Ltd

20 Fletcher Gate,
Nottingham,
NG1 2FZ
UK

angryrobotbooks.com
twitter.com/angryrobotbooks
Who would be king

An Angry Robot paperback original 2018

Cover by Larry Rostant
Set in Meridien by Argh! Nottingham

Distributed in the United States by Penguin Random House, Inc., New York.

Angry Robot and the Angry Robot icon are registered trademarks of Watkins Media Ltd.

ISBN 978 0 85766 737 3
Ebook ISBN 978 0 85766 738 0

Printed in the United States of America

9 8 7 6 5 4 3 2 1

For the dreamers...

"How last unfold
The secrets of another world, perhaps
Not lawful to reveal?"

JOHN MILTON, *PARADISE LOST*

One
BROTHERHOOD

"Look," Josef whispered. "There."

Neythan looked to where he pointed. The camp was less than a mile away. He could see the evening fires winking through the trees of the forested valley beneath them like light through a basket.

"I see it," Neythan said.

"Good. Good… I'll circle round for a way down. You stay here. Patience is the way."

"Patience is the way."

Neythan watched Josef go, the mist rolling up ghostlike from the basin below. It was still warm, quiet but for the croaking of insects and the murmur of the stream. A night like any other, save that he was to kill a man. The price of Brotherhood.

In truth, it had been just as Master Johann had said – no chance to plan, barely time to get ready, scrambling from their beds at news from Arianna and tumbling the same hour into the forest's knotted dark to find her. Should be grateful, Neythan supposed. They could be skulking about a cave by night, or down a canyon with only the moon for help. He'd heard tales of such from Tutor Hamir and Yulaan back at Ilysia, of boys his age on their first outing not making it back. But then with Hamir you never knew when he was telling the truth. The only thing he'd said before they left that Neythan knew he meant was, "The first time is always hardest."

"There's a way down."

Neythan looked up as Josef came trotting back toward him along the ridge. "Where?"

"Along the cliff, a half-mile. Steep though."

"How steep?"

"It'll do."

"You're certain?"

"It'll do, Neythan."

Neythan looked back along the ridge. There wouldn't be much time. The others were probably already in place. "Alright." He looked back to Josef, saw the calmness there, and nodded to himself. "Alright... Let's go."

By the time they made their way down the escarpment the campfires were dampening. The sounds of the camp itself – the ribald laughing, the chatter, the faint noise of bells and strings – continued to roll on as Neythan and Josef worked their way through the forest.

By the third watch they'd reached the settlement's edge and sat watching the camp from the long grass, Neythan fingering his crossbow nervously, two quarrels lodged taut against the whipcord. He glanced up at the half moon peeping from the clouds. Sweat prickled along his hooded brow, trailing down the groove of his spine. He felt Josef's hand on his shoulder.

"It's time, Neythan."

Neythan breathed deep and slid the crossbow up against his armpit beneath his smock. He removed his hood and stood, leaving Josef in the bushes, and began to walk, alone, toward the camp's clearing.

The space was a brief and grassless glade as wide as a tanner's yard. Gatherers had set a shelter on either side by the trees, no more than a shack's wood-roofing propped on log poles roughly a man's height, and between the two a sort of platform, overlaid with wool and what looked like bearskin and cowhides. Probably the altar. Neythan came slowly alongside the shelter nearest and leant against the beam, peering in at the crowd. One or two peered back.

"You have lingerweed?" a young woman called to him, slurring. "You have more wine?"

Neythan shook his head.

The woman frowned and waved him off.

Neythan scanned the gathering. There'd likely be guardsmen among them, armed soldiers, perhaps even a prince or two from the crown city, all for Governor Zaqeem, a king by any other name, or so it was said. Since there were no true kings save those in scribes' tales Neythan had never much liked the saying, but here, now, with the clamour of flesh and wine and finery, he was beginning to see its meaning.

Men and women wore armlets of brass and held silver goblets, dancing and laughing. The tart smell of wine filled the air like incense, mingling with the smoke of damp logs. There were no servants here, only rich men without their aides, just as Master Johann had said.

Neythan continued to watch the crowd and saw two young girls, neither one above seven years old, by the altar, studying the women as they danced. He finally spotted Arianna standing as part of the throng, dressed in fine linen, and began to walk toward her. He approached the altar where a turbaned old woman in scarlet was chanting with arms lifted to the sky. He saw Arianna's eyes meet his, saw her acknowledge him with her stillness. Then he saw her reach up, cupping the jaw of a silver-haired man beside her and drawing his lips onto her own.

He was the one.

Neythan let the crossbow slide from the crook of his armpit until he could feel the axel touch his fingertips, its coiled length against his forearm. He could hear himself breathing now, could hear the steady dull underwater chug of his own heart. The man Arianna had kissed – and thereby revealed as the governor of Qadesh, Zaqeem son of Tishbi – was gesturing behind to one of the young girls. The scarlet-clad priestess brought her forward, then made signs over her as others came to lift her, limp and without struggle, onto the altar, laying her on the cowhides like an upended doll.

The gatherers were shouting now, all of them on their feet. The governor smiled as the drumbeat doubled. The dancers and crowd whipped into a frenzy, staring at the child on the altar as the scarlet priestess approached with a flaming stave in her hand.

The crossbow fell fully into Neythan's hand. He lifted it level with the governor as the axel rolled and snapped into place, the whipcord flexing, the arrow ready. The sharp flinthead peeped above the sightline like a curious onlooker as he squinted along the quarrel's shaft. There was a slight tremor to his elbow, but that was alright – the first time's always hardest. *Just breathe through it. Be still, the way you've been taught.*

He heard the splash of oil as the priestess doused the child on the altar. Around him, the congregants were shouting and screaming even louder. *Be still. Breathe. Patience is the way.* The priestess was coming forward, ready to light the sacrifice, the din of the crowd growing louder, deafening, wordless. *Be still. Be still.*

And then... Arianna.

Neythan watched as she stepped in front to obstruct his view. She turned again to the governor, reaching up slowly, gently, as though to touch him – and then, as he dipped his head toward her, she drew her hand across his throat from side to front with a thumb-blade.

The man's head lolled violently as his blood leapt over the heads of those nearby. He went down gagging, pulling at the cloaks of those closest. The screams were immediate, distracting even the priestess, who paused with stave raised above the child on the altar. Neythan saw Josef's arrow thud into the meat of her breast as she turned toward the commotion, snapping her shoulder back as she fell into the mob.

And then everyone was running. Pot-bellied men scampering half-naked into the bushes, others rushing back from the altar to the shelter's corners for refuge, women squealing, bodies bumping, feet trampling as the gathering scattered. Cinders gusted upwards, luminous dust glinting red-gold against the night as a beefy man tumbled headlong into the campfire. Neythan went wading in, shoving his way through the fleeing crowd to find the girl. By the time he reached the altar the camp was almost empty, abandoned, the gatherers now scattered into the forest. A middle-aged man squatted in the corner of the far shelter, trembling in a thin cloak. The rest were gone, running through the moonlit undergrowth where Daneel and Yannick would be waiting.

He found the girl sitting behind the altar, rocking on her seat and humming tunelessly to herself whilst Arianna stroked her hair. The girl's eyes were still and empty, her expression as slack as a corpse. She wouldn't stop rocking.

"No need to thank me," Arianna said, looking up at him. "Had you waited any longer she'd be no more than roasted beef."

"I was about to do it."

Arianna rose to her feet, feigning a frown, before stepping toward him and smiling sourly. "Of course you were." She patted Neythan twice on the cheek and winked before walking away.

It was probably the thing Neythan found most annoying about her, how smug and dismissive she could be. As though the world owed her a kiss on the toes. Neythan was about to tell her that when out of the corner of his eye he saw the trembling man under the shelter rise to his feet, swaying and staggering as he did so. Maybe it was the anger from Arianna's barb, maybe it was something else, but by the time Neythan turned to see what the man was holding, he had, with barely a thought, levelled and loosed his crossbow, and in almost that same instant, watched the quarrel split the man's neck and lodge in his throat.

A perfect mark.

The dagger the man had been readying to hurl in Arianna's direction slid from his hand and clanked in the dust. The man took a step, pawed impotently at the shaft in his throat, and then collapsed.

Arianna turned and looked at Neythan.

Neythan stared at the man he'd felled.

No one spoke.

When Neythan eventually went to stand over him the man was already gone, his blood a dark puddle to one side of his slackened face. The eyes were half-open, everything they'd ever known or hoped now irrevocably expunged. Null. Forgotten. Although that wasn't really what unsettled Neythan. It was like the time he'd feared crane flies as a child, something about the way they'd fly, their legs dangling, like tiny drunken ghouls – until one night Yulaan had taken one, put it down the back of his smock and held him down. He'd screamed and kicked and wriggled until slowly realizing he couldn't feel it, not its dangly legs scrambling against his skin, nor its wings fluttering, nor any pain. Nothing. And that was what puzzled him now, this absence of feeling he'd expected to feel. His first time killing a man and he felt nothing. No fear. No joy. Nothing.

When Daneel and Yannick came wandering out from the forest's shadows an hour later the numbness was still there. Daneel, breathing hard, glanced at Neythan and then studied the slumped body of the governor first.

"So, this is him…" He then looked over at the dead priestess by the altar. "This one… I saw another just like her in the forest." He craned his neck for a better look. "No… Slightly younger maybe. Sister perhaps. Ran like a gazelle."

"So says the slug of the snail," Josef said, wiping his sword on the oil-drenched cowhides whilst Yannick stood off to the side, watching Neythan. Yannick flicked his hand and frowned, signing to him. Neythan nodded and shrugged back. He was fine.

"I mean it," Daneel said. "The woman was as quick as the wind. I had to use my sling to slow her." He turned to Neythan, glanced again at the governor's body, and smiled. "But what does it matter now? What matters is you got him, eh, Neythan? Your first. Governor Zaqeem."

"Actually, Arianna did that," Josef said as he came and stood next to Neythan.

Daneel's smile flattened. "Oh."

"Yes. Oh."

"But he did kill another," Arianna said. She gestured to the body slumped by the corner of the shelter, her gaze still on Neythan.

"That so?" Daneel put his hand on Neythan's shoulder. "So then you *have* done your first. Good. Finally. Well done. The first is always hardest."

Two
ILYSIA

A week later Neythan stood in the Forest of Silences staring up at the dry, fruitless boughs of his bloodtree, remembering the day he'd planted it, the same day he arrived here in Ilysia as a six year-old boy. *"The Shedaím say a thing's life, its essence, is its blood,"* Tutor Maresh had told him then. Then he had taken a flint knife, drawn it across Neythan's palm, and spilled Neythan's blood over a dull grey orb the size of a chestnut.

Welcome to the Shedaím.

To Neythan, the orb had resembled a decrepit eye. It wasn't until Maresh had marched him into the Forest and up its lush green slope to plant it here that Neythan had realized it was a seed. That was a whole sharím ago, eleven long years, and yet here the tree remained, barren as it had always been.

"I know what you are thinking."

Neythan turned from his bloodtree to find the short, thin-limbed frame of Master Johann behind him, his eyes black as onyx, glinting in the dawn light. The old man stood, as always, with his hands clasped loosely behind his back, the beginnings of a smirk in his eyes, observing Neythan.

"You're thinking if the outing had gone as planned," the master continued, "your tree would have its first leaf."

Which, Neythan felt, was a reasonable enough thing to expect. It had been three days since he and the other disciples

16

had returned, after all. It hardly seemed fair that his tree still remained the only one yet to bud.

Yannick's had gained its first buds years ago and was now thick with leaves. Josef's had grown to a long strong oak whilst Daneel's was one of the strangest in the Forest, with a slight kink midway up its trunk and sharp hot-coloured leaves pluming from it like fire. Even Arianna's was a spectacle, with its tiny blossoms that changed colour every month. Yet here Neythan's tree remained, the same as always. Bare, despite his having made his first kill.

"Your father's was the same, you know," Johann said.

"It was?"

"Well… Perhaps not quite as long in budding as yours, but longer than the others."

"But why? Why did it take so long?"

Johann shrugged. "There can be many reasons why. A seed, as with anything, needs for that which surrounds it to be just so. The right soil. Rain. Nourishment. The light of the sun, the heat or cool of the day. It needs help to become what it ought…" He nodded at Neythan. "Just like the one to whom it is bound." The master gestured to the other trees, nearly thirty of them in all, each belonging to a member of the Shedaím. Most of them died with their owners, withering to a brittle mass before crumbling altogether. But some, belonging to Brothers whose *sha* was greater, endured, living beyond the lifetimes of those to whom they'd been bound, and continuing to grow and plume regardless. Of these, none was greater than the tree of Qoh'leth. The First. A giant willow at the Forest's very centre, cresting the mountain's highest point. Qoh'leth's tree was the oldest of them all.

"Your problem, Neythan," Master Johann said, "is sometimes you can do *this*…" The old man smiled gently and tapped a finger against his temple, "…a little *too* much. It is as much a weakness as it is a gift. You must learn to still it. Once you are sworn and made a Brother, and then finally leave this place, you will understand."

"And what if I am *not* sworn?" Neythan said.

To which Master Johann cocked an eyebrow and paused. "You have spent almost every hour since you were six years old here in Ilysia, being taught to become what you now are. Do you think because you failed to fulfil a decree you'll be kept from taking the covenant?"

"My tree is barren."

"As are all things before their season, Neythan. Whatever the elders decide, your time shall come. But you must not lose sight of what matters most. It's true, you have been taught to wield a variety of weapons, and you do so skilfully, but all you have learned is for but one purpose – to *save* and *protect* life. It is *this*, above all else, that remains the goal of the Shedaím. The very goal you accomplished on your outing…" The master turned to face Neythan's tree, examining the branches. "The purity of our purpose, Neythan, and our devotion to it – this is what separates the Order of the Shedaím from the institutions of men. It is what *makes* one a Brother of the Shedaím, or not."

The master looked at Neythan to see he understood.

"Yes, Master."

"Good… you should go now. The gathering will begin soon, and you must join the others for breakfast."

So Neythan left Johann there and turned to walk down the mount, thinking, against the master's advice, about it all. His first day here when Uncle Sol brought him as a child, journeying halfway across the Sovereignty from the sunny shores of their fishing village in Eram, far to the south beyond the sands of the Havilah. Neythan couldn't remember much about the place now, only the countless stories Uncle Sol would tell of Watchers and lost gods and a thousand other things Mother didn't like him to hear. It was by Sol's tales that

Neythan first learned of the Shedaím. The Brotherhood. The Faceless. Everyone had a different name for them but to most they were no more than idle rumour, a myth half-whispered by evening fires to keep children from misbehaving. It had been strange when Sol first told him that the Brotherhood was real, and that both he and Neythan's father had once been of their number. But even stranger was the sudden month-long journey Uncle Sol took him on when Mother and Father died, all the way here, to Ilysia, so that Neythan could become one of their number too.

"Ravenous as monkeys, all of you!" Yulaan said as Neythan arrived. The others were already eating. Neythan took a seat next to Yannick and grabbed a bowl.

"You always say monkeys," Arianna answered between mouthfuls. "Why monkeys? Why not lions, or wolves? Or a bear. Ravenous as a bear."

"You've never seen hungry monkeys," Yulaan said as she ladled the muddy broth into their wooden dishes. "And that is what you are all like."

It was still early. The village flocks were bleating loudly by the yard wall as they went out to pasture whilst Yulaan cooked.

"Back home, in Livia," she said, her Low Eastern accent turning her voice to a song, "we have monkeys everywhere. In the markets, in the streets, in palaces. And there is nothing so wild as a hungry monkey."

Yulaan was mother-aged and full-bodied, with copper skin, crinkled eyes and a stout, fleshy neck. She'd come to Ilysia while they were children. She'd even told Neythan the story of it once, as reward for a quickly emptied plate, of how she had once been a harlot heading a brothel in the strait streets of Hanesda. Not a crime in itself. It was the secrets she'd learnt from those who frequented her house and then peddled to other interested parties that had brought about her exile to this high, hidden mountain village. It was the same for almost every villager here: Ghandry, the hot-tempered butcher from the High East; Jaleem, the woodworker, with his deep bronzed skin and still eyes, and that long scar down the side of his face he refused to talk about. Each were fugitives of some kind, rescued by the Brotherhood and brought to Ilysia to build, or shepherd, or cook.

"I *saw* a monkey once," Daneel said. "Yannick too, didn't we, on my first outing in Qareb."

Yannick nodded, slurping up another spoonful of Yulaan's soup.

"Funny little beasts," Josef murmured.

"Yannick tried to catch it," Daneel went on. "But couldn't. Too quick for him, wasn't it, Yannick?"

Yannick, looking down, took another slurp of his soup without responding.

"Is it true that a monkey can be as clever as a man?" Arianna said.

"Man once told me," Daneel said, "the souls of damned men are given to dwell in those furry little bodies of theirs, that's why they're so cunning."

"Pass me the melon there, Dan," Josef said.

"Who told you that, Dan?" Neythan said.

"A man in an inn during my outing last year."

"He meets everyone in an inn," Josef quipped.

"They're educational places, brother, you ought to try them sometime. Shouldn't he, Neythan?"

Neythan glanced up at the pair across the table: Josef, eating calmly, eyes down on his food whilst his twin brother, Daneel, jabbed a spoon at the air as he talked. It was the kind of thing, years ago, he'd have smirked knowingly at Arianna about. But it wasn't that way with them anymore. Not since Uncle Sol's exile. Neythan looked toward her at the other end of the table, thinking about the walks they'd take together in the evenings, after the day's training was done and the others had gone to their huts, and how they'd sit there, just the two of them, and talk and–

"Neythan?"

Neythan glanced up. Daneel was still waiting for an answer. "Who was he?" Neythan said instead. "The man in the inn?"

"I forget. He looked Haránite. Low Eastern. Like Jaleem, the carpenter, or Yulaan here. That's how he caught my eye. Anyway. So I was in this inn with Tutor Hamir and the Brother I was shadowing, third sharím I think he was, I forget his name."

"Is there anything you *don't* forget?" Arianna asked.

"The taste of good wine," Josef answered for him.

"You want to hear this story or not?"

"Go on, Dan," Neythan prompted.

"So anyway. I'm in this inn and this woman approaches from across the way."

Yannick rolled his eyes, nudging Neythan, his thumb tapping against downturned fingertips as he nodded at Daneel.

Daneel frowned. "I'm saying it as it was."

Yannick cocked an eyebrow, unconvinced.

Neythan couldn't help but smile, which was something Yannick had known how to make him do since they were children, back when Neythan was mute, stunned silent by the deaths of his mother, father and sister, deaths he'd apparently witnessed but remained unable to recall. For almost the entire first year in Ilysia it took for Neythan to regain his speech, Yannick, himself deaf, was his only friend, their silence a familiar shared tongue. Until Arianna taught Neythan to speak again.

"I'm telling the truth, Yannick," Daneel said, then turned his attention to the rest of the table. "She walks across to me. Good-looking woman. Hefty, you know..." Daneel winked, palms upturned. Arianna sighed heavily. "And she says to me, 'Where're you from?'"

"Doubtless she hoped to send you back there," Arianna answered.

"Funny, Ari, but I don't remember you being there."

"I don't need to have been there to know you can be a–"

"Disciples!"

They turned in unison. Tutor Hamir was standing by the threshing floor at the entry to the yard. His tall, bald scalp glowed in the sun as he cleared his throat.

"The elders have come down the mount."

Josef stopped chewing.

"Your summons has come," Hamir confirmed. "You will see the elders at eventide by the Tree." He turned to leave and then stopped, glancing back. "You ought to make ready. You are to cease your discipleship. You will take the covenant and become Brothers tonight, and be gone tomorrow." And then he looked at Neythan. "You as well."

Three
COVENANT

That night they went through the village on their way to the Elders' Temple whilst the villagers stood at the doors of their houses and huts holding candles and lamps. Ghandry the butcher. Yulaan the cook. Jaleem the carpenter, his long black hair combed back like a raven's feathers to mark the occasion. Just like the day he'd walked Neythan into the village after he'd been to plant his bloodtree, showing him to the hut that would become his home for the next eleven years. Neythan picked them out from the gloom as he walked, trying to ignore the memories each face conjured – Jaleem teaching him to read, Yulaan teaching him to cook – as somewhere an elderly woman sang a lament.

Eventually he and the other disciples, dressed in ceremonial black cowls, passed beyond the village into the Forest of Silences, the old woman's dirge sinking into silence behind them as they went up the slope toward the mount's peak and the Elders' Temple. It took just over an hour to reach it. The tree of Qoh'leth, the First Brother, loomed overhead and nearly blocked out the moon, a blunt hulking shape several times the height of any other tree. They were shown to a tall obelisk with the image of Sharíf Karel, the founder of the Sovereignty, carved into it, and then sworn in there as they bowed before the pillar and three hooded figures. The disciples touched their foreheads against the stone and then spoke the words of the covenant. Only then did one of the figures remove his hood to reveal himself.

"It's said our father, Qoh'leth, planted this tree nearly three hundred years ago," the man said. "After hunting down what remained of the old Orders to end the Priests' War."

The man was bearded, with cropped black hair smudged to grey around the temples. His head was heavy-looking and square, faint pockmarks pitting the upper part of his cheeks like dimples on lemonskin. His skin was a deep olive, same as Neythan's, although the man didn't share the same soft curled hair. Unlike Neythan he wasn't of mixed blood. More likely he was a native of Calapaar or Hardeny, darker than the pale-skinned Kivites beyond the Sovereignty's northernmost borders, yet lighter than the copper-skinned Low Easterners of Harán or Sumeria.

"Many forget that Qoh'leth was himself Magi," the man went on. "Yet willing to renounce his vows for devotion to his sharíf."

Neythan knew the story well. They all did. It was Qoh'leth who'd begun the Brotherhood nearly three centuries ago, and in so doing established the means by which every sharíf since Karel had maintained their throne, secretly rooting out the seeds of rebellion and war before they could begin and, having subdued their homeland of Sumeria, going on to conquer the lands of Hardeny, Calapaar, Eram and Harán to establish the Five Land Sovereignty.

"It is no simple thing for a man to shed what he once was," the elder continued. "To become what is required of him. Yet it is this example our father, Qoh'leth, has left for us. An example marked by the covenant he made here before Karel, the first sharíf, all those years ago, sealed by his blood," he glanced behind to the towering bloodtree, "to serve the sovereign throne forever. Like him, you too have renounced all this night, and are dead. All that remains of you now is the covenant you have spent your lives preparing to uphold, the covenant you have now become part of. *Qoh'leth's* covenant."

Neythan and the others answered in unison. "My life, my sword, my blood, I swear to this peace, this honour and that blood."

The man gave a bow of his head. "Then I am Gahíd. I am third elder of the Shedaím, mouth to this Brotherhood. I stand before the sharíf and speak our words to him, and carry his words from him. It is I who hold your decrees now."

The next figure removed his hood, revealing a slim elderly man with thinning white hair. "And I am Tarrick. I am first elder of the Shedaím. Ear to this Brotherhood. I abide this mount and hear what is and tell what is to be done."

Then the next, a small greyheaded woman. "And I am Safít, second elder of the Shedaím and eye to this Brotherhood. I abide the temple and this mount, and am sworn to never leave it. It is I who sees what is yet to come."

She stepped gingerly forward and bowed again. Neythan saw the cloudy paleness to her gaze as she straightened, and realized she was blind.

"And now, you are Arianna, Daneel, Yannick, Josef and Neythan," she said, her blank eyes passing from one to the next as though she could see them. "And you are *Brothers* of the Shedaím, the right arm of this Brotherhood. It is you who shall be and do what there is to be done. Rise now, Brothers. Let us be one."

In turn, the disciples each took a blade from the belt of their ceremonial cowl and cut along the scar in their palm where they'd first bled onto the seed of their bloodtree. They watched Safít do the same, then held out their hands and bowed as she pressed her own wrinkled bleeding palm against theirs.

"The life is in the blood, and our blood is one," each said with her as she took their hands.

Afterward Gahíd gave them each a flute of snowcane.

"You must remember, a decree is a sacred thing," he said. "Not to be spoken of. Not even among yourselves. You must realize everything is different now. *Everything*. It is important you understand this... Some, they leave this place and fail to understand what it is to be a Brother of the Shedaím and no longer a disciple. They discover themselves in strange lands amongst strange people and close their eyes, hoping to hear the counsel of their tutors telling them what to do, where to turn. But they hear nothing, only the beating of their own heart, the sound of their own breath. And so they *fear*... But fear can have no place with you or me. Fear is a wicked and deceitful fiend, a taleteller, his whisper as rot that weakens the bones."

"Gahíd speaks truth you will do well to heed," Tarrick said. "Especially where you are to be sent." He nodded at the flutes in their hands. "Your decrees belong to one mission. They are to be fulfilled together, in the city of Dumea: to the south on the Stone Road to the Summerlands of Súnam. It is rare Brothers are sent as one this way, but events have required it. You will go to the city and see that these decrees are fulfilled, each on the same day... Read them now, and then pass them over the flame."

The disciples opened the flutes.

"Remember," the blind elder said as Neythan tapped the rolled parchment free from his flute. "A decree is a sacred thing."

Neythan nodded and opened the roll. He read the instructions carefully, then lingered over the words that footed the page:

...The blood of Bilyana daughter of Yoaz of the house Hophir, wife to Tobiath son of Abner, chief scribe of Dumea. To be fulfilled on the new moon by sovereign decree.

Neythan stared at the page the way he'd been taught, imagining a face and life for the name decreed: *Bilyana daughter of Yoaz*.

He exhaled slowly and held out the parchment to the lamp to light the roll. Then he watched as the page coiled, blackened and shrivelled in the flame before gliding slowly to the ground in ashes.

The next day they all stood at the edge of the village, watching Josef and Daneel ready their provisions for the journey. They were to leave in separate groups – the twins in the morning; Neythan, Yannick and Arianna at noon – the better to dissuade attention. Two or three journeying together would be companions, five a mob. The two groups would take separate roads and come together again once they had arrived at Dumea.

"Almost doesn't seem real, does it," Arianna said as she handed Daneel his quiver, gazing at the village behind them.

"What doesn't?" Josef said.

"That we're finally leaving."

"*Finally*, yes," Daneel said.

"What do you think it will be like?" Neythan said. "Out there, by ourselves, without the tutors? What do you think we will see?"

"Cities," Daneel said as he checked his blade. "Markets. Palaces. Towers. Perhaps even the sea. I would like to see the sea."

"It's not like you'll have a say," Josef said. "Today I go to Tirash. Tomorrow, Qareb."

"I might," Daneel said. "The Brother I shadowed said you can go months without a decree. Plenty of time to roam. See things."

"What do *you* intend to see, Josef?" Neythan said.

Josef shrugged. "When I was a boy, I wanted to see where

Yulaan's honey was kept. Then I did, and soon tired of its taste."

"What about you?" Arianna said. Neythan turned to find her regarding him coolly. "What do you look forward to seeing?"

Neythan thought about it. "I don't know." He turned to the other disciples, these adopted siblings, the family who'd come to replace the one he'd lost as a child. "It will be enough to return here," Neythan said. "A year from now, and see all of you again, alive and well."

"Well, I certainly will be," Daneel said as he finished packing. "With talk as wet as that, I can't vouch that *you* shall."

He smiled as they took one another's arm and embraced. The others did the same, hugging as they said their farewells. And then Josef and Daneel were traipsing down the footpath, away from Ilysia, into the thick woodland of the mount and down to the stables waiting near its base.

Neythan, Yannick and Arianna followed suit a few hours later. The next day they were on horseback, loping along a low-hilled plain with Ilysia's mountain receding behind them.

"We should come to some villages by nightfall of tomorrow," Arianna said, tossing the words over her shoulder as she rode on ahead. "Tutor Hamir has said there are many beyond the grasslands."

Neythan nodded, then glanced at Yannick riding beside him. "No. She says by nightfall of tomorrow."

"What?" Arianna turned in her saddle to find Yannick signing and gesturing with his hands. "Oh. What's he saying now?"

"You can see for yourself," Neythan said.

"I don't understand him as you do, you know that."

"Only because you won't learn."

"No. Because *he* won't *speak*."

"He can't."

"He can't *hear*, but he's a tongue and mouth like the rest of us. If he won't learn to speak why should I learn his signs?"

Yannick glanced at her and slapped an open knuckle against his palm and flicked his fingers.

"And what does that mean?"

But Neythan just laughed.

"Tell me what he said."

And now Yannick was smiling too.

"Tell me."

Neither did.

They came to a village in the Calapaari foothills the following evening. The people called the place Godswell because of the cistern by the small temple ruin on the road in. The rest of the settlement was fairly plain – clay houses, the odd stone one, all scattered like tossed pebbles either side of the road. Along the slope behind, goats watched in silence as they passed. The only building of note was the inn. They went up the narrow rubbly street toward it, flanked by sheds and outhouses. A small old woman with a face like a prune scowled at them as she carried firewood into a nearby barn.

Neythan pushed open the stiff, chewed-looking door to the inn. Inside the space was dark and cramped. Small round tables littered the room, streaked by the sticky shine of dried wine. The smell of sweat and goat dung hung in the air. A handful of men sat hunched over mugs of sourwine. A few lamps were placed in the corners of the room, their dim lights mingling with the waning day through the windows at the back where a pair of guardsmen sat – tribute collectors, most likely. Probably journeying west to the coasts of Calapaar, collecting the sharíf's due from the port cities along the shores of the Summer Sea.

"Good day," the innkeeper offered as Neythan approached the bar.

"We'll be wanting a room for the night," Neythan said.

The innkeeper's eyes shuffled from Neythan to Arianna to Yannick, then, after lingering a moment with Arianna, back to Neythan again. "Yes," he said, having measured the quality of their custom. "Though we've not any too big."

"Whatever you have will be fine," Neythan said.

"Ah, a simple man. It is my custom always to regard well a simple man. He says what he wants. I give what he says. He is happy. I am happy." He smiled.

Neythan didn't smile back.

"My name is Zubin," the man said. "Follow me."

He took them to a stone outhouse near where they'd tied the horses. The ceiling was low; only Yannick didn't have to bow to enter. There was a chair in one corner and a thick narrow bedmat in the other. Arianna looked the room over, then gave Zubin a silver coin. He grinned and bowed as he left.

"'Whatever you have will be fine'?" Arianna said.

"It's not so bad," Neythan said. "It is dry at least."

Yannick sat in the chair, put down his bag and patted his chest with a nod.

"I suppose that leaves us the bed then," Neythan said.

Arianna sighed and dumped her sack by the mattress.

That night Neythan fell asleep quickly, wondering, as he drifted off, whether he too would see the port cities of Tresán and Caphás on the Summer Sea coast, or perhaps he'd even be summoned south, to the coasts of Eram, the land of his birth.

He'd slept no more than a couple of hours before he was awakened by a familiar and squalid smell. His eyes snapped open. The room was silent and black. He fumbled tentatively for Arianna on the other side of the bedmat. The bed was empty. Something moist and sticky lay in her place. Neythan's gut turned cold. He groped about. More of it.

"Arianna. Yannick?" he whispered loudly, but they didn't answer.

He sat up, rolled from the bedmat and stood. He was about to reach for where they'd stowed the lamp when the door burst open. The room flooded with light. Two men stood in the doorway holding torches, the tribute collectors from earlier. Behind them stood Zubin, wild-eyed and shouting.

"That's him! That's the one! Murderer!"

Neythan turned, squinting, to look at the space where moments ago he'd been soundly asleep. A dark puddle of blood stained the bedmat beside where he'd slept. In the corner Yannick lay slumped on the chair, his head hanging back, his lips ajar and his throat open, gaping wet deep red. Blood was everywhere. Splattered against the wall, pooling by the foot of the chair and mingled with urine. There was another streak of blood on the floor between the chair and bedmat. Arianna was gone.

Neythan's mind lurched. A heavy calloused hand gripped his shoulder.

"You'll be coming with us, boy."

Neythan slackened instinctively, letting his shoulder give as the man's hand pressed to grasp it. He spun violently back and pushed his shoulder free, grabbed a wrist and twisted, turning the elbow before thrusting his open palm against the upturned joint.

The man screamed as his arm snapped. Zubin froze, slack-jawed by the door, as Neythan shoved the man aside.

The other one came rushing in. Neythan ducked and jabbed his throat, watched him choke and gag, then grabbed his head and shoved it against the wall to make sure. Zubin now stood alone in the doorway, mouth open.

Neythan took him by the throat, pulled him in, and slammed him against the wall.

"Who sent you?"

Zubin just stared, panting, head wagging frantically side to side.

"Who sent you?" Neythan repeated. "Who killed Yannick?"

Zubin whimpered.

"Who. Killed. Him?"

"She said... you did."

"She? Who is *she*?"

"The girl who was with you... light eyes, black hair. Said you'd tried to kill her too."

"*What*? Where is she?"

But Neythan heard the answer before Zubin had a chance to speak, the noise of horses beyond the outhouse door. He ran outside and saw Arianna across the yard by the stables, clambering onto her horse in the rain. She stared back at him from beneath the hood of her cowl, held his gaze, then galloped up onto the road, away into the night.

Neythan stared after her, his mind awash, his thoughts groping like flailing limbs. He started back toward Zubin, still frozen at the door. Neythan stepped past him and the other men slumped against the wall and retrieved his sword and crossbow. Then he grabbed some provisions before looking a final time at Yannick's body hanging off the chair, eyes half-open, splattered in blood.

What had Arianna done? Why?

Neythan saw a window light up from across the street. Others were waking, voices stirring from the innhouse. He took what he had out into the rain and ran for his horse. In the blackness it was hard to see how far Arianna had gone, but in the quiet of the still sleepy village he could hear the hooves of her mare pounding the earth. Neythan swung into the saddle, rode up onto the road and sped off in pursuit.

Four
ROGUE

It took Neythan nearly a week but he managed to track Arianna to a ravine deep in the forests. He'd lost track of her a few days after the inn when she'd crossed a bridge over a brook ahead of him and then hacked away its bindings, letting the wooden planks disassemble into the rushing water beneath. He'd tracked along the embankment for close to half a mile before finally finding a place narrow and shallow enough to cross. It was only by the remembered teachings of Tutor Hamir that he managed to find her trail again.

Hamir, a man Neythan never thought he'd be grateful for. The tutor was Haránite, from Hikramesh to be exact, a city thirty miles inland from the South Sea Gulf, built amid the arid dust of the Low Eastern foothills back when the first crop farmers were still learning to reap their yields. Back then the worth of any dwelling place could be weighed by its closeness to water – a river, a coastline. But Hikramesh was built in a desert. Hamir liked to say the complex network of wells, irrigation channels and canals that coursed along the streets of his home city was exactly the kind of innovation only a Haránite could have come up with – a diligent and inventive people, given to curiosity. Which, Neythan thought, was the kind of thing only a Haránite would say. But perhaps Hamir was right. It was certainly one way of looking at it. The other was that Haránites – judging by Neythan's experiences with the tutor and Yulaan – were clever, yes, but also habitually busy and meddlesome, albeit in a more or less well-meaning way. Most of the time.

Perhaps it was because of this Neythan had learned to forgive Hamir for how he'd tell him and the other disciples to "think more like a Haránite" when they were children, and then have them spend weeks in the forests lower down the mount of Ilysia, leaving them to survive by their own means in order to teach them the skill.

"To hunt well, a man must know the country," Hamir would say. "He must be filled by it, breathe it, until every bough of a tree, every stone and blade of grass becomes a part of him, part of his soul, his *sha*. It's only then, when you know what ought to be, that you'll *feel* when something's wrong. And that's the secret… *feeling*. Only by feeling will you be able to see what *isn't* there as much as what is. The absence of a thing is as telling as the presence of another."

Like the absence of naturally arranged branches on the low boughs of a cedar Neythan found three mornings ago – branches Arianna had likely stripped as fodder and bedding for herself and her horse. Or the absence of disorder in the undergrowth of a clearing Neythan happened upon the day after – somehow too neat, too contrived, as if to distract from what had been a night's resting place. Then there was the absence of bark on a sycamore tree Neythan had spotted only yesterday – bark that had been removed by some recent passerby to access the nourishing sap beneath. Hamir always said they'd one day thank him for what he'd made them endure. Neythan had never expected that day would come so soon.

He let the memory fade, allowed another thought to rise in its place – Yannick, throat open and bloody, head hanging back on the chair with mouth agape and eyes staring.

Arianna had murdered their friend, a fellow Brother, breaking the first law of the Shedaím and transgressing the blood covenant she'd sworn only the night before. Neythan still couldn't make sense of it. That Arianna could have done what she did. That Yannick was now no more. That Neythan himself had been spared. Sorrow. Grief. Guilt. Each had taken their turn but more than these and overwhelming them all was the simple, inescapable question. *Why?* Neythan searched his memories, seeking clues to which he'd been blind, anything that would begin to make sense of what Arianna had done. Why she had done it. And why she had spared him. For spare him she had. He was sure of that much. She could have easily killed him, just as she had Yannick. In fact, Neythan was sure she'd taken deliberate steps to avoid doing just that, keeping him asleep. There were ways after all – incense, powders, certain elixirs. And what else could explain how he'd slept through his friend's murder? And if that was true, it meant she'd *planned* it this way. She'd *chosen* to slay Yannick. Which meant this was not some act born of whim or fear or anger. It was planned. Determined. It was her *design* to kill Yannick, and not him. A decision she'd made. But to what end? Why?

Only you have the answers, Ari.

Neythan peered through the rain, lying belly down in the undergrowth. He could feel the chilly downpour seeping into his spine and neck as he stared down into the ravine at Arianna.

The ravine was deep. A thin river flowed along its crag. A waterfall tipped in from the rocks above. By its foot Arianna sat on her horse, staring through the curtain of water as Neythan sighted her with the crossbow. It would be hard to be accurate from this distance but at least the downpour would slow the arrow, weighting its flight. He wanted only to wound her. Then talk to her. And then maybe kill her.

He watched her climb down from her horse. Then watched

her move to the edge of the river and lean over, gazing at the waterfall. *What are you doing, Ari?* But as he lifted his gaze from the sights to try to get a better look, she ran forward and leapt *through* the waterfall, vanishing into the wet rushing drape.

Neythan blinked. "Gods..."

For a moment, he remained still, waiting to see if she'd come out again. When she didn't, he rose to his feet and glanced about for a way down the ridge. He went along the clifftop and eventually found a tree rooted in the wall of the ravine. He took hold of the trunk and deftly lowered himself onto a foothold below.

It took half an hour for him to finally reach the bottom. Every foothold was slick from the rain and he had to keep stopping to make sure Arianna hadn't re-emerged. When he reached the ground he stood and watched the waterfall again. From here the crash of water was even louder than the rain. He could barely hear his own steps crunching on the loose flint and shale.

He walked slowly beside the river toward the fall and stepped up onto the broad stony ridge that banked it. Arianna's horse stood on the other side, ears twitching to the noise of the downpour. There was something behind the waterfall. Something bright or shiny, like brass, or some sort of jewel, shining out from the torrent as though caught in the sun. But there was no sun.

Neythan pulled his crossbow from his back and loaded the cord. He waited again, watching. Then went forward with the bow held low. He'd barely slept in three days. Possibly his eyes were playing tricks. More likely Arianna was. Some sort of trap. He moved closer. Carefully. Slowly. He was feet away when he saw the shadow moving over the fall, refracted by the rush of the water. He stared for a moment, trying to make sense of it, and then realized it wasn't a shadow at all. It was a reflection, of something behind him, in the sky, heading his way.

Neythan dived as the long shaft of a spear went flying past his shoulder and smashed into the rock behind him. He rolled, wheeled around with his crossbow.

No one. Nothing.

He heard the hollow sigh of something else fast approaching and dived again as an arrow whistled past and thudded against an oak. He scrambled into a crouch by a tree, saw movement in the woodland opposite, and took off sprinting toward it. He skidded to a stop as he neared the river, aimed and fired two arrows at the half-seen motion on the other side, then dropped his crossbow and continued running.

The river's water rushed beneath his feet as he leapt across and drew his sword. He could see a hooded figure on the other side now, groping in the mud for whatever had been dropped when they scrambled to avoid Neythan's volley.

The hooded person looked up and saw Neythan coming, grabbed an arrow and fumbled it to a bow. Neythan yanked his scabbard free and tossed it to gain time. The other ducked as Neythan closed in and swung his sword. Metal clanged in the rain. The hooded figure parried with a shield. Neythan swung from overhead, knocking the figure on their seat as they blocked again.

The impact dislodged the hood.

When the man sat up, Neythan's sword was poised at his neck.

"Who are you?" Neythan said.

The man was old and small. Smooth pale scars covered his arms, neck and head. Neythan watched as he wiped back long greasy strands of hair from his wind-chafed scalp.

"Now that *is* quite a thing," the man said. "A question like that? When *you* are the trespasser?" He ignored Neythan's sword and climbed to his feet, wiping mud from his sticky palms and thick shawl. "I suppose I shouldn't be surprised. That's the thing with you people, isn't it. You're all the same. Enter another's home and behave like the victim when he decides to defend it."

"Home? What home?"

"And then add insults, if that wasn't enough."

"You're calling this place home?"

"A home is wherever you make it. I thought they'd have taught you that by now."

"*They*? Who's 'they?'"

"You know. *Them*. *Your* kind. Faceless ones. Shedaím. No discipline these days, any of you. Not like before."

Neythan stepped in, his blade touching the man's throat. "What do *you* know of the Shedaím? How do you know what I am?"

Still wiping mud from his fingers, the man looked up at him. "Not the smartest, are you? Say I'd only guessed. I'd know now by your words."

"You will tell me how you know."

"And pushy too. Still, I'm the forgiving kind. So how about this? You tell me of your home, I shall tell you of mine, *and* how I know what you are."

Neythan didn't answer, blade still poised.

"Oh, come now. Me, I'll not be bothered by a little rain but I can see you would like some rest and shelter, no? Look. You're shivering. How long have you been out in this?"

"Long enough not to feel it."

The man laughed. "And would your lady friend say the same…? Yes. That's right. I saw her go on through the fall there."

Neythan's sword prodded the man's throat.

The man raised his hands. "Be calm, boy. You cannot follow her now anyway," he said, nodding at the fall. "That way is closed."

Neythan glanced back at the water and was about to ask what the man meant when he felt a sharp prick in the side of his neck. The sting quickly turned numb, then the numbness spread, over his shoulders, then his arms. Finally, Neythan dropped to his knees. When he looked up, the old man was standing over him, smiling, and then he was gone, along with everything else, blurry, then black.

Five
OATH

"Neythan. What are you doing?"

Neythan didn't think anyone knew this place. He'd spent the last three weeks, after he made the decision, trying to find the spot that would be just right. A quiet place. Where he'd be left alone, allowed his silence, somewhere still. He'd snuck out after the evening gathering, when the day's training was ended and the evening meal shared; when they were left to their chambers for the night, that sweet closeted nook where all the voices stopped and the demands and the disciplines and everything else finally ceased.

"What are you doing, Neythan?"

Like sleeping. He'd asked Jaleem about it once, and that's what he told him, though it could only be supposed. But Neythan liked to think perhaps that's the way it would be. Like sleeping.

"Put it down, Neythan."

And the blade seemed so right in his hand. And the night seemed so right, the stars above so clean and bright as if waiting to welcome him.

"Why?"

"You mustn't."

"Why not?"

But he knew he couldn't. Not while Yannick was there, and so he decided to hand the dagger, handle first, to his fellow disciple. But when he turned around Yannick wasn't there. A woman stood in *his place. Her eyes were golden, glowing. She began to reach toward him, calling his name.*

"Neythan."

Neythan woke up.

It was dark. The air was chilly. Overhead leaned craggy angles of rock, sharp-edged and glossy. The dream lingered in Neythan's thoughts as he stared up at them. Strange to have dreamt about that night. Nearly three years ago now. But then again perhaps not so strange. It was Yannick who'd found him after all, and if he hadn't…

It was the first time he'd heard Yannick speak – his voice slightly mangled, the syllables blunted around the edges but apart from that surprisingly good. Not that anyone else would ever know. No matter how much Neythan tried to assure him, Yannick still refused to try his words with others, even Master Johann. Neythan thought about that often: how seeing him that night, alone with the blade, one year on since Uncle Sol's exile from the Brotherhood, had been the only thing to push Yannick beyond his fear and make him speak. But the woman in the dream. Who was she?

Neythan tried to rise but he couldn't. His head felt heavy and strange, as though filled with water.

He was lying on a raised flatbed of stone. To his left, a stool stood against the wall. In the corner there was a pot of incense, likely the reason for his sluggishness.

"You're awake."

Neythan craned his neck to see. The small man from the ravine came in carrying a lamp. In the light from the flame he looked even stranger than before. His head was tall and scabby. His jaw was narrow and misshapen. Pouches of crinkly skin hung about his neck like a turkey's wattle.

He sat down opposite the broad stone slab where Neythan lay and put the lamp on the ground beside him. He regarded

Neythan silently, his eyes moving over his body like a merchant eyeing merchandise. After a while, satisfied, bored, or both, the man sighed and then folded one leg over the other, resting its weight on the other's thigh like some king's courtier.

"I know what you're thinking," the man said, head tilting to one side. "How did this happen, hmm? Why am I here? Who is this strange little tyrant sat before me?"

A wineskin of blond goat hide appeared in the man's hand. He looked at Neythan again, as if weighing a decision, then loosened the cap of the skin and swigged.

"Yes, I'm sure one like you, with your... breeding, your learned distaste for acquiescence, would have many questions, yes? You will be unlike most and so you must forgive me if I savour somewhat your being here. It's not often I happen upon prey so rare."

"I am not prey."

"Ah, but you are, young one, you are. Come. See around you. You are *captured* prey. A man mustn't be too proud to accept what he is."

Neythan looked around, his eyes adjusting to the gloom. Fronds of light and shadow shimmied along the wall like watery ghosts. Perhaps there was an underground pond nearby. "What is this place?"

The man took another mouthful from the wineskin. "My home, as promised in the ravine. A man of my word, you see. And, as I told you, dry. Though I admit, perhaps not so warm. But," he shrugged, "one can't have everything."

"How long have I been here?"

"Quite some time," the man admitted. His head bobbed in a slow drunken nod. "You've been lying here still as a corpse for just over a week."

"A *week*?" Neythan tried to rise again. The room lurched.

"Not the best idea," the man advised. "You'll need a few days yet."

"I've been here a week?"

"Give or take. The dart I used, you see." He shrugged apologetically, one palm opened in commiseration. "It was dipped in a little invention of mine, a mixture I use, very strong. Urdin berries and lingerweed and the heads of certain fungi, but you have to *ferment* the berries, which, by the way, are fairly rare in this season with all the rain. Then you must grind them together until just so. And heat them. And then... well, details, I shan't bore you. Suffice to say the mixture is quite potent. I usually keep it to guard against bears and wolves but... well, you had a sword. One must improvise."

Neythan laid his head back on the stone bed. The room felt as though it was spinning. "Why did you bring me here?"

"Where else was I to bring you?"

"But why? What do you want?"

"What do I *want*? Now *there* is a question. One might find a great many ways to answer were he to take his time. Truth is, a man seldom knows. I want gold, he says. Or to live in a palace. Or a thousand wives. A man wants for many things and perhaps sometimes gains them, without finding what it is he *seeks*..." He drank again from the wineskin and grimaced. "A dangerous question to ask really; what a man wants. Especially for the one who's to answer. Wiser not to. The hungriest of all beasts, you see – we men – and with less mercy than most. Still, seeing as you *do* ask, I suppose there might be a thing or two a man of my means would settle for. Especially from one like you... Shedaím."

Neythan looked at him. "You have not said how you know me."

"I know the Brotherhood."

"How?"

"The stench, perhaps."

"You are a spy."

"Hmph." The man spat.

"Then what? Who are you?"

"Caleb. My name is Caleb. I am… a merchant. Of sorts. Spikenard, spices, wines. I deal in what can be found, and sometimes…" He nodded at the pot of incense in the corner. "Things of my own making." He capped the wineskin closed and held it loosely between his knees as he leaned forward, elbows propped on thighs. "But you asked of what I want, didn't you, erm… your name. What is your name?"

Neythan didn't answer.

"It is only a name, boy. Hardly a dangerous secret. And you will need to tell it to me if you are to discover what I want and perhaps have a hope of leaving this place."

Neythan thought about it for a while. "My name is Neythan," he said reluctantly.

Caleb nodded. "Neythan… Well then, Neythan. I shall tell you how I know your precious Brotherhood. And I shall tell you what I want. I shall tell you it all. Whom else is there to tell, after all? There are so few a man like me can trust. But you… I know I can trust *you*, Neythan. I can. Because I know you are the rare soul who will understand what I'm going to say… You see, I wasn't always as I now am. I was once as *you* are…"

Caleb waited for comprehension to gather on Neythan's face.

Neythan said nothing.

Caleb coughed impatiently. "I was Shedaím. A Faceless One. One of your Brotherhood?"

Neythan laughed then realized Caleb wasn't smiling. "You cannot expect me to believe that."

"Is it so hard to believe, Neythan? Perhaps in time, should you live long enough, you will learn how deceiving appearances can be." The man's gaze wandered to the middle distance. "How sometimes you can think you know something, or even some*one*, and be deceived."

Neythan thought of Arianna.

Caleb saw Neythan's silence acknowledge his truth. "I was one of the most esteemed in my company," he continued. "A master by only my third sharím."

Which only made the story more fanciful. There are four sharíms in all, eleven-year seasons that mark a Shedaím's time. The first is spent at Ilysia as a disciple, beginning as a child and learning the disciplines and apart for a few trips each year to witness the wider world – cities, townships, plains – remaining on the mount. The second begins with the taking of the covenant, which is when a disciple passes from discipleship to Brotherhood and leaves Ilysia, returning once a year to begin with but eventually only returning when summoned. The third sharím is a Brother's strongest, when he is experienced, and yet still young enough to make best use of the knowledge he has gained. And then there is the fourth and final sharím. Although few survive to see it, it is during this period, as the strength of the body wanes, that the sha is believed to grow most. Those who survive it enter the tutorship at Ilysia or become one of the sharíf's bodyguard and eventually, beyond that, perhaps an elder.

To be made a master before the fourth sharím was unlikely. But then to even know what a sharím was without having been part of the Brotherhood was even more so. Neythan decided to hear him out.

"So what happened then?"

"Ah. Well, funny you should ask." He opened the wineskin and swigged. "I've asked myself the same question many times, Neythan. Many times... You know, it's said a man chooses his place in the world, but I'm not so sure. I often wonder if it isn't already set for him, like a seat at the banquet table, and his choice merely an illusion conjured to him by the fact he made his own way to the chair... But then, who can know? Only the gods perhaps, if there are such. If there are any, they are cruel. They do not smile on us. They did not smile on me, Neythan. They cursed."

"You're not making any sense–"

"Hikramesh," Caleb said. "That's where it happened, you see... I was sent there from a township north of it, along the Low Eastern foothills by the gulf. More than ten years ago now. Wild territory then. Desert lands, mostly. I was to seek out a scribe there – Sarwin, of the house Saliph. Fussy little fellow. Took me a few days to find him. I finally came upon the man at some night council where he was courtier to Jikram the Tirashite, the sharíf's vassal. It fell to Sarwin to make preparations for his journey north to Hanesda for Helgon's inauguration as sharíf. My decree was to deliver a letter. That was all. A letter that only his eyes were to see and afterward I was to destroy. Which, when you think about it, is a strange task to have asked of one like me – third sharím, a master?"

"And what did this letter say?"

"I never knew its contents. *Never.* I was not to read it. I was faithful to what I'd been decreed... I went to the council in the city's eastern quarter by the watergate. I was to find Sarwin, deliver the letter, watch him read it, and then ensure it was destroyed. I did as I was bid. I delivered the letter. But when I did..." Caleb frowned, his hands beginning to tremble slightly. He gripped one with the other at the knuckles to steady them. "Must have been a trap, you see. The men in that chamber... They tried to seize me. Five men, six perhaps. Armed... I managed to kill two or three but..." and then he grew still, he looked puzzled. "Then there was a fire." It came out almost like a question. He looked up at Neythan as if expecting him to answer. "From nowhere. A fire." Caleb pointed to the tight and shiny seared skin of his face. "How I got my scars, you see... It was then they took me."

"Took you where?"

But Caleb said nothing, staring at the ground.

"Where did they take you, Caleb?"

He tried for another swig from his wineskin and, finding it empty, grunted a muttered accusation at the flask.

"How did you come to be here?"

Caleb frowned into the empty skin, staring at the uncapped hole as if for the answer.

"Caleb?"

"What if I were to remove this incense," Caleb said. "Release you from its effects?"

"What?"

"What would you do?"

"What are you asking?"

"Perhaps I'm asking for you not to kill me, should I, against my better judgment, free you."

Neythan said nothing.

"I could even help you," Caleb went on, "to find this lady friend of yours. The one you were seeking by the ravine."

Again, Neythan just watched him.

"You see, I remember, Neythan. I remember many things about the Brotherhood. I remember it was forbidden to give one's word in oath and break it." Caleb rose from the stump and stepped toward Neythan. "That when one clasped hands with another the words spoken in that littlest of embraces were binding, just as any decree." Caleb came closer still until he was standing over Neythan's limp body on the stone bed. "I remember these things, and it occurs to me how intriguing the hand of Providence is. Fickle, but intriguing. And so I think to myself, perhaps she has come to me in hope of repaying a debt owed."

"Again, you are making no sense."

"I'm talking about a bargain, a contract, between you and me. Merchants together, Neythan. Stock and trade. I have

something you want, and you, you have something that may
be of use to me."

"And what is that?"

"Yourself."

Neythan frowned. "What do you mean?"

"I was *betrayed*, Neythan. That much has always been clear.
What isn't, is by who. And why."

"And you think I can help you."

"I think if you ever hope to see the light of day you will
swear to help me. You will swear to be bound to the answering
of these questions until such a time as I release you."

"It has been many years since what happened, Caleb. Isn't
that what you said?"

"Yes. More than ten. So?"

Neythan just looked at him, thinking about it. "And you
spoke of being able to help me?"

"With your lady friend."

"You know how to find her?"

"I do."

"If it is true you know something of how to find her, then
I will agree."

"It is."

"Then that shall be our bargain. You help me find her. And
I will help you find your answers."

Caleb smiled. "You are the one imprisoned. You cannot set
the terms. I will want my answers first."

"I *am* the one imprisoned. With no reason to trust you.
None. Whereas I, as you know, am bound by my word should
we take skin for skin in the speaking. You claim to have been
a Brother, but you are no Brother now. There is no covenant
in your tongue. The bargain can be no other way."

Caleb stepped away from the bed, thinking it over.

"What do you hope to do," Neythan said, "when you find
your betrayer? Talk with them? Reason? You free me, help

me find her, and I *will* find the answer to your questions, *and* render judgment as you see fit. The bargain can be no fairer than that."

Caleb stared long at Neythan. Then his hand slowly emerged from his ragged smock.

"It seems you are quite the barterer. It shall be as you say. We will find this girl you pursue. But afterward, Neythan, the answers. And, as you have said, *judgment.*" His eyes finally left Neythan's to glance down at his outstretched palm.

Neythan lifted his own hand and placed it in Caleb's. "Skin for skin," he said.

"Yes, Neythan. Skin for skin."

Six
DUMEA

The trouble with men is they never grow up. Some sort of childish instinct, stubborn as a weed, seemed to cling to their nature. Yasmin had told little Noah more times than there were stars in the sky that he was not to persist with his pigeons until after his Judgment. The ceremony was only two moons away. Seven years of schooling and the boy couldn't wait another two months for the sake of his future. But what truly annoyed her was his father, her husband Hassan. Rather than doing as he should and insisting that the boy study, he continued to indulge Noah's hobby. Hassan: son of Nalaam, steward of the citystate of Dumea, the fourth of his line to hold the title, and yet it seemed to Yasmin that it was she, not he, who was more concerned with ensuring their eldest son grew to uphold the traditions his forefathers had walked so well before him.

She shook her head and turned from the childish pair back to the house.

It was late afternoon. The sun was low and tawny. The reapers were still collecting in the wheat. She sighed and marched away through the already scythed part of the field.

It was ridiculous Hassan could be so irresponsible. Even more ridiculous, she was stuck in this backwater of a city.

She'd been the daughter of a consul from Kaloom, far

to the east, a month's journey from here. She could still remember accompanying her father on his long journeys south to Hanesda – the City of Thrones, as he'd call it – for the annual councils and First Moon festivals. They would journey to the crown city once, sometimes twice, a year and every time she loved it. The huge white walls gleaming in the sun, the narrow clustered streets, the sharíf's palace and royal gardens, and all the people, every one of them in a rush, each hour an event.

It was there she'd met Hassan, more than twenty years ago, at a banquet to celebrate the wedding of Játhon son of Sulamar, a prince of the house of Saliph and a kinsman of the sovereign line. Játhon had wed the young queen of Hikramesh the previous week. A particularly favourable match, Yasmin's father had said. Játhon, as both a relation of the throne and a member of the Calapaari gentry would now join the lands of Harán, Sumeria and Calapaar together by blood, consolidating their accord and strengthening the Sovereignty. It was good, her father said, for peoples, once conquered, to feel themselves masters rather than slaves.

It was an idea Yasmin had never liked. That a woman's affections should be no more than a tool to engineer the accords and affairs of men, that she too should be one day swallowed up in another's plottings and manoeuvrings for power. An ornament of convenience, an elaborate currency. That was what she'd liked about Hassan. His interest in *her*. The way he talked to *her*. It had been her cousin Tobiath who'd introduced them. Even now the memory remained fresh.

"The best gardener amongst the nobility you are likely to meet," Tobiath said, presenting him to her.

"Gardener? Is that not the work of servants?"

"My father," Hassan answered, taking her hand in greeting, "has always taught me that he who is to govern must first know *how* to serve."

"You'll find Hassan a man of pretty words," Tobiath explained.

"But true ones," Hassan added, smiling as he gazed at her. "And believe me, it is no lie when I say it is a delight to meet you, Yasmin."

She liked him instantly; the glossy shine of his black hair, his wide and kind mouth, his almond skin, his perfect height. The way his eyes – doleful, long-lashed, though a little too close together – fixed to her whenever she spoke, as if the room and its assembly of consuls and courtiers was, when compared to her, no more than an inconvenient distraction.

"Are you always so forthcoming?" Yasmin said, smiling.

"Often so. Though," glancing at Tobiath, "my friends tell me I ought to grow out of it." His eyes returned to her, measuring. "What do *you* think, Yasmin? This honesty of mine. Is it a vice or virtue?"

"I would say it has a certain charm."

"Then a virtue it must be. For you to be charmed it could be nothing else."

Yasmin laughed. "Well, perhaps your virtue might help us then."

"Oh?" Hassan slid another glance to Tobiath, then back to her. "I would like nothing more."

She drifted to Hassan's side, goblet clasped loosely in hand, leaning at his elbow to survey the room. The space was broad and dim and filled with people. Dignitaries from the cities of Caphás and Tresán along Calapaar's coastland reclined at low tables, wearing their typically elaborate and multicoloured flax-woven tunics. Yasmin had always loved the bold gaudiness of their designs, how lively and audacious they were. Fashions always seemed to move so quickly out there by the coast, but then they were seafaring cities after all, used to tasting of and exchanging with faraway places. And never ones to miss a celebratory occasion like this, despite the distance. A crowd of Low Easterners dominated the far end of the room, chattering loudly as was their way. Probably members of the newlywed queen's retinue. And of course there were plenty of Sumerians too, delegates and consuls from the nearby cities of Qadesh or Tirash as well as the crown city itself, no doubt here to jockey for favour and gain the ear of this new and influential union. Yasmin lifted her chin to Hassan's ear and motioned with her drink at the blithely peopled space. "Tell me. What do you think of them?"

Hassan raised an eyebrow, took a sip of his wine and shrugged. "Well, at a glance, some portly, some less so. Though, on the whole, finely attired."

Yasmin smiled and shook her head. "No." She leaned in a little, waited for Hassan to return his attention to her, and then pointed with her eyes and a nod. "I mean *them*... Játhon and his new wife. What's her name again?"

"Satyana," Tobiath supplied in a murmur.

"Yes... Satyana."

Satyana, queen of Harán's largest city, Hikramesh, and daughter to king Jashar of Harán. Tall, elegant and swarthy – she stood at the shoulder of her husband as he talked with a rose-cheeked and heavily bearded man – Játhon whispering, the bearded man guffawing, Satyana silent.

"What do you think?" Yasmin asked as they watched. "Are they well matched or no?"

"How could they be anything other? They are wed after all. As all this lovely wine testifies."

"Does that make them matched?"

"I suspect you have your own feeling on the matter."

"Yes. As does Tobiath, though our feelings differ, and so I ask..."

Again Hassan took a thoughtful sip of his wine. "I suppose it's no secret that agreement between Sumeria and Harán is often... well, difficult," he said. "That Satyana belongs to the house of Najir may remedy this. Everyone knows the sharíf desires a highway from Tirash to Hikramesh to better take advantage of their ports. It's not hard to see how he may profit."

"Mhm. An apt price for the building of a road then, a marriage?"

"For some."

"And what about for you?"

"Me?"

"Yes. What would be your price, Hassan?" Yasmin said, testing the sound of his name on her lips as he had hers. "Why would you marry? For duty? Or devotion?"

Hassan turned from the party and looked directly at her. "Who's to say the two cannot be one?"

They married less than a year later. They began a family, built a home, and, Yasmin felt, were to build something more. But that was before Hassan's father died. Before Hassan took up the stewardship of Dumea. Before the light in his eyes that had first drawn her began to wane and the man she knew withdrew. Now Hassan laughed less. Talked less. Worked more. And then, just days ago, there'd come the news about Yasmin's estranged older brother, Zaqeem, the governor of Qadesh and one of Hassan's oldest friends – found dead by an altar in a Sumerian forest. Hassan hadn't slept or eaten well since, but for Yasmin it was different. Her father had disowned Zaqeem before Yasmin knew how to walk or talk, exiling him for what had apparently become an unseemly preoccupation with the outlawed traditions of the Magi. Which Yasmin had always found strange. Nearly a hundred priestly orders, as many as ten thousand men and women, had been destroyed by Sharíf Karel in the Cull three centuries ago when the Sovereignty began, with the few who survived fleeing to Súnam. Why would anyone risk their life and those of their loved ones to pursue the very practices their sovereign's forebears had fought to eradicate? It made no sense. And yet that was what Zaqeem had done. And now he was dead.

To Yasmin, the news felt strange and vague, a thing she was meant to feel but couldn't. And so that evening she gazed mutely from the corner of the decree court as the harvest festivities began. She watched the colourfully festooned drapes marking the square and the smiling people who filled it, feeling like a stranger. Like she didn't belong.

"So glad to see you, sister."

She looked up to find Bilyana approaching from the crowd, waving as she came. The festival was small, but Bilyana had come dressed in rich blue-dyed cotton as fine as any found in the high bazaars of Qalqaliman. She was dressed fit for a king's table, her arms braced with twin armlets of polished bronze. Yasmin smiled despite herself. "A fair sight you are, Bilyana, for a fair evening."

"Is it? You must be yet to taste the wine, sister."

"A mistake you have not made."

"A mistake I shall never make. What else is a feast for if not wine?"

"Quite."

"Mock all you like, but in this place we must scrounge for our delights wherever we can find them. Though I admit, this time 'delight' is no way to describe the wine. Perhaps gutterwash or dregs. A right-minded man would not offer it even to his oxen."

"A right-minded man would not offer *any* wine to his oxen."

"Well, perhaps he ought. They may work harder knowing how poor the end of their labour has been."

"Oxen till for crops, Bilyana, not wine."

"What? Oh. Well, then useless beasts they are. I'd always

wondered why they seem so glum. But at least they have an excuse. You, on the other hand..."

Yasmin balked, frowning, and looked at the other woman. "You are not kind, Bilyana."

"And never aim to be. Its charm is thought too much of, you know. Now honesty, honesty is a better way, kinder than kindness. Are they not the words of some poet or scribe? Anyway, you *are* glum, and without excuse, having not endured the wine."

In truth, Bilyana, of course, was not Yasmin's sister but rather the wife of her cousin, Tobiath, who, after fostering as a boy with Hassan and Zaqeem at the home of the crown city's scribe, had elected to follow Hassan here and serve in the schools and library rather than remain in Hanesda. A decision that had built in Bilyana – whose affection for the crown city mirrored Yasmin's – a sort of wry boredom, but one she wore well, or at least better than Yasmin managed to, tempered by wine and food.

Bilyana sniffed diffidently, her nose ring shivering, and turned her square pudgy hips to glance around at the gathering.

"So," she persisted, bullish from the wine, "what is it? Your face is longer than a mule's."

Yasmin thought about her argument with Hassan that morning. "Noah," she lied. "The Judgment is so close now. Not that one would know it to see him. All day long he is with those pigeons. It is not good for him. He doesn't study. He rarely even *speaks* with the other children."

"I'd not speak with them either; good-for-nothings all of them. You should leave him to his way."

"Easily said."

"Easily done."

"For you perhaps."

Bilyana only paused but it was enough to make Yasmin

regret the words. Bilyana's barrenness was the other reason for her taste for wine.

"Yes. Well," she replied, before Yasmin could pity her with apology. "We all have our troubles... Which reminds me. I have a favour to ask."

Yasmin nodded meekly, stung by her own callousness.

"It's my brother, Zíyaf," Bilyana said, leaning in conspiratorially.

"Is he well?"

"Hm, well, the answer to that is less than simple..." She stopped abruptly and smiled, waving at someone in the crowd. "Old hag," she muttered to herself, still smiling as she waved. "Smiles to my face and then preens and coos whenever Tobiath is around, laughs like a hyena at all his jokes. A *drunken* hyena. As though she could be any less subtle. I mean, fathers bless him, your cousin's a good man but he's as much wit as a mayfly... Anyway. Zíyaf."

"Is he alright?"

"Well. He's taken with a Súnamite, some woman he came upon when your husband sent him down there to collect a Saori staff for the library."

"Came upon?"

"He likes her... well... is convinced she ought to be his wife."

"His *wife*?"

A goblet of the offending wine had somehow appeared in Bilyana's hand. She sipped it and nodded, the tiny bauble of her nose ring dangling vigorously.

"I see."

"No, sister, you do not. This Súnamite, it happens she is the daughter of a chieftain."

Yasmin grimaced.

"Yes," Bilyana replied. "Exactly. You know our situation."

And Yasmin did. The reason for Bilyana's willingness to

follow Tobiath to Dumea in the first place had been the fall of her own house and the debts it had crippled her and her brother with. The humiliation of coming to Dumea had been a welcome choice compared to the unforgiving ire of their creditors.

"You're worried about the dowry."

"I'm worried about all of it. The visit, we have none to speak for him. Tobiath and I, we are too young, and we have no titles... But Hassan," she said hopefully. "Well, he is *steward of Dumea.*"

"Oh, no–"

"They would receive him, Yasmin. He could sit and talk with their elders, decide the brideprice."

"Bilyana, Hassan is very busy."

"I know. I know he is. But if he could do this..."

"I doubt he would be willing. The journey alone, there and back, is at least two weeks, likely three with the rainy season just beginning. And the heat..."

"Yes, I know, but there would be good reason for him to."

"What reason? We have Noah's Judgment, after that we are at court in Hanesda. I see no way he could–"

"Governor Zaqeem," Bilyana said suddenly.

Yasmin frowned. The name of her dead brother hung in the space between them. Somewhere a minstrel and strings had begun to play. The crowd were starting to clap. Yasmin stared at the other woman. "That is *not* funny, Bilyana."

"And I play no game, sister." She leaned in further. "What if I told you I knew things, about Governor Zaqeem, about why he died?"

"Zaqeem died because he tried to have a pair of orphan girls put to death on an altar like goats. Should it be any surprise he was come upon by robbers? Everyone knows raiders always seek those disgusting gatherings, all the gold to be had there, and–"

Bilyana touched her arm, gave a short sad smile. "No, dear sister. That wasn't why. Speak to Hassan. Tell him what I have said. He will understand. Then ask him to favour my brother. He listens to you, Yasmin." Bilyana finished the wine in her goblet and glanced back to the crowd. "Now, I have to go. I can see Tobiath trying to leave. We have so few parties in this wretched place and always he seeks to leave. To go *where*, I ask?"

With that, Bilyana briskly walked away. She turned once and offered another tight nervous smile, mouthing the words *he listens to you*, before disappearing into the shallow throng of people without looking back.

Seven
FAMILY

Daneel stood beside his brother and watched Tobiath and Bilyana leave the gathering. He watched as the couple squabbled in the street. Then he tried to imagine the things they'd be saying to each other as he and Josef went on ahead to wait at the library, where they knew Tobiath would eventually go. It had become a habit of late for Daneel. Imagining things. Daydreaming.

He'd had plenty of time for it, after all. Days, in fact. That was how long he and Josef had been here, stuck in Dumea, discreetly following the city's officials around like stray dogs. Studying them. Waiting. Daneel had never been good at that. Both his strength and weakness, Master Johann liked to say. At the moment it was proving to be the latter. Even Josef was growing tired of his complaints about being here. It had got to the point he'd taken to roaming the city alone each morning to avoid Daneel's company, learning the streets, or else simply meditating in the safehouse. Which was the other thing Daneel was sick and tired of – the safehouse.

The housekeeper was an old blind woman who'd been a beggar the Shedaím redeemed, granting her the small hovel she now kept for sheltering the strangers they sent. The Brotherhood kept many like her, in every city; always blind, always old, though not always as forgetful as this one, forgetful of how many times she'd told her story, how many times she'd praised the mercy of the strangers who'd redeemed her. Too many times for Daneel to hear again. He'd rather follow this Tobiath around and imagine what he and his wife might be arguing about.

Besides, Daneel had never been much good with meditating anyway, the first discipline they teach you. Unlike Neythan, who could contentedly sit still with his eyes closed for over half a day, Daneel had never been able to build a taste for it.

He shrugged.

What of it? As Master Johann would always say: each tree has its fruit, and Neythan's bloodtree had little, for all the meditating he did.

Where *was* Neythan anyway? And what of Yannick and Arianna? How long were he and Josef expected to keep following around city officials in Dumea to pass the time?

"Something is wrong," Daneel said.

Josef sighed and continued to watch the library. They'd found a good place to wait. It was early evening and at this hour the library cast a deep shadow along its eastern side.

"I can feel it," Daneel said. "The others ought to have arrived by now."

"We don't know that."

Daneel looked at his brother. "Of course we do. What's that even supposed to mean? *We don't know that.*"

"It means the decrees."

"What of them?"

"None of us were privy to each other's edicts."

Daneel thought about it. Say what you want about Josef, he always had another way of seeing things. "You think there's more to what they were ordered to do," Daneel said. "Before coming here."

"Perhaps."

"Like what?"

"I don't know. That's the point."

"We were not told of that. Master Johann said nothing of that."

"No. He didn't."

"You think it a test."

"Probably."

"Because we are not to discuss our decrees, what we are each to do."

"Perhaps that's the test."

"Whether we will or not."

"I think so."

"So what were yours?"

Josef chewed.

"I'm your brother, Josef."

"I haven't forgotten."

"You're not going to tell me?"

Josef didn't answer.

"Fine. Don't tell me... but I know something's wrong."

Josef didn't say anything. Neither spoke for a while. They listened to the faint sound of music as it drifted across from the harvest festivities in Dumea's main square. The celebrations had been going on for some time. It seemed to be all they did here, indulge in celebrations and spend the rest of their time in debates, waffling on about the meaningless writings of dead men stored in their library. To be expected in a place like this, Daneel supposed. Jaleem, the woodworker, had warned them as much back in Ilysia. Not a talkative man but one of the few things he'd shown a willingness to speak at length about was Dumea, the city of his birth. What it was like now and its history.

How Seth of Hophir, the eighth king of Dumea, had built the library before the Sovereignty's birth. How his grandson, Sufjan, later sought to fill it with works and writings from every known land, beginning a tradition that would be handed down through his line for generations until news of it reached even to Kosyatin, the sixth sharíf, who, when he came upon Dumea to raze it, couldn't, for fear of destroying the sacred library. In the end Dumea became part of the Sovereignty in nature if not name, ceding fealty to Hanesda in tribute without adopting its laws, and thereby turning its line of kings into stewards. Since then it had become little more than a hinterland on the way to Súnam to which Sharífs banished the disfavoured and undisciplined as ancestral penance for the city-state's resistance to full sovereign rule. Which, Daneel thought, only added to the scores of babblers and wastrels already here.

He sighed. The tale of the place was as boring as being in it. He leaned over to his brother. "I am to kill Hassan, the city steward," he said. "When the others arrive."

Josef looked at him, still chewing, then back to the library.

"I told you my decree."

"You did."

"You're still not going to tell me?"

Josef said nothing.

"I can't believe you're not going to tell me."

"They're here."

"What?"

"They're here. Look."

They watched the men they'd been waiting for go into the library, and then got up to follow. They climbed the wide steps of the entrance and entered, passing beneath the tall arch of the doorway into a short high-ceilinged anteroom. Dense patterns covered the walls. Through another doorway and beyond the anteroom, the space swelled higher and wider still, a yawning expanse of shelves and scaffolds. Rolls of vellum and scraps of jaundiced parchment poked out from sills dug into the walls.

"There they are," Josef whispered.

Daneel followed his brother's gaze. Two men sat opposite one another at a small table across the room. Josef and Daneel wandered in their direction to a shelf filled with wooden artefacts, each etched with unfamiliar markings and scribbles.

Daneel picked one up and turned it in his hand, showing it to his brother.

Josef glanced at the piece and cocked an eyebrow. They conferred like this quietly from a distance, just close enough to hear some of the muttered speech of the pair they'd followed in.

"You're not listening to me. How can you be sure he was there?"

"Hassan, I know this is difficult…"

"*Difficult*? Do you, Tobiath? *Can* you?"

"My *brother*, Hassan, my brother, my own flesh and blood, he saw him there with his own two eyes. I know he can be… well…"

"He is a drunkard."

The other man lifted a finger. "He is my brother, Hassan. He knows what he saw. Governor Zaqeem was lying there among the others with his throat cut."

Hassan sighed. Looked away. Looked back again. Said something too quiet for Josef or Daneel to hear.

The other man, Tobiath, waved him off. "It's nothing… just… listen to me, my friend. You must listen to…" More murmured words, placating gestures.

Hassan was shaking his head.

Tobiath was becoming more animated. He grasped Hassan's forearm. "You must see," he said, just loud enough to hear. "Zaqeem was not a simple man. You didn't know everything about him, neither of us did. You said it yourself, for more than a *year* he'd been hiding something. Perhaps now we know what that something was."

"He was not one of them."

"Yet he was found among them." The man lifted his hands. "I loved him too. But it is where he was found. He was mere feet from the altar."

Hassan shook his head again. Their voices dropped once more from earshot.

Tobiath was murmuring intently. He seemed to be doing most of the talking now.

After a while Hassan leaned in. "And Yasmin?"

"No," Tobiath said, a little louder than intended. Both glanced around the room before turning back to one another. "Do not tell her, Hassan. She *cannot* know."

"You are doing as Zaqeem did, Tobiath. You are keeping things from me. And now you ask I do the same with her?"

Their voices lowered again. Josef looked around but there was no way of getting closer without making their listening obvious.

The Brothers continued to move around the library, pretending to examine its various artefacts and texts whilst remaining within earshot of the two men until midnight, when the library closed. When Tobiath finally left, Josef and Daneel followed him from a distance. They watched him go along the side streets by the sheepgate. They followed him through the narrows by the city's west quarter and then out into a deserted street.

From the adjoining alley, they could see Tobiath walk the street's length to the walled end on the other side. The man reached the cornerhouse, stopped to look around, and then retrieved a key from beneath a pot beside the door.

"Same as yesterday," Josef said. "He will be in there for an hour at least, alone, then he will go to sit with the old men by the city gates."

"What do you think he is doing in there?"

Josef shrugged. "Whatever it is, he offers us now as good a chance as any."

"As good a chance for what?"

Josef paused. He looked at Daneel a long time and then exhaled. "To do what I have been bid, brother... He is my decree." He went back to looking at the house.

Daneel kept watching him.

"What?" Josef said.

Daneel was smiling. "You told me your decree."

Josef shrugged. "Yes. Well. Like you said, you are my brother after all... and besides, I will need your help if I am to fulfil it here." He looked at him again. "There can be no blood."

"I thought all was to be done the same day, when the others get here."

"All but this one."

"Nothing was said of that."

"Will you *help*, brother?"

Daneel looked from his brother back to the street. He shrugged. "I suppose there will be little else to do until the others arrive anyway."

"Good. Come then."

They crept along the road toward the cornerhouse. It was about the size of a stable-booth and joined to an overlapping terrace behind it. There was one window, a tiny muslin-draped portal without shutters.

Daneel slowed as he came to the door, back against the wall. He crab-stepped along its length as he glanced up to the flat-roofed porch above to make sure no one else was looking out. He could hear the scrape and shuffle of Tobiath's movements within the cornerhouse as he approached the window and peered through the muslin. He could just make out Tobiath's shape kneeling by the far wall in the gloom, his elbows propped on a ledge, head bowed, facing the wall. The man seemed to be writing.

Daneel dipped his head and climbed into the window, carefully squeezing through the tight fit. He rolled in shoulder first and slowly lowered his weight onto the dusty floor.

The chamber was dim. Two clay cups and a dish on the ledge by a tumble of scrolls. A lamp on a sill in the corner opposite with another pile of scrolls beside it. Tobiath remained oblivious, on his knees facing the wall, scribbling frantically.

Daneel rose and crept across the room. He could feel Josef beginning to scrape his way into the window at his back. Tobiath was murmuring to himself as he wrote. He stopped abruptly as Daneel approached and stood over him.

"I knew you would come eventually," Tobiath said.

Daneel had been reaching toward the man's throat but now froze.

"Yes," Tobiath said. "Just as you did for Zaqeem... She will rest easy then, her secret safe."

Daneel was about to ask what he meant when the man moved suddenly, leaping back, pushing with his feet from the wall to thrust back and try to shove Daneel over. Daneel saw it coming, rode the impact and let the man's weight carry them to the ground. He got on top quickly, grabbed an arm by the wrist as the man scrambled, then wrenched it back, twisting hard. The man screamed as the bone crunched, then shot out his other arm. Only afterward would Daneel realize he'd thrown something. The wall beside them crackled like cooking fat, then erupted with hot wind and jagged rock as sparks flashed, knocking Daneel sideways off Tobiath.

He blacked out for a moment and when he came to, Tobiath was on top of him, trying to strangle him with his remaining healthy hand. Daneel reached up and fended off the grip easily as Josef came in and hauled the man up from behind and tossed him against the wall.

Josef struck Tobiath once, hammering into the side of Tobiath's neck with the blade of his hand. The man sagged, dazed and choking, and slumped to the ground beside Daneel.

Daneel got on top and clasped him by the throat, then proceeded to do to Tobiath what Tobiath had tried to do to him just a moment before.

By the time Daneel loosened his grip he was breathing hard and sweating. Tobiath wasn't breathing at all, his spittle-frothed lips open and still, his gaze frozen. Almost peaceful, Daneel thought. He passed his fingers over the man's eyes and pressed the eyelids shut as Josef got up behind him.

"What *was* that?" Daneel said.

Josef had gone across the room and was examining the wall on the far side. There was a scorched patch of stone, and a small shallow pock where the fragments of rock had erupted from the wall.

Josef just shook his head, unable to answer, trying to rehearse it in his thoughts – the sound, the heat, the curious way the stone had come apart.

"I don't know."

Daneel climbed to his feet.

Josef turned to examine the scrolls on the sill.

"Whatever it was, it was loud," Josef said. "We shouldn't linger here." He pulled a sack from his sleeve and tugged it open. He put the scrolls inside then turned to the ledge where Tobiath had been writing when they came in.

"What are you doing?" Daneel said.

Josef swept his hand across the ledge, pushing the contents – letters, scraps of vellum, scribbled parchment, etched shards of clay – into the sack. "We must move quickly." He nodded at Tobiath's body on the ground. "We are to bury him. He is not to be found."

"Bury him? Where?"

"You will need to fetch the horse and cart. It will be easier to get him out of the city that way."

"*Out of the city*? And you couldn't have mentioned this before?"

"I hadn't expected for there to be..." Josef gestured loosely at the small scorched crater on the wall. "Whatever *that* was. I thought we'd have time. The noise will have drawn others. The sooner you go and get the horse and cart..."

"Fine, fine, I'm going. But you should mark this, brother. The list of favours I'm owed..."

Josef nodded and waved him off.

Daneel unlatched the door and peered through the crack, then went out.

He didn't see Josef go to the window and push the flimsy drape of muslin aside to watch him hurry across the street in the dark. Nor did he see him wait until Daneel had rounded the corner of the alley opposite, and then wait a while longer to be sure his brother hadn't forgotten something or found some other reason to return.

Once he was sure, Josef turned back to the room and went straight to the second pile of scrolls on the sill in the corner. He rifled through them carefully, checking the names and titles stitched into the leather and goat hide coats of each. He found the one he was looking for and lifted it from the others. He held it to the lamplight by the sill to be sure as he read the name stitched along the cover.

"*Magi Qoh'leth.*"

Just as his decree required.

Josef carefully unrolled the scroll, then tightly rerolled it and tucked it into the sleeve inside his cloak, out of sight. Then he waited for his brother.

Eight
FALL

Neythan felt like he was climbing from the belly of some vast beast as he looked up to the small circle of daylight above him. He could see sharp outcrops of pumice and flint overhead where the passage twisted up toward the exit.

"How'd you ever bring me down here?"

Caleb turned and looked down on him. "Your horse was very strong," he said. "Amazing what can be done with a good horse and a length of rope."

"And where is the horse now?"

"Well, a man must eat."

Neythan grimaced as he watched the little man skip deftly from one foothold to the next. It turned out the stony hollow where Caleb had kept him all this time was joined to a series of underground caverns that led to the outside through a lengthy and convoluted tunnel. Caleb had warned he would need a week to regain his strength in readiness of it. After so long stuck in that hole, Neythan had had no intention of waiting. Now he was beginning to regret how quickly he'd spurned the other man's advice. His joints ached. His muscles were stiff and burning.

"How much further?"

"Not long."

Neythan sighed with the effort as he reached for another

handhold. "You said that last time I asked."

"Then it is truer now than it was then."

The man wasn't even out of breath.

The daylight thickened as they neared the top. Neythan could feel the freshness of the air on his skin. He squinted as he reached the surface and poked his head into the dawn. The sky was cold and pale. Rain stung icily on his head. He lifted his face to it, mouth open, and let the drops tingle coolly on his tongue.

The tunnel had led out onto a smooth flat of stone edged by woodland.

Caleb clambered out quickly and stood as Neythan swung his knee up onto the rim of the opening, before rolling himself clear and onto his back. He lay there like that for a few moments, exhausted and face up in the light rain and thin, frigid air, watching his breath plume out above him like steam. Caleb looked down on him chirpily.

"Here, let me give you a hand up," he said, smiling.

Neythan waved him off and rolled onto one knee before forcing himself to his feet. He looked around at the skinny trees surrounding the plateau as the morning sun winked through their branches. And then turned again to the little man and waited for the explanation of how to find Arianna he'd promised before they began the climb.

"So." Neythan jutted his chin out impatiently. "How?"

"It's simple," Caleb answered. "The waterfall."

"The waterfall... where I last saw her?"

Caleb nodded.

Neythan just looked at him.

Caleb raised a palm to explain. "You see, I often hunt by the fall, Neythan, for rats and voles. It's what I was doing when you and I met. You'd disturbed me as I was about to catch the fattest beaver a man ever saw. There'd have been meat enough for five men, he was so fat. You can imagine my annoyance."

"Inconsiderate of me."

"Well, *I* thought so. But let's not dwell."

"What has this to do with Arianna?"

"I was hunting there, three years ago perhaps. Again, it was winter. The rabbits grow scarce with the cold and so I go again to the fall for the rats. One night I see a man come that way."

"What man?"

"I don't know. It doesn't matter. The point is not who he was but what he *did*."

"And what was that?"

"The very thing this Arianna of yours did. He came to the waterfall, peered at it, then jumped through to the other side, and didn't come out."

Neythan thought about it. "You're certain he didn't come out."

"I am."

"How long did you wait?"

"I did better than wait. I followed. But when I went through I found nothing, just a sort of small empty space, a hollow behind the water."

"He'd gone?"

"Just so."

"Where?"

Caleb grinned. "I don't know."

Neythan was expecting him to say more. Caleb didn't.

"You said you knew how to find her."

"I said I could help."

"What you've said is neither."

"*Neither*? There is a door behind the waterfall, Neythan. Some sort of hidden opening."

"And you saw this door?"

"I couldn't find it then but there must be one. It's the only explanation."

"Even if there is, it was days ago. Am I to expect for her to be there now?"

"Of course not. But it's a curious thing, is it not, a door behind a waterfall? Finding it will likely tell you *how* to find her, where to look. That's more than a good Brother ought to hope for considering the time that has passed."

In truth Caleb was right and Neythan knew it. This was the best he could have expected, and yet he'd hoped for more. He swallowed his annoyance and looked at the barren trees. He sighed.

"This fall, then…"

Caleb smiled. "Follow me."

It took them most of the day to reach it. They traipsed down the soggy hill beyond the plateau, and into the grassless vale beneath. Neythan's thighs, still thawing to life from the incense, burned with every pace. Noon came and passed, the occasional faraway caw of a crow the only sound.

Caleb grew tired of the quiet and began to talk, about everything, about nothing. He spoke about the five realms of the Sovereignty, the forested mountain lands of Calapaar to the west and north, the dry plains of Harán to the east, the fertile riverlands of Sumeria and Hardeny to the south, and the coastlands of Eram that lay beyond. He continued on like a scribe, telling Neythan about their customs and histories. Which Neythan didn't mind. It passed the time.

The land turned greener as they neared the stream. They followed it through more scrubland until they stepped beyond the sparse shrubbery into a ravine lined by batches of tall thick oaks. The rocky basin was familiar, split by a gurgling brook flowing from a tall waterfall on the other side.

This was the place.

Neythan could see the spot where Arianna had clambered from her horse on the outcrop beside the river.

He walked slowly toward the brook and stepped up the ledges of slate and lichen to the top of the bank. The waterfall and brook were quieter than they'd been when he was last here.

"Do you see anything?" Caleb said as he struggled up behind him.

Neythan looked up at the sky. It was getting dark. He looked again at the shallow brook, and then back to the fall. There was a ledge of stone protruding from behind the cascade. The brook was a three-foot drop from where he stood on the outcrop. Caleb finally made it to the top and came alongside him.

"What is it?" the older man wondered.

"I don't know."

The ledge must have been hidden by the heavy rain last time. Arianna would have had to have known exactly where it was. Neythan looked around and measured his options.

"I suppose there's only one way to find out."

He jumped in.

Neythan gasped as he hit the water. It came to his thighs and quickly numbed his legs. He waded through stiffly, arms high and wide, until he reached the waterfall. He felt for the stone sill he'd seen from the outcrop, and then bounced up from the water to pull himself through the fall onto the ledge.

"What can you see?" Caleb shouted.

To which the answer would have been not much. The ledge was short, no more than a few feet. Water spat at Neythan's head and nape as he stood up in the space behind the fall.

"Anything?" Caleb said.

"Why don't you come down and tell me?"

The older man grumbled and proceeded to scramble down the outcrop. He got halfway down and then slipped, tumbling into the brook back first. Neythan turned, smiling as Caleb struggled to right himself in the water and slowly waded toward him.

"Here," Neythan said. "Let me give you a hand."

Caleb took his hand grumpily and let Neythan yank him up.

"How did you manage to get up here last time?"

Caleb ignored him and began to feel along the wall. "It must be here somewhere."

"So you say, but I've been looking. I can find nothing."

"There will be something."

"As I said, the–"

"Ah." Caleb pointed.

"What?"

"There… do you see?"

"Where?"

"There."

Neythan crouched a little to bring his line of sight level with Caleb's. "I don't see anything."

"Just… there."

Neythan followed the other man's gaze. Then, seeing, he cursed. "What *is* that?"

Nine
WATCHER

Neythan stared, dumbfounded, at the glowing fissure in the rock. Soft blue light seemed to be leaking out of a narrow cleft in the wall like dawn through a morning drape. He'd never seen anything like it.

"What by the gods *is–*"

He was leaning forward to touch it when the faint light blinked and then suddenly exploded. It was like lightning, a sustained surge of blue-white radiance that seemed to widen the cleft into a breach, peeling at the wall to part the rockface. The noise was deafening. Neythan felt the ground quaking as the light began to suck at the surroundings like a gale. Chunks of rock ripped away from the opening, yanked back into its shining vortex. Then everything began to collapse. Neythan watched in awe as trees, boulders, and even the water itself lifted from their places, snatched into the vortex whilst he stood there, somehow cocooned in stillness. He tried to catch sight of Caleb in the blur of flying dirt but the light was too bright, and growing brighter. Behind him the waterfall had disappeared and he could see the tall black oaks from the ravine's edge being ripped from their roots. They popped free in the gale and hurled toward the gleaming breach, toward *him*.

Neythan dropped to one knee, lifting an arm to shield

himself, eyes clamped shut.

Then everything stopped. The noise, the wind, the shuddering earth beneath him, all of it fell into abrupt silence, like speech stilled mid-sentence.

When Neythan opened his eyes he found himself standing alone, surrounded by an endless cloudless sky. Or at least that's what it seemed to be. He couldn't be sure. Stars spangled the expanse overhead but seemed to be swaying. The sight was so captivating it took a moment for him to realize the ground had become a metallic and silky plane, undulating slowly like a half-frozen sea. The ripples seemed to move across both it and the strange sky as one, as though they were somehow joined, their pulses spreading from some hidden point on the horizon. Neythan stood there, frozen, staring at the bizarre luminous vista all around him, trying to make sense of it.

"Your presence is welcome, Neythan."

The woman's half-whispered words echoed against each other, her voice like a chorus. Neythan turned around and when he saw her, almost forgot to breathe. She stood more than a full head and shoulders above him, dressed in white sheet-thin garment that began at her shoulders and swathed her body like bandages, spreading at her ankles to rest on the slowly moving floor. Her arms were poised slightly away from her body, sheathed in the same thin white fabric. Her eyes were golden and fluorescent, like jewels. Her hair, white and straight, swayed gently in the breeze. Neythan tried to speak but no words would come.

"You took longer to come than I'd hoped," she said.

Her voice, strange as it was, seemed familiar. Neythan looked up at her and made another attempt at speech. His tongue felt heavy, his lips cumbersome and dry.

"Who... are you?"

The woman paused, seemed to frown. "Why do you ask who I am?"

Neythan had no answer.

"All that matters of the witness is what she sees. The time is short, Neythan. You must seek what must be known. To seek anything else is meaningless."

Neythan nodded hesitantly. The words didn't make sense, his thoughts still frazzled by the surroundings. He glanced at the strange liquid floor, then back to the woman, who just stood there, still and immense with that unerring golden gaze.

"What is this place?"

"A breach."

"But... Where are we?"

"Everywhere."

Neythan hesitated. "I don't understand."

"This place is the world you know."

Neythan looked at the swaying velvet sky. "It is not."

"A part of your world," the woman clarified.

"It is no part I have known."

The woman's eyes seemed to shift, as if about to smile. "It is not the way a branch is part of a tree, or an arm part of the man... this place is as the sap that *sustains* the tree, the blood that sustains you."

She raised a hand and, as she did so, seemed to block out the moon, hiding it from view. She looked at the resulting shade on the cool molten ground. Neythan followed her gaze.

"The realm you know is a shadow cast by the light," she said. "It does not know the light that made it." She looked up at Neythan. "Just as you do not know this place."

Neythan tried to make sense of it, of where he was.

"But... I was..." He shook his head. "There was a waterfall."

"Yes. I called you there."

"*Called* me?"

"Yes. You remember... Don't you?"

Her voice *was* familiar. He squinted in thought. The answer unfolded slowly, clearing like stilling water, though what eventually emerged made little sense.

"My… dreams?"

In the cavern with Caleb's incense, he'd dreamt strange things, of memories and shadows and at each turn he'd heard a shallow beckoning, a woman's voice in a half-whisper. *This* woman's voice.

"You…" He spoke the word slowly, almost accusingly. "How?" He shook his head and looked up again at the woman. "This cannot be."

But the woman just tilted her head, as though watching a rare animal or small child. "A thing is as it is," she said. "It owes nothing to the ways of the one who has learned of it. To think so is deceit and folly, *man's* folly, taught by the shadow wherein he abides. You must seek what must be known."

Neythan had no answer. He glanced again at the silent stars, then the slow-moving liquid ground, and nodded again, as if willing himself to accept it. *Seek what must be known.*

"You called me here," he managed.

The woman said nothing.

"Why?"

The woman's gaze, for the first time, seemed to approve. She gave a single slow nod then pointed a finger. "See behind you."

Neythan obeyed and turned around. In the distance, at the point from which the pulses seemed to be spreading across the sky and sea-like ground, there was a small dim light sitting on the horizon, each ripple moving outward from it as though from a dropped stone in a lake.

"What is that?"

But the woman didn't answer. The light continued to wink, then seemed, as Neythan stared at it, to fill his thoughts, his vision, encompassing everything until there was only it, its blank white canvas before him. He saw strange shadows moving across it. He heard sounds of war, of horse and rider, as the light continued to blink to the rhythm of his heart.

"What is this? What's happening?"

But again the woman didn't answer. The images simply continued, their sounds growing louder: the braying of beasts, the screams of men, the howling lament of the wind. Soon the shapes began to merge together, gathering into a hulk of black smoke that seemed to reach toward him.

Neythan tried to move but couldn't. He watched as the arm turned to long gaseous tendrils and took hold of him, wrapping around his wrist. The grip burned as the shadowy creature continued to grow and merge with the sky, whispering words Neythan couldn't understand, louder and louder, until Neythan finally closed his eyes and buried his head in his hands.

When he opened his eyes again he was standing before the woman. The creature was gone. The woman watched for a moment as Neythan gathered himself.

"The shadows shown to you tell of what is to come," she said. "They tell of darkness."

Neythan looked down at his wrist where the thing had touched him. The skin had striped red and was stinging. "What darkness?"

"This too you shall learn. But there are laws between you and me. Things that can be told. Things that cannot. You must know what to ask."

"What do you mean? I do not know who you are, or even where I am. How can I know what I am to ask?"

"A man's sha knows what *he* does not, though he seldom listens to what it tells; this too is his folly."

"My sha?"

"You must still it, Neythan. The way you have been taught. It is why you are here."

As she spoke her arm stretched out and, though it did not reach him, somehow touched him. Neythan stared into her eyes and saw a calm there that, as he continued to gaze, seemed to pass from her to him. His breathing slowed, deepened, turning heavy and quiet until after a while he closed his eyes to gentle his sha the way Master Johann had taught.

"This place," Neythan said, opening his eyes again. "It is not the light of which you spoke, is it?"

The woman smiled. Neythan watched her. It was as if the words had offered themselves to him from the silence.

"No," she said. "It is not. Just as the moon is not the sun." She raised her hand as she had before, again covering the moon's pale glow. "And yet..." This time she parted her fingers, allowing some of the moonlight to press through and pierce the shadow on the ground in front of them. "By observing one, the other can be known."

Neythan looked at her hand and the parted fingers. "A parting," he said. His mind suddenly felt clear. "A breach," he nodded to himself. "That *is* what this place is, a tear, as in a garment."

"Yes, Neythan. But that is not why you are here."

"Why *am* I here?"

The woman said nothing.

Neythan thought about it, back to the waterfall, the long journey from Caleb's cavern. "I was seeking someone... A girl, she was–"

"Arianna," the woman answered.

"Yes... Yes... You know her?"

The woman didn't answer.

"Did she come..." Neythan gestured tentatively at the surroundings. "To this place?"

"Arianna has chosen her path, Neythan. You must choose yours."

"You know where she is."

The woman said nothing.

"Can you tell me where she is?"

"I can tell you whatever you wish. The heart receives no more than what it desires."

"Then tell me, where will I find her?"

The woman said nothing for a long while, staring at Neythan as if into some revealed secret. "The crown city will lead you to her," she finally said.

"The crown city. Hanesda. You mean Hanesda."

Something like lightning flickered silently across the sky and shimmered in the clouds. The woman looked up at it.

"It is time for you to return, Neythan."

"Return?"

"To your place."

"But... I have questions. You spoke of darkness."

The woman's face, though still, seemed to grow solemn. "The question you have desired is answered. You can receive nothing more. There are laws between you and me. You must return. The time is short."

And then her garment burst into light, shining with increasing intensity until it hurt too much to look at. Neythan turned away, back toward the dim lamp on the horizon. The light from the woman spread out like an unrolling scroll to envelop the sky, until everything – the stars, the lamp, the horizon itself – was eclipsed, swallowed in her burning bright wake. Neythan closed his eyes.

When he blinked them open again, everything was dark and blurred. A smudgy round shape moved at the top of his vision to muffled sounds.

He blinked again. The smudge was a face, hanging upside down.

"Neythan! Neythan, wake up. Come. We don't have time for this. Get up. Get up!"

Caleb's upside down image was standing over him.

"Caleb?"

"You speak? Finally you *deign* to speak?"

"What are you doing?"

"What am *I* doing? You fell from behind the waters as though *dead*. I had to *drag* you out of the brook. I've been trying to wake you for over an *hour*. Get up!"

Neythan rolled his head to look around. "We're still here?"

Caleb shot him a murderous look. "Get. Up."

Neythan rolled onto one elbow. He shook his head, everything was so fuzzy. "What happened?"

Caleb stared back wide-eyed before jabbing a finger at Neythan's chest. "You listen to me, boy. I told you we were to be gone by nightfall. I carefully explained to you my concerns."

"You didn't explain any–"

"And lo, it is nightfall. And we are still here. Now, we don't have time for these games. You ought to count yourself fortunate I didn't leave you here to them."

"To who?"

"Just get up."

Neythan climbed groggily to his feet. The forest was dark. The moon was three-quarters full, the same as it had been with the woman in the... where? Where had he been? Had it been no more than a dream?

"Come, Neythan," Caleb hissed. "The time is short."

The time is short. The words echoed strangely in his head. His wrist was hurting. He looked down and saw the trace of a red mark striping his forearm, like he'd been lashed with an ox goad.

"Neythan!"

Caleb was frantically gathering up their provisions from the riverside. Neythan went over to help. A rustle from across the river behind them. They froze and looked beyond the water to the woodland on the other side. Nothing. Caleb eyed Neythan.

"Time to go," the little man whispered.
Neythan decided he was right.

Ten
SHARÍF

To be king is to be a slave. That's what they don't tell you. The ingratiating bows, the absurd luxuries, the sweaty obsequious smiles of strangers with flabby fingers and ruby rings: all of it is an extravagant pretence. Something Sidon's father, for all his gnomic sayings and sage looks, had failed to tell his heir and son. Come to think of it he failed to say much of anything those last few months, bedridden most days, half-mad on the others.

And so when Sidon found himself, a year ago today, standing a quarter-mile beyond the city walls by the sepulchre as they rolled the stone, it was almost a relief to know the old man was finally gone. His mother, Chalise, had stood alone off to the side, her pale face tearless and blank as stone. Sidon, just thirteen, had stood with Uncle Játhon and his father's chamberlain, Elias, as they sealed the tomb with the palsied body of the old man inside. And afterward Sidon had tried to pretend he wasn't glad. Glad he'd no longer see the handmaids cleaning his father's emaciated flesh. Glad he'd no longer have to hold that frail veiny hand as he lay murmuring in his bed. Glad he'd no longer have to pretend it was fine when the old man forgot his name and seemed to scarcely recognize who he was. Glad it was all finally over.

He stood in the Judgment Hall looking out over Hanesda. From here he could see as far as Pularsi's amphitheatre and the southern quarter baths, and the pyramid of the city forum beside them prodding from the blockish rows of housing. They'd anointed him there, in the forum, a week after his father's burial. And although Sidon had trembled with nervousness throughout the ceremony he'd felt strangely exhilarated too. Sidon son of Helgon, sharíf of the Sovereignty, ruler of the Five Lands. No more Father commanding him what to do and when to do it. No more Mother ordering him around and telling him what to wear. He was ruler now. He was a man. He'd be able to do things his own way. Or so he'd thought at the time.

"*There* you are."

His mother came walking across the Judgment Hall as he stared out the window. He was looking at the way the aqueducts tracked along the eastern wall to meet the Swift on the other side.

"It would be better if the water's channels came in by Kaldan's Tower," he said. "Or even the circus, don't you think? It's strange that they don't."

His mother came to a halt at his shoulder. "The seamstresses have been waiting for you, Sidon."

Sidon turned to face her. She was dressed in a long blue robe. The garment draped neatly from her slender shoulders to the floor. Too young to be a queen mother. She'd been a girl of eighteen years when she'd wed his father, Helgon, to become sharífa. His father had been a man of fifty at the time.

"You are beautiful, Mother. All the council say so. They say you will wed again."

"It is *your* wedding we ready for, my son."

"Yes. Some Tresánite you have chosen who is old enough to be my aunt—"

"She is only eight years older than you."

"–and who I've seen but once, and never met, and probably won't much like."

"She is a good match. Joining with her house will secure your throne."

"You told me last time I'd grow to like her."

"Yes, well, perhaps a sharíf ought not require the childishness of pretence to do his duty. Now come... my king."

She turned and strode away. Sidon reluctantly, followed, walking out to the adjoining corridor which led toward the throne room and then to his bedchambers on the other side of the palace. The walls were marked with multicoloured ink drawings of Umar of Saliph kneeling to Theron the Great, the third sharíf – the mural was Father's favourite. The Birth of the Sovereignty, he liked to call it, depicting the moment when the king of Calapaar had ceded his vast territories and throne. The moment when Theron king of Sumeria became Theron the Great, a king of kings and true sharíf – fulfilling the dream of his grandfather, Karel, and beginning the line of sovereigns whose territories would continue to expand from one generation to the next as they conquered the High East, then Harán, Eram, and eventually Hardeny to the west; all the way to Dumea and the borders of Súnam lying south of it.

Sidon's gaze passed on from the drawings as they rounded the corner and moved toward his bedchamber. A small audience had gathered. They turned in unison as Sidon and his mother entered. A plump balding man with hairy forearms came forward and bowed.

"The choices have been prepared, Sharíf."

The man clicked his fingers and ushered several young women forward, each holding swathes of satiny fabric draped over either arm in varying colours and patterns.

"They are from Caphás, Sharíf, the finest that can be found. You see the fabric, how tightly woven it is. It is done by the hands of children, very skilled, their fingers are nimbler than any–"

"The blue, the red, and this one, the purple with the dyed yarn stitching."

The man bowed again. "The sharíf chooses well." He turned and clapped. Two of the girls hurried to a dressing area that had been set up in the corner. Another servant girl came alongside Sidon with a platter of fruit as he walked toward the screens. Sidon took a grape and, seeing his mother, the hirsute dressmaker and the house servants still standing behind him, paused.

"Don't worry, Mother. I think I will manage to dress myself."

She smiled thinly and went toward the door. The others followed her out.

It was a common thing for dressmakers to employ mutes as attendants. Sidon had even known some to cut out a slavegirl's tongue to better suit her for the role. A dressmaker could seldom expect to be present when a customer was trying on his wares. It seemed sensible to keep those whose company he'd have to leave them in from saying anything foolish. All of which meant it was a surprise when one of the girls actually answered Sidon. He'd been talking to himself as she helped him disrobe and put on an undercoat.

"What did you say?"

"I said I think you are right. That one *does* look better."

He looked at her, then to another slavegirl – apparently customarily mute – who looked back blankly, and then hurriedly stepped back behind the screen.

"It wouldn't usually do for someone your age but you've a man's shoulders already, my king."

Which was enough to keep Sidon from flinging the backswinging knuckle of his hand across her face and calling her master in to flog her.

"You've a bold tongue," he said.

The girl gave an apologetic dip of her head. "Forgive me, my king. My mother always says I can be dull-witted that way, given to speaking out of turn."

"Yes, well..." Sidon glanced at the cut of her dress, the way the fabric collected tidily between her breasts like a weir. "I suppose some follies, given time and mercy, can be learned from."

"Thank you, my king. Sorry, my king."

Sidon turned back to the brass dish to examine his reflection. He glanced hesitantly back to the girl. "But you say this one is better?"

The girl smiled shyly. "Yes, my king. The seam runs wider, here." Her palm brushed slowly across his shoulder blades as he looked at his reflection. "You have strong shoulders, so the fit is better for you. It is a man's fit, not a boy's."

Sidon nodded. Perhaps her counsel wasn't such a bad thing. "What is your name?"

"Iani, my king."

"Your master has taught you in these things?"

"Master V'lari teaches all of us, my king. But I've always had an eye for it. I'd fix my mother's dresses for her when I was a child."

Sidon turned from the brass to face her. She was slender, with rich dark hair that clung in soft curls to her neck like hanging baubles. She was only a few years older than him, younger than the girl he'd been promised to. Her dress was plain but clung around the hips so her–

"Sidon!"

The door to the bedchamber swung open with a thud, loud enough to make Sidon flinch. "What under the sun..." He pushed the girl aside and looked out from behind the screen to find his mother striding across the room toward him.

"What are you *doing*, Mother? I told you I can dress my–"

"You must come quickly," she said. "There has been word from Gahíd."

The doorkeeper to the throne room was a tall Súnamite with wide round shoulders that bulged from his sleeveless tunic like dark pommels. He bowed and held the door as Sidon and his mother entered.

The throne room was Sidon's favourite chamber; he loved the lofty ceiling and the elaborate paintings of his predecessors, Arvan the Scribe and Tsarúth the Brave, that covered it. He loved too the long windows that strafed the west wall, tall oblongs of nothing open to the sky and emptying the waning day into the chamber in thick shafts of dim sunlight that bronzed the wall on the other side, illuminating the detailed murals of the red-armoured armies of Theron the Great at the Battle of the Crescent.

Sidon's chamberlain, Elias – a small and wiry old man with large watery eyes that reminded Sidon of an owl – sat alone by the long council table. Uncle Játhon, governor of the city of Caphás and a prince of Calapaar, stood by one of the tall windows opposite, facing out to the palace court and marketplace beneath.

Elias stood and bowed as Sidon came in. Játhon turned from the window and gave a cursory nod.

Sidon noted the pair of courtiers in the middle of the room and looked at Elias as he climbed the steps to his throne.

"They have the herald's letter," Elias said. "The herald did not think herself worthy to enter your throne room. She made these two swear to keep the seal unbroken until you were present."

The queen mother raised her eyebrows. She'd followed Sidon up the steps and lowered into her seat beside him.

"The herald is one of Gahíd's *own*," the chamberlain explained.

Sidon caught his meaning and smiled. "*Is* she? I've never yet seen one face to face. Is she still here?"

"She waits by the reflecting pool to deliver your words to Gahíd."

"I'd like to meet her."

"It would be her honour, Sharíf," Elias said. "But that Gahíd would send one of them, and not a ranger, or dove… it suggests the matter is urgent."

Sidon nodded. "Very well. I am here now."

Elias bowed, showing the bald tanned dome of his scalp, his white hair curved in coarse tufts about the sides and back of his head like a fluffy halo. He turned to the courtiers and slipped a palm from the warmth of one of his deep sleeves to beckon them forward.

"Open the seal and read the words."

The younger courtier nodded. "Yes, sire." He cleared his throat, peeled the seal from the flute and took out the thin piece of vellum inside. "It says only: *The shadows sent out have turned on each other.*"

Sidon saw his mother stiffen beside him. One of Elias's horny feathered eyebrows hitched upwards. A silence stretched.

"*Turned*, you say…" the chamberlain said.

"Yes," the courtier answered. "That is what the letter says."

"Show me."

The courtier stepped forward with the epistle in hand. Elias took it and read. He looked back at Sidon and nodded.

"Was there nothing else?" Játhon had now stepped in from the far wall, frowning. "Did the herald say nothing else?"

"No, sire. The letter was all."

Sidon's mother leaned her forehead against her fingers.

Játhon waved the courtier away. "Leave us."

"No." The queen mother spoke. "They shall stay." She stood and walked slowly down the steps. "You have both taken the vow," she said to the courtiers. "Let it be known that should you break it and utter anything of what is spoken here there will remain nothing of you nor those of your house that shall not be broken tenfold in like manner. Do you understand?"

The courtiers nodded. A cloud passed the sun outside.

"The herald," she said. "How long was her journey?"

"Seven days, she said," the younger courtier answered. "She rode from the north, through the ash plains."

The sharífa nodded and glanced at Játhon. "It will have been a moon past at least then."

"Yes," Játhon said. "Unfortunate."

She turned back to the courtier. "I trust the herald spoke of where she learned Gahíd's tidings."

"Yes, Sharífa. Gahíd sent her from Godswell; a small Calapaari village a few days south of the Black Mountains."

"And does Gahíd remain there now?"

"The herald said he planned to stay, to study the place."

"I will need to speak with her, this herald."

"Yes, Sharífa," the older courtier said, speaking for the first time. "I will see to it."

The queen mother flapped an assenting palm.

The courtier bowed and exited the room, leaving the other standing alone. The sharífa went to one of the windows and looked outside. Her desire for a census had been refused by the council that morning, opposed, no doubt, by governors Sufiya of Qareb and Malkezar of Sippar, unhappy at having a boy on the throne too young to properly wield power and a queen mother who was, to them, an outsider. Chalise was a daughter of Saliph, the ruling house of Calapaar to the west and north, rather than a native of Sumeria like the late Helgon the Wise who'd widowed her. First Laws or not, for many it was the old ties they still held to. That was something young Sidon still failed to understand. Yes, he was sharíf. Yes, his forefathers had won vast territories. But to hold and wield them still required the influence of the Sovereign Council, an assembly including the rulers of every major city throughout the Five Lands, many of whom happened to be the offspring of old royal lines, with breeding and egos to match. Chalise understood it; before marrying Helgon to become sharífa she'd been one of them too, daughter to an old and noble line now reduced to bowing to sovereign edicts like an eager housemaid. Raised to rule, forced to serve, with the echo of the ancestral surrender and failure that had led to it splayed across the palace walls in celebratory murals like a constant taunt.

It took the tact of a general to avoid prodding these inherited wounds in council members whilst trying to coerce them to her own ends. To court the favour of Jashar, the king of Harán, without trampling the interests of Qalqaliman or Hikramesh. Every promise of an extra five hundred measures of grain to one city was a slight against the interests of another, every commitment to better trade for one land's merchants along the Ivory Pass would be at the expense of another's. Chalise had hoped the preparations for her son's wedding would lighten her mood, and now *this*. Her head was beginning to ache.

"You are new, are you not?" she said.

The courtier, realizing he was being addressed, nodded. "Yes, Sharífa."

"Phanuel, isn't it?"

He looked up, surprised to be known by name.

"You will perhaps find all this... a little confusing."

Phanuel didn't answer.

"You know the tidings, yet do not understand them... Talk of shadows and so on..." She made a lazy gesture with her hand, she was still looking out of the window. "It is something to which you will grow accustomed."

"My duty is only to obey, Sharífa."

"Yes, obey. Of course." She sighed wearily.

"Though… I *would* know my queen's disquiet if I were able to still it."

She cocked an eyebrow and looked at Phanuel over her shoulder. Phanuel bowed his head.

"Would you indeed," she said, then glanced at Elias at the table, and then back at Phanuel.

Again Phanuel didn't answer, unsure now why he had the first time. Yaron, the other more experienced courtier, had advised prudence in the throne room, it was always best to let one's words be few. Phanuel bowed his head.

"Well then," the Sharífa said. "Perhaps you *shall* know it…"

She turned from the window and began to approach him.

"Your king sent wolves on an errand, Phanuel," she said, gesturing vaguely to Sidon sitting quietly on the throne. "Expecting them to do what instinct has taught them to do." She walked along the lengthy table toward the courtier. "Yet these wolves defied what they'd been taught, they defied their master."

Phanuel remained silent.

"What do you think of that?"

Phanuel looked at the others in the throne room, then the sharífa again. "I know little of wolves, Sharífa."

"Even so…" she gestured mildly, waiting.

Phanuel hesitated. "I would think a wolf without instinct is more a dog than a wolf, my queen."

The sharífa smiled. "I would agree, Phanuel, I would agree. Yet even a dog is obedient to his master. What fate should await the one that is not?"

"Punishment, I would suppose."

She glanced behind to Játhon this time, then smiled again. "Quite," she said. "Yet these dogs are no ordinary beasts, they are a more savage kind than their kin, and now run free who knows where."

She had made her way around the table and taken several further steps toward Phanuel as she talked. She stood before him now with her hands clasped in front of her, gaze fixed, like a stablehand inspecting a new bought horse. Phanuel looked to Elias but his sleepy gaze stared back, indifferent. He looked back at the sharífa. She was smiling mildly, though her eyes remained hard, scrutinising. Phanuel fumbled for an answer.

"Then perhaps a trap? I've known men to catch wolves with traps."

"Perhaps these are too cunning for traps."

Phanuel said nothing.

"Come Phanuel, speak,"

"He is young, Sharífa," Elias answered from the table. "He does not see his impudence, but I will teach him of it."

She smiled more broadly now. "There is no impudence, Elias. He merely desires to please his queen." She turned to Phanuel once more. "Isn't that right, *courtier*?"

"I..." he looked to Elias again, then to Játhon, who too was watching, amused. Then to Sharíf Sidon on the throne, who was peering back curiously. "I am sorry, my queen."

"What need is there for apology? I ask only a question; you need only answer."

"I..."

"Come, let me know your counsel. How to catch a wolf, hmm?"

The sharífa had stepped closer, no more than a foot or so from him. He could feel the warmth of her breath.

"Will you not comfort your sharífa?" Her voice was quiet, yet rising.

Phanuel looked again to Elias, pleadingly.

"How to catch a wolf?"

"Sharífa, forgive me, I–"

"How to catch a wolf?" she repeated mildly.

Phanuel was panting now. "I cannot…"

"Don't look at him. Look at me. I am your queen."

"Please, Sharífa."

"Answer me."

"I…"

"Answer me!" she erupted, eyes wide with rage.

Phanuel felt the cool spray of spittle across his cheeks and on the bridge of his nose. He shut his eyes, trembling.

"Answer me!"

"Another wolf," he blurted.

Silence. Phanuel eventually opened his eyes to find her staring at him, her face now suddenly impassive. There was no trace of anger, or even feeling.

She spoke gently. "What was that?"

Phanuel's chin was buried in his chest. "I… I would say, perhaps… another wolf?"

The sharífa looked on him a long while, then smiled. "Indeed." She brought her hand to Phanuel's face and allowed it to hover over his cheek a moment before patting it softly. "Another wolf." She sighed happily and walked away back along the side of the table, past the tall windows and up the steps to return to her seat. "Very good, Phanuel," she said as she settled back beside the lofty bronze and ivory throne of her son who was now watching her curiously.

It was then the heavy scrape of the doors came again and the doorkeeper ushered the returning courtier into the chamber. He came and stood beside Phanuel and bowed.

"The herald awaits your enquiry, Sharíf."

Sidon peeled his gaze away from his mother and nodded.

"Very good," the queen mother answered. "Tell her to send word."

"My queen?"

"To Gahíd. She shall send word. Tell her…" She pondered a moment, looking off into the distance, smiling faintly. "Tell her, the Sharíf says to ready the pack, a wolf to catch a wolf. He will understand."

The courtier looked at Sidon, then Phanuel, and then the others in the room, and then bowed. "Very good, my queen."

Eleven
VAGABOND

Neythan couldn't help but look over the satisfyingly plain terrain with a hint of giddiness, glad to finally be out of the forest. Ridges of dried molten rock jutted in small dune-like rises across the horizon, stretching out beneath a pale, colourless sky to signal their arrival to the famed Ash Plains of Calapaar. Or, as some liked to call them, the Black Lands, named for their endless stretch of dark shale where Theron the Great, the third sharíf, had extended the frontiers of the Sovereignty into the vast territories of Calapaar more than two hundred years ago, taking the shipping lanes along the western coastlands that would later fund his grandson's conquest of the High East. Neythan could still remember the history lessons in Ilysia, Tutor Hamir slapping a stalk of willowcane across his knuckles every time he confused Tsarúth the Brave's exploits with those of Kosyatin the Bloody. Not that any of it mattered now.

Both Neythan and Caleb were exhausted. Barely a word had passed between them since they'd departed the ravine, although that was as much to do with the sulk Caleb had slipped into along the way as it was the work of the journey. For the three days since leaving the forest he'd limited himself to the occasional mumble and tut. His protest against the way Neythan had abruptly fallen asleep at the waterfall. Never mind that Neythan had about as much control over that as when he'd been pricked by Caleb's darts. Never mind that it was Caleb himself who'd persuaded Neythan to visit the fall in the first place.

Still, at least they were out of the forest, and after having journeyed a whole night to escape, Neythan was too tired to bicker anyway. In the end, he'd left Caleb to his stubborn silence and turned his thoughts instead to the encounter with what he'd now come to believe could only have been a Watcher.

Yes. A Watcher. It had to be. What else could she be but one of those mercurial spirits Neythan remembered from childhood chatter and Uncle Sol's stories? From before the time of men, Uncle Sol had said. Too old to be marked by age. Although Neythan had loved every tale told about them he'd never thought them anything more than fodder for fables. Not until seeing *her*.

Already his memory of the whole thing – the way she'd looked, the things she'd said – was beginning to fade, turning foggier with the passing of each hour. But the blueness of the place he'd stood in, and beyond that, her counsel to reach Hanesda, remained clear. And that was enough. More than enough. Because the more he thought of it the more certain he became of what she was, and the more certain he became of that the more uncertain did everything else become. For if she was a Watcher then the very world was no longer what he'd once thought it to be, or *more* than he'd thought it to be. And if the world itself could be so different from what he'd always thought, then what else?

The questions felt dizzying and perilous. It was a feeling he'd usually have taken hold of and expelled quickly from his mind, the way the disciplines taught, but *now*...

"Look."

Caleb's voice startled him. Neythan glanced over to find

him pointing ahead to a scant cluster of ruins in the distance.

"Shelter," Caleb said. "Looks empty too."

Neythan arched an eyebrow. "So, he speaks at last."

Caleb didn't answer. Neythan shrugged. They wandered slowly toward the broken structures. Three buildings, one beside the other, each built entirely of slagstone. The roofs were flat, the walls pebbly. In place of doorways there were small misshapen openings.

"Nomads," Caleb muttered. He nodded at the bump in the horizon miles to the east. "In times past men would settle in places like this. They'd wait until the volcano had its say, then take a smoothing stone, driven by oxen or mules, to some plot like this while the ground was still soft, and ready it to be built upon."

"Strange place to live."

"No, child. They did not build to dwell here. This place was made by wanderers, men without country."

"Well, if not to dwell, then for what?"

"Therein is the mystery. It's no simple thing to know the mind of the dead. The only ones who would were priests, and they are gone from these lands." He looked up at Neythan, squinting a little despite the dim sky. "You can thank your Brotherhood for that."

They wandered around the plot but it was mostly plain. The terrain left little need for a threshing floor and whatever other tools or structures there may have once been had long since gone, taken by time or the roll of the wind. After a while they looked around the houses too. The floors were smooth and flat, as if paved. The first two had an opening for a door and another for a window, admitting little daylight. The last house had no window but was almost roofless, with segments of what had once been its ceiling scattered about the ground in polygonal slabs of stone. A rubbly stack of rocks sat in the corner next to the biggest gap.

"Perhaps some sort of temple," Caleb said, standing beside the heap as Neythan stared up at where the roof ought to have been.

"Anyone would think you a scribe," Neythan said.

Caleb didn't answer.

Neythan was about to pry further when he heard the distant whinny of a horse. He went to the small doorway at the front of the building and saw a band of men approaching from the east.

"We're not alone."

Caleb came to the doorway and peered out to see. He stared for a long while, then grunted, took off his sack, and dumped it on the ground before pulling Neythan's crossbow out. Neythan stared at the bow, then Caleb.

"That's my bow."

Caleb glanced down at it in his hands. "So it is."

"All this time you've had my crossbow?"

"Where else did you think it'd be?"

"I thought it lost at the fall, when you took me."

"Well. Think of it as payment in kind, till the bargain is up."

"You've been stowing my bow this whole time and all–"

Caleb put his finger to his lips and pointed at the doorway and the approaching strangers, smiling.

Neythan glared back, then turned to the door and drew his blade.

There were four of them – three men and a woman – each dressed in long robes, all on muleback, save the leader who rode a horse. Neythan watched them as they neared, their mules loping across the dry plain with their tongues out, great long heads nodding as if in time to a rhythm only they could hear.

The woman was old; a Súnamite with dark ebony skin so cracked and sunbaked it resembled charred timber. She rode in the middle behind the leader, her head hung like a starved plant's. The man at the front wore a pale and dirty turban. Stubbled narrow jaw. Wide shoulders. A sword's sheath low-slung on his right thigh. A second man rode by the old woman. Heavy-set. Thick beard. Broad back. His legs dangling either side of his mule like tassels, his gut keeping him stiff and upright in the saddle. He talked and japed with the rider at the rear, a young man Neythan's age, gangly with a long neck that made his head loll in step with his mule's.

"Bandits, likely," Caleb whispered as he crouched at Neythan's elbow with the bow. "Makes sense for them to use this pass. Unlikely they'd see men or anything else for at least a day's journey in either direction."

The turbaned leader climbed from his horse in front of the ruins. He untied a gourd from his saddle and slowly eyed the grounds before murmuring something to the man behind him and pointing toward the broken houses. Then the man opened the gourd and lifted it to his lips. Neythan saw the woman's eyes flicker to life, gazing at the drinking man as he poured the water down his throat.

"Captive," Caleb whispered.

Neythan nodded, a common enough thing. Tutor Hamir had taught them of how bandits would wait on known trade routes, especially here in the north where there were fewer roads. It made it easier to guess the way a bounty might take. In the riverlands of Sumeria further south there was Qareb, Hanesda, Qadesh – each of them large market towns, which meant more merchants, more roads, and more cityguards and soldiers to watch them. Trickier work if you wanted to rob a man as he travelled, which was why bandits preferred to raid in the north.

The turbaned man wiped his mouth and stowed the flask, slipping it back among his provisions on the saddle. He smiled at the old woman, who slumped as he put it away. The man gestured again at his companions impatiently. They began to slowly climb down from their mounts. The old woman leaned forward on her beast. She looked exhausted. Neythan looked at her and decided.

"We need a horse," he said.

Caleb glanced up at him from the shadows. That they were backed into a house with one exit would make it hard to surprise the men. That they were both weakened, having walked with little rest for three days and eaten sparingly, would make it even harder.

"Whatever you may be thinking, Neythan, you would do well to forget it. The odds do not favour us. Look. The day is not far gone. With luck they will do no more than look around then continue on their way. If we can go without disturbing them then let us try."

"Give me the crossbow."

Caleb hesitated, but something about the way Neythan said it – so calm, and firm – made him obey. He handed the bow to him. Neythan put his sword in its sleeve and took it. He checked the stock and selected two quarrels, fixing one snug in the groove against the whipcord and the other beside it in the spine. Caleb watched him, saw the cold stillness in his gaze as he stared out at the bandits.

Outside, the men had begun to move about the ruined plot, looking around. Neythan looked out of the doorway again and saw the broad bearded one entering the house on the far side, chatting bawdily with the lanky youngster as he went in. Neythan would have liked an arrow in the leader first. He had the horse. He'd have the choice to flee, and had the look of one able to fight. But from this angle Neythan could no longer see him.

Neythan stepped out from the small doorway and looked around. There was only the old woman on the mule, head stooped and back hunched. Her gaze rolled up from beneath her headscarf to see him. Neythan nodded. The woman said nothing, as silent as the two mountless mules beside her. Neythan moved along the wall toward the gap between the houses, and then on to the low doorway of the adjacent house. The wind picked up, rolling grit from the ashy stone slope, rattling drily against the slagstone.

Neythan guarded his eyes as he reached the doorway and crouched to peek in. Daylight streamed in through the battered roof. He went inside. He checked the corners, his feet crunching on the dislodged grit from the crumbled ceiling. No one here. The big man let loose a loud belch outside to the sound of laughter. Neythan looked through the window at the back of the house. Still no leader, only the barren, slate-coloured landscape rising up on the other side. He went back to the doorway to check the next house.

Outside, the youngster was shouting at the old woman. He'd pulled her from the mule. She lay on her ribs, groaning, her wrists still bound as the youngster muttered insults before wandering away to the far corner of the plot to urinate. Neythan stepped out and moved to the last house as the boy stood with his back to him, showering the ground. Neythan stayed close to the wall, creeping in its shadow with the crossbow cradled low.

The big man came out yawning before Neythan reached it, a sop of dry bread in one hand, his other lazily scratching his gut as he squinted east to where the boy stood. He stretched and looked idly back along the wall away from the boy and toward Neythan. Saw him approaching in the wall's shadow and froze. He saw the crossbow in Neythan's hand; then, the bread dropping from his mouth, he reached clumsily to his waist for his sword.

Neythan quickly stepped away from the wall and shot the man through his beard. The arrow pierced his throat and lodged there like a signpost.

The boy turned at the man's grunt and yelped. Still

moving, Neythan skipped forward and swung the crossbow, pounding the bearded man's skull and then turning to the boy as the arrowed man crumpled to the ground, reaching feebly for the shaft in his neck as his shawl filled blood-red. Neythan thumbed the next arrow into place and moved to sight the boy.

Whisper of wind at his ear.

Neythan left off from his aim, dropping the crossbow, and turned abruptly to duck away.

The sword of the turbaned leader crashed from behind through the emptied space as he tried to plough through Neythan's shoulder from overhead. He was turning to swing again but Neythan had already unsheathed his blade. Was already pivoting, allowing his momentum to carry through into his backswinging arm and sword. The blade swung through the turbaned man's neck, separating his head from his shoulders in one savage swipe.

The dislodged head fell and rolled, coming to a stop between Neythan and the boy as the turban unravelled like a loose ball of thread.

Neythan remained still for a moment at the end of his follow-through, sword outstretched. He watched Caleb tentatively step out from the temple entrance and then turned to survey the carnage. The thick, bearded man lay slumped against the wall, his hand loosely clasped about the shaft in his throat as he wheezed and spluttered.

Neythan looked down at him without expression.

Then he turned his gaze to the headless body at his feet and the blood pulsing from it, puddling against the wall. The boy was still standing toward the edge of the plot, eyes wild and wide, fixed on Neythan. Neythan just looked at him. It was strange really, fascinating even, how other he was in that boy's gaze, how alien, though they were more or less the same age.

The boy panted, his breaths snatched and jittery, like an injured bird. He was still holding his member in one hand from urinating. His legs gave out as Neythan sheathed his sword and turned to walk toward him. Then, when he saw Neythan collect the crossbow from the ground, he began to scramble backward on his hands and feet, pleading, whimpering, begging for his life to be spared. Neythan aimed the bow and shot him in the chest from no more than a few feet. He stood and watched the boy bleed and grow still before turning back to the plot to face Caleb.

"Perhaps some warning in future?" Caleb said quietly as he approached, looking over the thick man with the arrow in his throat against the wall. The man was still now, no longer breathing. "Only I like to be somewhat ready when about to witness a bloodbath. Easier on the bowels."

Neythan walked to the beasts and took the bearded man's flask. Then he went to the old woman and squatted where she lay on the ground. He undid her bonds and handed her the flask and rose and returned to the beasts. He began removing the supplies hung over the mule-saddles but then, remembering, looked about for the leader's horse. He saw it idling at the corner of the front house. He threw the satchel he'd been rummaging through at Caleb.

"Only the necessities," he said. "We cannot take too much, we must make good time."

Caleb checked the satchel as the old woman, still on the floor, drank from the flask and watched Neythan. He approached the lone horse, talking to it softly. He stroked its long muzzle and rubbed the throatlatch. Its broad wet nostrils flared and snorted nervously as it eyed him, wary of this bloodspeckled stranger. Neythan patted its neck gently and led it toward the three mules and checked its saddlebags.

"A strange one," the old woman said weakly, but she said no more before closing her eyes to rest on the ground.

Neythan looked at her, and then at Caleb, who eyed him back for a moment but then looked away. Overhead, a lone vulture called, marking the meal to come.

Neythan stood there in the quiet, pondering the old woman's words, and then other things too: the way Arianna had looked back at him through the rain from her horse that night in Godswell. The way the room had smelt when Neythan awoke to find Yannick's blood splattered across the walls and floor. Caleb's cave. The Watcher's sayings. All of it was so unreal, as shapeless as the outhouse doors before him. He looked at them now and the ruined buildings they invited entry to, these grey neighbourless structures built by men who'd long since turned to dust. And he wondered at what they'd known or not known about the world and whether they'd ever too felt as he did now. Then he turned back to the sacks and bags at the horse's saddle and continued to rummage, still thinking of those nameless builders. *Wanderers,* Caleb had called them. Men without country.

Twelve
SEER

In the end, they decided to stay the night and make use of the shelter. Caleb was coughing like a toad and the old woman was in no ready state to travel. Caleb had agreed, though reluctantly, to allow her to stay with them until they reached the townships further east. They'd let her keep the mule she'd ridden on, sell one of the others, and use the remaining beasts to journey south toward the crown city. Which seemed reasonable to Neythan. He was tired anyway, fatigued by lack of food and the work of moving the bandits' bodies.

He sat propped up against the ancient wall of the ruin, staring at the sky as he breathed in the smell of the bandits' blood. Strangely comforting, the familiarity of it. Like a memory of home, because that was precisely what it was. He could still remember how, as a child, they'd make him and the other disciples gut goats and pigs to accustom them to the scent, the blood and offal mingling together until it finally became like nature to them. Like dawn and dusk and clouds and sun. Which was confusing, because a life is something more, isn't it? That's what Uncle Sol would say. Neythan missed him now more than ever, the way he'd sit with him, all calm and still but with an answer for everything, answers that were usually questions. Or stories. The old man was forever telling stories. When Neythan was a child even his reprimands came in narrative form, fables that would sketch and then admonish whatever behaviour he'd been found out for. That gently thrumming voice chiding and enthralling him at the same time so that Uncle Sol never had to shout or order or scold, the stories alone always enough. In Ilysia they called it a talent of his blood. Sol was a Súnamite after all, and tales and storytelling were common to their ways, almost a kind of language to them. But that was before Sol began to share the things he saw in his meditations, and the Shedaím decided the things he said shouldn't be told.

"What troubles you?"

Neythan was still watching the clouds overhead, the way their undersides reflected the sun as it lowered toward the horizon beneath. A buzzard glided still-winged across it all despite the hour, one slow black arrow moving over the shining amber dusk. He dropped his gaze to find the rheumy grey eyes of the old woman peering at him.

"Sorry?"

"What troubles you?" she repeated.

Neythan just looked at her as he sat there on the ground against the gravelled wall of the outhouse. Caleb had busied himself with fettering the horse and mules whilst Neythan remained propped against this ancient wall resting from the work of moving the bodies, thinking, of nothing, of everything.

"What makes you think I am troubled?"

"The question on your face," the woman said. Her voice was deep and dusty. "You are carrying something within you. Like... a knot, inside, tight... you did not know how to *loose* it... yet now you have found... a direction, a way to what you seek... yet you are troubled... What troubles you?"

Neythan looked her over; the dark leathery skin, the deep long wrinkles. Black freckles lay either side of her wide flat nose where lines stretched from broad nostrils to her thick rubbery lips.

"Who are you?"

"A question with a question," the woman said wonderingly. "And twice too..." She tilted her head and smiled. "You shun the answer... But why? What troubles you?"

"Well, the beasts are secure," Caleb said, ambling over from the far house. "Though it's true what's often said of mules, stubborn as a maid's mother, and too picky it would seem to abide the company of a horse, lest they offend their delicate tastes. We'll sell the worst of them when we reach a village. The takings along with these spoils will see us the rest of the way south. Especially the blankets and..." He trailed off, observing Neythan's distracted gaze. He followed it to the old woman. "Ah. So you are awake at last."

But the woman didn't answer, her gaze fixed on Neythan.

Caleb looked back to Neythan, who was still staring at the woman. "I am interrupting?"

"No." Neythan slowly peeled his gaze away from her. "No. You are not."

Caleb nodded and glanced between the pair. No one spoke.

"It's good to see your mood has finally lightened," Neythan said to break the silence.

"My mood?"

"Since this morning... Well, in truth, since the forest."

"Ah, that's right. My *mood*. Such a strange thing, isn't it. Nothing to do with the fact you nearly had us killed in that forest, of course."

"So you say, yet tell nothing of how."

"Why should I? You're not exactly the kind to listen, are you?"

"What's that supposed to mean?"

"Supposed? There is no *supposed* about it. You couldn't be less heedful if you tried." Caleb's head wagged as he tugged a blanket free from the pile of belongings they'd gathered from the bandits. "I mean, after all that waiting and peril you put me through whilst you slept blissful as a baby in that forest, you awake only to say, '*Hanesda.*'" He paused, looking up at Neythan. "*Hanesda.*" Then he continued his rummage through the spoils for another blanket. "That was the best you could do? The sum wisdom you were able to glean from such an encounter? I mean, you spoke with a *Watch*–" He stopped and glanced at the old woman, then back to Neythan. "You ought to have learnt far more," he added quietly. "Far, far more." He shook his head again as he spread the blankets to sit.

"You should not speak so fiercely," the old woman said.

"Oh?" Caleb cocked an eyebrow. "Is that so?" He looked at Neythan, then back to the woman. "You are his defender, then," he said. "Well, perhaps it is to be expected for the modest price of a gourd of water and the death of a few captors. Time was mere thanks would suffice. But no, not so any longer, I see."

"I speak for the sake of the dead. We sit on a grave. You see the markings there on the wall."

Neythan and Caleb turned to find thin scratched etchings marking the cornerstone of the middle house.

"The line across, it tells that this place is a grave. The plumblines tell of how many rest here. There are four."

"Why would men build houses to bury the dead?" Neythan asked.

"They are storehouses," the woman said. "They were built long ago, when the winters were harsher. Longer. Men made these shelters so they would not perish on the way if they journeyed in that season. Like a well in a desert. Although," she nodded at the markings on the cornerstone, "sometimes men still perished."

"Storehouses, you say," Caleb said.

The old woman nodded.

"Not a temple."

"No."

Caleb frowned.

Neythan smiled.

"How do you know this?" Caleb said. "It is not a common thing to know."

"I am Súnamite. Many among my people still keep the old ways, the traditions of the Magi. There, it *is* a common thing to know."

"You are a priestess?" Caleb said.

"I didn't say that."

"Priests are outlawed in the Sovereignty," Neythan said.

"They are," the woman answered. "A strange thing. My people have always spoken of the lands that killed their gods, but it is still another thing to have come and witnessed your ways for myself."

Neythan smiled. "It is the priesthoods that were destroyed. There *are* no gods."

"Is that so? Then where did your first laws come from?"

"They were written by men, the most learned among us."

"And yet many of them resemble those formed by the priestly traditions you killed."

"Many wars were formed by those same traditions."

"So there have been no wars since they were destroyed?"

Neythan smiled thinly. The centuries-long enmity between the Sovereignty and Súnam had erupted in war many times, and well after the Cull, as the Five Lands tried to invade where the few surviving priests had fled to. Since then the conflict had simmered as little more than a vague wariness, punctuated by the occasional skirmish whenever a Sovereign patrol strayed too far beyond Súnam's borders – which was why the Shedaím had first tried to recruit Súnamites, like Sol, in the first place.

Neythan sighed. "You know there have been."

"Yet you blame the gods for your wars and praise men for your laws." She tilted her head to one side, puzzled, amused, it was hard to tell which. "In Súnam we do the opposite."

Caleb shifted his weight, tired of the game. "How did those men come upon you? Where were they taking you?"

"For judgment, so they said, to the nearest city. They hoped to fetch a purse as their prize."

"Why?"

The woman looked at them and smiled. "They thought me a priestess."

"Quite a coincidence."

The woman shrugged. "As men endure so does what is in them. They thought my words strange, said I knew things too well. And they see I am Súnamite."

"Knew what things too well?" Caleb asked.

But the woman only smiled and fiddled with her headscarf, tucking in the black tufts of fluffy hair that peeked from the hem.

"What is to stop us completing their errand and fetching the bounty?" Caleb said.

"You will not," the old woman answered simply. "It is not in your heart. There is some other path before you."

Neythan just looked at her. "Who *are* you?"

"Filani. My name is Filani."

"Filani," Neythan repeated.

"Yes." She was looking at him strangely now, as if at a puzzle or tiny detail she had to squint to see. "Though I see you will not answer what I ask of you…"

"Of me? What do you ask of me?"

"I ask what troubles you?" she said, her gaze still curious, her round head even nodding a little. "But you do not answer because you *cannot*… Yes… For you do not yet fully know."

They slept that night in the middle house, huddling together for warmth as the night stared down at them through the hole in the roof. They took three blankets from the spoils and used two to cover the ground and the other to cover them whilst they slept.

The smell of blood settled in Neythan's nostrils from his stained knuckles. Blade and blood, the same no matter what. It had felt that way as he slew the bandits; a sort of easy normality to it – solid, safe, known. Against all that had gone before it had almost felt like cleansing. Caleb had seen it too, the peace that had settled in Neythan's eyes afterward, and looked away. Neythan was unsure what to think of that. He dismissed the thought and turned beneath the blanket to face the roof instead, gazing up through its gap into the night's cool black diffidence.

"What do you think is out there?" the old woman said, lying beside him.

Neythan rolled his head to see her watching him, the whites of her eyes visible despite the dark. They'd spoken little the rest of the evening, which was the way Neythan had wanted it. He found being around her uncomfortable. Strange, even. The way she'd looked at him earlier, as if her eyes were peering through to something else, a secret she knew and he didn't. He was beginning to see the bandits' point. He rolled his head and looked back to the darkness overhead.

"What do you mean?"

"Out there, in the sky."

"Nothing… moon and stars."

"But you cannot see them."

"The night is cloudy."

"It is."

A quiet moment passed. He could feel her gaze still on him, as it had been throughout the evening, watching when he sat, watching when he moved, watching when he ate. "What do you want?"

"Just moon and stars, Neythan."

When he rolled his head to look at her, she was smiling. "I think I'm beginning to see why those men thought of you what they did. You speak in riddles, like a priest would."

"Riddles are the way of wisdom, Neythan. Of answers waiting to be found."

"Why should an answer need to be hidden?"

"All things of value are hidden. Like treasure. Like the world itself, too broad and vast to be fully revealed." She rolled her head to look up and through the broken roof. "Just like this cloudy night. I have always known this. But you, you have *seen*. You have seen above the clouds to what hides behind..." Her gaze rolled to him again, mild yet watchful. "Haven't you?"

Neythan remained silent. Even in the darkness those old grey eyes seemed to pass through him.

She sighed an old woman's sigh. "Yes. You have seen. Yet you are not Magi..." She rolled onto her shoulder, turning her back, as if to return to sleep. "And you are not a witch... You are a strange one, Neythan... You make an old woman curious."

"Curious of what?"

But only silence answered, and then a moment later, the soft gentle sawing of the old woman's sleeping breaths.

Thirteen
SUMMERLAND

In the end, Yasmin waited until one night after supper when the children were asleep before telling Hassan everything Bilyana had told her: her strange notions about why Zaqeem was killed, her claim of knowing more, the price she'd asked to share her secrets. It all seemed so surreal, ridiculous even. Yasmin found herself smiling a little at the absurdity of the words even as she shared them. And so when Hassan, having heard it all, sat back in his chair and after long thought simply answered, "Very well," Yasmin was confused.

How could Bilyana's fanciful claims be, to Hassan's mind, believable enough to warrant – just two months from Noah's Judgment – a twenty-day journey on the whim of Bilyana's brother to visit with his Súnamite fancy's kin and speak on his behalf?

The fact Hassan had agreed to the trip and Bilyana's request was almost as hard to believe as Bilyana's claims. And yet here they now were, traipsing through warm clothy air and luminous green bushes on the way to some Summerland village.

It had been years since Yasmin's last journey to Súnam. The circumstances then had been so different, travelling with Hassan to recover some tired artefact for the library he'd been gushing excitedly about. Back then, accompanied by Hassan's enthusiasm and sense of adventure, it had been easier to ignore the constant shrill cries of the gypsy bugs. Or the suffocating and sweaty cling of her clothes when she moved. Or just the sheer brightness of everything, of leaves, of water, of earth, all hammered white by the excessive gleam of the sun. It made her head ache.

"Are you well, Inchah?"

Yasmin glanced up at her handmaid, Lusana, and smiled weakly.

"We will be there soon, I think. Mulaam said this morning we would reach the village by midday."

Yasmin gave a small appreciative nod and tried to push her mind from the queasy sway of the camel beneath her. She could feel the shifting fat of the beast's hump through the saddlestool, drifting side to side with each long, lazy pace.

Hassan was at the front of the caravan with the assigned men of the cityguard. Bilyana and her fool of a brother, Zíyaf – who, having inflicted all this upon them, had the gall to laugh and joke with his sister all the way here – went behind. Then there was Yasmin herself with her handmaid, Lusana, followed by two of Hassan's bodyguard; both of them, like Lusana, Súnamites, driving a cart of gifts for the would-be bride's father and kin.

"When I was a girl we'd play along the river and talk of the village of Ulan and how pretty the women are there and how great the festivals are. My mother's mother was from there. I think you will like it, Inchah. I think you will like it a lot."

Again, Yasmin attempted another smile, though from the uncertainty in Lusana's eyes it may have appeared more a grimace. The young girl nodded and smiled dutifully and then turned to busy herself further up the caravan.

In the end the estimate proved false. The caravan reached the village closer to late afternoon. Children greeted them as they arrived, prancing beside the camels before a light-skinned

Súnamite strolled across from a hut at the front of a horseshoe arrangement of mudbrick houses. Short, scanty shrubs dried leafless by the heat sat around the village's periphery. A long straw-roofed pen, surrounded like an island by the resultant clearing of pale dirt, stood in the middle of the plot with villagers sheltering beneath.

The Súnamite man, long-limbed and languid, approached Hassan at the head of the caravan. Yasmin watched as the two conferred briefly before the man then pointed and waved the caravan in. They went across the clearing toward the pen. Most of those sheltering beneath were women, each dressed in brightly coloured dye-stained fabrics they wore wrapped around them from the armpits to the knees like cocoons.

Yasmin dismounted from her camel beyond the shelter. Hassan helped her from the saddlestool as the animal lowered.

They were led to a large hut at the plot's rear where more houses sprawled out into the jungle.

"Wait here," the Súnamite said before going inside.

"They are deciding how much will be given for Hassan to sit with the elders," Bilyana said. She'd drawn alongside Yasmin, apparently inserting herself as guide to Súnamite custom in Lusana's absence. Perhaps to keep her thoughts off the disappearance of her husband, Tobiath. Missing for a while now. Likely seeking respite from Bilyana's constant fussing, Yasmin thought. Yasmin watched her now as she sidled a podgy shoulder against her own and leaned in like a co-conspirator.

"They will ask a gift for the privilege to sit with him," she said. "Then a gift to discuss the brideprice, then there is the brideprice itself. They make marriage a rich business here. It's enough to make a man favour daughters over sons. Almost makes you envious of their ways, doesn't it?"

"Just as well you'll need not worry yourself of the cost."

Bilyana glanced sideways nervously. "We are grateful, sister. Beyond measure. Do not think us otherwise. To have come here on our behalf… well… our recompense will be worthy of the kindness. Yours and Hassan's."

"I hope so."

Bilyana nodded zealously. "It shall, sister. It shall."

Eventually the man emerged from the draped doorway of the hut, squinting. He pouted as he readjusted to the brightness and beckoned Hassan in. Yasmin moved to join him, earning a cocked eyebrow from the man.

"No." The man extended his palm gravely. "You must stay."

"I will not," Yasmin said.

Hassan looked at her.

"I've been three weeks in the bush, mites and mosquitoes and whatever else nibbling me like dog scraps. I won't be waiting in this ridiculous heat for my trouble."

Hassan sighed and looked to the man and nodded. The man eyed him dubiously, then disappeared once more into the hut. He emerged again shortly after and mumbled something in Hassan's ear, no doubt adding to the price of their audience with whoever waited within. Not that Yasmin cared; the trip was Hassan's choice, not hers. Why should she be brought all this way only for him to keep hiding things from her?

They ducked as they were ushered inside.

Within was blackness, the hut's dark made denser by the brightness they'd come in from. Eventually their eyes adjusted so they could see the baked mudbrick walls, dingy grey and mottled with stray feathery strands of cobwebbing and grass. The only window was a misshapen hole toward the top on one side. A dusty beam of sunlight knifed diagonally across the room, making it hard to see much of the chamber behind. The floor was tidily swept. The air was spicy, riddled with the sharp niggly scent of a pepperish meal.

"There is an old story I learned as a boy." The voice was parched and croaky, its owner shrouded in the shadows. "The tale of the cidlewoods… You will know of cidlewood.

Strong wood. Your people covet it, for your palaces and summerhouses." The man made a smacking sound with his lips, probably finishing a meal.

"In the story, it is said the cidlewoods were once oak trees, but one day tired of their lot, and so cast off their roots to roam the earth as beasts do and make of themselves a greater name. When the other trees heard it, they bickered with them, telling them to return to their place. But the oaks ignored them. 'The other trees speak from jealousy,' they said. Then came a Watcher, commanding them: 'Return to your place.' But the trees would not hear him. 'Our great strength can defy all,' they said. Then the river heard of it and told the oaks to keep their roots lest her banks flood when the rains come. But the oaks would neither heed her, and grew bold, seeing no creature was able to resist them.

"Then one day there came a drought. Every creature was weakened, but seeing as they'd kept league with the river, even as she shrank she did not refuse them her water. Yet of these oaks, who'd insulted and defied her, she allowed not a drop. When at last the drought grew so fierce that those mighty oaks starved of water began to wither and die, they came again to the river. 'River, will you let us drink?' And so the river told them: 'When the rains were plenty, you were strong and your roots kept me from flooding, then you left your place and I struggled to keep my banks. When I asked you to consider and return, you scorned me. Now times of plenty turn to times of need and I no longer need your roots as you did not need my waters. Why then should I grant you drink?' And she would not let them drink.

"So the oaks turned to their brothers, the other trees: 'Bid the river let us drink.' But they too refused, for the oaks had despised their counsel when they were strong. Finally, they turned to the Watcher. 'We beg, bid the river let us drink, for without we will die.' And so for mercy's sake, the Watcher commanded the river to give of herself, and she obeyed and gave them drink. Then the Watcher commanded the oaks: 'You may drink. Only let it be that you return to the ground that bore you, and dig your roots deeper than before, that you never again seek to leave your place.' And so the oaks obeyed, and drank, and dug, and in so doing surrendered the freedom they'd claimed. No longer would they roam as beasts do.

"Over time, as they continued to abide by the Watcher's command, they changed. Their deep roots made them taller and stronger than every other tree. So tall and strong they could be called oaks no longer. They were greater, and so were given a new name... This is how they became cidlewoods."

The voice paused, resting a moment in the silence as the hidden eyes of its owner watched them from the shadows.

"It was my father's father who taught me this story," the voice said. "He told me there is no greater folly in a man than for his heart to be lifted in pride, and there is no greater weakness in him than to depart from the way of his ancestors. He said, if a man forgets his roots, he forgets his very life..." More wet tuts and smacks of the man's lips.

"Our people," he eventually resumed. "We have a root. Ways that keep us, ways we must hold to. It is not this way with all people, but with us, it is this way... do you see?"

Hassan nodded. "I understand."

"Good. That is good."

The old man clicked his tongue and gestured through the gloom to the guide at the door. The man stepped outside through the drape and returned a moment later carrying with another the chest of tribute Hassan's men had brought. They took it through the shaft of light from the window to the chamber's rear and put it down and left. Hassan and Yasmin listened as the faceless old man callously shuffled the lid aside to view its contents. He made an approving sound in his throat and then clapped the lid shut again.

"Come closer," he said finally. "Both of you. We will see one another's face as we speak."

Hassan and Yasmin obeyed and passed through the sunny shaft to find a mat on the other side. They didn't notice the men until they'd seated themselves. Three elders sat there, squatting side by side on stools in the corner.

"This boy, he has gone against our ways," the elder who'd been doing the speaking said. The man was old and slim and sat with his elbows leaning on his knees. A small woollen hat rested on his thin shiny skull. His eyes glimmered like coins in the dark. "It was not his place to speak to the girl without the permission of her father." He swung his hand limply, gesturing to the elder on the far right. "You offend a man's house to do this."

Hassan looked at the father. The father said nothing. Hassan looked back to the first elder.

"The boy was not familiar with these ways," Hassan said. "He meant no offence."

"Even so, such a thing cannot be allowed, lest trees learn to roam."

"Perhaps the father's offence might be eased," Hassan said.

The elder again looked across to the father.

The father was slightly younger than the other two, darker skinned, with a thick cap of densely coiled hair. Black wiry hairs sprouted from his forearms and the tops of his broad flabby shoulders. He eyed Hassan and Yasmin boldly, his chunky nostrils flared. "I will take five measures of palm oil," he said, his voice loud and deep. "And ten goats, and four measures of cornwine."

Yasmin looked to her husband.

Hassan gently cleared his throat. "He is very upset, of course," he said, careful not to address the father, whose face he'd yet to purchase. Instead he looked to the elder who'd first spoken to him. Hassan was more familiar with Súnamite custom than

Zíyaf had evidently been. "Yet perhaps the kindness of leniency would indebt the boy further."

The elder, pleased both by the deftness of Hassan's answer and that he continued to address him rather than the offended party, smiled. "Perhaps so," he said, and looked again to the father.

The father shrugged unhappily. "Two measures of cornwine then," he said.

"The father is a generous man," the elder said.

"He is," Hassan said. "Perhaps too generous… let it be three measures."

The elder looked to the father. The father nodded, accepting the offer.

"Obasi accepts," the elder said, naming the father for the first time to indicate Hassan's right to now address him directly. His offer of more cornwine had been enough to pay for the father's face. He would now have the chance to discuss the suitability of Zíyaf, and beyond that, if Obasi proved willing, the brideprice.

"I see you are familiar with our ways," the first elder said.

"Only some," Hassan answered. "They are noble customs."

"Though costly ones?"

Hassan smiled wryly. "Perhaps some would say so. But sometimes such a thing is good. A man holds precious what he has paid for. And in these matters this is important."

"Ah." The elder smiled again, his eyes closing as if to music. "You see, Obasi. This man speaks well; if the boy is of his stock he may not be so bad."

Obasi grunted and sucked his teeth.

"I and the boy do not share the same blood, but I have known his family well and can speak for them."

"Where are they?" Obasi demanded. "The boy comes with no people of his own."

"He has only a sister. His mother and father are no more. He did not think it fitting to visit with only cousins, men who are of age with him."

"As are you," Obasi said. "The boy has no grey-haired man to speak."

"It is true. Yet, in the city of my home, I am an elder nonetheless."

"Then your city is poor, that children are elders there."

"Obasi," the other elder said. "Your tongue should mind the company of a prince. This man is steward of Dumea."

Hassan was lifting his hand to wave off the insult when several tall men – barechested and dark-skinned – suddenly barged in through the stringed drapery of the doorway. They wore graven armlets and patterned knee-length skirts with coloured threads tied around their elbows and ankles. They were not villagers.

Hassan, instinctively, got to his feet. Yasmin rose beside him, looking to the elders for guidance. Perhaps it was another custom, one they were unfamiliar with. The old men only frowned and gawped at the intrusion… and then they saw the young woman step into the hut behind the men.

"Inchah," Obasi gasped, and then bowed toward her. The other elders did likewise.

The woman's skin had the colour and polished sheen of an eggplant. Her long arms, bared midriff and tapered waist were smooth as a child's. The whites of her eyes seemed to shine in the dimness like a cat's against her glossy dark skin. Bangles of gold and turquoise ringed her tall neck and wrists like armour.

She dropped her chin to acknowledge the bowing elders.

"Forgive me, fathers," she said. "It is not right I enter unbidden." Her gaze swung toward Hassan. "But I have come from my mother's side to speak with this man." She glanced back to the elders. "And I must speak with him alone."

To Yasmin's surprise, the elders rose gingerly from their seats and began to move, wordlessly, toward the doorway to be ushered out by the barechested guardsmen. Then the young woman turned and looked at her.

"You must leave also."

Yasmin frowned, part fear, part affront. She looked to Hassan.

"It is alright, Yasmin…" He was eyeing the woman carefully.

Her hair was coiled and short, cropped close to the skull and covered by a gauzy cap of laced gold that hung to just above her shoulders like a wig of jewelled cobweb. Yasmin had seen the style before, loosely sketched in some of the scrolls Hassan was always encouraging her to read back at the library in Dumea. It was the fashion of Súnamite royalty.

"Wait for me outside," Hassan said to his wife.

Yasmin's gaze switched between Hassan and the dark-skinned young woman. "I will not," she said.

The woman glanced at her. The guard by the door came striding forward and then stopped abruptly as the woman raised her hand. "No," she said, smiling a little, her eyes still on Yasmin. "It is good… We will let her stay."

The guard gave Yasmin a narrow glance and slowly stepped away, returning to his place by the door.

The young woman's gaze slid from Yasmin to Hassan. Her royalty was obvious. Why she was here wasn't. Yasmin and Hassan had come to the Summerlands several times before and never encountered Súnamite nobility. Nubassa, the crown city, was as far south of here as Dumea was north. Probably farther.

"You are Hassan, son of Nalaam," the woman eventually said.

"I am."

She paused, pursing her thick lips as she looked him over. Her voice was deep and smooth. "They say your line were kings once, in Dumea."

"Then you know more of my line than we can know of yours," Hassan said.

The woman smiled fractionally, acknowledging the implied question. "I am Imaru, daughter to Queen Umani, ruler of Súnam."

Hassan digested that with a slow intake of breath. "Your mother's throne lies far from these outskirts, highness."

"My mother takes interest in every corner of her land, even its outskirts," she inclined her head, watching him carefully. "Watching for those who come, those who go."

"Then she will know our coming here is innocent."

The speculation in Imaru's eyes seemed to disagree. "Yes," she said nonetheless. "It would seem so... at least for now."

"And for hereafter. I carry no ill intents. We have come only to–"

"You misunderstand me, son of Nalaam."

Hassan frowned at her interruption.

Imaru appraised him. She began to slowly stroll around the edge of the room, watching them as she walked. "It has been near to one hundred years since your Sovereignty last sought to enter our lands and take what does not belong to them. There are still those among my people old enough to remember... We have a saying – the jackal cannot be tamed. It shall be as it has been. What it has sought before it will in time seek again. My people say the only true way to be safe from a jackal is to learn his ways, or kill him..." She completed her circuit and turned to face them. "And there is no better way to do either than by one who belongs to his pack."

It took a moment for Yasmin to understand, and then suddenly she saw it, the reason why Súnam's queen would send her daughter all this way to a small village in search of Hassan.

"Yes," Imaru said it slowly, recognizing the comprehension in their silence. "We have spies along the Narrow, son of Nalaam. It is how we knew you were coming here. But we have no spies in the Sovereignty. No way of knowing what moves in the Five Lands."

"You are asking me to… *spy*, for Súnam?"

"You are the governor of Dumea," Imaru said. "The nearest city to the Narrow in the Sovereignty. It almost borders our lands and will be a stronghold in any battle between my people and your sharíf. What better watchman could Súnam have?"

"And why would I agree to that?"

She smiled. "I know about Dumea, son of Nalaam. The Sovereignty never conquered it. Never broke its walls, never pillaged its people. Your father made a covenant with the Five Lands to protect the library, and in so doing robbed you of your birthright. Now they call you steward where once they would have named you king. Because of the Sovereignty. Your ancestors weep for you, son of Nalaam. Because of the Sovereignty. And yet you ask why you would agree to what I have asked…" Her smile soured, became pitying. "Still," she added. "If you need another reason I shall give you one. You will agree because whatever favour you thought precious enough to journey two weeks south of the Narrow for…" She glanced at the chest of tribute in the corner. "With trinkets and treasures for these village elders – shall be granted or refused you by *my* command." She returned her gaze to him. "So. Your aim in coming here *can* be fulfilled, son of Nalaam. But only if you agree."

"You're asking me to commit treason."

Her lips tautened in amusement. "I am asking you to be as a watchman. No more. The queen desires but a small thing, to know when the Five Lands bring their armies to the Narrow. Should it not be so in your lifetime, you will have no need to act. We seek only to protect our lands, our people. Is that not a small price for the prize your long journey has sought?"

Yasmin thought about the elders who'd moments ago sat before them discussing the brideprice; Bilyana, who'd promised to divulge secrets of Zaqeem's death in return for their favour. But *what* secrets? Why had Hassan even countenanced the offer? Why had he considered it worth all this – the journey, the tribute? And why, even now, was he deliberating over this woman's request to spy on her behalf for its sake? What could be worth such risk? What mystery concerning her brother's death could be so vital? What was Hassan hiding?

"I will do it." It took a moment for Yasmin to realize she herself had spoken the words.

Hassan turned and stared at her. As did the princess. Then Imaru smiled. "Good. Then it is agreed." Her gaze lingered on Yasmin. "You see? There was profit in your staying after all, little dove."

It was only afterward, once she'd emerged from the hut with Hassan and found Bilyana rushing toward them from beneath the pen, that Yasmin felt the weight of it sink into her.

"Well?" Bilyana said as she came to a stop in front of her.

For a moment Yasmin couldn't speak, her thoughts in a fog. She regarded Bilyana grimly as she dipped beneath the shelter's shade. Hassan walked on beyond the pen to the other side of the clearing in silence. Yasmin watched as he sat down on the far side with his head in his hands.

"Well?" Bilyana said again. "What is it? What happened?"

"It is all agreed," Yasmin said numbly, hardly able to believe the words even as she spoke them. "We have come to agreement. The elders will receive your brother."

Bilyana's eyes widened. She gasped, grinning. "Thank you!"

"We have paid heavily for what you have claimed to know, Bilyana," Yasmin said. "It had better be worth the price."

Fourteen
S E C R E T S

Strange place, Súnam. The territory bordered the Sovereignty's southern reach, hedged up against the low lands to the north and south of the Narrow Sea by the twin desert passes on either side. Beyond that, what was known of the place itself was limited. A collection of largely rural provinces scattered across jungly forestland and stretches of desert, punctuated by a few great cities deep within its boundaries that no one from the Five Lands had seen firsthand for more than two centuries. Beyond that, no telling how far south the land stretched, or its population. Which was why, Daneel thought as he squatted beside Josef in the undergrowth, it was strange for Hassan and Yasmin to be here.

True, Dumea in many ways was a city unto itself, abiding by its own laws, just as it had since the day it was stripped of being crown city of Hardeny when Kosyatin the Bloody conquered the land half a century ago. He'd left Dumea as the country's only surviving stronghold, a walled island surrounded by nothing but villages and homesteads for miles. Apparently, it had been his one act of mercy, and that only because his scribes begged him to resist destroying the place to preserve the famed library of Hophir that sat within its walls. So for Dumea's ruler to have now journeyed here to Súnam, the one land to have successfully defied the Sovereignty since the Cull was, well, unexpected. Perhaps even concerning. More so given the journey now seemed to have involved meeting a young Súnamite who, by the looks of her, was probably some kind of dignitary. A noblewoman perhaps, if they had such things here.

From their vantage point, Daneel and Josef watched Hassan and Yasmin step out from the hut and wander beneath the shelter at the centre of the clearing. Hassan went to the far side, leaving Yasmin, and stood by the endpost, staring out toward the road that had brought them in. The Súnamite noblewoman exited the hut a few moments later and signalled to her guardsmen, preparing to leave.

"Interesting," Daneel said.

"Very," Josef said.

Daneel glanced to the rest of the group beneath the shelter. There was Bilyana daughter of Yoaz, fanning herself with a banana leaf she'd had set with twigs. Her brother, Ziyaf, sat beside her, scratching his neck and muttering in her direction. Several handmaids and servants were gathered together on the other side, laughing with the colourfully dressed locals whilst their masters brooded in the shade.

Tracking them here had been easy enough. No need to follow too closely with a party this size, especially with the trail of debris and camel dung they left in their wake. More difficult had been the heat, along with the unfamiliar animals and plant life. Choosing what fruits and leaves to pick and where best to bed for the night was a continual guessing game. In the end they'd settled for following the choices of those they were tracking, using the discarded shells, twigs and skins of Hassan's travelling party as a guide for what to eat. This wasn't the Dumean's first trip down here after all.

Daneel watched him now, leaning to one side for a better look. Hard to see Hassan from this angle, a pair of claybricked huts on the periphery blocking the view, and Hassan kept passing in and out from behind them as he stalked agitatedly around beneath the canopy.

"They were in there quite a while," Daneel said.

"They were."

"Who do you think she is, the Súnamite?"

Josef shrugged. "An emissary maybe. Perhaps a princess."

"You think she is *royalty*?"

"You saw the elders leave when she entered. And she was wearing turquoise. Only those of royal blood are permitted to do so here."

"Interesting."

"Yes."

"We should follow her."

Josef looked at him.

"What?"

"That would be risky. Not to mention your decree is Hassan, which, since I'm here with you, makes it mine too."

Daneel snorted. "That was before we witnessed him consorting with the throne of *Súnam*."

"We don't know that."

"You just said she may be royalty."

"Only maybe."

"Then we should make certain."

"We have our decrees, Dan."

Daneel looked at his brother as he would a stranger cracking a bad joke. It had always been this way with Josef, even since childhood. No imagination. Given to stubbornness. Take this scroll he'd been carrying, hidden in his coat since Dumea. Daneel had noticed it several nights before amongst Josef's things when they'd made camp on their way here. The edge of a page prodding from a hidden inner sleeve when Josef had got up to relieve himself. So of course, Daneel had gone over to look at it. Why not? Why would he expect his brother to keep something from him? Secrets were for others. Not for them. They were blood. Twins, no less. Two souls in one flesh, like Mother used to say, back before Ilysia, when they were still a family and she was still alive. Back before Father did what he did and then forbade his little sons from ever speaking of it or her. That was a vow Josef kept but Daneel wouldn't, no matter how many times Father beat him, which was something Daneel still hadn't forgiven Josef for, his continuing refusal – out of obedience to a man who was now dead – to speak of their mother.

"I'm going after her," Daneel said. "The Súnamite."

Josef glanced sidelong at him. "You can't do that."

"Take it you're not coming then."

"We need to stay with the steward."

"*You* need to stay with the steward. The advantage of there being two of us is we can divide our interests. We can keep to our decree *and* investigate at the same time."

"*Daneel.*"

"I'm going." Daneel spat the words, saw his brother's eyes shift to him in what, for Josef, could almost have passed for a flinch. Daneel couldn't even make himself feel bad about it. Why should he? For days he'd waited for his brother to show him the scroll. To share it with him, explain the strange markings and items stitched into the page, speculate on the fact it bore the name of Qoh'leth, the father of the Brotherhood, of all people. For Daneel, just failing to confess he knew of it had been a struggle. Josef, however, had seemed able to remain his usual serene self, as though keeping things from his brother was the easiest thing in the world to do, a way worn smooth with habit. Daneel was beginning to think it was time he got some secrets of his own. He stepped back from the hedge of bushes in front of them.

"I'm going," he said again.

"Dan, you can't just go and…"

But Daneel was already moving, striding out of earshot, too

far for Josef to call out to him without raising alarm. He quickly clambered down a shallow verge in the undergrowth and worked his way south in the same direction the noblewoman had arrived from, angling away from the settlement and deeper into the cover of the jungle that surrounded it to flank her travelling party as they journeyed further in. Fat-leaved saplings, greener than any green Daneel had ever seen, slapped at his waist and thighs as he jogged through the vegetation, weaving his head to avoid the low-hung boughs weighed down by the foliage. He soon caught up with the noblewoman's party, watching them in the distance ahead of him as they marched on through the undergrowth. Daneel slowed his pace and kept low, just like Tutor Hamir had taught him. That old bald tyrant had made Daneel and the disciples do this sort of thing a thousand times or more back in Ilysia. Mountain deer, doves, hares and any other skittish animal he could think of, Hamir had had the disciples stalk them all, watching to see how close they could get without disturbing their prey.

Thick pillars of sunlight shone down into the forestbed like giant gleaming blades where the canopy parted, glinting off the gold in the young Súnamite's glittering headdress and vestures and making Daneel squint. A minor problem. If he kept following much longer he'd have bigger things to worry about. It was going to be dark soon, and this place wasn't like the Sovereignty. In the Summerlands, the sun didn't leave by degrees. Instead day turned to night like a snuffed-out candle. Which meant if Daneel was still following this... whoever she was an hour from now, he was going to struggle to find his way back.

He watched the woman step clear of the forest into a broad clearing of broken rocks and ruined walls. Her guards didn't follow, remaining along the fringe of the glade and turning away to stare back out to the forest. The place seemed like some kind of ancient shrine. Markings were dug into the large bulky stones of the walls on the far side, grooved divots so deep it was hard to imagine what sort of tool could have made them. The stone-carved head of a bull lay upended in the centre of the space on a paved platform, lying on its cheek as though trying to hear secrets of the earth. Daneel stayed low and still, staring at it, and then realized the head had more than one face, a bull on one side, the face of a woman on another, and who knew what lay on the side facing away from him. It reminded him of the temple ruins near his home as a child, and the ancient defaced monument of Gilamek that lay near it – a huge full-body likeness of the old god with his torso bared, and his arm cocked back like a javelin thrower's as he clasped a spear. Daneel had always liked it, the way the whole thing had been carved deep into a cliffside the size of a palace too many centuries ago for anyone to remember how or why. It wasn't until he was brought to Ilysia that he realized the country was littered with the things – broken, scratched out murals on the outskirts of cities, huge defaced statues in forests, ancient rubbled walls with strange markings sitting in open plains – fragments of a time before the Sovereignty, scattered throughout the Five Lands like tombstones from another world.

He was crawling nearer on his belly, trying to get a better look when a hooded figure seemed to suddenly emerge from behind it. And that was when things got confusing.

Daneel watched as the supposed Súnamite royal stepped toward the hooded figure and – after saying a few words, and still decked in her gold and turquoise accoutrements – knelt, bowing her head. Daneel frowned. As unfamiliar with Súnamite custom as he was, he felt certain royalty were *not* in the habit of bending their knee to any man or woman who did not themselves sit on a throne, and even then they mostly only did it when compelled by conquest or the threat of death.

He stayed and watched as the hooded figure moved forward, resting a hand on the Súnamite's shoulder and gesturing for her to rise. She got slowly to her feet, and then walked away with the man beyond the ruins and into more jungle on the other side, leaving the guards by the clearing to bar the approach for any who might attempt to follow.

Daneel stayed for what might have been another quarter hour, watching the guardsmen and hoping for the royal or the hooded figure to return. When neither did, he crawled through the brush and out of sight before making his way back along the route he'd taken as the sun swiftly lowered and ushered in the night. It took him longer to return than it had to go, only the glow of fireflies and whatever moonlight managed to slip through the dense canopy overhead there to guide him. By the time he'd made it back to the village he'd been gone for several hours.

Josef eyed him carefully as he finally returned to their camp. "So," he said drily, as Daneel sat down. "You decided to come back."

"Well, you know me, brother. Wouldn't have you lonely."

"So, is she royal or no?"

"Hard to say."

"Why? What did you see?"

"That's hard to say too."

Josef looked at him.

Daneel just turned and held his gaze for a moment, daring his brother – after having hidden this scroll of his and who knows what else – to insist on the full truth. "I followed them into the forest," he eventually said. "Watched them make camp, and roast a rat or two. The woman is an able cook. As for what else she may be... well. Like I said, brother. It's hard to say."

Fifteen
COUNTRY

An old man with one eye and beer-stained teeth tried to sell Neythan a limping goat as they came into the village.

"He is a fine beast. Good meat. Sweet. See?"

The goat was speckled. It had sleepy, jaundiced eyes and a loose lower lip, hanging a little from black gums whilst flies congregated in the air around its tired head, making the animal's ears twitch.

The man hopped and danced alongside, following as they went along the village's main street.

"I have figs too. Fresh. See? Good figs. Sweeter than honey. You try? No? Spices. Good taste. Look. Smell. Good spices."

Two little boys, with streaks of dried snot or saliva on their cheeks and crusting their eyelashes, scampered at the old man's hip, switching to his hand a calabash, a gourd or some other sample of whatever he wanted to show the visitors. It had been the same in the last village, stone hovels squatting along the roadside like waiting sentries, mostly deserted but every so often surrounded by old women and solemn staring children who gazed without expression as the strangers passed by.

"This, this you will like." The man's sore-ridden hand lifted, dangling wood-beaded bracelets. They were actually well made, the beads smoothed and brought together by a thin bind of twisted leather. The man proffered them, his malnourished eye bulging from its sad wrinkled socket as he grinned with stained teeth. "You like?"

Neythan considered them briefly. "We are looking for a place to stay."

The man pocketed his smile like a rejected trinket.

Caleb, still on his mule, came alongside. He glanced dubiously at Neythan before bending to flip a silver coin for the man to catch and then lifting the bracelet from his fingers. "This is good."

"I have more." The man turned to beckon the children.

Caleb lifted a hand. "My friends and I, we've come a long way. We're weary, looking for a place to stay, shelter and fodder for the beasts. Perhaps later, when we are rested, we will look to other things."

The man looked again at the silver coin in his hand, then back up at Caleb's wrinkled face, then nodded. "There." He pointed vaguely. "There is a house and a keeper," he said. "A goatherd, the only flock and pen in the village. He'll have shelter and fodder for the beasts."

Caleb nodded thanks.

The man went on his way.

Caleb turned and saw Neythan watching him. He shrugged. "Likely he sees real custom no more than once or twice a year," he explained. "Yet he'll dance about this place, offering what he has, all of it of no use to anyone here."

"Why?"

Caleb shrugged again. "To pretend," he said dully, and then looked out over the dilapidated settlement, the children stooped on their haunches picking idly at the beetles in the dust and the dry weeds sprouting through the cracked ground. "To pretend."

He nudged his mule onwards and went the way of the old man's counsel. Neythan lingered and watched the old man dole his trinkets and mouldy figs to the dull-eyed women sitting in front of the hovels along the street, each one waving him away like they might a persistent fly or bad smell.

"These outlands are not pleasant," Filani said, hovering at Neythan's shoulder as he watched. "But for those here they are refuge."

Neythan glanced at her briefly before turning back to watch the children as they followed the old man. "Strange kind of refuge."

She followed his gaze. "There'd be no life for an orphan in Hanesda or Qadesh but that of a slave or harlot. Some become so, and find kind masters. But not all masters are kind, and it is from these they flee to here. For the widows it is the same, they flee from creditors. Then there are the mad, the lepers, they flee too. All are of one infirmity or another, and so will dwell here or places like it... Brokenness, Neythan. It makes bedfellows of those who know it."

They continued along the main street to the settlement's back side where the buildings turned from hovels to wooden shanty sheds, some with small yards next to them. They were beyond the ash plains of Calapaar now, likely no more than a few days from the crown city of Hanesda and the other Sumerian river towns, and yet here, away from the Swift's fertile banks, the land was as hard and desolate as salt.

They found the goatherd's house on the next backstreet, the only house in the street to be built of cut sandstone. A large pen stood beside it. A stable adjoined the corner. A young girl, no more than six or seven, stood in the dry grassless yard alongside, clutching a squawking hen by the feet.

"I caught it myself," the girl said. She stood there grinning, waiting for them to approve.

Only Filani smiled back. "Well done, child."

"Nadia. Come."

The girl's father came walking slowly up from the house. A

paunchy man, blotches of sweat on his caftan, hanging loose from his gut like a drape. He squinted up at them on their horse and mules, then rubbed his beard, awaiting an answer.

"We are looking for somewhere to stay," Caleb said. "Ourselves and the beasts."

The man stared at the scars on Caleb's face. A habit of almost everyone who met him, Neythan noticed. He wondered how Caleb felt about it, but Caleb just showed the man his purse, hefting it gently in his palm to allow the dead bandits' silver to clink.

The man grunted and nodded. "I will show you the place for the beasts."

"My father, he was a goatherd too," the man, whose name was Bazra, said later between mouthfuls.

They were sitting on the ground as they ate, settled on mats of hemp beneath the large juniper tree at the house's rear. The fire they'd been sitting around was beginning to grow dim and small.

"He'd a large flock, larger than this," he went on. "I inherited mine from him when he died. These are all offspring." He gestured across the yard to the goat pen. "Save that." He picked out an old he-goat standing nearest the fence watching them. "That one was his. The old man's been dead near twenty years but this one's too stubborn to follow."

"Didn't know goats lived that long," Caleb said.

"A goat, if he's stubborn enough, can live thirty years," Bazra answered. He took a loud slurp of his soup, tipping the bowl to his lips. "But then there's much men don't know of goats. Noble animals, though men seldom think so. They favour sheep, just because sheep are heedful and goats are not. As if that makes sheep nobler." The man laughed drily. "All it makes them is more cunning. They heed only because they've no choice. Blind as bats. Barely able to see a ditch from a duck. May as well heed if you've not eyes to test what you hear. But tell a goat to come or go and he'll watch first. Speculate." The man tapped a finger against his temple. "A thinking animal, you see. Eyes of his own to consider a thing, weigh it up. Men don't like that. Don't like aught that'll think for himself."

They ate out of wood bowls from a pot of lentil soup the man's wife had cooked. She stood by the house with their daughters watching whilst the sons, three of them, not much younger than Neythan, sat around the juniper tree on the mats with their father and the strangers, listening to Bazra hold court.

"You're a strange band though," he said, looking them over. "A Súnamite, a leper, and a boy."

Caleb considered the man's assessment. Filani continued eating.

"What's your business?" he asked. "Where are you going?" He munched loudly on the soup, then waved his spoon. "Ah, no, don't tell me... You're going south."

Neythan and Caleb exchanged a glance.

"Only two ways from which men come to a place like this," the man explained. "North. Or south. There are no other roads, you see... and you," he pointed with his spoon, "you don't have the look of southerners. You're not so... polished."

"Polished?" Caleb said.

"They who'll come this way from the south, they smell of rose oils and honey balms and spikenard. You three... you smell of country."

Caleb cocked an eyebrow.

The man raised a palm. "Pay it no mind, though. Don't. I like the smell of country better. The other rankles my nostrils, makes me itch."

"They come this way often then?" Neythan asked.

"Southerners? Not often, no. Just now and then. Exiles,

you see. They never say so but you can always tell. They come flanked by soldiers. The soldiers are happy for shelter and somewhere to put the horses, but the exiles, they're here in their fancy robes and frankincense and signet rings, you can see their noses twitching at every turn. They are courtiers and councilmen and high-minded house servants. Not used to country."

"Why are they exiled?" Neythan said. "From where?"

"From Hanesda," Caleb answered. "They who fall from the sharíf's favour, or perhaps that of his chamber."

Bazra laughed and nodded at Caleb, glancing at Neythan. "Your friend here regards the crown city a little darkly perhaps, no? They who pass here would be at fault for more than lost favour. The last one to come this way, the soldier guarding him said he'd been caught in a bribe. They're weak-stomached down south, you see. My father, he'd have had such a one scourged. When I was a boy, he had the herdsmen marked up for far less. Hired hands, he'd say, hired hands have two sides to them, one is to work, but only the scourge keeps the other from cheating you."

"Where do they go?" Neythan asked.

"Who?"

"The exiles. Where do they take them?"

Bazra shrugged. "You'd know better than I. They go north. Always north."

"No," Filani said quietly. "They go west, to Dumea."

Neythan looked at her. The old dark-skinned woman was sitting beneath the shade of the juniper tree, chewing and cracking the shells of pram nuts and spitting them out into a small dish of stripped bark. She didn't look up. Just let the word hang in the air. Dumea. Weeks since Neythan had thought of the place, weeks since he'd thought of his decree. Both had fallen away from his thoughts the night he looked on the bloodied body of Yannick. Josef and Daneel would be there now, waiting for him, his absence noted. Did the Brotherhood know? Did they know yet of Yannick, of Arianna? He glanced up at Filani again, as if she would answer. The old woman cracked another nut in her mouth and spat out the shell.

"Dumea?" Bazra said. "Passing here would be a strange way to take. May as well go by the river." He shrugged and slurped another spoonful. "Worse places to be exiled, though."

"You have been?" Caleb asked.

He bobbed his head and tapped his ear as he downed another spoonful. "To Dumea? No. Heard only, from travellers like you. No bad city from what they say. An unusual place though. Murals on every wall and clerics on every corner. But then that's Hardeny for you. Talkers and artisans and not much else. Still, I'd like to go and see for myself one day. Always better to trust the eyes in your head than the words of others. Like the goats do."

They left early the following morning, riding up into the hilly pastures behind the house as the sun rose ahead of them. They carried on southwards until nightfall, beyond the cattlefields to where the grass grew wild and long. The sky thundered when the darkness came, clattering overhead like the moving of furniture, the storm clouds lodged invisible in the blackness. As a boy, Neythan had feared nights like this. Even now, the lightning flickering to the east, shimmering violet-white beyond mountainous clouds, unnerved him. It was as if the sky was cracking, another world trying to push its way in.

They wandered on through the rainless tumult until the sun came again, its golden eye peeping above the foothills along the horizon. Neythan took a gulp of water from his gourd as Caleb slumped, sleeping, in the saddle of the mule ahead of him.

"You will need to sleep soon too," Filani said.

Neythan turned to look at her and offered the gourd. "As shall you."

She took it and opened the cap to drink. She nodded thanks and looked around. "The Pepper Hills."

Neythan glanced around at the sloping field of black poppies. The snatch of dry grassland interrupted the dusty plain like a giant rug.

"You will be a few days from Hanesda," she said. "But just half a day from the next town. I have friends there who will provide you with food and shelter. I will stay with them as you go on your way." She drank and then reached over to hand the gourd back. Neythan took it and fastened it with the other provisions behind his saddle.

"You know the land well," he said.

"I have had to. I am a merchant, a seller of purple. Or at least I was before the bandits took me."

Neythan looked at her.

"You are surprised," she said.

"You're a little old for that kind of work."

She laughed. "Perhaps you are a little young for *your* work. It's uncommon for someone your age."

"What do *you* know of my work?"

But she just turned to look at the horizon as if she hadn't heard him. Her skin, as dark as Uncle Sol's, turned black against the light of the sun rising beyond her.

"Tell me," Neythan said.

She turned back around and considered him for a long moment. "I know that you are troubled, Neythan," she said finally. "And I know that you cannot understand why. Because you do not understand yourself. What you are. Why you feel things you wish you did not, why you *can't* feel things you think you should. I know that your sha knows what you do not: that you belong to a war you have never seen or heard, or touched, but a war nonetheless. Around you. Within you. Everywhere."

"What do you mean? What war?"

But the woman said nothing.

"You're a seer, aren't you? Like in the stories my uncle would tell me."

She smiled. "A seer? I did not know they told such stories in the Sovereignty. I'd thought them all locked away in Dumea's library, along with everything else... Tell me, Neythan. Do you know the tale of Dumea's last king?"

Neythan nodded. All the disciples had been taught the story, along with many other histories of the Five Lands and First Laws. How King Nalaam had ceded the kingship of Dumea to Sharíf Helgon nearly twenty years ago, paying double fealty to the throne and impoverishing his city. The agreement turned the city's ruler to no more than a steward, all to preserve the Dumean laws and the famous library those laws had allowed Dumea to build and curate.

"Some say it was foolish for Nalaam to sell his throne for the sake of books," Filani said. "They do not see that he sold a coin to keep a treasure. And that even now it remains the only place beyond Súnam where your dead priesthoods' writings can be found... Perhaps it was there your uncle learned his stories. Perhaps that is the place you *should* be going in search of your answers."

"And what answers am I searching for?"

The woman leaned forward slightly in her saddle, then paused, her eyes shifting, looking past him. Neythan turned to follow her gaze. There was a tree stump in the patch of grass on the other side. A pair of crows perched on top of it.

"There is something there," Filani said.

Neythan frowned at her, and then stopped the horses and climbed down from his saddle.

"What's going on?" Caleb asked, jolting awake. "Why have we stopped?"

Neythan drew his sword. "Wait here." He stepped into the little field, stalking through the skinny reeds of wildgrass.

It was only as he neared the stump that the smell hit him. He coughed violently, pulled a rag from his sleeve and held it to his mouth. It was as he heard the greedy buzzing hum of the flies that Neythan began to widen his approach, stepping around the thick, pale stump and leaning his head to see around it.

He saw the hand first, cadaverously grey, an open pallid palm with dirty fingers resting in a relaxed claw, as if beckoning him near. Neythan obliged and stepped closer. Then he saw the stained cowl, the torn flesh, turgid skin, gashed skull, dry teeth, the single up-staring eye, the empty socket beside it where the crows had already been.

"He is Shedaím."

Neythan glanced aside to find Caleb at his shoulder, peering down on the body.

"There," Caleb said, pointing. "His palm. You can see the trace of the scar from his bloodseed, and from when he took the covenant."

Neythan coughed and spat to the side. By the look of him he'd been dead no more than a week, which was concerning enough, but it was the killing wound that bothered Neythan more. A wide and neat gash arced across the throat from right to left where the man had been seized and slashed from behind. The work of a left-hander, identical to the wound that had killed Yannick.

He glanced back to the road to where the old woman waited on her mule. Nothing but plains and scrubland in either direction for miles. This was the only highway south. If Arianna was truly in Hanesda it was likely she had come by this very road to get there. He turned back to the body, eyeing the wound, rehearsing the events of the past month – Arianna missing. Now *two* Brothers dead. Both killed the same way, the inconvenient truths twining together in his mind like cords of rope, along with the growing sick feeling there may be more on the way. Caleb's words in the cave came back to him. *Sometimes you can think you know something, or even someone, and be deceived.*

Neythan stared down at the corpse.

But would you do this, Ari? Can you truly be doing this?

Only the crows answered, cawing lazily as they scratched at the bright timber of the tree stump.

"Come, Neythan," Caleb said. "We're not far from the next town. There's nothing to come from tarrying among the dead."

Sixteen
BUTTERFLY

"Tell me something, Neythan."

Neythan suspected that's where it began. But then he couldn't be sure. Funny thing memory, will of its own. Even now he wasn't exactly sure what Arianna had meant to speak of that night. Looking back, the sense of something ulterior, beneath the surface, beneath the words, had always lingered. They'd sat with their feet dangling on the lip of the Great Dry Lake that Master Johann had shown them as children when they first came to Ilysia. They'd stayed there for a long time, chatting, staring into the jagged shadow the crater spread beneath them. A warm starless night, benign sky above, still forest behind. How different Arianna had seemed; strangely coy, nervous even, almost a different person. Tell me something, she'd said; her voice soft, insistent, opening to some foreign part of her Neythan had never seen before, his admittance a privilege. Tell me something you have never told anyone before. *And that thought, that sense of privilege, of a secret between them, tugged at him, made him want to prolong the spell, play along, and so he answered.*

"I dream sometimes."

Arianna had regarded him suspiciously, waiting for the joke to spill. "Dream?" *Her nose wrinkled like a rabbit's.* "Everybody dreams."

"The same dream," *Neythan clarified.*

"Hm. And what is it you dream of?"

147

"Of night," Neythan said slowly. *"Of flames... of blood. And someone there in the dark, dying. Someone I don't want to die."*

Arianna had studied him, fiddling her tongue at the back of her front teeth in that considered way of hers, emerald eyes atwinkle, fronds of dark hair askew. "And you've told no one?"

Neythan shook his head.

"Why not?"

Neythan shrugged with another shake of the head.

A corner of Arianna's mouth twitched to a half-smile.

"What?" Neythan said.

"I'm trying to imagine what Master Johann would say."

"About my not telling?"

"About your dream."

Neythan shrugged again, a thought he'd already considered. "He'd say it's my sha."

Arianna nodded. "He'd say it's trying to teach you."

"Teach me... Teach me what?"

"Helplessness." The answer was quick and, though she said it quietly, emphatic, like something she'd known a long time, like wisdom. "That there are things you cannot do. Things you cannot stop, or control."

"You almost sound like him."

Arianna shrugged and glanced up at the night. "And he'd be right too, Neythan," she continued, speaking to the sky. "There are things we cannot control, can't wield, even of our own selves, no matter how many disciplines we are taught."

"What things?"

"Things like the mind... What is in it. What it chooses to want. Even when you don't want it to want what it does..." She continued to stare into the muted constellations above where puffs of cloud were now gathering to block out the moon. "Do you ever wonder, Neythan?" She turned to look at him now, eyes narrowed, accusing, pleading, it was difficult to tell which. "Do you ever wonder what it would be to simply go where you please, do what you want?"

Neythan hesitated. The words seemed prickly, hot to the touch. "Go where?" he said, holding the question at arm's length. "Do what?"

"Anything," she said. "Anywhere."

"But the teachings…"

"Never mind the teachings."

Neythan balked but tried not to let it show, tried not to disturb the spell, this quickened nameless something, fickle as a perched butterfly, lingering in the space between them. "The teachings," he repeated quietly. "The creed… it is what guides us… what makes us. It is who we are."

"What do you know of who we are? You do not know who you are. Or who I am. And neither do I. They – the tutors – they make us fearful of knowing. But why ought we be frightened, Neythan?" Her voice lowered. She moved closer, whispering, as if the woods might hear. "Why ought we fear the things we want?"

He'd hesitated then, a growing habit of the exchange, the two of them treading carefully into where these flighty words of theirs had ushered them. He gazed at her face, the large jade eyes almost luminous, their whites curious and glowing. The dainty nose and small expressive mouth and her dark hair, usually tied into a single braid, now loose and unfettered and falling messily. And she seemed so timid, so unlike herself; innocent, fragile. And so, after a long pause, almost experimentally, just to see if the words could be said, he answered. "Perhaps you're right." And it was these words Neythan had come to both regret and cherish the most.

Another smile had shivered on Arianna's lips then, like a skittish bird – disbelieving, grateful – and Neythan saw that his agreement had freed her somehow, had affirmed what she had not allowed herself to believe before. A secret, some private madness he, by agreeing, had saved her from. She leant forward. The space between his face and hers – precarious and bewitching and agitated, like the air before a storm – closed. She neared, eyes flitting nervously – to his nose, his ear, his cheek, his eye, his forehead, his lips… A twig snapped behind them. Neythan turned *around. Nothing. No one. Too dark to see. He turned back but it was too late, the spell broken, the butterfly unnerved. Arianna was running away to the safety of the thickets, away into the milky blue night.*

"If you're not careful you'll turn to salt, you know," Caleb said.

Neythan glanced up from the deep, shadowed tunnel of the well he'd been staring into. Nearly four years had passed since that night he'd sat with Arianna at the crater, feeling known by her in a way he'd not been known before or since, like there was some fleshless umbilical thing between them, pulling from inside, a secret bond. More than Brotherhood. *Tell me something you've never told anyone before…*

"What were you thinking of just then?" Caleb said. "It was like you were a world away."

Neythan blinked, smiled thinly, then tossed the rope-tethered pot down the pit again to draw more water for the animals. "Did Filani say how long she would be?" he said. "Or who these friends of hers are?"

"Cousins, I think she said. Or *a* cousin."

"A cousin…" Neythan tugged on the rope, pulling it taut against the mooring post by the well to check its bind. They'd been here for close to an hour now, waiting at the edge of the township for Filani to return. "… in a Sumerian town? I thought Súnamites did not like to settle away from their homelands."

Caleb scoffed. "Sayings and proverbs. Rarely trust them, especially that one. When we reach Hanesda you'll find plenty of Súnamites. There, you find many of any and everything that can be found."

"You don't speak fondly of the place."

"Should I?"

Neythan shrugged. "You're a merchant. They call it the

merchant's home."

"Like I said, not all that is said can be counted true."

"No," Neythan said. "I suppose not."

Caleb watched as Neythan's gaze grew still again.

"Who is she?"

Neythan started, looked at him. "What? Who?"

"This girl you hunt… She is your decree?"

Neythan tugged at the rope, bobbing the vessel beneath to tip and collect its water.

"Come now, Neythan. I have told you the story of my cause."

"Little of it."

"I've told more of it than you have of your own."

"Only whilst you were in your cups, aided by the sourwine."

"Even so. I have told."

Neythan pulled on the cord and began to yank the vessel from the water. He grunted. "There is nothing to tell."

Caleb laughed. "Well of course there isn't. We journey halfway across the Sovereignty in pursuit of her for mere sport. Half-starve ourselves on the way for the same reason… I may no longer be of the Brotherhood, Neythan, but we are still covenanted you and I, in words as binding as blood. You know what binds me in my part, I ought to know what binds you in yours."

Neythan, straining, pulled the vessel to the lip of the well. He looked at Caleb and nodded at it.

"Ah, sorry." Caleb came and reached across to hold the pot's handle as Neythan let go of the rope to grip the pot's other side. They heaved it over the well's ledge together, then set it down against the nearby trough, allowing the water to pour in as the mules and horse drank.

"So," Caleb resumed. "Is she your decree?"

Neythan let out a long slow breath. "She is a rogue," he said. "A betrayer."

Caleb's eyebrows hopped up on his long forehead. "She is Shedaím?"

Neythan didn't answer.

"Strange of them to have sent you, one so young, after a heretic. And alone."

"I was not sent," Neythan said, already regretting the conversation.

Caleb frowned, then gestured for further explanation.

Neythan sighed heavily. "We were sent out... a decree to fulfil... She turned on us."

"Us? How many of you were there?"

"We were three."

"Three? All Brothers? For a single decree?"

Neythan started lowering the pot once more into the well.

"Where is the third?"

"Dead. She slew him."

That stopped Caleb. He shifted. Paused. Then spoke again. "Why?"

The pot touched and bobbed against the well's water, bouncing softly along the rope. Neythan removed one hand and looked at Caleb. "That is what I intend to ask her... Perhaps the last thing I will ask her, before I require at her hand the blood she's taken from the Brotherhood."

Others arrived at the well, a few shepherd boys settling a flock at the bottom of the low footworn slope beneath and walking the shallow incline to draw water, a group of young girls coming out from the town with buckets, a large company of men coming in from the country.

"What do you imagine will be the answer?"

"What?"

"Why she did it."

"How should I know?"

"You above all others *can* know. You, the others of your sharím, you will have spent every day since you were children together. You will be like family."

"Yet she saw fit to kill one of us."

"So, there was nothing? No sign? No hint that might point to–"

"You think I haven't thought of all this? Haven't wondered? You think every day, every *hour*, all this has not come to me? She killed my *friend*, Caleb. Butchered him. Carved his throat like a lamb before a banquet. Listened to his gags, listened to him choking on his own blood as he died, slow, and in pain... *Family*?" He laughed sourly. His jaw bobbed, as if to continue, but he stopped and shook his head instead. He turned to the well, tugged the rope to dunk the pot, then yanked again, put one foot against the ledge and gripped the cord two-handed, bracing to draw it out.

Caleb watched silently, letting Neythan settle as he pulled the pot to the top of the well. He reached across and helped lift it out and over, then stepped back as Neythan put it once more to the trough for the beasts to drink.

"What kind of girl was she, this Arianna?"

Neythan glanced sidelong at Caleb, irked by his persistence, but saw no malice there. He sighed again and looked out over the empty land leading to the town gates.

"I don't know," he said. "She was always... different, I suppose."

"In what way?"

Neythan shrugged. He sat down on the ledge of the well, thought about it. "I don't know... For the rest of us, the disciplines, the training, it took all our strength to master. Eleven years... there was rarely a day we ended without sweat and exhaustion. But it never seemed like that with her. It was as if everything to her was a kind of game, to be made light of... I remember one time, the tutors and Master Johann take us down the mount, half a day's walk from the village. They want to teach us a new weapon. The shentak, it is called. You carry two of them, blades, like daggers sort of, but the hilt is curved, doubles from either side of the handle, around your knuckles and down your arm to the elbow..." He lifted his hand to demonstrate and looked at Caleb. The old man nodded knowingly. "Of course. You will know it... So you know then that the thing with it is the blades move, they swing, are weighted in the handle so you can sort of feel, after a while, the way they will swing. Not easy to master.

"So Hamir and Master Johann have brought us all this way so our sha will be clear and still, undistracted by the village and its people, so we can remain there for a few days or weeks to learn it. We can't have been much older than twelve or thirteen years at the time... Well. By nightfall of the second day Arianna is wielding these things as if born to. The rest of us are still just trying to make sure we don't chop off our own arms. Meanwhile she's telling Master Johann, 'let's go back, I'm missing Yulaan's sweetsoup.'"

He turned back to face Caleb. The little old man smiled a little, which seemed strange, until Neythan realized it was he who had been smiling, at the memory, and that Caleb was simply smiling back. Neythan shed the smirk like something dirty.

The approaching girls from the town had come near the well, giggling bashfully, glancing at Neythan. There were three of them, sisters by the look, ages close together. Neythan stepped back and handed over the rope. The eldest took it with a grateful nod and began to carefully let it down as Neythan stepped away to stand by Caleb.

"There was sometimes something else with her," Neythan said. "A sadness... or fear."

"What was she afraid of?"

"I don't know... It never really made sense."

Neither spoke for a while. Neythan glanced over to the town gate where Filani, less than an hour before, had wandered in on her mule to search for her cousin. He glanced back at the well and the girls drawing their water and the men coming in from the country. Neythan could hear the soft clink of metal on them as they moved. One or two acknowledged him with a nod as they sat tiredly down at the other side of the well. Neythan nodded back.

He looked at Caleb. The little man was frowning in thought. "What?"

"You say she was afraid."

"So?"

"It can be a fearful thing, to discover the sins of your father."

Neythan eyed him with a frown of his own. "What are you talking about?"

"A father, a mother, they are all a child knows of the world. But one day perhaps that child grows, learns things, sees things. When young, the sins of a father, to a child, are not sins, they are the right acts, but when older, they see them as they are. They see their father as they are. It can be a fearful thing."

Neythan didn't answer.

Caleb stepped closer. "For you, me, her, our father has been the Brotherhood. We come to it as children. It teaches us, tells us what is to be thought, what is to be believed."

Neythan shook his head. "No."

"A man imagines the world to be whatever he has seen of it and nothing more. But a man can be wrong. Like you were wrong, before you discovered the Watcher."

"No, that's not the same. You're twisting things."

"Perhaps she discovered things too, Neythan, about the Brotherhood. Perhaps that night, she wanted to escape."

"You would defend her?"

"Perhaps your friend woke to discover her fleeing. Perhaps she panicked."

"You would defend her, because you hate the order."

"And ought I to love it? After it betrayed me?"

"You don't know what was or wasn't done. Yet you want me to hate the order as you do."

"I want you to *think*, Neythan."

Neythan turned away from him, back to the well. He was about to turn back and suggest, just to change the subject, that they go into the town to find their own shelter, when he glimpsed him. The cocoa-complexioned face, those long oval solemn eyes, bronzed skin, wispy long black hair, and that one thin long scar trailing from beneath his eye to under his jaw – the man who'd taught Neythan to read, who'd welcomed him to the village in Ilysia as a child, standing amongst the men who were not herdsmen. Neythan stared. The man's name dropped like a query from his lips.

"Jaleem?"

The man looked up, turning toward him, expressionless, his blank black gaze coming to rest on him and then, in that slowed and still moment, firing some unlooked-for instinct of alarm in Neythan. Jaleem's long arm lifted, pointing.

"There," he said. "That is him. He is the one."

The other men turned to regard Jaleem, and then turned again, following his outstretched arm and pointed finger, to see Neythan. Then there was a lull, a brief fragment of time in which they looked at Neythan and Neythan simply looked back. Then one of the men reached beneath his sheepskin coat, breaking the lull. The men began to slowly come forward, like hunters to prey, drawing swords, axes and maces as they approached Neythan.

"Get the beasts, Caleb."

"What is this?"

"I don't know." Neythan drew his sword. "Get the beasts."

The girls squealed at the sight of drawn blades, buckets of water upended as they began to flee.

Caleb backed away and started to quickly untether the

horse and mules. The first man saw and stepped closer, his stance coiled and low, shoulders hunched, scrawny under the bulk of the sheepskin.

He lunged forward, his blade swinging toward Neythan's leg.

Neythan stepped back, hopped, and stamped down hard as the man's sword passed beneath his foot. The blade clanged to the ground as the man stumbled forward.

Neythan swivelled his hips, lifted a knee. Crunch of bone. The man's head caromed backward as he twisted and splayed to the ground.

Now everyone was shouting, the shepherds running into the town. Sheep panicked, bleating and hopping around the well. A dog somewhere barked.

The second man rushed in, burly and heavy-handed, swinging a mace from overhead. Neythan sidestepped and spun, swinging his sword as he pivoted. The blade sliced across the man's cheek beneath the eye, sending him back into the next onrusher, hands clutching his bloodied face.

Neythan stepped in and shoved again. Both men went down.

Neythan turned to parry a sword from behind. Clang of metal. Swords locked. The blade bit at Neythan's shoulder and drew blood. Neythan threw an elbow, freed an arm, then followed with a kick to the gut. He watched the man stagger back and hit the well's ledge, legs and feet kicking upwards at the impact as he fell heels up and headlong into the hole.

Caleb shouted from the saddle of his mule, holding the reins of the horse and other mule beside him, each animal now untethered. There were at least ten attackers, and more, seeing the chaos, now running in from the sloping plain beyond the well. Jaleem was nowhere to be seen. Neythan turned and sprinted toward his horse, waving Caleb to flee. An arrow whistled at his ear as he ran.

"Come on!" Caleb screamed.

Neythan leapt, one foot into the stirrup, swinging his other leg over. An arrow thudded into the horse's rear. The horse whinnied vengefully and started with Neythan barely in the saddle, hanging on sideways. The other mule was already down, two shafts sticking out from its neck, its mouth wide and panting.

"Into the town," Neythan shouted ahead to Caleb. "We will lose them there."

"No. They don't have horses. We'll go to the country."

Neythan, still side-hung on the horse, tried to pull himself up, yanking on the reins for leverage. He pulled on the bit and twisted the horse's head, curving its way back to the well, the horse already limping from the shaft.

A man caught up and leapt onto the other side, clawing at Neythan, trying to pull him off.

The horse sagged. Neythan's foot was tangled. The other attackers swarmed around, one coming from the other side to hack at him.

Neythan heaved his weight and hit the man on the other side of the horse, jabbing his knuckles into the eye. The man hung on, old hand, fidgeting in his belt for a blade. Neythan reached for his own and tugged it free as the one on foot came near.

He parried as the horse swung around again, hiding him from the onrusher. Turned back to find the hanger-on with dagger raised. Then a fleshy thud and grunt and the man turned rigid before slumping from the horse's limping flank. Neythan glanced over the saddle to find Caleb opposite on the mule with his bow at the ready, having shot the attacker.

"Hurry up! I'm always waiting for you."

Neythan kicked his heel up over the horse's back, hauled himself into the saddle, parrying again as another ran in swinging at the horse to hamstring her. Then they were galloping away, Caleb on the mule, Neythan on horseback, as the men chased and harried. Neythan looked over his shoulder and saw Jaleem behind the men, still as a tree and watching calmly as the others gave chase.

"They have called it madness for me to be as I am. To have done what I have done and to seek what I seek. But of what matter is that? Why should sparrows expect to understand the ambitions of a swan?"

KAREL THE YOUNG, KING OF SUMERIA AND FIRST SHARÍF OF THE SOVEREIGNTY, AT THE BATTLE OF A THOUSAND BANNERS

BOOK III OF *THE WRITINGS OF NAJJIB SON OF ROMESH, FIRST SCRIBE OF HANESDA, IN THE THIRD YEAR OF OUR KING*

Seventeen
DECREE

The marketplace seemed to hum around Chalise as she walked along the aisles between the stalls. Hands wagged and clapped. Vendors and merchants shouted as the crowd jostled and shouldered through the narrow passages of the bazaar.

"Rugs for you. Finest oxhide. Twenty shekras. For you, ten."

"Silk from Kaloom."

"Five shekras, then. Now I rob myself."

Chalise let the loud bartering and bickering wash over her, ducking occasionally where the canopied stalls stood too close together.

Sidon was soon to meet his bride in Qadesh. Chalise had decided it would be good for him to select a gift to greet her with. He'd decided asking the dressmaker's attendant, Iani, to help him choose would be a good way to rankle his mother. And so he walked on ahead with the slavegirl in tow as a dozen guardsmen pushed a furrow through the mob.

The boy was so unlike his father. Helgon had always refused to venture among the stalls. The baying bustle of the traders was an unruly chaos to him, a riot waiting to happen. Or so he'd call it. Always so cautious that way, Helgon. Stiflingly so. Sidon, it seemed, didn't share the habit.

"He is young, Sharífa."

163

Chalise blinked and looked down to find Elias at her elbow, watching her as she watched her son.

"He does not have the luxury of being young," she said as she turned her attention back to Sidon. He was standing at a potter's stall up ahead, talking to the dressmaker's girl as she nodded excitedly. Chalise sighed. "He is sharíf."

It was another half hour before they neared the west quarter. Fewer stalls. More people. An amber-cutter sat with his tools in a stone alcove on one side. Tawny feathered chickens preened in the doorway. The damp mesh of old netting hung overhead, crossing the narrow span between the wall and the stalls opposite and casting plaited shadows as Chalise and the guardsmen passed beneath. She'd ordered most of the men to stay with Sidon, along with Casimir, one of two Shedaím Gahíd had sent to guard them. Apparently, the elder was growing nervous of the renegades he was still yet to find.

The other Shedaím, Abda, walked beside Chalise. A tall angular woman with black hair tied in thick muscular braids fastened so tight they seemed to pull her face taut.

"Sharífa."

Chalise looked down at Elias again. The diminutive chamberlain gave a small jerk of his head and strayed from the corridor of people into the din of stalls. Chalise and Abda followed whilst the palace guard, as instructed, continued on with Sidon.

Elias led her through a clutch of stalls and then on beneath a large canopy. The vendors fell still as they passed, glancing away from Abda's flat cold stare as she followed behind the sharífa.

They eventually emerged at the market's fringe, passing the last of the stalls and coming out onto the traders' square. Chalise squinted as they stepped from the stall shadows. She glanced at the children running along the tops of the high walls of housing, the sandstone tenements set against one another like pebbles in a purse.

It was then she saw Gahíd.

The elder stood by a low wall fencing the street. He met the sharífa's eye, nodded once, and then leaned back against one of the wooden support posts that marked the lengths along the market boundary.

Chalise drifted across to him. Gahíd gestured at Abda, who'd come trailing behind. The Shedaím peeled away to stand watch on the street beyond the low wall. Which was annoying, Chalise thought, Gahíd's commanding her like that, reminding Chalise the bodyguard was not her own.

"Good to see you, General," Chalise said.

Gahíd grimaced and bowed.

"I always forget you do not enjoy the title. But how else for your comings and goings here to not be thought of? Do you wish we'd never given it to you?"

Gahíd scanned the shore of stalls she'd approached from.

"Yes. Of course you do. But then we *all* wish for a great many things, don't we, but how often do we find them?" She glanced at the empty street. "Must we always do this?"

"Prying ears are the rot of any throne, Sharífa."

"Yes... So it is said." She lowered slowly to the low wall and sat.

Gahíd did the same.

"So," Chalise said. "What does the blind woman see?"

"She sees little."

Chalise looked sidelong. "Is that so? That's not like her."

"No. It is not."

"Is there a reason?"

Gahíd shifted on his seat. "She says it is my fault."

"Your fault?"

"She warned us of this, Tarrick and me, three years ago."

"Of *this*?"

"Something *like* this. She said Arianna would prove difficult. Tarrick and I believed she could be taught. The girl is gifted; we did not want to discard her talents needlessly... Safít says our refusal has closed her sight in the matter. She has no counsel."

"So, what do you plan to do? One dead Shedaím is discomfiting enough, but a second? And now you say there is a third? Maybe more? It's almost slovenly, General. I will abide a day of snow in summer, but when there is a second, one has questions."

"I know."

"No. You do not. You've weeds in your garden. Such a thing makes one wonder at the habits of the one keeping it."

"Weeds are not the fruit of the gardener."

"No, though they are often evidence of his neglect. The Shedaím are meant to *prevent* these things, not become the cause of them... What is the counsel of the elders?"

"They are yet to convene."

"*Yet to convene*?" Chalise's gaze snatched back from the market. "More pressing concerns, have they? Some other engagements they must first keep?"

"The eldership convenes just once a year, Sharífa."

"Three of you were together barely a month ago to anoint this new sharím of yours."

"We anoint a new sharím but once every eleven years, as you know. In any case, it takes more than we three to declare a heretic."

Chalise stared at the elder. Slowly it dawned on her. "You've yet to give the order."

"All must be there to decree against them. Not just the Three."

"You've two of your..." Her jaw shivered and clenched. She glanced around and forced her voice to lower. "Those two are running free about *my* lands, killing and pillaging and who knows what else, and you are yet to send after them?"

"I have sent some."

Chalise's gaze narrowed.

"It's why I've come."

Chalise, still watching, exhaled heavily through her nostrils.

"Thirty men, soldiers from Calapaar. Very capable. And a ranger, Jaleem, from Ilysia. He knows their faces and ways well. They have been hunting them together."

"Thirty men and a ranger? After the countless times you've lectured me on how feeble the sword of a soldier is before one of your vaunted Shedaím? And now you say foot soldiers are what you have sent after them? Why not send pups after wolves?"

"The betrayers are young, Sharífa. Talented, but young. And Jaleem is... special. With these soldiers in his hand he will find and at least slow them. It will give us time to prepare to send those of the Brotherhood."

"And when will that be?"

"The council has been called. I am returning to Ilysia to meet it. From there word will be sent to the remaining Shedaím. The betrayers will be declared heretics, and the Brotherhood shall hunt them. And then there shall be no way of escape."

Chalise stared at the elder for a long time and then stood. She surveyed the terraces. "Why, Gahíd?" She turned and looked down on him. "These betrayers – Neythan and Arianna – why are they doing this?"

"I do not know, Sharífa."

"And the blind woman, Safít, she does not know either?"

"She does not."

The sharífa shook her head. "What use a mystic who gives no answers?"

Gahíd watched the market.

"And you are certain these two are the ones responsible?"

"I have seen the bodies of the slain myself, those that have been found – Yannick in Godswell, Sha'id in Parses. Qerat's too, not far from where the first was found. Each slain by the same method." He lifted two fingers to his throat, drew them across to demonstrate. "And each time the work of a left-hander, just as Arianna is. And then there is always the bruising, where they've been held down by larger hands – Neythan's hands... I too would rather it were some other way, and that these two were not our enemies, but with each passing moon another body or two of the Brotherhood is found. To take the life of one from our order is an uncommon thing, Sharífa. To take the life of more than one... Well, unless by a troop, a very large troop, there are none who can. None save those who have *belonged* to our order."

Chalise paced restlessly, watching the terraces again. "You will fix this," she said. "It is nearly new moon. My son is to wed less than a month from now. Nothing can be allowed to disrupt this." She turned to face the market, staring at the endless motion of it, the men and women going back and forth pursuing their trade.

There were twenty-two seats on the Sovereign Council, including the rulers of every major city in the Sovereignty and, by law, the mother and wife of the sharíf. With both Játhon and Chalise's father, Sulamar, already on the council, if all went well her family would control nearly a quarter of the court by the end of the month. And it was control she needed. Sufiya, the governor of Qareb, was already agitating for a return to the old ways and the supremacy of Sumerian blood. And there was King Jashar of Harán to think about, whose house had been a rival to the house of Salíph since before even the Cull.

Never mind that Jashar's daughter, Satyana, was married to Játhon. Jashar and Sufiya still wanted more. More say in whose grain stores went where, and their pick of the best crop yields and trade routes, or cidlewood and cedar for whatever Haránite creation Jashar was seeking to build next. And the problem was they were gaining it. Influence. The favour of the court. Elia, the governor of Qalqaliman, had already turned to them, and there were rumours Geled's governor, Zikram, was preparing to reject Calapaar and do the same. Two more council members to cause further delay and opposition to Chalise's aims. Her only comfort was that she had finally chosen Sidon's bride. A girl she had handpicked carefully, who would soon sit on the council, and who Chalise would be able to groom and prepare until she was ready to...

"Sharífa."

Chalise started. She turned back to face the general.

"Did you hear what I said?"

She looked at him blankly.

"Dumea," Gahíd said patiently. "What of Dumea?"

"What does Dumea have to do with anything?"

"The decrees there are yet to be fulfilled."

"And those you sent remain in the city?"

"More than that, Sharífa. Those I sent saw the steward, Hassan, *leave* Dumea and go beyond the Narrow, into Súnam."

"The Summerlands? When?"

"Less than two weeks ago. I received word only today. They say he met with one of the daughters of Queen Umani."

"*Umani?*" Chalise watched the ground as she resumed her pacing.

"Sharífa?"

"I'm *thinking*..."

Gahíd leaned back and turned his gaze to the street.

Chalise, after a few moments, came to a stop and turned to face him. "The ones you sent to spy on Hassan," she said. "They are of the same sharím as these rebels?"

"Yes."

"Then you will have them return. If there are any who will know why these betrayers are doing as they are it will be those who've spent most of their lives with them. They may be able to tell us something of their aims, even unknowingly, perhaps we will learn what they plan next. You will question them, and then send word to me."

"And Súnam?"

"Súnam will wait," she said. "For now, at least." She turned to start back toward the market. "The Sovereign council is against me, Gahíd. They will not agree to act against the Summerlands. When the time comes, it will be the Brotherhood that shall be called upon to do what must be done. Which is why we must first take the thorn from our *own* foot before we seek to tread on another's."

With that she strode away across the clearing. Gahíd watched the chamberlain, Elias, come to her side as she turned again and beckoned to the waiting Abda. The bodyguard glanced to Gahíd. Gahíd nodded at her, releasing her to return to the sharífa. It was only as she obeyed that Gahíd noticed the chamberlain watching him, the old man's gaze lingering for a moment across the distance before he too finally turned to follow the queen.

Eighteen
CARNIVAL

Melodic jangling sounds floated over the giant walls of the city as the drivers hailed the gates. Shouts and laughter from men and women inside the walls. Neythan poked his head out of the carriage, watching as the long-awaited high doors of Hanesda slowly parted.

The watchmen waved them through with a caravan of cloth and spice merchants he and Caleb had joined in the hill country after fleeing the men at the well. Caleb, it turned out, knew one of them – a balding and diminutive spice seller by the name of Nouredín. A man with an annoying habit of leaning in too close as he spoke, voice always hushed, as though he was about to suggest robbing those nearby. It was a manner all the more irritating for the sharp niggling scent of cardamom, cumin and some other smell Neythan didn't recognize that wafted from the man whenever he opened his mouth to speak. He leant toward Neythan now, nudging his thigh with a fist, falsely familiar.

"Seems our timing is good, my friend," he said, pointing upwards. "New moon festival. There will be many delights within for a man like you." His lips, thin and crinkled, twisted into a narrow smirk as he winked, making his mouth look like a wound. Neythan ignored him, as he had for most of the journey. He had other things to think about. Like what had happened back at the well, the sheepcoated men who'd attacked him, and Jaleem, who'd pointed the finger.

"They hunt you," Caleb had observed not long after in the plains.

"So I saw."

"The Shedaím must think you in league with Arianna. Understandable, really. You did not return to Ilysia. You didn't tell them what happened. You went after her unbidden. They would have found only the body of your friend, you and her both missing."

"Yes, I know…"

"Natural for them to suspect you with the time that has passed. The question is what you will do now."

"I should return to Ilysia."

Caleb had leaned in quickly then, almost tipping from his seat as if to snatch the words from Neythan's lips. "But you will not," he said. "We have a covenant, as binding as blood. If you return they will punish you because you should have returned the night it happened. Then you shall be kept from fulfilling what is agreed." Then, slowly, Caleb leant back again, eyes wide and staring. "We have a covenant, you and I," he'd said again. "As binding as blood."

Neythan grimaced at the memory as he sat swaying in the carriage. He was bound to the words he'd given, and now it seemed they would lead to his being hunted by the Brotherhood. His only comfort was that the men who'd come for him were soldiers, not Shedaím. But Jaleem – why had they sent Jaleem?

The carriage jolted, tipping Neythan from his thoughts. The carriage was moving again, rolling through the city gates. The music grew louder as they entered, drowning out the crunch of dust beneath the cartwheels. Neythan lifted a corner of the canvas walling the cart where he sat, tugging it to one side with a finger to peep through. Outside, the night stuttered by to the bumpy roll of the wheels. Pale ribbons hung droopingly in messy festoons across houses and moorposts and stall roofs.

The streets were filled with people: women, midriffs bared, clothed in loose, skimpy livery; men chasing, laughing, grinning, cavorting through the streets and upon walls and in narrow alleys to the sound of flutes, cymbals and timbrets and somewhere the steady thud-patter of drums. Along the road Neythan saw a sinewy old man, half-naked, jumping in erratic hops and leaps, tossing his limbs wildly as if on fire as those nearby wandered in wine-staggered steps around him. A troupe of small children stood on a long foot-high wall in an alley, each gazing at Neythan as he passed by in the cart.

Another street; a pair of beggars on hands and knees tugging at scraps of dropped meat, the street panning away to the side, another jerking into view. More people, colourfully dressed, single-shouldered robes, hips and waists jigging, dancing to a band of shirtless drummers, their drums – long kettles of hollowed wood – slung at shoulders and hips, marching as gambolling bell-tethered ankles skipped and bounced over the ground to the rhythm of their pitter-patter beat whilst one gleeful woman in the middle of them all, dressed in red, tambourine in hand, turned endlessly.

Neythan replaced the drape. He turned to face Caleb as the carriage rounded a corner.

"Every new moon is like this?"

"Yes," Nouredín invited himself to answer, leaning in again, grinning. "It is why we come, all of us. We do our best business at the new moon. Is that not so, Caleb?"

Caleb gave an obligatory nod.

"You can sell spices in this?"

Nouredín looked at Neythan as if he had something on his face, and then started laughing raucously. He laughed a while longer, his head wagging, before seeing Neythan staring flatly back.

"Spices," Nouredín sighed. "Ah, no… no, no my friend. I have spices yes, but here, we sell jewellery, garments, and wine, lots and lots of wine." He flopped a palm on Neythan's shoulder. "The wine is the joy of it; the quality is the worst kind, but during the carnival it will sell as though plucked from the very honeyvines of Tresán."

Neythan shrugged the man's palm from his shoulder and grunted, turning again to peer outside at the passing streets. Each one was busy and narrow, every house and terrace pressed together. It was hard to believe they were finally here. Hanesda. The Crown City. Seat of the Sovereignty. Home of the Founding Council and the First Laws, and throne of the sharíf himself. For years Neythan had heard of its lavish buildings, the resplendence of the palace, the greatness of the forum and amphitheatre. What he saw now, one eye peeping through the narrow slip his finger opened, bore little resemblance to what he'd imagined.

"Quite a sight, isn't she," Nouredín said.

To which Neythan, as had become his habit, made no reply.

"But her bosom is deep, with many a sweaty cleft and corner, and as craggy as a catacomb. Your task will not be easy."

Neythan glanced back over his shoulder.

"Caleb has told me why you are here," Nouredín explained. "That you are looking for someone."

Neythan turned fully now and looked hard at Caleb, who simply shrugged.

Nouredín smiled placatingly and again leant in, his thick nose prodding. "So happens I have a cousin in the city, you see," he murmured. "He is a ranger, and good at it. Would find a tadpole in the Swift if need be."

Neythan ignored him and went to sit by Caleb. "What is this?" he hissed. "You told him why we are here?"

"Nouredín is a man who can help."

"So you will speak secrets to the unsworn?"

"Unsworn? Am *I* a Brother?"

"You know what I mean."

"I told no secrets. Only that we're seeking someone."

"You should have told me."

"You wouldn't have agreed."

"With good reason."

"Without reason enough. What did you think, Neythan? That we'd come here and seek her out by our own means? You see what it's like out there. This is not Ilysia. A man could seek a stranger for a year here and not find him."

"We'd find a way."

"There *is* no other way. The Brotherhood hunts you now. You cannot do as you once might have. There isn't the time."

Neythan's jaw clenched.

"We have the purse, Neythan, and he *can* help us."

"So *any* man would say when silver is offered."

"Perhaps. But we have little choice. And the fact remains..." Caleb nodded at the waiting Nouredín across the carriage as he leaned forward, straining to hear. "He *does* know people. People who can help us."

Nouredín managed to pick out this last part over the noise of the music. "My cousin, as I have said, is a ranger. He'll know the one you seek or how to find them. It would be my pleasure to introduce you... for a small price, of course."

"Of course," Caleb replied.

Nouredín smiled. "Good. So, we have an agreement?"

Caleb looked at Neythan. Nouredín perched on the edge of the bench, waiting.

Neythan finally looked up at the spice seller and sighed. "A ranger, you say."

Nouredín grinned. "Ah, my *friend*..."

The carriage slowed and came to a halt by a square filled with tent booths. They peeled back the drape and clambered down from the cart. Caleb stretched and rubbed his numbed backside. Neythan stood and looked along the length of the parking caravan, ten donkey-drawn carts in all, driven by Nouredín's men. Beyond the square of tents stood whitewalled houses, flat-roofed and piled one atop the other into terraces, rising high over the narrow alleys that squeezed between them.

"Your first time in the city?"

Neythan turned again to find Nouredín watching him. He nodded.

"It shows."

Neythan looked over the square of tents. There was a quarter-mile or so of them. "Why all these booths?"

Nouredín looked across the square and sniffed. "Sippar, Qareb, Qadesh, some from Calapaar and Qalqaliman perhaps. Marketers mostly, like us, they have come to sell. There's rarely space for us all at the inns, and so we use the square to pitch our tents."

"This is where you will sleep?"

"Sleep?" Nouredín grinned. "We will not sleep on a night like tonight, my friend. Neither should you." He smiled and began to move away toward the hired men unloading the stock and the other merchants alighting from the carriages behind, and then stopped and turned back. He looked Neythan over. "You know... you should come with us."

Neythan glanced at Caleb, still stretching, and then back to Nouredín. "With you where?"

"Here you are, in the city of cities for the first time. What a poor friend I should be if I failed to introduce you to its many qualities. We *are* friends now after all, eh? And do not say you have Caleb here for your guide. He is poor counsel when it comes to the treats of Hanesda, and besides, since we have an agreement, there is little reason why you shouldn't meet my cousin *tonight*."

"The ranger?"

"Yes, the ranger."

Neythan looked at Caleb. Caleb, doubled over, shrugged and waved him on.

"You'll not come?"

"Let him rest, he is weary," Nouredín said. "The journey was long. His bones are not as young as yours. Come. I will show you the city, then you will meet my cousin. Caleb will still be here when you return."

Nouredín, true to his word, led Neythan along countless alleys, deep into the city, along with his company of vendors, sellers and brokers, each one with their quick smiles and slippery eyes nodding and laughing at Nouredín's jokes and stories.

They visited and exited underground dens with drinking men and giggling women. At every corner another stranger who knew Nouredín's name saluted his coming and going with a happy deferent bow or a brittle embrace and kiss, before ushering his party into whatever festivities waited inside.

They entered the third or fourth place Nouredín took them to through a narrow low door, one by one, and descended what seemed a hundred or more steps into a broad dim-lit space. The room was split by rainbows of thin sheet drapes, muslin and cotton. Slow ripples billowed across them from the wafted heat of the potted fires in each corner, along with the shadows of dancing women. Bare-bellied girls sauntered about the narrow smoky space carrying platters of fruit and wine. Smiling hosts whispered in ears. Bronze lampstands flickered and breathed. Flutes and hand-drums played. Nouredín was handing Neythan a brass goblet. Neythan eyed it doubtfully whilst Nouredín smiled.

"The best wine you are likely to taste."

Neythan raised a palm and shook his head.

Nouredín, still smiling, cocked an eyebrow, puzzled.

"I do not drink it... I don't like the taste."

"Ah, then you should taste this, my friend. All other wine is as pigswill next to it."

"You are kind... perhaps later."

"Take. Drink. What kind of host should I be to have you dry?"

Neythan didn't take the goblet.

"It is but one cup; you needn't have more unless you wish but I will not have you my guest and not partake of such good stock."

"I thank you, but no."

Nouredín's smile lingered, his eyes shifting toward onlookers. He stepped forward and leaned in yet again. "It is not right to refuse the gift of your host."

Others were starting to take note of the exchange. Neythan glanced around, and then back to the rigid, hard smile of his host. Nouredín's hammy gold-ringed fist was wrapped around the offered goblet, waiting. Neythan, reluctantly, took it.

Nouredín remained, continued to watch.

Neythan, looking around and then back at his host, cleared his throat and sipped from the goblet.

Nouredín frowned, gesturing impatiently with his hand. "A mouthful at least. You will not get the flavour."

Neythan took a mouthful, swilling it, and then swallowed. The sweet tart taste fell down his throat. He looked up again. Nouredín, satisfied, nodded knowingly.

"I told you there would be delights did I not. It is good, uh?"

In truth, the wine was very good. Neythan examined the goblet and nodded.

"Then drink. It is but one goblet. And this is a party."

Neythan took a larger sip. Not too large. But then again, what would he know? He'd never taken wine before. It was only after he swallowed he began to think his estimate may have been generous. He could feel his lips tingling and his cheeks beginning to numb. They continued on down more corridors, past more lampstands. Some moments later, perhaps longer – he was finding it difficult to tell – Neythan found himself sitting in a curtained chamber. His lips felt cool and turgid. He pressed his fingers to his scalp, trying to massage feeling into it. He was sweating. The music seemed to be pitching from loud to soft, leaning from one to the other like a sliding bucket on a wind-tossed ship. The low woody whistle of a flute bounced in time to light drum patter and the dainty rattle of bells. The room seemed to be gently swinging back and forth. People talking over it all, quiet chatter, murmured voices, then, the vague sense that one of them was speaking to him.

"… And so Caleb told me of your concerns. You must understand, he and I have been friends for many years, often partners. Our talents are of mutual benefit to one another. He is an able courier of goods, I have many goods to courier. A healthy partnership. Always, the best ones must be this way, each party of shared aims though differing means. My wives, they can never understand this. Always they are expecting me to be as they are – chattering, talking. I try to explain. I am a man. You are women. We don't have the same ways, the same temper. Ought I to wear dressgowns and anklets? Or ponder nose-rings and bracelets? It is the fashion of Parses, yes, but let us not call those of that city men and mar the name. We are different, I say, let us rejoice in it. But no, they will not understand and so always, *Why don't you do this? Why must you do that?* Ah. A nagging woman, my friend… such a thing, I will tell you, it is not good, will drive you from house and home. Keep but one wife if you desire peace. It is what I tell my sons, but one wife… Where was I… ah, yes, Caleb, he has explained it all to me. You must find someone, yes?"

Neythan slouched; he was struggling to follow the other man's speech. The words seemed to smear into each other. "I uh... I am." Neythan puffed his cheeks; the air felt thick and warm, his words sticky in his mouth. He sighed, hiccupped. "I'm looking for my sister," he said slowly. His throat was dry. He could have done with another drink. A young almond-skinned girl with frizzy hair appeared, presenting a silver platter with a single brass chalice as though summoned by his thoughts. Neythan smiled lazily, at least he thought he did, the muscles in his face were growing steadily less compliant. He took the vessel and nodded his thanks. The woman smiled back, her gaze lingered on him, then she moved away through the sheet-draped walls into another corridor.

"Your sister, you say. How does a man lose a sister?"

Neythan shrugged, groping for another piece to the lie. "She was to come here," he said, slurring. "And then return home. But she did not return... and has sent no word... my mother... she worries." Neythan, satisfied by this last improvisation, sat back and reclined on his elbow.

"Ah, what mother does not, my friend? These things happen of course, but it needn't follow that harm has come to the girl. Perhaps she has enjoyed the city and wishes to remain. She'd not be the first. It can be a seductive place, no?"

"Still, I must know one way or the other."

"Of course you must. Our having happened upon one another is good. I knew so from the beginning. It's the very reason I wanted for you to meet my young cousin here." Nouredín gestured toward a man sitting in the corner.

The man was sitting upright with crossed legs, perched like some king on a cushion. Strange Neythan hadn't noticed him there. The man was golden-haired, something Neythan had seen just once before. He was big too, though not in a bulky way; lithe and muscular, his build as much a dancer's as a soldier's. Stranger still, he had blue eyes, as blue as the sea, and skin paler than Neythan had ever seen. He stared steadily at Neythan. Unlikely this man was truly Nouredín's cousin. Neythan wondered about his origins, wondered vaguely about why Nouredín would say they were kin. After a while he could no longer summon the effort to care. He propped himself up again from his slouch and watched the man tip his head in acknowledgment.

"So, you…" Neythan pointed, his finger swaying unsteadily as he did so, "are the ranger."

The man considered him a moment before answering. "Huntsman, I prefer," he said, gently.

Neythan glanced at Nouredín, who made a quibbling shrug.

He looked again at the man. "Huntsman…" the word dragged. His lips were starting to feel swollen.

The man looked down into his lap, examining his fingers as he spoke. "As I have been since my youth. In truth, my work has changed little from then till now."

"No?" Neythan looked at Nouredín, then back to the man. "A strange sort of prey you hunted then."

"Some might say so." The man's voice was soft, yet somehow carried through the din. "It was given to me to provide for the dining tables of the princes of Tresán, in Calapaar."

Neythan frowned, trying to sit upright, the room sliding as he did so. "Tresán is a long way from here."

"Yes."

"Do these princes not have men of their own to hunt for them?"

The man lifted a thumb-sized cup from his lap and sipped at something steaming within. "They do," he said. "But they are princes, and princes, especially those of Tresán, are extravagant banqueters. When their spirits are especially high, their tastes run to mammoth meat and mountain cats, things not easily found, and harder to kill."

"Takes a skilled hand."

"Quite so."

"And so they employed you."

The man gave a bow of his golden head.

Neythan smiled, looked to Nouredín, who smiled back, dropping a nervous, single-syllabled laugh.

Neythan looked back to the man and squinted. The room was beginning to blur. "So, there you are, in lovely Tresán," he said. His words were growing increasingly untidy, tripping over each other. "Having the favour of princes... and then..." He dangled his goblet in the air as he formed the thought. "You somehow come to be here, all this way... Did you tire of your mountain cats?"

A corner of the man's mouth twitched. "Let us say I discovered a bounty more rewarding. Princes pay well for mammoth and cats, but men pay better for men."

"Hmm." Neythan finished off his drink.

"Besides, in the end they are not so different, men and beasts."

Neythan looked up from the dull worn brass of the emptied vessel. "No?"

"No. A man's appetites..." He glanced at Neythan's emptied cup. "His *habits*, they rule him as well as do a beast's. They shape his wants, his acts, his comings, his goings. A man is as much a slave to his belly as any creature."

"That so?"

The man's still blue eyes held Neythan's gaze. "Yes. It is." He put his small cup carefully to one side. "It is his only weakness, but the only one needed to join him to every animal. And it is this weakness, as with every beast, that often tells the way he will be found. Or caught. Or killed."

The words hung awkwardly, chased by the quiet patter of the music. Nouredín, his eyes working between the pair, pushed out another hesitant chuckle to fill the void.

"All this talking, when you ought to be drinking." He clapped his hands and beckoned back the young almond-skinned girl. "More wine for them," he said. "There will be time for talking and business later. Now is time for celebrating. Drink. Drink."

From then the evening slid by in bits and pieces, each sloshing, like poured wine, into the next.

Nouredín cackling at something Neythan has said as he hands him yet another goblet of wine. Women dancing in low skirts, bodies turning like ribbons through the air. Blurred light. Men arguing, Neythan joining in, something about camels, a needful point being made. Food passing around on wooden platters, berries and red grapes. Everyone dancing, drumbeat hammering loud and quick.

Then outside somewhere, shivering in the cooling air. Clear starry night, pulsing overhead as if in time to the music's constant throb.

Staggering, arm wrapped around a stranger, no, the almond-skinned girl from before. She's laughing, telling stories, people she's known, patrons – men, women, old, young, blind, seeing.

Somewhere else, a tavern, seats and tables, raised drinks, shouting and toasts, Nouredín's cousin calling, that strange blue gaze no longer watchful but lazy, peering back through heavy eyelids and a sluggish smile.

A slumped man, face hanging over an empty mug, muttering, weeping.

A tapped pan drum and bells and cymbals, the almond-skinned girl pulling him to dance, Neythan falling back down. More wine. The steady thud of the drum, shrugged shoulders and raised hands, all bouncing in time.

Nineteen
RANGER

"I saw the night speak to me, Neythan. I saw the stars draw near as doves. When the moon was black, with a ring of light around it. And that was when it fell, into the sea. The moon, I mean. I saw it, watched it sink to the very bottom like a rock. It was then the stars told me I must follow, I must go and retrieve this fallen dark moon. But when I looked down into the sea, in place of my reflection there was an animal, like a jaguar, only bigger. Its eyes were like suns, and its coat, so dark, as black as the night around us. It leapt out from the water to stand against me, to keep me from the dark moon beneath the sea... It was then, as I looked into the beast's eyes, that I understood, Neythan. The jaguar was me, a shadow of me, and it was also the Brotherhood. It did not want me to do as I ought. They do not want me to discover the dark moon."

Neythan awoke to the cloying heat of what felt like an oven and the sounds of children playing outside. His tongue felt chafed. His throat, clammy and dry, as though he'd swallowed a meal of feathers.

He'd dreamt of memories again. Memories he'd forgotten he had – this time of Uncle Sol, sitting with him back in Ilysia by the forest beneath the village as he shared one of his visions. Neythan couldn't have been much older than seven at the time, fascinated by the vividness and detail of

Sol's words but unable to make sense of what they meant or why he shared them. Sol had always said he'd explain when Neythan was older, teach him the meanings. But he never did. Never could. Time ran out...

Neythan blinked and looked around. There was hushed amber light glowing from the low canvas walls surrounding him. A goatskin blanket lay draped across his body. Something similar lay on the ground beneath him. He was in a tent booth. He lifted his head to see what else there was and flinched at the stray slips of sunlight wickedly breaching the entrance by his feet.

"Gods have mercy..."

So this *is what it felt like.* Memories of a snoring Tutor Hamir lulled to sleep by too much of Yulaan's summer brew came to mind. Neythan groaned and yanked away the goatskin blanket to find himself dressed in a wrinkled tunic that didn't belong to him. He tried to remember the night before, where the tunic had come from, then gave up and tried to lever himself upright.

He could hear the sounds of ambling routine from outside – the proud clucks of a hen, the distant murmur of voices, the soft crunch of footsteps passing by, and riding over it all a deep aching throb at his temples and along the back of his scalp.

"Aha, alive to the world at last."

Neythan grimaced and squinted, lifting an arm to shield his eyes from the light as Nouredín poked his head in.

"Ooh, sorry. Still delicate, are we?"

Neythan grunted grumpily.

"Well. I hope you'll be better in an hour. You will need to be. Yevhen is to meet us in the market."

"Who is Yevhen?" Neythan croaked.

Nouredín blinked. "My cousin... You met him last night."

Neythan, slit-eyed, stared back blankly.

"The *ranger*?"

Neythan, still squinting, sighed sulkily and muttered.

Nouredín just chuckled, shaking his head, and then withdrew.

After nursing his headache for a while, Neythan manoeuvred himself onto his hands and knees and crawled gingerly toward the tent's exit, taking a breath before pushing his head through to the outside. The sun whited his vision. He squeezed his eyes narrow, shading them with the flat of one hand as he came out and rose to his feet.

Sunny. A sea of tents stretched out in every direction, billowing gently in the weak breeze and backed by the familiar sprawl of piled up terraces behind them. Beyond the tents to the east the broad shore of the marketplace extended out in rows of low stone buildings and stalls.

"So, you finally decide to join the land of the living."

Caleb was sitting on a stool nibbling a dish of nuts and berries next to the tent.

"How do you feel?"

"I've felt better." Neythan picked up the vessel of water at Caleb's feet and swigged heartily. He wiped his mouth and looked down again. The water was warm from the sun. "What hour is it?"

"Guess."

"I've not the stomach for games, Caleb."

Caleb looked at him as if to see if this was true, then shrugged and chewed on another berry. "Noon."

Neythan rubbed his jaw.

"You are to meet Yevhen soon?"

Neythan glanced down at him. "You know of this Yevhen too?"

"Of course. It was you who introduced me to him... here, last night."

Neythan stared.

"You don't remember? You were very eager for us to meet. Woke me up even, which I wasn't grateful for. You said you'd made an agreement with him of some kind, that he was willing to help us; and that you would meet today to discuss payment."

"Payment? We gave the last of the silver to Nouredín."

"Funny, that is *exactly* what I said to you last night."

"And what did I say?"

"Not to worry. All was agreed. You were quite cheery about it all. I was looking forward to your waking up just so I could hear all about why."

Neythan's headache was worsening. He rubbed his neck.

"You remember nothing?"

Neythan shook his head.

Caleb kept looking.

"You find this funny," Neythan said.

"A little… the way you were last night. It was… well… unexpected."

"Glad you found it entertaining."

"You should eat."

"I don't think so."

Caleb smiled. "Ah, that's right, perhaps not the stomach for food yet either. No need to look so dark though. I'm sure you'll remember what you must soon enough. Let's hope it's in the next hour though, Nouredín says he is to take you to Yevhen then."

Nouredín was true to his word. He arrived just as Neythan was finally managing to make himself eat, tentatively scooping shallow spoonfuls of lukewarm porridge from the pot Caleb had made that morning. His headache had dampened down to a dull simmering pressure behind his eyes. He badly needed to go back to sleep. Nouredín duly led him into the marketplace.

The stalls were huddled together in tight rows. People moved hurriedly in the narrow gaps between. A small copper-skinned boy walked on ahead of them in the crowd, bare-chested and barefooted, leading a young goat by a rope and every so often nabbing items from the stalls – small trinkets mostly, and at one point what looked to be an expensive ornament of ivory – and slipping them into the goat's mouth. Neythan watched, waiting for the goat to gag or choke. It didn't. Well practiced, apparently.

His gaze drifted to a troop of women wandering through the narrow aisles between the stalls in pale-coloured shawls like Filani had worn, hiding from the sun. Two turbaned marketers were arguing with one another from behind opposing counters, their heads leaning over and around the passing crowd to continue the dispute. Neythan found himself ducking as he passed between them.

They continued on through the stalls for around a quarter of an hour, shoving and shouldering through the glut of shouting men and women like tadpoles against the tide.

They eventually found Yevhen in a clearing at the heart of the market. He stood with his back to them observing the Stone of Arvan: a broad column of carved slatestone marked by the Sovereignty's First Laws on every side and crowned by the tall blade of a sundial. He was wearing a white sleeveless coat of linen that hung to his ankles and a pale vesture beneath, revealing muscled forearms. His conspicuously long golden hair was tucked beneath a turban, pulled fast around his head and tied into a ball against the back of his skull.

"King Karel the Young, son of Yusan of Hagmeni, Lord of Sumeria, first sharíf and father of the Sovereignty, author of peace, prosperity and hope..." Yevhen glanced over his shoulder as Neythan and Nouredín approached. "What do you think? Are we feeling especially prosperous or hopeful today?" He turned fully, saw the weary ill look on Neythan's face and smiled. "Perhaps not so much."

"Good day to you, cousin," Nouredín said. "How are you?"

Yevhen nodded at Neythan, still smiling. "I think the question is how our new business partner here is. Let us hope you carry your blade better than you do your drink."

Neythan looked away to the market and sighed impatiently.

Nouredín took the hint. "Speaking of business…"

"Yes, of course," Yevhen said. "Let's walk this way."

From the clearing the market split into quarters along four main roads extending away from the column. Yevhen led them along the easterly street into the quadrant of the market furthest from the square of traders' booths they'd come from. Neythan watched him walk. Something in the way his hips moved, the balance of his weight, the stillness in his shoulders. The gait of a combatant. Neythan had suspected as much the previous night as they sat together, though only vaguely through the fog of the wine.

"I feel you are a man acquainted with conflict," Yevhen said softly, echoing Neythan's thoughts. "I felt it so when we met last night. It was because of this I agreed to help you."

Neythan, walking at his shoulder, just looked at the taller man. Yevhen turned to Nouredín. "Cousin, how about you let Neythan and I get acquainted properly? Now, in the light of day."

Nouredín hesitated, cleared his throat, and then peeled away, wandering reluctantly into the crowd. Yevhen glanced at Neythan over his shoulder and smiled.

"I understand your reticence. He is a good man truly, but his ears at times, well… they can be as keen as his lips are loose."

"Is he really your cousin?" Neythan said.

"Ah, well, that depends. Most say kin is chosen by blood, some say by other means. I am one who believes the latter. As do you."

"Do I?"

"Of course. All your kind does."

"My *kind*."

"Yes, those of the Brotherhood. The Shedaím."

Neythan stood still.

Yevhen had walked on a few paces before realizing Neythan had stopped. He turned, looked at him standing there, and then walked back to him.

"The lapdog knows the voice of his master, Neythan. Rangers, some of us, the most skilled of us, have worked so often for your kind – ferrying word, spying decrees – we cannot help but grow familiar with your ways. I am a watchful kind, I suspected you might be one of them the longer I sat with you. Though I could not be certain, until now."

Neythan didn't speak.

Yevhen, again, gave that thin and easy smile. "It is perhaps the Shedaím's only flaw; that they entrust some of their work to youths. Like you. It betrays you. You have the bearing and manner of a man twice your age, yet the face of a boy. And your eyes, Neythan, even when taken with the wine, are always so watchful. Full of mistrust. It's an uncommon habit. To the man who is looking, these things can be noticed."

"What do you want?"

"Not to anger you, or any others. As I've said, I know your kind, your *works* as well as your ways. I seek no quarrel." Yevhen glanced at the crowds passing either side. "But please, let us walk."

They resumed.

"And what of Nouredín, your loose-lipped cousin?"

"He knows I am a ranger, yes. But he knows little of my business beyond that – nothing of the Brotherhood. Your kind are no more to him than a child's tale to be grown out of."

They turned off the road into an alley of stalls. The canopies of the tables were nearly touching each other. Yevhen leaned in close, closer even than Nouredín would have, and spoke into Neythan's ear as they went.

"I know of the one you seek," he said. "Your 'sister.'"

They turned to pass by a table of hens. Their clawed feet were tethered to a nearby beam supporting the high roof sheltering the stalls beneath. They were clucking and shrieking and flapping their wings. Blood and dismembered chickenfeet and scattered feathers lay on the table by them, and the vendor, a foot away, worked with a cleaver.

"I hear rumours of her."

Neythan looked at him. "What kind of rumours?"

"Rumours of how she turns on her own kind."

Neythan placed a hand on the other man's forearm as they rounded another stall. "That is strange talk for a ranger to hear."

Yevhen looked down at Neythan's hand, then to Neythan. "Nevertheless, from time to time such things are heard."

"From whom?"

"You needn't concern yourself with that." He slowly eased his arm from Neythan's grasp. "Those who speak of such things are few – lapdogs, like me, who from time to time hear the talk of their masters above the table. Such whispers, for us, are of little worth. After all, who would we tell? The Brotherhood itself knows that we whisper, and that we dare not go beyond that. We're as fond of breathing as we are the silver you pay us... but then I happen upon you, one in pursuit of her. And, as in all my dealings with your kind, I seek for my services to be had, to deal my secrets. Yet you have no silver, no gold. And so how, as is custom, are you to pay?"

"I have the feeling you are about to tell me."

"What better price is there than your skill?"

Neythan smiled wryly. "You want a favour."

"A favour, yes. The perfect way to put it."

"And in return?"

"In return… I will tell you where she is."

Neythan stopped.

Yevhen, again, waited for him.

Neythan glanced at the passing crowds and then stepped toward the ranger. He spoke quietly. "Say that again."

"I will tell you where she–"

"You *know* where she *is*?"

"Yes."

"The Brotherhood seeks this girl and is yet to find her, and you… How could *you* possibly know where she is?"

"I am a ranger, Neythan. My business is to know and find, just as yours is to seek and kill. It has always been this way. In truth, it's strange the Brotherhood hasn't already come to me. Ashamed perhaps, because she is one of their own. But this failure is to our gain, should we make this bargain."

Neythan just stood looking at him.

"I suppose your doubt is understandable," Yevhen said.

"How did you learn her whereabouts?"

"That will be part of the bargain, Neythan. I cannot–"

"If you want me to trust your claim then you will tell me how it is you're able to make it."

For a moment, they just stood there with people moving either side of them. The ranger eyed Neythan for a while. And then, abruptly, smiled gently. "Very well."

"Very well, what?"

"The answer is simple – a tailor. One with whom your 'sister' has visited. One who has helped her, and who knows of where she has been and where she will be, who may even know something of her plans."

"And who is this tailor?"

"He is one of your Brotherhood's tailors, just as I am one of its rangers. Just as there are those who are its innkeepers, smiths, and who knows what else. Your kind, you have people in every city. Some, I have learned of; many I have not and never will. But this man, he is one of them, and she visited with him for two nights and two days."

"You are certain."

"I saw them myself. Sat with them. Ate with them."

"*Ate*? When? Where?"

"They are good questions, Neythan, truly. But their answers have a price."

Neythan's gaze had fixed to the man now. There was no more market, no more people or headache, just this man who claimed to know the whereabouts of the person Neythan had been seeking since that night at Godswell. He spoke slowly. "Be careful, Ranger. You should be sure of what you say. It would be unwise to trick me. I am just a youth, as you say. We are not given to temperance when slighted."

"I don't doubt it." He turned to resume the walk. "But come. We must yet walk."

They passed a stall kept by an old woman with no teeth and a black shawl wrapped tight to her head like a widow. Two monkeys sat in wooden cages on the counter, each clothed in small vestures like little men, one clapping a pair of tiny cymbals, the other playing a drum.

"I will tell you all you desire," Yevhen said. "Even take you to the tailor should you so choose. All I ask is a favour."

They passed through a screen of beaded strings, into a small sheltered square of fruit stalls walled off by leaning planks of wood and tattered drapes. Yevhen stopped at one of the stalls and nodded at the man behind the table, taking a couple of pears. The man huffed and nodded back grumpily. Yevhen smiled and turned to face Neythan, a pear in each palm.

"So... will you hear my request?" he said.

Neythan thought about striking Yevhen in the throat with the blade of his palm, thought about wrestling him to the ground there and then and pressing his thumbs against his eyes until Yevhen let go every last secret detail Neythan desired – where she was, how he knew, why they'd eaten together. He glanced about at the crowd and understood now why Yevhen had insisted they meet here, in the marketplace. He looked again to the taller man and his glassy pale blue eyes.

The waiting ranger cocked a thin eyebrow. "Will you?"

Neythan exhaled long and quiet through his nostrils, and nodded.

Yevhen smiled. "Good." He handed Neythan a pear.

He wandered away from the stalls and stood in a less busy corner, leaning against another support beam. Neythan followed, stopping close by, watching the people come and go around him as he bit unhappily into his pear.

"I seek a jewel," Yevhen said.

Neythan smiled humourlessly. "I should have guessed."

"A very *particular* jewel. Very precious."

"You want to steal it."

"Retrieve it, yes."

"And so would have me play the thief."

"In a way."

Neythan bit again into the pear, which seemed to be turning sourer with each mouthful. "You seem an able enough man. Why should you need me?"

"The jewel is kept in a certain place, a chamber in the palace."

Neythan stopped chewing. "You mean the *sharíf's* palace."

"Yes."

"You're saying you want me to steal from the sharíf?"

"The jewel is not his. In truth he barely knows of it."

"Yet it is in his possession."

Yevhen nudged himself forward from the support beam where he was leaning and stood in front of Neythan. "You asked of my kin," he said. "Earlier – 'is he really your cousin?' you said."

"Yes. So?"

"No doubt you wonder about my origins," he gestured lazily. "My hair, my eyes, my skin."

Neythan waited.

"You'll have guessed my blood is not of the Five Lands... I am a Kivite, Neythan. From beyond the Reach, north of the twin seas."

"A barbarian."

Yevhen parted his lips to answer but then thought better of it. He gave a wan smile. "This jewel was stolen from my people in the time of Sharíf Theron. I simply wish to return it."

"And you tell me? A servant of the Sovereignty?"

"The Sovereignty you serve has more pressing matters than a stone it took two centuries ago. Matters that you, by an agreement with me, can easily remedy."

"You've waited a long time to rob a trinket. A hunter in Calapaar, a ranger for how many years, yet only now you seek to take this jewel."

"It's taken many years to even learn its whereabouts. I discovered it just days ago. It's why I came to the city, only to find, thanks to the efforts of your 'sister', that the sharíf has elected to keep two Shedaím by him in the palace at all times."

"Two Brothers? Here in the city?"

"Two that I know of, yes. You can imagine my surprise to have found you, a third, and one who may yet strengthen my hand."

"I have agreed to nothing."

"You have agreed to listen. You know as well as I it is the reasonable thing. A trinket – as you call it – in a crypt, a forgotten one at that, is of no worth to the throne compared to a betrayer, a Brother turned against her own, killing one after another. You know what you must do."

Neythan took another bite of the pear, chewed slowly. *Killing one after another* – so there *had* been further deaths. He wondered how many. *Three? Four?*

"It is a royal tomb," Yevhen continued. "Its contents are rich. I want only the stone, a black pearl, fixed in a pendant; whatsoever else you come upon you will be free to add to your bounty."

"I am no thief, Yevhen. We are not alike."

Yevhen considered him. "No... we are not... ill of me to say so." He took another bite of his pear and chewed, looking out again to the gathering customers opposite them beneath the shade. "Nonetheless things are as they are. I have something you want, you have of me the same. So. What is your answer?"

Neythan looked at him and then back to the crowd. He took a final bite of his pear and tossed the bitter seeded core to the ground. "Let's go back," he said. "I must speak with Caleb."

Twenty
TRADE

Neythan sat next to Caleb at the tent booth and watched the people bustling along Hanesda's narrow walkways as though it was a sport – builders and masons from Harán, merchants from Calapaar's coastal market towns, garment-makers from the High East. There were even Súnamites here, just as Caleb had promised, selling spices and fabrics from the Summerlands – the whole world, it seemed, packed together in one place, and all of them moving hurriedly along the city's streets and gangways as though they were being chased.

It was a similar story in Sumeria's other cities – Qadesh, Sippar, Qareb – each one filled with too many people and not enough time, the fruit of having sprung up along the ever-fertile banks of the Swift back when the neighbouring Harán was little more than dirt and sandshrubs, before the Low East discovered bronze and iron and how to forge them, and then how to dig deeper wells, further inland, and build their settlements around what they'd dug. Still, Hanesda remained the biggest, built atop a sloping valley on its north and eastern sides and overlooking the Swift to its south and west. A sprawling whitewalled network of terraces, alleys and squares where friends behaved like strangers and strangers sought to make friends, all in the name of trade. It took some getting used to. Not the kind of adjustment a golden-haired

Kivite, unaccustomed to the warmer weather and heavily peopled streets and a native of the barren city-less scrublands of the Reach, should find easy to make. But then that was just one of the many strange things about the ranger, how comfortable he'd seemed strolling through the cluttered passageways of the marketplace and laying down his wishes.

"Do you trust him?" Caleb asked.

Neythan glanced at him, then back to the street opposite. "Not really. But then how much can I trust a man I've known a day?"

Caleb gave a conceding shrug. "His price is steep – go rob the sharíf himself."

"I know… What of Nouredín? How well do you trust him?"

Caleb shrugged again, made a wry face.

"You've known him long?"

"Years. But time isn't always a teacher when it comes to people."

"How did you come to know him?"

"He's a broker. Came upon him in a village in the High East, south of Tirash. I was trying to find buyers for a cage of peacocks I'd brought up from the Narrow. The man I'd gone there to meet had refused to do what was agreed. Wouldn't buy. So there I was, stuck on the back side of the desert with this cage of birds and no buyer. One of the hirelings knew men in the town, sent word, not the kind of thing I like to normally do. I like to know whose silver I'm taking ahead of time. But, as I said, it's desert land, ten days' journey at least from almost anywhere. If I go on with the stock how am I to feed them? And they are nervous creatures. Two had died already on the way. So anyway, word comes back from the town, this man Nouredín has taken an interest – which is a relief – and what's more is willing to come out from the township to meet me and see the stock. Which, well, he didn't have to do, did so as good faith, to make life a little easier for me. As I said, the creatures are skittish.

"He wanted and took a hard price, of course. I mean, I had four birds in the cage, all strong and healthy. But we are in the desert. Who else am I going to sell to? He knew this… so anyway, he was impressed with the stock, asked if I was able to get other beasts besides, which I was, and so he partnered with me at a better price to take what I brought him every three moons – monkeys, camels and so on… He was a reliable buyer, more so than the first, always on time, always with silver."

"You trust him, then?"

Caleb grimaced mildly. "I trust him to pay for goods when he has agreed to do so, nothing more. We've seldom eaten together. I do not know his kin. It is not like that with us."

Neythan grunted.

"When does he want to do it?" Caleb asked.

"Ten days from now. The sharíf is to visit the south corner of the city to see the school before he departs to Qadesh to wed. The ranger thinks that if the sharíf goes, so ought the Brothers who are guarding him."

"Should it be a difficult thing to take this jewel?"

"Not the way the ranger tells it. The sharíf's guard are twenty men but most will go with him when he journeys. In the palace will be only cooks and servants, perhaps a handful of armed guards, or so he says."

"Even so, this is the crown city. The cityguard is what, maybe a thousand men?"

"I said the same."

"And what did he say?"

"He claims the jewel won't be missed, that the sharíf barely knows of it. It is kept in a tomb he never visits and is of little or no value to the Sovereignty. He claims as long as our trespass goes unknown we could leave with the jewel and abide a year in the city without it being noted missing."

"Seems unlikely."

"I said the same, but he spoke as if all the more certain."

Caleb grunted and continued working on his sandal as they squatted together on stools by the tent booths. He'd been at it for a while. Several thongs had come loose around the toes. He was taking the remaining thongs, bound from further back on the sole, and dipping the thing whole into a bucket of water, trying to make the leather stretch to tether them at the front.

"Would help, of course," he said as he continued to work, "if you were able to remember more of the Watcher's words."

"So you have said."

"To come here and nothing more... it's slim counsel. Bones without meat."

"We've been over this."

"If we knew, at least, whether your heretic is here."

Neythan sighed.

"It would be helpful were you to remember."

"Yes, I know. But I do not. The sticks are as they are."

"You say he met her, the ranger?"

"Ate with her, he said."

"And you think he speaks the truth?"

Neythan shrugged again. "He described her likeness to me well. He's seen her, if nothing else."

Caleb nodded, turned the sandal over, shook his head. "What *is* this jewel anyway?"

"A pearl... No, a *black* pearl, he said."

"Black?"

"Yes."

"Strange."

"Yes."

"And whose tomb is to be raided?"

"A wife of Sharíf Karel."

"Karel, you say... Analatheia? Queen Analatheia?"

"You know of her?"

"Of course. As *you* ought, it is the wife he killed… But the Brotherhood these days…"

"Yes, I know, they teach us nothing."

Caleb looked up from the sandal. He smiled sheepishly. "I say it so often?"

Neythan shrugged.

"I didn't know I said it so often."

"Why would he kill his own wife?"

"Ah, well. Whose story would you hear? There are as many as there are years to have passed since her death. Most say for infidelity. The intrigue is in knowing with whom the betrayal was, or, for some, with what."

"What do you mean?"

Caleb put down the sandal. "It is said of some she practised the ways of the Magi, and that Karel commanded her to cease and keep his law. When she refused, he had her killed."

"Loving husband."

"There will be a secret or two for every man or woman of the royal line, Neythan. Of that you can be sure."

"This too, you say often."

"What does he want with this pearl, anyway?"

"He is Kivite. He says it belongs to his people, that Theron stole it when he conquered them."

"And he's waited until now?"

"I know, that too I questioned him of."

"And?"

Neythan shrugged. "He said he'd only recently learned its whereabouts."

Caleb frowned and shook his head. He dunked the sandal once more into the bucket. "Well. So, how would the deed be done?"

"The ranger and I would enter together."

"He knows the palace?"

"He knows a man who does, a courtier. He'd be our guide to the tomb and out again; the ranger has bought him."

"And he is reliable, this courtier?"

"So he says."

"Must be quite a price the ranger paid, for the courtier to be so bold."

Neythan nodded.

"What then? Where is the tomb?"

"There are many. Some beneath the palace, some in a crypt beneath the gardens behind. The ranger thinks the one he wants will be under the palace."

"How does he know?"

"The courtier."

"Right."

"The courtier is to take us to the door of the tombs. The ranger will wait there to keep the watch, and I will descend."

"How does he know this courtier?"

"I don't know. I didn't ask."

"There's not much to like about this."

"Again, we agree."

"The pearl, it will be somewhere in the tomb? Does he know of its place?"

"It sits in a pendant, joined to a necklace the queen wore. He says it will be with her."

"What do you mean, *with her*?"

"With her... She... well, her corpse will be wearing it."

Caleb snorted. "No wonder he'll stay and keep the watch."

Neither spoke for a while; Caleb puzzled, lifting and turning the sandal before putting it to the ground, pinning the sole there with his toes and yanking on the thin threaded leather of the thongs.

"I keep thinking there ought to be another way," Neythan said. "To find Arianna, seek her out."

"Like?"

"I don't know. You know people in the city, people we could speak to... find a beginning."

"I know the same people as Nouredín, except he knows more, and knows each one better than I. Were you to remember more of the Watcher's words, *that* would be a good beginning."

"What's your advice then? That I do it?"

Caleb shrugged, then tutted, dropping the sandal as he yanked again on a thong. He picked it up. "Strange he doesn't do it himself. He has the courtier, he has the day for the deed, why should he need you?"

"He fears the Shedaím, fears one of them may remain within the palace."

"Why would they?"

"I know. But he doesn't want to take chances. Thinks my being there will help, should anything go awry."

Caleb frowned again.

"So, what *is* your advice?"

Caleb tossed the sandal to the ground grumpily. "I'll have to buy another or pay for it to be mended, not that we have the silver." He looked up from the battered and soggy leather sole. "My advice..." he looked around at the tents, at the market across from them, then, finally, back to Neythan again. "We cannot know whether the ranger speaks the truth or no... But what other means have we? Perhaps he *does* speak the truth. In which case how else, other than doing as he's asked, might we come to learn what secrets he knows, where to find your heretic?"

He sat and stared for a while. Neythan waited.

"I do not trust him," Caleb said evenly.

"That makes two of us."

"It is a hard thing."

"Perhaps we agree to do his bidding, but then find a corner somewhere, on the way to the deed, and take hold of him.

Gain what he knows by force."

Caleb shook his head. "But how then would we flee the city? And what if what he knows requires us to stay? We would have to kill him just to make sure whatever friends he has didn't hear of it. And besides, he could as easily choose to lie."

"I would bring the truth from him, Caleb. You can be certain of that."

"Be that as it may, it would be less than wise… It would be better to do the task he has asked."

"Rob from the sharíf?"

"That or bleed the ranger, each are as hopeful as the other."

It was Neythan's turn to sit and think.

"Perhaps our choice is this," Caleb said. "Let us rob the tomb and hope the ranger's words true, and if his steps prove false we simply put a blade in his back first, and then leave the city second, and seek some other way to find your heretic."

Neythan thought about it for a moment. "No."

"No?"

He picked up Caleb's sandal, dusted it off. "A blade in the courtier, second," he said distractedly as he tugged at the thongs. "Leave, third."

Twenty-One
GATHERING

Dawn. Honey-glazed light leaked sleepily through the leafy canopy overhead like water through fingers, beaming down in thin, pale shafts that dappled the ground light, dark. The Forest of Silences was more a garden than a forest, Gahíd had always thought; the sloping gaps between each tree were too big and airy, too neat, though he'd always liked it that way. He gazed up at Neythan's bloodtree.

"It's strange that it would finally leaf now, don't you think?"

Master Johann glanced sideways to the elder and scratched his chin. "Perhaps. Perhaps not. I always wondered about when it would... Maresh used to say teaching this sharím was like teaching the elements. You had Josef, who was like stone. Strong. Determined. He was a slow learner as a child but once he'd learned a thing, come to understand it, you could not easily dissuade him. You cannot shape or carve stone quickly. So it was with him. His brother, Daneel, was the same, though for other reasons. More like fire; unruly, wild. With him the thing was not so much to teach as tame. And then there was Arianna, who was *always* changing, *always* seeking, like wind, unable to dwell long with one thing. Easily distracted. With her, many things came easily – the way to handle a blade, wield a bow – but other disciplines, less so... and then..." He sighed and looked at the tree.

"And then what?"

"Then there was Neythan... He was *always* quick to learn. *Easy* to mould. Like clay. But like clay, also easily weathered. Yielding. Sometimes fragile... but then that's the trouble with clay. It can become anything a man may choose, which is often the very thing that keeps it from taking a shape of its own. It's why his bloodtree was always slower than the others. Just like his father's. I always knew it would pass in time, that he'd become very able, perhaps the most able of them all... Perhaps it is beginning with him now. Perhaps that is why his tree now leafs."

Gahíd nodded and looked around, surveying the slope, glancing at other trees for comparison. It had been a while since he'd come here. He'd forgotten how dense and strange the quiet was – no breeze, no birdsong, nothing. Like death. Peaceful somehow, and yet eerie too.

"How long has his tree been like this?" he said.

"The first leaf sprouted weeks ago. The others followed thereafter. It has been growing quickly since."

"And you don't know what it means?"

"I have told you, Gahíd, each disciple is different. To say would be a hard thing."

"But if you were to guess."

"If I were to guess I would say only what I have already. His sha is discovering and choosing its shape. He is becoming what he will be."

Gahíd approached the tree. The girth of the trunk had widened. Thick boughs were spreading from it in every direction, each branch clothed with small leaves. He was reaching out to touch the bark when he noticed Safít standing beyond it, facing them, a stone's throw away, waiting. Gahíd stepped out from around the tree and walked across the short distance toward her.

She was standing in a plain ankle-length smock and headscarf, hands clasped loosely behind her back, her pale sightless gaze staring into a vague middle distance somewhere between Gahíd's chest and navel.

"How was the sharífa?" she said as Gahíd approached.

Gahíd glanced up at the bloodtree behind her. One he recognized. The tree of the exiled Master Sol, a tall spare cypress with naked boughs and thick clusters of foliage resting on its high branches like giant nests. "As you might expect," he said. "She asked after you."

"Kindly, no doubt."

Gahíd smiled, his gaze lowered to her. "Do you know how many Brothers remain?"

Safít's head turned a fraction, indicating the space around them. "Roam the Forest. You will see for yourself."

"I don't like to stay here long, Safít. You know this."

Safít said nothing. A frequent habit. A woman prone to silences.

"What does Tarrick say?" Gahíd said.

"He says little."

He was about to ask further when the dull blast of the village horn bumped the silence. Birdsong abruptly resumed with the sound.

Safít stepped back and turned toward the Forest's incline, ready to return to the temple. "The last of them has arrived," she said. "You should go. They will be waiting for you."

Gahíd lingered for a moment, and then nodded and turned away, leaving her by the bloodtree as he began to make his way down the lush grassy slope. By the time he cleared the cover of the Forest, clouds were gathering overhead and to the west, drifting in on the wind in a thick grey pall. The signs of rain seemed to weigh on the villagers as he passed along the narrow walkways of the settlement, the solemn way they stared after him, or perhaps it was just his being here. They knew why he'd come.

He reached the village's fringe on the other side to find Tutor Hamir waiting for him by the brakes of sycamore shrubs and wildflowers near the path in.

"Are they all here?" Gahíd said.

Hamir nodded and turned to lead the way.

They went through the woodland to the slab of naked rockface that framed the door to the catacombs of the Shedaím. Hamir made a show of lighting the oil lamp when they reached the opening, conjuring flints from his sleeve and blowing reverently as he kindled the wick. Gahíd followed him in, stooping into the passage. The tawny crown of Hamir's bald head glowed in the lamplight as they moved further in. They continued along the narrow tunnel one by one until it broadened, leading into a small low-ceilinged lobby with a door at the end. Hamir leaned in to push it open and then stepped aside for Gahíd to pass through.

The dull stench of trapped air and incense was familiar. Gahíd saw the dim bulk of the Creedstone in the middle of the room and the stony bench that ringed it, sitting there like a gigantic toadstool. A lampstand of carved ivory stood on top of it like a waiting visitor. The engravings of the Shedaím doctrines were spread across the Creedstone's table, illumined by the dim light. Gahíd could see the others standing by the wall opposite, just beyond the glow.

"Sit," he said.

They obeyed, stepping into the shallow hue of the lamp's light and lowering to the bench.

Gahíd looked at them. So few. It was worse than he'd thought.

Josef and Daneel sat together on one side. They'd arrived only an hour before, passing the Empty Fountain on the way into the village and gazing at the familiar puddle of water within the raised sink of stone carved in the shape of an upturned palm. Daneel had seen the chipped middle finger where he'd once thrown a pebble to try to splash the water when Neythan and Yannick were bowing to drink. He could still remember the hiding he'd caught that day from Master Johann for his mischief, and the balms and ointments Neythan and Yannick had later sneaked to his bedchamber to take the sting from the wounds. Neythan still taller than him then. Fond memory. Ilysia had many of them. Which was why it was strange, after having journeyed all the way from Dumea, to be greeted so sombrely by Tutor Hamir on their arrival and ushered in silence to the cave's entry, passing along its tunnels to this chamber to wait and stand with two other Shedaím – a man and a woman. Third or fourth sharím. Silently awaiting Gahíd's arrival and the explanation he would bring.

The elder ran his fingers through his beard. "You four are the only swords remaining to the Brotherhood," he said simply. Then waited.

Daneel looked at his brother to see if he'd heard and understood any better than he had. He looked at the two older Shedaím sitting blank-faced on his other side.

"Yes," Elder Gahíd said. "You heard correctly. This is all of you. The question you will ask next, of course, is why."

But no one asked anything, so Daneel glanced again to the other Shedaím. The man had cropped grey hair and bland flat features as though his face had been bashed in with a rock. The woman beside him was a Haránite, High Eastern by the look; the light honey-skinned complexion, the snub nose, the slight compact shoulders and narrow eyes. Both of them were staring intently at the elder as though they fully understood his words. Like they were all playing a game Daneel just didn't know the rules to.

"Let me explain why you are here," Gahíd said. "Before you were each last sent out there were eighteen of you.

Eighteen Brothers. Now there remain only eight – you four seated here, two others guarding the sharíf, and two others retrieving the next sharím."

"I don't understand," Daneel said.

"Well, of course you don't. Where are the other ten, hm? Well, I shall tell you simply... Eight of the ten you do not see here are dead. The other two are their killers."

Silence.

"Betrayers?" whispered the Haránite.

Gahíd nodded.

More silence.

"Who?" asked the greyhead.

Gahíd looked at Josef and Daneel. "Their names are Neythan and Arianna."

"*What?*"

"They have murdered eight of our kin, eight of their own Brothers."

Daneel was about to answer again when the Haránite cut in. "Who are the fallen?"

Gahíd nodded. It was a question he'd expected. "Qerat. Tanith. Eliab. Vanya."

The Haránite's eyes seemed to drop further with the mention of each name.

The elder looked at the greyhead. "So too Sha'id, Majad and Nassím." And then he looked at Josef and Daneel again. "...and so too, Yannick."

Daneel half-smiled, half-frowned, disbelieving. "Yannick is dead?" The words seemed absurd. "You're saying Neythan and Arianna have *killed* Yannick?"

"Yes. I am. Because that is what they have done. They murdered Yannick in a village on the way to Dumea. It is the reason they failed to meet with you in the city. From there they went east, and then north, and have since gone on to kill seven more Shedaím: Qerat, in a fishing village not far from Godswell, the village where Yannick was killed. Sha'id, in Parses a few days after that. Nassím, two weeks later, in Çyriath…"

"But that makes no sense," Daneel said. "Why would they do that? To what end?"

"Ah, now *that* is the question, and, as it happens, the reason for our being gathered here. That we may know. More important shall be *how*, but I do not expect to discover that here. Only when we find the betrayers themselves shall we know by what means they learned the whereabouts of those who've been their prey. But as to why, this we expect to be enlightened of by those who know them best."

Gahíd looked pointedly at Josef and Daneel. They felt the gazes of the other two Brothers at the table turn toward them too.

"Of all of us," Josef said, "none could be more devoted to the doctrines of the Brotherhood than Neythan. I hardly find how to believe what he has done, how should I be able to understand it?"

"Then you say Arianna will have led him to it?"

"No. She too wouldn't–"

"But you spoke only of *Neythan's* devotion."

"I meant only that–"

"Josef. Is that your name?"

Josef glanced at the greyhead.

"I understand," the man said. "I do. It is difficult to think how *any* would betray the creed, much less spill the blood of his brethren. Even harder for that betrayer to be of your own sharím. I'd struggle to accept that too. I am yet struggling. But eight lie dead, one from your own sharím, and one who was my own flesh and blood. None of them less devoted than any of us. Eight, Josef. Think on that. An uncommon enough thing for one to fall at the hand of a troop. But *eight*? It can only be the work of one belonging to this order, or, more likely, two. If it is not by their hand, how else could it be so?"

"Salidor speaks truth, Josef," Gahíd said. "I *went* to Godswell. I saw what was done to Yannick. I spoke with those who'd witnessed it. They described the betrayers' likenesses well. With my own ears I heard their witness, and with my own eyes saw Yannick's butchered body. Do you think I was not as you are now? I too would sooner believe it not so, but each week word comes to me of another slain. In the end, a man must accept the truth is the truth. We cannot allow what we'd hope or prefer to blind us from what is. We cannot afford to."

Daneel was still shaking his head. "But where is the reason?"

Gahíd looked at them and sighed. "Not with you, it would seem. But perhaps that doesn't matter for now. Most important is that they are found. Until they are, they remain a threat to the order."

"But surely you cannot believe they would–"

Daneel barely saw it. Metallic glint in shadow and his chin lifted, suddenly bracing away from the blade at his neck. The Haránite was on the table, squatting over him, face inches from his and eyes hungrily looking him over like some strange unfamiliar prey.

"Who is this one?" she said. "With words so many and sense so small?" She'd somehow swung from her seat and mounted the table so quickly that Daneel had barely time to blink. "He calls himself a Brother," she said, peering at him. "Yet despises the words of an elder and defends betrayers. Perhaps we should cut him, and see if he will defend us also."

Josef's voice was firm. "Let's not."

Daneel, blade still at his neck, smiled at the woman as she looked down to find his brother's shortsword pressed against her ribs.

"Put it away, Jasinda," Gahíd said. "You too, Josef. Our

enemy is elsewhere. And you will not defile this table with the blood of more of our kin."

Jasinda lingered. Her eyes passed from the still smiling Daneel to the cold staring Josef before she slowly withdrew the shortsword and climbed back down to her seat.

"You may find this difficult, Daneel," Gahíd said, "but you are a child no longer, and neither are they. For whatever reason they have chosen to become betrayers, and they will soon be named heretics. Whether you would wish it some other way or not, they have no part with us now. They are not of this order. They are *not* Shedaím. They are rot, and are trying to eat away what remains of the tree that bore them. This rot must be found, swiftly, and cut out. The matter is simple."

"So we are to hunt them, then."

Gahíd turned to the greyhead. "Yes, Salidor. We are to hunt them."

"Where?"

"Where the last of our fallen was found. The Calapaari foothills to the north. The four of you will go as far as Geled and track them from there."

"You're sending us together?"

"Yes. I am. It will be unfamiliar to you, I know. But I have already sent Casimir and Abda to guard the sharíf. And Johann had already sent Zora and Shimeer to gather the new sharím before any of this began. After them, you are the last swords left. And after you, there are only the tutors. And so, as you can see, we cannot afford for any others to be lost. If you go together the betrayers will not be able to do as they did with those who are fallen."

"And if we *do* find them?" Jasinda said.

"I and the other elders desire to speak to them, yes. But they are talented, these two. And those they have slain were strong. So..." Gahíd placed his hands on the flat scarred rock of the Creedstone. He felt the shallow grooves of the doctrines that marked the stonework. "If they cannot be brought to us," he said, lifting his eyes to regard those gathered, "they must be killed. Swiftly. The rot cannot be allowed to go any further."

Twenty-Two
TOMB

It turned out it was the sharíf's custom to visit the Sovereignty's schools once a year before the early rains. There were four in all, spread out through the Five Lands and housed in buildings built by one sovereign or another. The largest and oldest was the School of Hanokh in Hanesda, and according to the courtier, Sharíf Sidon would begin there and then go on to Qadesh and Livia, meeting the teachers and scribes who were its custodians, as well as the best of the students.

"He will go to all but Dumea," the courtier said. "He does not like it there. The sharífa is not friends with the city's steward, and the sharíf is to be several days in Qadesh for his wedding anyway."

It had been Neythan's insistence to meet the courtier before the day of the deed. If he was to rob the sharíf he wanted to be sure of the man who would be his guide in doing so. Yaron, his name turned out to be, an older man with a plump fussy neck and hairless face and a shaky querulous voice that began to grate from almost the first moment they met: *We shouldn't meet like this. Do you know what I risk in helping you? We cannot be seen. You must not be caught.* Every chivvying word made Neythan want to slap the man's pudgy nervous face. Instead he had him talk through every corner and corridor of the palace's interior in as much detail as he was able to.

Afterward Neythan met with Yevhen every day leading up to the agreed one, going over what would be done and when and how. He spent the evenings watching the palace guard from the marketplace that fronted its gates. He wandered the city's streets, growing familiar with its passages and alleys and buildings, and now, finally, he sat here with Yevhen and Caleb watching the sharíf vacate the palace, parading through its main gate and along the street toward the south corner of the city to visit the school.

"There," the ranger said, nodding. "The woman, the tall one, walking before the sharíf, she is one of them."

Them meaning Shedaím. And this Neythan could tell, even from this distance, just by the way she moved.

"But I do not see the other."

"He will be elsewhere," Neythan said. "Somewhere distant, where he can see everything. Somewhere like this."

They were perched atop a roof overlooking the main road between the walls of the palace grounds and the market. It was early evening. The sun was blood red, sinking down through a clear sky to touch the mountains to the west.

"He may be in the palace," the ranger said.

"He may, though to be so would make him a poor guardian. He cannot keep guard of the sharíf from where he is not… Still, we'll be careful either way. Rain does not always fall in its season."

"No," the ranger said. "It does not."

They climbed down from the wall as the parade moved on. The crowd followed the sharíf as he mounted a heavily jewelled camel and went along the south street.

The palace courtyard was cobbled stone, cordoned off from the rest of the city by low rough walls of sand-rock, half a man's height. The wide frontage sat atop several broad steps. A colonnade stretching the length of the building upheld by a row of twelve pillars supported a broad balcony above.

They approached from the north side, away from the market, hopping the wall and walking, their shadows pulled long by the low sun. They came around the building to where the front entrance waited on the western face. A huge doorway stood above the pillared porch like a giant affrighted mouth. They passed by without sparing it a glance. According to Yaron the twin doors were a foot thick and manned by a pair of guards waiting behind the entrance. Better to enter by the slopdoor on the south side, he'd said. With the sharíf gone there'd be no cooks in or around the kitchens.

They followed Yaron's advice and continued around to the back corner to find his sweaty bloated face waiting for them when they reached the slopdoor. He slipped a wary glance through the crack before opening to let them in.

"You are late," he said breathily, and looked out behind them, side to side.

The ranger jutted his chin. "Lead on. You've said the way to the crypts is long."

The courtier turned and led them through the kitchens, weaving between the wide benches of hollowed stone where the stoves seeped their ashy odour.

"Ten guards have remained," he whispered as they went. "Two by the entry door, others by the sharíf's chambers and the way to the gardens. I saw one in the courtyard, some others here and there."

"Here and there, where?" the ranger said.

"They roam about the place."

"And what of the sharíf's own bodyguard, do any remain?"

"I've not seen them if they do. I'd imagine they've gone on with him to the school."

The ranger grunted. Neythan and Caleb followed behind.

The palace was huge, built in broad arcades about an inner atrium with a reflecting pool. Each gallery undergirded a series of flat balconies with houses built along their length and then, on one side, a tall minaret crowned building that housed the sharíf's chambers. Yaron took them along the south side by a narrow corridor marked with drawings of each past sharíf. Karel the Young, Arvan the Scribe, Theron the Great... Neythan wondered what would be done half a century from now when there was no more space, or whether this place would still even be here.

"This way," the courtier said.

They rounded a corner and turned into another corridor. The passage was wall-less on one side and open to the atrium that centred the palace where the reflecting pool sat in long cool shadows, calm as stone. The dry rattle of scurrying lizards hissed vaguely from the walls. Their own footfalls were silent.

"Wait," Neythan whispered.

They froze, listening. The murmur of voices floated somewhere ahead. The courtier gestured. They stepped to the wall and waited. The voices grew louder, nearing. The courtier turned jittery. He came back on himself toward a door close by and fiddled for a key. Out along the courtyard opposite Neythan could see a shadow shifting as a guard moved along the roof balcony just out of view.

"Be quick," he said quietly.

The voices were clearer now, two or three men, accompanied now by the sound of their steps and the clink of weaponry. Neythan put his hand to his sword. Yevhen did the same and turned anxiously to the courtier.

"Hurry."

Yaron's hand fumbled; the key slipped and clinked against the ground. The shadow in the courtyard stopped, then moved again, quickly. The voices ahead were within a stone's throw, the courtier scrambled to the ground for the key. He reached clumsily as the shadow along the roof angled for a view. The courtier was rising, trembling hand on key, probably too late, the shadow nearly at the corner, the voices close by.

Neythan pulled his sword clear of the sheath and stepped toward the corner, lifting his blade. The voices were at the wall now. Maybe more than three of them. Ribald chatter, coarse men. Neythan would have to... Suddenly he was grabbed from behind, yanked backward into darkness. The door to daylight swung closed as he tumbled back into a new chamber.

He landed with a bump by what may have been a table. The room was small and windowless. A thin, luminous beam at the door's foot was the only thing dampening the dark. It was Yevhen who'd pulled him back into it. The ranger turned to the courtier and cursed.

"Will you have us die here for your dithering, Yaron?"

"Sorry. Sorry." The courtier, still by the doorway, was shaking. The sweat on his chin shimmered dimly from the light beneath the door.

"Be calm," Neythan said.

The courtier nodded, his fleshy chin shuddered.

Neythan got up and moved him gently from the door. Stood there and listened. He heard the steps of the chattering guards passing outside. Their feet swept black bars across the crack of light beneath the door.

"How far are we now?" Neythan said, turning again to the courtier. "From the crypt?"

"There is only the Judgment Hall and handmaids' chambers, the length of the east wing."

Neythan nodded. "And the door is away from the rest, you say. Out of sight."

"Yes. Yes. There are steps by the corner of the vestibule. They keep it hidden."

Neythan turned back to the door. "We will need it to be so." He cracked the door open and peeped through.

The corridor was empty. The waning yellowed light of the sun strafed the walls. It was quiet but he couldn't spy the guard patrolling the balconies from this angle.

"Is there any other way from this room?" Neythan said.

"Yes... yes, there is."

"Where?"

The courtier stepped hesitantly from the wall and pointed to the room's other end. "There are two."

"Where do they lead?"

"This one, back to the kitchens. The young men carry what is stored here to the cooks." He turned to the opposite wall. "This one leads to a second pantry at the corner of this wing."

"Will anyone be there?"

The courtier hesitated. "There shouldn't be."

"Good enough." Neythan eased the door fully closed. "We will go to the pantry and remain out of sight, and then find our way from there."

The courtier nodded and fished about the folds of his garments for another key. "This way."

The passage was short and well swept and ran along the outer flank of the palace's south and east wings. It opened on the other side to a pantry bigger than the first, filled with broad pots of grain, a man-sized pestle leaning against one wall, and a series of smaller clay jars standing in rows in the corner like guards awaiting command.

"The rear foyer is on the other side," Yaron said as he went to the pantry's outer door and turned the key. "It is a large space. I will walk to the other end where the entry to the steps below lie. If all is well I will turn and beckon you with my hand. Like this. Then you will come."

"Good," the ranger said. "We'll watch for your signal."

Yaron breathed deep. His chin and neck were flushed red. He swallowed and went out through the door.

They peered through the gap as he walked across the tiled-floor lobby. Neythan watched the daylight from the atrium beyond view, scanning for shadows and movement as Caleb crouched at his hip and studied the courtier. Yaron reached the other side and turned around. Then waved nervously.

They went out and jogged toward him, wide steps, bent double. By the time they'd crossed the foyer the courtier had stepped down into a short bay cubbied in the wall. He found the lock and angled the door open before turning to wave them in. They stepped down into the recess and quickly through the entrance as the courtier followed and pressed it shut.

They'd entered a dark cold space with a long stairway stretching down into blackness. The courtier, jitterier than he had been, seemed to feel the chill, the sense of trespass.

"Alright, I've done what you asked." He said it almost immediately, spilling the words as though from held breath.

The ranger saw and nodded derisively. "Go back to your duties. The rest of your monies shall be with you tomorrow when we have departed, and I can be certain you have not shrunk back from what was agreed."

The courtier's eyes darted between them uneasily and settled on Neythan. "It is the sixth door," he said, then pinched his thin lips together as though to hold his breath, and stepped out, leaving the door ajar to let the light in.

"Well, you heard the man," the ranger said. He lit the stave lodged on the wall, closed the door, then hefted the torch from its fixture and handed it to Neythan. "I will wait here and keep the door," he said, and then nodded at the stairway. "Tarry no longer than you must."

Twenty-Three
AFTERLIFE

It had been near to three hundred years since the Priests' War, and just as long since Karel, the first sharíf, did away with the old faiths. He'd killed the last priests, outlawed their practices – the observance of the moon, the speaking of ancient tongues, the strifes about special books and sacrifices and all the wars these and a thousand other superstitions had led to. By the end, Karel allowed only the ancestral prayers to remain and replaced the rest with worship by way of fealty to a new and singular god – the *sharíf's* throne.

It was said he burned the priests' bodies on a giant pyre heaped to the height of a hill, and that its summit was crowned by the collected scrolls of every order and tradition from Hanesda to Hikramesh. It had disappointed Neythan as a child, to learn that. To think that all that could be done without a whisper from any of the gods Uncle Sol's stories always talked about. When he'd asked those at Ilysia why, everyone would offer a different tale. Some said there were never gods to begin with. Others said there used to be gods but then they were no more, like isles subsumed by the rise of the sea, ushered to extinction by the inexorable roll of time. Master Johann would say gods are a dream you count true in sleep and forget when you wake, and that you can tell which a man is by what he believes. Which troubled Neythan, but when he told Uncle Sol, he said Johann's words were true, but that a man doesn't truly wake until he gives himself to slumber anyway, and thereby surrenders all he thinks he knows to discover the truth. In the end, it was only Jaleem's counsel that made any sense; there wasn't much use thinking about it either way, the Haránite had told him.

"As many stories about that as there are about death, and besides, Sharíf Karel may have said there are no gods, but when he died he still filled his tomb with treasures ready for them just in case."

Neythan wondered if they'd find Karel's tomb here as they went along the crypt's slim passages. The walls were craggy and tight enough to bump shoulders. The ceiling, wherever it was, vaulted high overhead like a canyon, sucking the torch's glow into its narrow black maw. The stairway they'd descended was probably as deep as the palace was high. Like the whole thing had been built atop a huge enclosed ravine, or cave.

"Joram, of the line of Karel..." Neythan read as they passed another door. He lifted the torch for a better look. The flame crackled and breathed at his ear like a slow, crumpled storm as he squinted at the inscription. It had been the same with every doorway, a slim arched opening with a name ornately etched in the stone above. Except with this one he didn't recognize the name. He turned to Caleb. "An uncle perhaps? I'd thought they housed only those belonging to the sovereign line here."

"Joram *is* of the sovereign line. He was heir to the throne, before Sidon. The boy was to be sharíf... you didn't know?"

"I'm not a scribe."

"And needn't be to know histories barely set. Joram was Sidon's brother."

"*Sharíf* Sidon? He has a brother?"

"*Had.* An elder brother. He was to rule. Sidon was to be his regent."

Neythan turned back to the doorway, glancing in at the edges and corners of vague shapes as the light from the fire grazed the obscure contents within. "So what happened to him?"

"Sickness. Both were still children. Each fell ill with fever. Sidon recovered. Joram did not."

Neythan grunted.

"It doesn't matter. Let's just find what we've come for and leave. I've no mind to tarry among the dead."

They continued on and came shortly after to the door the courtier had told them of. Its narrow shape broadened with the angle as they neared. They stood and examined the tall arched opening and read the inscription to be sure it was the right one – *Sharífa Analatheia, of the line of Harumai* – and then stood there as though waiting for something, an instruction, perhaps.

Caleb looked at the tomb's doorway, then up at Neythan. "Well... you're the one with the torch."

Neythan grimaced, glanced once more back along the passage, and stepped inside.

The inner wall, illumined by the fire, hovered dimly into view as they entered. It was marked by elaborate drawings that seemed to narrate some event. Neythan mostly ignored them and stared instead into the room's dark void, sweeping the torch back and forth as he slowly crab-stepped his way deeper into the chamber. He flinched as the light snagged on the shape of a man. Tall. Upright. Still. And then a second. And then, as he neared, several more, emerging from the dark into the torch's glow. Statues. Heads bowed like supplicants and circled around a long stone chest. Neythan stepped carefully between the rock-carved figures – two men, three women, all crowned, and each half a foot taller than him.

"The ranger wasn't lying after all," Caleb said.

Neythan turned around to find Caleb standing on the

other side of the chest, looking out to the opposing wall. Long shelves had been dug into the stone and each hollowed sill glinted dully, filled with metallic items. The little man was smiling. He saw the look on Neythan's face and sighed.

"Fine, fine, I know. We are not graverobbers. But there's little harm in at least taking a look."

Neythan stared flatly back.

Caleb turned and wandered over to the wall anyway. "And bring the torch, I can hardly see what I'm looking at."

"We've no time for this."

"Better to come over quickly then. I'll not be visiting queens' tombs again any time soon. If my penance is to be here, I'm going to see all I can."

Neythan sighed and followed him to the wall.

The shelves were filled with vessels of all sizes, mostly silver, some brass. A pair of seamless garments and a long woollen overcoat lay neatly folded further along the shelf, both covered in dust. Neythan stood impatiently by as Caleb ogled the contents. The wall's entire length seemed packed with costly keepsakes of one kind or another – gold, silver, bronze.

"They'd have counted much of this cursed, you know," Caleb said. "That's why it is all here. Some pretty pieces, no?"

Neythan walked along at Caleb's shoulder. He saw a fold of parchments on one of the higher shelves, stacked vellum overlaid with a cover of hardened leather and piled into the short space. It was the only messily placed thing they'd come across. He left Caleb softly rubbing dust from a golden lamp and wandered over to examine the stack more closely. He tugged it out from the shelf. There were several scrolls placed together. The pages had begun to fall loose. Neythan decided to take one out to reroll the page and place it properly. He lifted it carefully from the shelf with one hand.

"Here, take this," he said, and held out the torch.

Caleb came across. "What have you there?"

Neythan shrugged. "Scroll."

Caleb took the torch. "What does it say?"

Neythan turned its coat, eyeing the coiled barrel of leather that encased it. A strange emblem marked the covering – what looked like a jaguar, its body elongated and set in a circle as though prowling after its own tail, except the tail was the head of an eagle. Elaborate patterns ringed the emblem and words were stitched at the corner.

"*Magi Harumai*?" Neythan read.

He lengthened the page, unrolling it from the pin. It was filled with glyphs and markings like nothing Neythan had ever seen. He turned it to Caleb.

Caleb squinted. "Some sort of writing?"

"A strange sort."

Neythan shook his head and rolled the page again. He put it back on the shelf next to another leather-coated scroll. He craned his head, curious to read the words stitched at the corner of that one too, and then, reading them, frowned.

"What is it?"

Neythan tugged the hem of the coat an inch from the shelf to show him.

"*Magi Qoh'leth*... now that *is* interesting."

Neythan tugged it free and opened it. The markings inside were as the first, unfamiliar, indecipherable.

"A puzzle for another day, though," Caleb said. "As you've said, we cannot tarry long."

"No..." Neythan said quietly, lingering over the scroll, looking at the stitched name of the father of the Shedaím. "We cannot."

He slowly rerolled the page and put it back on the shelf and looked at it. He then turned and took the torch from Caleb and went back over to the chest and statues. Caleb remained by the shelves, stroking a jewelled silver pot.

"Are you going to help me with this or not?" Neythan said.

The chest was twice the length of a man. Caleb walked along its length and swiped at the cobwebs tangling between the lip of the ledge and the chest wall.

"Be sure to put that down somewhere safe," Caleb said, nodding at the torch. "Somewhere it won't go out. Lose its light and we'll be stuck in here a while longer than either of us would like."

Neythan carefully propped the torch against the foot of the statue behind him, letting the flame lick against the stone. He went to the chest and braced against the ledge. Caleb came around to the same side.

"Together. Now."

They pushed hard. The ledge shifted, snagged, then scraped loose, opening a narrow triangle of space into the cavity beneath. Neythan collected the torch and lifted it over the opening. A glitter of brass and gold winked up at them from the gap as a waft of warm spongy air gasped free. Caleb, on tiptoe, saw and giggled.

"Perhaps we ought to reconsider this no graverobbing thing. I mean, that's more gold than either of us will ever see again."

"Do you see her?"

"I see many things, darkly, but the corpse, no, I do not. She may be underneath. Perhaps you ought to... I don't know... rummage a little."

Neythan looked at him.

"I would myself but my arms are too short."

Neythan gave a wan smile. He looked again at the disordered trinkets of gold and copper – goblets, necklaces, rings, a diadem, a moth-eaten garment of purple slovenly spread beneath and through it all, tangled and silken despite the dust. There was even cutlery, and a strange rod of silver, like a sceptre, long and jewelled. Neythan leaned down and grabbed it, and then used it to feel around, searching for the queen's corpse.

"I think I have her," he said.

"Can you bring her up?"

"Perhaps."

"Be careful, she'll be little more than bones. If you catch on an eye socket and yank too hard you'll bring only the skull and not the rest."

Neythan grimaced.

Caleb smiled.

"You're joking."

"Of course I am. She will be bandaged, likely."

Neythan shook his head and slowly lifted the snagged sceptre. The trinkets and ornaments spilled away around it. The sceptre emerged clinging to the hole of a woollen mantle. Caleb reached in and helped. They pulled out a bandaged stiff mass of head and shoulder and propped it against the inner wall of the chest on top of the gold. The lower body, wrapped in starchy bindings, looked hollow and caved in.

"Didn't think she'd be so heavy," Neythan said.

"It's not her, it's her dress, her jewellery. Of all you see in here the best of it will be worn on the body itself, wrapped in with the bandages."

Neythan shook his head. "Sovereigns have so much they must be buried *in* it?"

"Likely they just can't abide the thought of it falling to others. Now, hold her still." Caleb brought out a small dagger. "The bandaging will be hard, difficult to cut, so do not drop her."

He put the blade to the rot-dried cloth swaddling the neck and jabbed it in and began to carve – hacking and sawing and tugging – upwards along the neck's flank to its nape.

Neythan pulled a face at the smell.

"What did you expect? Myrrh and spikenard?"

"I expected bones. Dry ones."

"The way they treat the body at burial preserves the flesh, at least partly. She'll be bones, yes, but not dry ones. Not yet."

He cut a square and pulled it away; sticky membranous strings clung after it to reveal a mess of black putrified grime at the collar and neck on one side.

Neythan coughed.

"You see why the ranger chose to stay by the door," Caleb said.

He cut another square, this time around the front beneath the jaw. A gob of rotted tissue pulled away, clinging to the cloth. Caleb held it up, looking for the glint of metal – the pendant – then, not seeing anything, tossed it back into the chest.

"You seem to have a talent for this."

"I've seen and done many a thing, Neythan. But graverobbing? I'll confess this is my first."

Neythan watched as Caleb cut and tugged and dug, ploughing through the bandaging and the clammy moist fabric of the queen's graveclothes beneath as the putrescent stench of decay wafted up with every new ribbon of rot and rag he sliced off. Neythan's grip of the corpse was starting to cramp. He was beginning to doubt the stone was even there when Caleb allowed himself a half-happy sigh.

"Look."

"Do you have it?"

"Perhaps."

Caleb held a pendant and thin chain. He took a rag from his pocket and cleaned them and then held them to the torch.

"Yes, I think this is it. Let go of her. Take a look."

Neythan let the bandaged corpse slide back into the chest.

"See the jewel? Have you ever seen anything like that?"

The pendant was a half-globe of misty black stone prodding from a large pebble-shaped seat of gold, like the burr of a chestnut cracked open.

"Finally," Neythan said. "Keep it in your pocket and give me a hand closing the lid."

They shut the chest, pushing the ledge back across the opening. Neythan looked around the chamber to be sure they'd left nothing behind and, taking the torch, went toward the doorway, Caleb following, and then stopped.

"What is it?"

Neythan went back in, around the chest and statues to the shelved wall opposite. He examined the scrolls and tugged free the one named *Magi Qoh'leth*.

"Oh? And what happened to 'we are not graverobbers'?"

Neythan put the scroll under his arm and came back toward the doorway.

"If you are to take something you could at least let it be something of worth, like all this *gold*."

"Come on," Neythan said, walking quickly past and back out into the dank tunnel with the torch so Caleb had to follow. "Let's get out of here."

Twenty-Four
R O B B E R

As it often is, the way back seemed quicker, as though the tunnel had shortened. They quickly found themselves scrambling up the cool stone steps and making their way toward the doorway at the top where the ranger waited. Neythan was carrying the torch in one hand and the battered roll of vellum in the other. Caleb, at his side, trying to keep up, hopped up the steps in twos, his fist thrust deep into his pocket clasping the amulet and chain. The stairway curved upwards into the airy cold until they arrived to find Yevhen still at the top, squatting on the first step like some grim beggar.

"Finally... I was of a mind to come down after you."

"A thousand pardons," Caleb said. "The swaddling of the dead makes heavy work. Feel free to go down and see for yourself."

The ranger ignored him. His tongue danced nervously behind his teeth as he gathered to the torchlight. "So. Do you have it?"

"The amulet? Yes. We do." Caleb lifted it from his pocket and held it up. "And a pretty little thing it is."

The ranger smiled hungrily. "Let me see."

Caleb handed it to Neythan. Neythan looked at it and held it out to Yevhen. The ranger squinted, his eyes still adjusting;

he'd been sitting there for over an hour in the dark. He took the amulet, stood by Neythan and the torch, and examined the jewel carefully, before, with obvious relief, exhaling and smiling again. He looked at Neythan and Caleb. "I thank you."

"You'll have your chance to do so," Neythan said. "When you show us the tailor's dwellings."

The ranger nodded, still smiling. "Indeed I shall. Now, let's be gone from here."

He took the torch from Neythan to return it to the fixture on the wall by the door. And then, before lifting it to its place, doused it with a damp rag stowed in his hand, putting out the light, turning everything dark.

"What are you–?"

Neythan heard the blow and the gasped grunt and soft muffled tumble of weight and limbs at his side.

"Caleb!"

The door swung open, a brief blink of waning day into the stepped shaft, the ranger running out, Caleb behind, sprawled on the steps, groaning.

"Caleb."

"Go…" Caleb's voice was weak. "I'm alright… go after him."

Neythan fumbled for the closing door and pulled it open. The evening lamps of the foyer glared brightly. He squinted to see the ranger sprinting away along the promenade by the atrium.

He looked back into the shaft. Caleb, bloodied head, breathing hard, trying to lift himself.

"Go," the old man commanded weakly.

Neythan went out into the back foyer. The atrium was to his right. He could see the ranger running along the arcade – darker now, the sun setting – and turning into the corridor on the other side. Neythan ran into the open, across and through the atrium and beside the reflecting pool to try and cut him off.

"You there!" The guard on the roof. "You! Stop!"

Neythan ran on to the other side and entered the corridor the ranger had disappeared into, the guard still shouting, calling to others. He arrived in the passage to see another door closing. He ran to it, yanked the door, went in.

Dark room. No windows.

The stave came at him from the side, hammered into his ribs, knocking him over a table and to the wall, the scroll dropping from his hand as he fell. The ranger hurled the stave at him. Neythan parried it, pushed himself up from the wall, picked up the scroll, and followed as the ranger rushed back out of the room.

Across the atrium a pair of guards approaching, the one on the roof still bellowing commands. Neythan turned right, sprinting along the gallery's walkway to the corner after the ranger.

A dagger clanged against the stone wall ahead, weak and wide, the guards not armed with bows. Neythan ran past it and around into the passage at the end. He leapt down a short stairway. He could see the ranger ahead, scampering through the foyer, the image bouncing before him as he chased. Neythan was gaining when a sudden dull thud of weight abruptly drove against his shoulder. The impact shoved him sideways, nearly upending him, then a hot throbbing interior ache. Neythan looked and saw the long shaft of an arrow protruding from the top of his arm.

"I'd hoped I'd be the one to find you."

He looked beyond the arrow to find a man approaching, strolling across from the other side of the hallway. He was tall, similar height to the ranger. Broad, sloped shoulders. Short dark hair and greying beard. Neythan brought himself to his feet.

"Worse than a rat is a man who betrays his own words, his *creed*, and his Brothers." The man dropped the bow in his hand and drew a thick broadsword, still speaking as he approached. "A man who has no covenant in his tongue is no longer a man. He is accursed, as are *all* who betray what words they've spoken against themselves. Such a man must be judged... I *am* that judgment."

"Shedaím," Neythan said.

"Ah, so you do not forget the name of the one who bore you... *heretic*."

The man lunged forward, swinging his sword.

Neythan spun away. Then reeled back as the man's foot hammered his ribs and drove him off his feet, wincing at the dig of the arrow in his shoulder as he hit the ground.

He stood and drew his sword as the man rushed in again. Blades locked. Neythan tried to hit him with the scroll. The man dodged, countered, punched Neythan's ribs, then shoved him back again.

"Child's tricks," the man smiled. "I'd expected more from you – the famed son of Ruben, the nephew of Master Sol? They were of my sharím, you know. I see their likenesses in you now, the same betrayer's blood."

"I am not a betrayer."

The man grinned. "Do you await your companion? Is that it? Tell me, where is she? Perhaps she has betrayed you too. Seed sown one season and reaped the next. It can happen that way."

He rushed in again.

Neythan ducked and stepped in this time. Too close for swords. Arms tangled. He batted down a strike, worked an angle and leapt, letting his head crack hard against the man's jaw before he spun away, slicing back with his sword as he stepped out of reach.

The man staggered back and went down on one knee, bleeding from his mouth and flank. He looked down at the gash, spat out what may have been a chunk of his own tongue.

Neythan was about to speak when he saw more guards approaching from the rear. He turned and sprinted across the foyer to the kitchen door they'd first entered through. The door was locked. The man, still bleeding, was coming after him, the guards at his back chasing. Neythan ran out of the foyer into the palace's main antechamber. Two guards stood waiting by the main door. The others were chasing from behind.

Neythan ran on into a flanking passage that fronted the palace, running parallel to the arcades on the west. He leapt through one of the empty windows head first, landing hard and skidding against the arcade's paving.

Outside, the sky dimming and deep blue, few clouds, dull smudges lit by the moon, lamps and torches in the street, evening coming on. He got up quickly, sheathed his sword, picked up the scroll and ran hard again to the low walls of the grounds, the shouts of the guards behind him, his breaths hot in his lungs. He swung his body over, leaping and planting down with one hand; stumbled a little as he landed and kept on running into the city street.

The alley was crowded. Dim forms. Lamplit faces. Shadows from the tall housing, pale adobe walls heaped high and looming, darkening the oncoming night further, all of it rushing by as he ran.

He turned down another alley, thinner than the first. No torches. No people. The narrow way guttered and dipped inwards like a shrunken valley, slime slithering through its middle. Neythan felt the stray splash of puddled sewage against his ankles as he ran along the passage. He came to a corner and crouched, panting, waiting, staring back along the alley and willing his breaths to quieten so he could listen for pursuers.

He waited there for a while, watching the passing by of men and women at the alley's end as he squatted in the dark.

Word would soon go to the city gates. Likely less than an hour to get out that way. Caleb had looked badly hurt in the dark of the stairway. Had he been caught? Might he still be there? Was their theft yet known? The ranger, he'd be trying to depart the city too. Perhaps by the gates, perhaps by some other way – an advantage for him in that he'd planned this all along. Neythan would need the horse to make it to the gates swiftly but it was still by the tent booths near the market. Too busy, too many people. And then what of Caleb?

He took hold of the quarrel still sticking out from his shoulder, grasped it tenderly, wincing with the touch. The arrow was hard to reach and get hold of, aside and to the rear of his shoulder. It would be difficult for him to pull it himself without tearing across the flesh, if at all. He snapped the shaft instead – painfully – and tossed it into the slow-moving river of sewage and watched it float, resting on the lubricious froth of the water as it carried along the sewageways to be dumped out of the city.

Out of the city. The sewageways.

Neythan stood and looked along the alley to see where the water was going. He began to walk, keeping pace with the broken shaft as it drifted along the greasy current. The alley continued along as a back street between the housing until coming to a crossway where other rivulets had converged. At the centre was a hole into which they were all pouring. The opening was smaller than he'd hoped. He crouched down on hands and knees to examine it, gagging a little at the rancid waft of the sewage as it poured in. He stood up again and looked around. No other way.

He took the hem of the vest he was wearing, sooty and stained from the tomb, and tore it, ripping an untidy piece of cloth from the front and tying it around his face over his mouth and nose like a robber. He looked in the hole again to see how deep the drop was. Hard to tell with no light. He took off his sandals and placed them at angles to one another around the hole to form a corner, then stood opposite with his feet angled the same way, hedging the opening to stem the water. He bent down, turned his ear to the hole and lifted one sandal to let the water slide in again, listening for the splash beneath.

The water sloshed into the waiting current below.

"Not too deep," Neythan muttered.

He put his sandals on again, sliding his now grimy soles into the thongs as he listened for sounds of pursuit. He then, with a deep breath, took hold of the wet rims at the hole's edges and lowered himself through as the sewage splashed over his head and shoulders.

He dropped down into the dark. He could hear the skitter and squeak of rats as he landed, and the continuing gurgle of the water running to an exit. He used the limited moonlight from the opening above him to check the current's direction, and then began walking. The sewageway was a tall and slim passage. He steadied himself against the walls as he walked, moving slowly and allowing his hands to slide over the sweaty rock on either side. He felt the wet furry scurry of something over his foot in the blackness and flinched, then carried on, deeper into the dark.

So perfect was his blindness that it was a shock to feel the sudden cold bite of a blade against his ribs, pressing warningly, and then a whispered voice.

"I could split you in two from here as easy as gutting fish," it hissed. "Leave you catching your innards before you've chance to ask if it was worth chasing me... one chance, go back now and you die another day, old and in your own bed perhaps, instead of in a sewer with no one to come and fetch you out, and only the rats to offer you burial."

Neythan spoke carefully, slowly. "I chase no one... I do not know you."

A silence.

"Neythan?"

And then another.

"Caleb... is that you?"

"Ah, of all the... why creep up on me like that? I thought you some overzealous palace guard."

"How did you get out?"

"I could have killed you."

"And how did you find your way here?"

"Ah, so *now* you worry for my welfare?"

"You told me to chase the ranger."

"Did you get him?"

"No."

"But didn't come back for me."

"How could I? More guards in that palace than there are rats here. And a Shedaím."

"In the palace?"

"*Yes.*"

"So, one *did* stay."

"Yes. No... I think he *knew* me. I think he was *waiting* for me."

Caleb paused briefly. "We'll speak of it later. We must get out of here, out of the city. I'm just surprised you had the sense to know the waterways would be the only way."

They walked together along the passage, Caleb ahead, Neythan a little behind. The tunnel walls bent and wound mildly for what must have been several miles before they finally felt the gentle cool of evening air from an outlet somewhere up ahead, likely where the sewage emptied out from the city. It was true night by the time they reached it, too cloudy for stars. The tunnel opened above a small pit, part quag and part lake, gouged into the mount beneath and beyond the city walls. Neythan dropped down into the puddled mud first.

"Orgh!"

The sludge came to his knees.

He looked up to Caleb standing at the tunnel's lip. "Might be best to remove your sandals first."

Caleb did so, then dropped down after him. The muck rode up to the middle of his thighs. They waded across to the pit's end and kept going, on down the mount, making their own path away from the road.

"You should mark this, Neythan. Mark all I have done. This is far beyond the duty of our bargain. I smell like a mule's slopbucket."

"Qadesh is not far," Neythan said.

"Qadesh? I'd say it is. I'd say it's farther than most would like to go by night and on foot, covered in this load of–"

"We will wash in the river. Then we will go there."

"And then what? The ranger will be on horseback already, on his way north most likely, not to be found. And as for Arianna?" Caleb huffed a derisive laugh.

"I don't know. I need to sit and think... This whole thing... The ranger, the Brother in the palace..." Neythan looked down at the muck covering him. He flicked a gob of it from his hand to the ground and shook his head. "I need to think."

Twenty-Five
T R U S T

By the time Sidon made it back to the palace there were people everywhere, crowding along the gangways of the atrium, pressed up against the foyer's torchlit walls, murmuring agitatedly in corners or milling around the mosaic-floored lobby. Sidon had seen the blood as he was ushered through the main doors, smudged blotches of burgundy scattered across the patterned paving of the antechamber like dashes of paint from a child's hand. A clutch of cookmaids hunched on their knees, scrubbing vigorously as Abda, Sidon's bodyguard, led him through the flustered throng.

The main hall was mostly filled with soldiers. Some standing idly, watching, others bickering, relaying competing accounts of the evening's events to the captain of the cityguard to try to dodge blame. Handmaids whispered on the fringes behind them, pretending to console one another in the moonlight from the atrium whilst angling for gossip of what would come next. Everyone quietened as Sidon entered and looked around.

The middle foyer and main hall were a mess. Broken pieces of ceramic and clay littered the floor from a pair of upended vessels. Divots of dislodged grass lay strewn beyond the court from the sliver of green beside the pool. There was a lampstand lying against the near wall that no one had bothered to return upright. And yet, as untidy as the place looked, and as anxious as he was at the thought of intruders, as Sidon looked over it all he couldn't help feeling strangely exhilarated too. Something about the disorder, and all these people being here at so uncommon an hour, the excitable whispers of the handmaids in the walkway, the hurried stride of courtiers and guardsmen as they looked for signs of entry and escape, the silver hue of the moon as it glazed the brickwork by the atrium, glinting in the reflecting pool's silkily calm surface and casting eerie blue shadows over everything and everyone. It was like the air itself was heightened somehow, alive, itching with expectancy, like during the new moon festivals.

"We're still not sure how they got in." Sidon's mother appeared at his shoulder against the wall, surveying the hall with him. An hour before, they'd been at the School of Hanokh together, listening to the chief scribe explain the pupils' normal practices and routines and admiring the ribbed sandstone columns of the amphitheatre when Yaron, one of the courtiers, had arrived, interrupting to tell them of what had happened.

"Elias says he spoke with Casimir," Chalise added, still beside him. "The Shedaím who stayed behind. He saw and engaged one of the intruders. He is certain it was the betrayers."

"The betrayers? Why would they come *here*?"

"Not for you, my son. Elias is certain of that much. The Shedaím, they study the movements of those they hunt. Had they sought to come on a day you would be found here in the palace, they would have."

"Then what did they come for?"

"That, we do not know. Not yet… But come. You must rest. And not worry of these things. Fifty men will foot the palace guard tonight, and Abda and Casimir shall remain also."

• • •

Sidon slept in fits nonetheless, and only lightly. It took no more than a muffled thud for him to start from sleep, eyes wide and heart racing. He glanced to the shuttered windows. Narrow slats of night sky peeped in darkly; a star or two glimmered faintly between the gaps. Perhaps he'd imagined the sound. Or dreamed it. He rolled over, adjusted his pillow, and was closing his eyes when he heard what may have been scuffed footsteps somewhere outside. He stared at the door, waited for the silence to swell and comfort him. Instead he heard another soft scrape, or was it a sneeze, distant but definitely within the palace.

The sharíf's bedchambers were a dome-roofed house, reasonably sized, lodged with several other smaller buildings on the palace's flat roof and all hemmed within a balustrade that edged the lengths and corners of the balcony. *The palace's crown*, as Elias liked to call it. From here, if the rest of the palace was quiet enough, Sidon could sometimes hear through the open cutaway of the atrium to the ground floor beneath. He waited a further few moments in the bed, listening for more noise and wondering if his mother had been lying to him earlier about the betrayers having not come in search of him. Gahíd had sent Abda and Casimir to lead his bodyguard after all.

When only silence answered, he climbed from his bed and ambled around in the dark for a robe and then, finding one, shouldered himself into it. He found the dagger his uncle Játhon had given him the day of his anointing and went to the door and unhooked the latch. He lifted the beam from its crook and pulled it slowly open.

Outside, the porch was empty. The night was breezeless. The bushes marking the strip of plants that ran along the rooftop's walkways sat poised and still. Sidon could feel his heart pulsing as he looked across the balcony. Usually there would be someone manning the narrow railed path that went around the upper level, whilst the remaining guardsmen kept watch in the courtyard and gardens surrounding the palace. Abda and Casimir had taken to watching over the ground floor, taking turns each night and roaming or sitting somewhere within the main hall and middle foyer. With Casimir's wounds still healing, Abda had volunteered to take the whole watch herself, which in turn had made Sidon wonder whether, beyond midnight, she'd be too tired to guard him. *Shedaím are not as ordinary men*, his mother had assured him. But Sidon was now beginning to wonder.

He couldn't see the guard on the upper level. He opened the door of his bedchamber fully, trying to get a better angle and view the rest of the rooftop. No one. He stepped out onto the walkway with the dagger. The moon had turned gloomy, shrouded by cloud. He could see the glow of torchflame from the broad rectangular opening of the atrium in the centre of the balcony, the light leaking up into the night like the mouth of a tamely simmering volcano. He was wondering whether to return to his bed and stash the dagger beneath his pillow when he heard what sounded like whispers. He blinked, frozen to where he stood, listening for more.

Silence.

He crept with held breath toward the edge of the atrium to peer over the handrail to the floor beneath. From here he could see the reflecting pool and the edges of the middle foyer, all bathed in dim lampflame. But still no one. He straightened and glanced over the courtyard to see if the palace guard were still standing watch on the outer grounds. At least a dozen men stood or wandered the yard on the west side, staring out to the sandstone terraces of the city as it slumbered. He considered calling to one of them but could think of nothing to say that wouldn't end in him appearing cowardly, or childish, and being embarrassed as a result. He decided to go downstairs. If there was need to, he could summon the guards with a shout. If there was no need, he would return to his chambers feeling safer, and with his dignity still intact.

The palace seemed so different in the dark. Each drawn shadow turned the usually familiar spaces strangely foreign, as though the angles and lengths of everything had shortened, narrowed by the night. Objects and furniture seemed to shift shape with every step he took.

Sidon heard another scuffed sound as he came down the final step of the stairway to enter the rear lobby. He turned the dagger in his grip, resisting the foolish urge to call out, and followed the sound. He went quietly across the lobby until he reached the corner and turned into the adjoining corridor. He began to hear the whispers again, this time clearer, closer. Two men, sitting in the deep shadowed alcove at the end of the passageway.

"We should consider it, Elias. The truth is we should have considered it from the beginning."

"You are impatient."

"And what if I am? Do you think doing nothing is a better course? They entered the *palace*."

"Explaining things to Gahíd won't change anything, Játhon."

"And doing nothing will?"

"I didn't say that. What I say is we ought to tread carefully. Things are finely balanced. A wrong step now could spoil everything."

"Uncle?"

The chamberlain's old head snapped toward Sidon like a flicked ox goad. Játhon, Sidon's uncle, bolted to his feet beside the chamberlain.

"Sorry. I didn't mean to startle you... I heard voices."

"Sidon..." For a moment Játhon's lips remained poised, as though he'd forgotten what he was going to say. "You struggle to sleep too?" he said, finally.

"Yes... a little."

"Well," Játhon licked his lips and coughed a short laugh. "As you can see, you are in good company."

Elias, the chamberlain, bowed. "We were just discussing the betrayers, my king... and whether Gahíd..." The chamberlain's rheumy eyes glazed for a moment, sliding to the corridor's borders. "Whether he ought to send another Shedaím to abide here with you, keep you safe."

Sidon looked at the chamberlain sitting there in the shadows. He seemed unlike himself, somehow. Restless. The lateness of the hour, perhaps.

The chamberlain gestured loosely at the alcove around them. "I expect this must be a new and strange thing to you – men whispering in the night like this. I assure you it is not an uncommon thing. You are sharíf now. The hopes of us all hinge on your wellbeing. Do not think it strange that some of us steal away to see how it may be more readily sought."

Sidon glanced at his uncle, who was smiling reassuringly, and then back to Elias. "I see," he said.

The chamberlain dipped his head once more in acknowledgment.

"I suppose I should say thank you," Sidon said.

And now both men smiled. "No, my king," Elias said. "It is as it ought to be. We are your servants, after all. In truth, we would ask you to join us, but I know you are to be very busy the next few days, preparing for the wedding. You will need your rest. Were we to deny you that, the sharífa would not be as accommodating of our intentions as you may be willing to be."

Sidon smiled a little himself, mostly in relief. The palace had not been invaded a second time after all. The betrayers had not, as he'd thought, returned in search of him. Silly of him to have thought so. "You are right as always, Elias," he said.

To which the chamberlain, again, smiled gratefully and bowed. "Good night, my king."

"Good night, Elias." Sidon nodded at Játhon. "Uncle."

"Sleep well, Sharíf."

Sidon turned and made his way back through the lobby to the stairway and up the steps, pondering the exchange. When he came to the top he found the missing guard lying in one of the beds of the roof garden on the balcony, head tipped back, mouth cavernous, great gulps of breath sliding sloppily in and out. Sidon nudged him with his foot on the way to his bedchamber, snapping the man awake, spluttering "Sharíf" as he rolled clumsily to his feet. Sidon ignored him and passed on to return to his room. He would have the guard disciplined and removed tomorrow for the lapse. It was the night following an intrusion after all. Strange how easily those who ought to be awake slept, whilst those who ought to be sleeping remained awake. Sidon returned to his bed and lay down. Then got up again, to take his dagger from the table and place it under his pillow instead.

Twenty-Six
QADESH

Neythan could still remember the day Uncle Sol left, the solemn way he'd stared deep into Neythan's eyes, hands pinned to his young shoulders as if nailed there whilst behind him the darkening sky gleamed along the horizon like molten bronze as he spoke those cold black words. Leaving. Exile. Forever. Neythan had tried to ignore them. There were larks frolicking overhead despite the hour, behind Sol. Neythan had turned his gaze to watch them until it seemed as though they were entering and leaving Sol's head, like living images of his thoughts. So Neythan had stayed like that, trying to pretend that what Sol was saying wasn't real, until he could no longer remain deaf to it, the words pushing in at the seams of his fragile make-believe and pressing their relentless way into his ears, his heart, like the stab of a blade, each solemn syllable piercing in and dripping its slow bitter truth like shedding blood.

"Are you the monkey man?"

Neythan awoke with a start to find a boy staring down on him. The child was small, no more than six or seven years old, with deep olive skin as dark as Neythan's, and large dark eyes.

"Well? Are you?"

Neythan just stared at him, still groggy from sleep, then looked past him to the surroundings. The house seemed smaller in the daylight, the pale cracked walls, their skinny fissures zigzagging upwards from the cornerstone, all dimpled and crummy and staining yellow toward the awnings like the aged vellum of the scroll under Neythan's hand. He glanced down at it and picked it up. He brushed the dust from the leather covering and shook it to spill the rest from the rolled page.

The plot was narrow and mostly empty save for a few items here and there – a rusty pan with clods of dried clay fixed to it, leaning against the wall. Beside it a grotty edged wooden bucket, and beside that several half-finished vessels of clay, each well formed at their bases but spilling from shape into ruddy blunt mounds.

Neythan stood. He worked his jaw and spat. His spittle, sticky and dry, rested in the dust like a snowflake. He felt queasy.

"You're not the monkey man," the little boy concluded. His face was remarkably calm. "Zahia said he'd be here, but he isn't."

Neythan glanced around. Where was Caleb? He looked back to the boy, his words now making sense, and nodded. "I'm looking for the monkey man too," he said. "Maybe your friend Zahia knows where he went and can help us find him."

The boy continued to stare, then frowned a little. "You're not looking for him. You were asleep." And with that he turned and calmly walked away into the house. Neythan watched him go and looked around the plot, then back at the wall behind him where he and Caleb had climbed over the night before, exhausted and cold and still damp from the river they'd washed in.

The plot was so quiet – like the stodgy, lonely silence of midday in Ilysia, the time of day Neythan used to love most, that stale thick stillness when all the villagers would disappear, migrating to the shadows to nap a while from their work as the sun climbed to its bright searing zenith, leaving him free to roam.

He turned as the nervous cluck of a hen somewhere interrupted the quiet, then the muffle of voices. There was a second doorway at the side of the house. He brushed himself down again and went toward it. A foot-long pestle leant by the near corner of the wall, heavy looking and wooden, like a club. The coppery smear of smashed lentils or spices crusted its blunt weighty end. Neythan picked it up, then winced, feeling the forgotten spiteful ache of the arrowhead still in his shoulder. He craned his neck and squinted at the snapped shaft jutting from the top of his arm, and then hefted the pestle in his grip, wielding it like a mace. No telling how many occupants within: the boy may have alerted a father, or someone else who'd be wary of a stranger lingering unannounced on the grounds. Trespass on a man's dwelling and he loses all reason.

Neythan patted the wooden pestle against his palm a few times, weighing it – less harmful than his sword, better to cripple a man than kill him – then walked with it around to the side of the house where the doorway waited.

The door was open. The voices, muffled before, drifted out to him along with the smell of cooking vegetables. Neythan cocked the pestle two-handed at his shoulder and edged slowly toward the door. He'd just glance in, see if he could pass by unseen to the street. He steadied himself by the jamb, shifting his grip like an axeman's, and took a crab's pace closer, about to peer in, mace lifted in case, when Caleb's jaunty voice leapt up from the mild din of chattering others inside.

"Well, that's why I said a monkey – fleet of foot, hand and thought," he said.

"But they're ugly," came the voice of a woman. "Those little faces of theirs, like a starved baby. And who'd want to look like a starved baby?"

"You're asking *me* that?" Caleb said.

More laughter, all female, some of it childish sounding.

"What about a giant ape?" A girl this time.

"A *giant* ape? There's no such thing," the woman said.

"There is."

"Where?"

"The Summerlands, in the mountain forests."

"No doubt you've been there."

"I was told."

"Oh, well if you were *told*..."

"You hear the vendors talk sometimes," the girl persisted. "By the baudekin on market day. I heard one say he'd seen them himself, twice the size of any man, and black, apart from some, the biggest ones, the oldest. He said the hair of their backs grow grey, just like with *your* hair, mama."

"My hair is not grey."

"Well, if the vendors speak of it," another girl, sardonic whining singsong, "it *must* be true."

"It *is*."

"True or no," the mother said, "I'd not want to be one."

"Why not?"

"Me neither. What would you eat?"

"Whatever's in the forest."

"There's no sheep in the forest though," the little boy's voice. "No goats or anything."

"You and your meat–"

"Leave him alone, Yoani."

"I think a lion would be best, that way you'll have your fill of meat and not too many others to bother you."

"I don't think that's quite how it is for lions, Zahia."

"I'd be a hare," the boy said. "Hares are fast and you can't catch them."

"Hares don't get to eat meat, Petur."

"I only like meat because I'm a boy. If I was a hare I'd eat grass and other things."

"Hares don't eat grass either, silly."

"Yoani. I said don't speak to your brother that way."

"Ah, Neythan."

Neythan stood halfway in the door now, watching.

"We thought you'd never rise. This is Neythan, everyone. Neythan, the discussion is wild beasts, and which we'd want to be if we could choose."

Neythan looked at Caleb, then the others. A young girl, twelve, thirteen maybe, sat in the corner with a weaver's pin and a patch of cloth, staring at him. Beside her stood the little boy from the yard, clutching a fistful of the girl's dress. Caleb sat at the table in the middle, slouching forward, gazing at Neythan like a friend at a banquet. Neythan looked at him. Caleb said nothing, only smiled. Neythan dipped his head through the doorway to find two others, an older woman with a brazier and skillet in her hands, standing over a stone hedged bench against the wall piled with ashes, frosted white from use. And next to her another girl, slim, older than the weaver in the corner, around Neythan's age, holding a pot of stew or soup. They were all looking at him.

Neythan, still grasping the makeshift mace in one hand beyond view of the doorway, slowly lowered his arm and dropped the weapon by the outer jamb.

"Come. Sit," the mother said quietly, and nodded him in. "There's a seat by your cousin at the table."

Neythan looked at Caleb. *Cousin?*

Caleb smiled.

Neythan went in and sat at the table. No one spoke for a while. The older girl with the pot decided to break the silence.

"Your cousin says he'd make himself a monkey," she said. "I say a lion is best. But Yoani," she nodded to the smaller girl on the stool in the corner. "Well..." she trailed off, shook her head.

"A giant ape," the girl said from the corner.

"Beasts that are *real* are the rule," Zahia said.

"Giant apes *are* real."

The mother's head wagged wearily.

"She's right," Neythan found himself saying. He must've been tired. It'd been a while since he'd sat to meditate. He looked around. Everyone's gaze had settled on him. "I mean... there *are* such beasts."

The girl grinned triumphantly. "S*ee*."

The mother looked at Neythan disapprovingly and shook her head, then to Caleb. "What is it with these young ones today? All of them, so given to fanciful things."

Caleb nodded in commiseration.

"What about you?" Zahia said, still looking at Neythan. "Which beast would you choose, if you could?"

The room turned to him. The mother had put down the brazier pot and was now placing a bowl of soup in front of him.

She nodded for him to eat. Neythan again looked to Caleb for guidance but he said nothing. Neythan looked back to the bowl of soup; it smelled good. He picked up the spoon.

"And we will have to see to *that* later," the woman said, gesturing at the broken shaft in Neythan's shoulder.

Neythan looked again to Caleb, who still remained silent. He looked at the woman. "Erm. Thank you." And continued quietly with the soup, resolving to eat the food, say as little as possible, and wait for the chance to speak with Caleb alone to have all this explained to him.

"Go on," the girl on the stool was saying. "You've not answered yet."

"Don't be so rude, Yoani. Let him eat," the mother said. "He needs to eat."

"It's alright," Neythan said. The soup was good. He decided to play along. "Perhaps an eagle," he said.

"Why an eagle?" Yoani said from the corner.

"You see?" the mother said. "You shouldn't encourage her."

Neythan swallowed his mouthful; the soup was stocked with beans and some sort of root vegetable he didn't recognize. "They can see long distances," he said. "And they can fly."

The boy nodded sagely. "I think that's a good choice," he said, and then to the rest of the room, "Eagles eat lots of meat."

It carried on this way for a while, the merits of almost every beast under the sun being announced and bounced between them. The mother's name was Gaana, it turned out. Though there was a silence concerning the whereabouts of the father.

"Dead," Caleb told Neythan outside when he was finally able to speak with him alone. "Sickness, apparently. Gaana says he started coughing one day, and never stopped. A year later he was dead. You can imagine how nervous she'd have been when she found us in her yard like that, thinking we were robbers. I awoke to a pestle hovering over my head, ready to crush my skull should my explanation for being there prove less than satisfactory. A widow can be a skittish sort. A widow with children to keep and feed, even more so. I told her we were revellers. That we'd got drunk and been robbed on the way here from Hanesda. When she looked us over, both of us covered in mud and you with an arrow in your shoulder, she believed it. Probably *wanted* to believe it. So, I told her we'd work for our keep, if she'd let us stay a few days. Of course, when I say '*we*' I mean you."

"Work? At what?"

"I don't know. At whatever she wants. Oh, and teach the boy fishing. His father was a fisherman and a potter. They still have his things but the boy no longer has anyone to teach him. Too young when he died. He's no more than five or six now, and they need whatever income they can get. Do you know anything about fishing?"

"A little."

"Good. That'll do. You work, teach the boy fishing, lick your wounds, recover your strength."

"And what are *you* going to be doing, exactly?"

"Thinking up what we are to do next, of course. Someone has to do the hard work around here."

Twenty-Seven
REVELATION

Yasmin hadn't expected tears. She sat watching as Bilyana, slumped on the chair, whimpered quietly from the corner by the candle, which was low now, a soggy stump of wax, slick and wasted and waning on the dirty shelf by the door. Hassan had told the chamberlain the night before to see to it but he must have forgotten. Less than an hour's worth of light in it now, and they'd need more time. Bilyana had entered mere moments ago, cloaked and hooded, stepping cautiously into the chamber like hunted prey. Her face seemed different, paler. She'd looked briefly around the chamber, a small empty house Hassan kept in the city's eastern quarter for discreet meetings not wholly unlike this.

"Zaqeem used to do the same," Bilyana had said, not bothering with greeting. "In Hanesda, in Sippar, Qadesh, Qareb, he was a man of means after all, as you know. Who knows how many cornerhouses he kept, and in how many cities. And how many women... like me." And then the weeping. Thinking about it, it made sense – Bilyana; Zaqeem's mistress. Yasmin had often noticed there was something in the way they were together, something bashful and smiling and coy, a secret swapping between their timid smirking glances. Poor Tobiath. Perhaps it was this he'd discovered. Perhaps it was why he'd gone missing. Over a month and still no word from him.

The chamber was short and empty mostly. Windowless. A table, a couple of chairs, the flattened candle, an old basin of dirty water in one corner with a towel that neither Yasmin, Hassan nor Bilyana had felt inclination to wash their feet with. Bilyana sat on one side by the door, Hassan and Yasmin on the other, watching her cry.

"Now," Bilyana said, her eyes flicking up to them, clearing abruptly, sober though still moist. "You mustn't tell Tobiath, there would be no need."

Yasmin nodded, the simple gesture somehow inviting more tears. She waited for a pause in the whimpering before asking. "He has never suspected?"

Bilyana, sniffing, shook her bowed head. "Tobiath is a trusting soul," she said.

"When did it begin?"

"With Zaqeem? Oh, a year or so before his death... that time he came to visit his vineyard and invited us all to taste the produce. Tobiath was in Tresán. I forget why. And... I don't know... I'd been so *bored* that summer... Zaqeem was kind to me."

Yasmin nodded. In the end they'd had no choice but to wait until they'd made it all the way back here to Dumea from the Summerland village to talk with Bilyana of what she knew. Yasmin, as eager as Hassan to hear Bilyana's divulgences and unwilling to allow him to speak with her alone as he wished, had argued with him throughout the entire journey back. Which was difficult. Hassan had never been the argumentative kind. He seldom even got angry. When he did he'd grow quiet and affect a slightly condescending smirk, as though you were part of some game or ruse he'd seen before. Or he'd simply walk away. But now they seemed to be arguing about everything. About the burden she'd agreed to on their behalf. About what he knew and was refusing to tell her.

And then there was the journey itself, which became longer and more difficult than the one there. There were heavy rains the first and second day. The guide had decided to change their route, delaying them an extra few days, so as not to be caught along the muddy passes of the Súnamite plains where the red and runny dirt would be poor footing for the camels. And then when they finally managed to return to the city they had to wait a further week with all the preparations around Noah's Judgment. All of which granted Yasmin more time to argue with Hassan, eventually persuading him they should speak with Bilyana together. She deserved to hear her secrets too.

She looked up at Bilyana, whose gaze had slipped to an uninteresting stain on the wall. The lids of her eyes were pink and swollen.

"Something I don't understand," Yasmin said. "Zaqeem was often away, at court, in Qadesh, or the crown city…"

"My trips there or to Qalqaliman for dresses…"

Yasmin nodded, *of course.* Yasmin had always wondered how Bilyana was able to afford the garments she returned with. "You were in truth going there only to see him."

"Yes…" Bilyana sniffed and heaved an exasperated breath, looking up to the ceiling. "The first few times, it was so much fun. I'd go and we'd eat and then he'd send me off to the bazaars or the city market with some measure of gold. Fifty, eighty shekras, it mattered little to him. Spend as you please, he always said." She smiled sadly; her gaze dropped to the floor. "Make your heart glad, he'd say. Then I'd come again by night when the gold was spent and show him the things I'd bought, and then, well…"

Hassan, sitting beside Yasmin, nodded and sighed, lifting a palm, needing to hear no more.

"Toward the end he became different," Bilyana said, quietly. "He was quieter… stiller. I'd ask what was wrong but he'd only smile, say he was an old fool, that nothing could be wrong when I was near... Then, there was one time I came to him and he was so anxious it frightened me."

"Anxious how?" Hassan said.

Bilyana's shoulders lifted halfway to a shrug, her neck thickening with the gesture as she slowly shook her head. "Every room we entered, he'd look out the door to see if anyone had followed before he closed it. Even when he closed it, he'd get up again to see that it was shut fast. He'd be asking me, how was my journey, did I see anyone on the way. Of course I'd seen someone. I'd seen many. How can a journey be made without doing so? It worried me... like how, if you see a spider sometimes, or beetles, it makes you itch. That was how it was with Zaqeem, the more anxious he became, the more nervous did I. And so I told him... I made some excuse, I cannot remember what it was, I told him I couldn't see him anymore, that Tobiath was growing suspicious. The thing had only begun for fun." She looked up at Hassan like a plaintiff before a judge, eyes wide and wet. "There was no more fun," she said, looking at him, waiting, though for what Yasmin couldn't tell – understanding? Appeasement? Forgiveness? "That was when he started... talking, saying things. He was like a madman, crazed, just talking."

Hassan sat forward. "What did he say?"

Her head was wagging slowly, her gaze fixed to a spot on the floor. "*It's because they know, it's because they know.* Over and over again, he kept saying it. He was so frantic. I'd never seen him that way before, he'd been feverish that night, his skin was like fire. I reasoned it was the fever."

"What else? What else did he say?"

"He said he knew things, had learned things, things to do with the sharíf."

"Yes?"

"He said the sharíf's throne was not truly his own... He

said... he said there were secrets, things that had been kept hidden, about the sharíf, about his line and blood. He said the sharíf's throne is false." Bilyana's voice dropped to a whisper. "He has a brother, he said, the sharíf does, an older brother, who is the true heir."

"Sharíf Sidon's brother died when he was a child, these things are known."

Bilyana shook her head, trembling. "No. Zaqeem said it is a lie, he was never taken ill, he never died. They put him away, secretly, because his father was displeased with him, some flaw in him, he said, some kind of strangeness."

"What strangeness?"

She shook her head again. "I don't know."

"Where is he then, the brother?"

"Zaqeem never told me," Bilyana said. "I don't know if he knew. He said only that he'd been banished. Put away."

"And he was certain the brother lives?"

"He was."

Hassan just stared, disbelieving, thinking.

"I thought it all meaningless, what he'd said, that his words were because of fever. But he kept saying it. Repeating. And he was so scared. He kept saying: *They know I know.* He said they were going to come for him, kill him, to make sure no others would learn what he had... I thought he was just trying to frighten me. Make me stay. It made me so angry. To think that he'd lie like that, to *me*... And so I left. I left him." And then she started to cry again, louder this time, but muzzled, burying her growled sobs in her shawl as she held it by the collar against her face in clenched fistfuls. "It was the last time I saw him... It was only... it was only when I heard the tidings..." Her tear-streaked face gazed out at them, cheeks reddened and glistening. "That he'd been killed... it was only then that I knew that he'd been telling me the truth all along... How hard it must have been for him to finally tell me, how alone he must've felt, and my only answer was to call him a *liar*." And this time she cried aloud, not bothering to hamper and hide her sobs with the shawl.

Yasmin stood and went across to comfort her. After a while, Bilyana's sobs quietened, small choked snivels coming between her coughs and sniffs.

Hassan spoke gently. "You must tell me, Bilyana. How did Zaqeem come to learn these things?"

"I don't know."

"Perhaps he mentioned names, people he'd spoken with, anything."

Bilyana's teary eyes stared into nothing, lost in grief. Her voice, when it came, was high and childish, as if about to cry again. "I don't know."

Hassan sat back in his chair with his knuckle against his lips.

"Sometimes he spoke of friends. A group of friends, he said. The Fellowship of Truths – that's what he called them, this group. But he only spoke of it sometimes, when he'd taken wine."

"The Fellowship of Truths?"

"He said he and Tobiath were part of it. Sons of the Fellowship, he said. He said he was going to tell you, Hassan. He said only you would understand... would hear him... know what to do."

It was then the candle went out, the short limping flame shivering to a stop on top of the diminishing pool of wax on the shelf. The abrupt dark made Bilyana gasp.

"It's alright, the wax was low, I told the chamberlain to replace it yesterday but he must've forgotten." Hassan stood to his feet in the blackness. "The hour is late anyway, we ought to take you home before your brother, Zíyaf, begins to worry."

"Home. Yes."

"Come."

Bilyana flinched as Hassan rose and touched her arm in the darkness.

"Come, Bilyana."

Outside in the street the night was relatively bright, the half-moon shining through a clear sky. Bilyana hunched her shoulders against the chill, grasping the collar of her woollen cloak as Hassan and Yasmin guided her.

"What will you do?" Bilyana said.

"I'm not certain," Hassan said.

"But you believe me, what I've told you?"

"I do."

Bilyana smiled a little despite her tears, sniffing again. "I thought you would but I wasn't sure... I know it sounds fanciful."

"Not so much. Not to me... The week before he died, I received word Zaqeem was to visit. He wanted to be sure I would be in the city. He said only that he had urgent things to tell me, too urgent to be written... He was dead a week later, the night before he was to travel... Perhaps now I know why."

He guided her by the elbow along the street. The hollow coo of an owl prodded shyly at the dark. The street, a narrow passage flanked by blocky terraces, was empty except for a mule tethered by a mooring post on one end, sleeping whilst it stood, its tired huffed breaths pushing small funnelled clouds into the darkness. There was no wind, no sounds other than the shuffle of their footsteps in the dust and the quiet snorts of the mule as they went along the road.

"I was afraid," Bilyana said. "If his life was taken for what he knew, then what should become of my own, since he'd told me? For weeks I feared, and then after a while that fear passed. But tonight, now, after speaking of it, after telling you, I'm afraid once more."

Yasmin could have said there was no need to be, perhaps she would have in other circumstances, but instead she remained silent as they walked her all the way back to the street of her house and waited at its corner as Bilyana reached the door and went in.

"In the one who has become both sage and fool, both elder and child, in this one lies the way of the sha, and the road to mastery."

THE SAYINGS OF QOH'LETH, THE NINTH
DISCIPLINE OF THE SHEDAÍM

Twenty-Eight
S H A

To get the arrow out had been difficult and painful, and despite the meditations a niggly hot ache pinched in Neythan's shoulder whenever he moved it. He expected it would be that way for a while. Gaana and Zahia had done it mostly themselves, sawing the quarrel shaft down before dousing the wound with sourwine and then, with Gaana's timid voice at his ear, gentle as a hummingbird, warning, "This will hurt some," cutting with a slim blade of flint around the injury to open the wound and slide the arrowhead slowly out. That had been the easy part. Worse had been the cleaning, Gaana dousing the bleeding sore with more sourwine and water and slipping her cloth-capped finger in and around to push out the dust and silty dried mud left over from the quag and river. And then, worse, much worse, sealing it, pressing the iron rod handle of her cookpan – left to rest in the fire until glowing – into and against the bleeding, its searing touch hissing as it cauterized the flesh.

It took Neythan a while to sleep that night, and a while longer to realize why Gaana was later nervous of him. There was a simpering wary quiet that hadn't been there before – there when she put food before him, or came to check on the wound, dabbing softly with honey and wine. In truth only this morning, several days on, had he understood why.

He'd been too quiet, silent in fact, when she took out the arrowhead and tended the wound. An oversight on his part. Force of habit. The disciplines ran deep.

"I've been thinking," he said.

Caleb, walking beside him, glanced up. "Oh? Well. Good. Thinking. Never a bad thing."

Neythan watched him. He'd been that way all morning, his thoughts elsewhere. "Hanesda," Neythan said. "There are a few things that did not make sense."

They were walking back for the fourth time that morning from the watersprings near the city gate. Neythan was waddling in small quick steps with a pail of fresh water held on either side, their sloshing weights swinging at his knees. Gaana needed a water carrier for the day but her daughter, Yoani, had taken ill with fever.

"The Brother knew I would be there," Neythan said. "I'm certain of it now. In the palace. He was expecting me... He called me a heretic. He knew who I was, knew me by name. And then he asked where *she* was, meaning Arianna, as though he was expecting us to be there together, thinking us one party, like the men by the well did."

Caleb didn't answer.

"And then there is something the ranger said, of what he'd heard, that Arianna had turned against her own kind, against the Brotherhood... Are you listening to me?"

Caleb's gaze swung back around from the street. "What? Yes... she'd turned against the Brotherhood..." He looked up at Neythan, and then away. Then glanced back again. "No bad thing, by the way."

Neythan sighed. "It's certain she's been killing others of the Brotherhood, Caleb. Yannick is not the only one. That's what the ranger meant. I'd suspected it was so back when we found that body after the ash plains but now I am sure. I could see it in the Brother's eyes in the palace, the way he looked at me, thinking me party to her."

Caleb kept walking, saying nothing.

"The thing that bothers me is, how did he know I would be there, in the palace?"

"The ranger," Caleb said, still looking away. "He must have betrayed us. Warned the Brotherhood."

"I thought that too. But if it was the ranger, why would the Brother in the palace think me of one party with Arianna, seeing the ranger knew, by our very bargain, that I am not?"

"I'd not think it the first lie he's told, Neythan."

"But why lie about *that*?"

Caleb finally turned back and glanced at him.

"If his aim was only to smooth his escape, by letting them know I would be there, what profit was there in saying I was to be there with *her*?"

Caleb thought about it. His gaze drew back from the street to Neythan. "You think someone else told them? Not the ranger?"

"Perhaps. I don't know."

"Who else but the ranger would have known? Or had means even to tell?"

"I don't know."

"Or would think you with Arianna?"

"Or know me to be without her but want it told otherwise?"

Caleb's brow spiked, paying full attention now. "Now *there* is a thought... Perhaps you've been spending too much time with me."

Neythan laughed drily. "If by that you mean having questions without answers, I agree."

The street, mud-black and cracked, was narrow, the paving a half-foot above the slender roadway the carts trundled over and hedged by a slim shallow ridge as if to keep those walking from spilling into it. It made the walkway difficult to pass along. Neythan, holding the rope-handled buckets on either side, had to keep turning his hips to sidle around and past the others on the street, tiptoeing sometimes along the ridge like some bored playful child whilst balancing the yaw and swing of the pails. He swooped, stepping up onto the thin ledge around an old man clumsily wheeling a small cart of chickpeas and sumac cuttings, and then nipped down again in time to avoid a wider cart of pomegranates being drawn along the road – where the old man should've been – in the opposite direction. Caleb followed, dancing nimbly up and down again.

"How many more of these have you to get?"

"Two more," Neythan grumbled. "I'd never known clay could be so thirsty."

"Not all of it will be for the potter's work. Gaana plans to bathe Petur later. And you will save her the trip for the cooking too. How's the shoulder?"

Neythan vaguely danced his head, part nod, part shrug.

"I suppose work like this won't help it much," Caleb said.

"You could always lend a hand."

"And ruin my back? Then we'd *both* be partway crippled. No sense in that."

They turned the corner and walked along the road past the sheepgate, dodging the stumpy bollards that lined the paving where mules and donkeys were often tied. Not far from here Neythan had had his first witnessing by the market square where they set the giant baudekin on the last day of each week. He could still, even now, remember it like it was yesterday – the dry tang of spices chafing the air, the bickering din of trade, lowing of livestock, a busy place but not as bad as Hanesda, not *too* busy. Hanesda – something still bothered him about it, niggling his sha, though he couldn't place what. He needed to meditate. To try to retrieve it. He glanced down to tell Caleb but the older man's gaze had already drawn away again.

Caleb started, seeing Neythan watching him. "What? Did you say something?"

Neythan shook his head slowly, still watching.

Caleb started to say something, then stopped. He gestured apologetically. His gaze drifted away again. "You ever have things... people... bring things back to you?" he said quietly.

Neythan, fighting the swing of the rope-tethered pails, almost had to lean in to hear.

"Remind you of things, I mean. Things from before..." Caleb's hand lifted as though to finish the sentence, shaping into a claw in mid-air before dropping impotently to his side. Then he shook his head and looked away.

Neythan, puzzled, spoke to interrupt the silence as much as anything, to try to catch whatever thought Caleb's flopping hand had dropped. "Smells," he said. "Smells often do that. For me, I mean... like every spring, in Ilysia, when the blueberries begin to fruit, there would be the smell of mandrake in the clay gardens by the tutor's fields. The smell would always make me think of Tutor Maresh. Even after he was gone."

He looked at Caleb, whose gaze had now reeled in and fixed to him, listening.

"I told Master Johann of it once," Neythan said. "How they made me think of Maresh. He said such things are like the smoke that lingers when a flame dies. Like incense, he said. *Lingering shadows*, he called them. Every soul known truly by another will have one. And a man's sha shall feel it, just as it does all things, though we forget its voice."

Caleb's face twisted a little.

Neythan saw it. "Though... Master Johann often spoke strange things."

"No," Caleb said. "No. He speaks truth this time."

Neythan watched him carefully. "It is a truth familiar to you?"

But Caleb looked away.

Neythan let the question lie there awhile. Then, not knowing what else to say, he was about to change the subject back to Hanesda, that elusive something still bothering him, something half-remembered. But then Caleb answered.

"The daughter," he said. "Gaana's daughter, Yoani," he smiled sadly. "This morning – she must've been dizzy with the fever – she asked me if I am her lost grandfather... She says he was lost before she was born and so has never met him. She thought I might be him."

"She is fond of you," Neythan said.

"Yes." Caleb's smile faded. "A daughter is a wonderful thing."

"Is it?"

Caleb didn't answer. He looked away across the street again, watching the gaggle of fruit pickers carrying their produce-laden baskets on the other side. Neither spoke. They continued along the street, turning at the corner to head to the house.

"I had a family once," Caleb said. "Your Brotherhood took that from me. After Hikramesh... I returned to my home, to my wife and children... they were all... they'd... they were dead... but they *took* my daughter, my firstborn." He looked at Neythan. "Yes, as though I were a heretic. Though I'd committed no betrayal they took her, hid her, denied her burial... Little Yoani reminds me of her. Of my Yva. Like the *lingering shadow* you speak of."

"I'm sorry," Neythan said. He knew little else to say. They carried on in silence along the street.

"Johann speaks truth this time," Caleb finally said, quietly, almost to himself as they rounded the corner. "The sha remembers, even what we would sooner forget."

Neythan dropped the pails of water and stopped. The buckets clattered to the ground, one to a flat dead stop, water sloshing over the rim, the other tipping over and spilling into the street.

Caleb, startled, turned and looked at him. "What's the matter with you?"

"That's *it*."

"You've spilt the pail, lucky to have not done so the other too." Caleb came forward to collect the toppled bucket. "Surprised you've not broken the thing."

"Hanesda," Neythan said.

Caleb righted the bucket on the pavement and set it down. Most of the water had already run out onto the paving. "That'll be no answer to satisfy Gaana when you return one bucket light. You'll have to go back again."

"Yes... we must go back."

"Well, that's what I'm trying to... Wait, what?"

"We must go back... to Hanesda."

"Back to Hanesda? Best I remember, it was no easy thing to leave. Why would we go back?"

Neythan was looking elsewhere. "The sha always remembers," he said, mostly to himself. "Yes," he smiled, laughed a little.

Caleb looked at him blankly. "Finally. You are finally going mad."

"Back there. In the tavern. I was with Yevhen and Nouredín. I was drunk... and there was a girl."

"You're talking of Hanesda?"

"A harlot."

Caleb sighed, palm raised, head shaking. "I've no interest in hearing about–"

"No. I mean. She was just talking to me, telling me stories, of those who visited there, those she'd entertained. Vassals, princes sometimes, all kinds, and then she says..." Neythan's head wagged with disbelief as he remembered. "She speaks of a strange visitor, less than a moon ago, she says. An old woman. Very old. And blind, cataracts thick as fingernails."

"Well. Strange place for one like that. That I'll grant. But, well, there are all kinds of people in the world…"

"No, Caleb. Listen to me. The harlot told me. She *told* me. She said the woman was blind, but was like one who could see – the way she moved, the way she turned, the girl couldn't understand it. But I could, Caleb, even then, even with all the wine. Though I didn't remember it afterward, then, when she was telling me, I understood."

Caleb was eyeing Neythan seriously now. "What did you understand?"

"I've seen a woman like this but once before. Old, blind, yet as one who is not, one frail, yet able… I saw her the night I was sworn, Caleb. The night we received our decrees… I've known none like her before or since. That woman was an elder of the Shedaím."

Twenty-Nine
CROWN

"So, you want for the slavegirl to be your whore. Well, it shall not be so. Not now. All must go well with this wedding. Do you understand? Nothing shall upset it."

Sidon's mother hissed the words to him in the darkness. She was leaning over him as he lay in his bed, the blue hue of the moon illuminating her face from the shadows, her fingers pressed against his chest. A strange thing to wake to, but then she'd been behaving strangely ever since she learned about the graverobbing, and stranger still since he'd insisted the slavegirl, Iani, join him in going to Qadesh to meet his betrothed. The girl was an able seamstress, she had an eye for the right cut of a robe, she'd be a good aide in readying his wedding garment, but no, to Mother, the motive could only be ulterior. Sidon barely slept the rest of the night.

At least the road into Qadesh was a pretty one. The windless lake sat like a giant dish of glass to one side, still as ice, staring a blank white eye up to the pale sky it reflected. The city walls were topped at their corners by stone-carved bears, their open, angry mouths pierced by the gaze of watchmen so that at night, or even in the dim cast of a cloudy evening, the hollowed throats glimmered in the gloom with the yellow flicker of a watchman's fire. They glimmered now as Sidon sat in the carriage opposite his mother, thinking of the night before and waiting for the wheels to roll them through the city to the governor's Judge House to finally meet his betrothed.

The market was closing as they passed through the gates. The bazaar stretched out along a row of city houses flanking the roadway. The quiet stalls spilled from its nub onto the main thoroughfare as vendors ambled lazily along, proffering their wares to the drunken fishermen who'd come in from the lake as they japed with one another from their sprawled seats outside the terraces. Beyond them, others gathered along the roadside to stand and watch the royal caravan pass by as what remained of the day's light waned.

Sidon watched it all without really watching. An hour from now he would meet her. A day from now he would be wed, the wayposts of his future marked out for him like the walls of a rat's maze. Mother, Elias, even Uncle Játhon, they all spoke only of duty and necessity. His power and rule would come once he was secure. This was the way things had to be. He was too young to see it now but later he would understand. *Later. Too young.* Their favourite song. Only Iani seemed to listen to him, dipping her head in that abashed way of hers that morning as she helped him dress, apologizing as if the whole thing were her fault. Ridiculous to think about, a slave sympathizing with a king.

Sidon tossed the thought aside as the car came to a halt beside the Judge House. It was getting dark. The broad bulk of the building towered over the surroundings, rivalling even the royal palace for size. Since Governor Zaqeem's death every vassal of the Sovereignty had coveted his place here and even in the dark it wasn't hard to see why. The broad-stepped colonnade stretched the length of several houses, propping up the ornate entablature with its carvings of bears and pomegranates. In the middle, a high arched doorway with the carved likeness of Sharíf Kaldan at its apex dominated. For a governor, being seated here was the closest you could come to living like a king without being one. Which was funny, Sidon thought, since he *was* a king yet seldom felt like one.

"King of kings."

The city steward came waddling out from the huge building with a welcoming grin plastered across his pink panting face, followed by a small crew of house servants carrying oil lamps.

Sidon stepped down from the car. "Hello, Yassr."

"Ah, and our glorious mother, Sharífa Chalise. Both of you here at last." He gasped as he made his way down the steps and across the courtway, his jowls shaking despite a persistent grin which abruptly dropped away as he gestured impatiently to the servants with him. Several guardsmen and attendants obediently hurried forward to unload the caravan. Yassr retrieved his grin like a momentarily dropped keepsake and looked Sidon over.

"The last time I saw you, you were..." The governor lifted his hand, palm down, and measured to just beneath his broad saggy chest, squinting. "And now see you. Near enough a man grown. Lord and ruler." He clapped a hand on Sidon's shoulder and turned to lead them into the house. "Now, Sharíf," he said, pronouncing the title with relish. "I will not have you worry. I have seen to everything. The food. The ceremony. You will find your chambers comfortable and in order. And the bed, believe me, my king, you will *love* the bed, that or I shall have men flogged." He laughed heartily. Several of the servants flinched as they carried the luggage. "And of course it will be my delight to show you the rest of the Judge House, Sharíf. It was your forefather, Sharíf Kaldan, who first built it, you know."

"Yes, Yassr."

"It was to be his–"

"Personal summerhouse, a second palace of sorts. I know, Yassr. I haven't forgotten your lessons. And even if I had, his likeness above the doorway would soon remind me."

Yassr giggled in his throat. His flabby neck quivered. "Always such a clever child. You'd have made an able scribe, Sharíf, if you were not to make an abler king."

They stepped through the tall, broad doorway and into a wide pillared lobby with the queen mother and servants following behind. The ceiling was tiled in chequered blue and terracotta squares. Patterns and animals painted in the same colours adorned the walls whilst bronze lampstands lined the chamber like lights at a mourner's vigil. Yassr led them through to an adjoining passage at the end of the lobby that in turn led into another corridor.

"The ceremony will be perfect, Sharíf. *Perfect.* There are five hundred bullocks from Hardeny. The finest honeywine from Tresán. Enough livestock for half the city to sound like a herdsman's field. Many of the vassals were here by midday, you know. Only Fatya of Tirash is yet to arrive. Although…" He paused and turned to face him. "There has been word your betrothed will arrive on the morrow."

"*Tomorrow*?" Chalise said from behind.

"Yes, Sharífa. Regrettable, I know."

"They are to *wed* tomorrow."

"And so they shall. The princess and her party were delayed on the way by sickness. The girl's father was good enough to send word." He resumed walking. "Merely a precaution, he says. They will be here in good time. Doubtless the princess simply dislikes the idea of meeting her sharíf and future husband for the first time with a twitchy gut and sickly look. Which is understandable. Always better to rest rather than travel with such things, I think. She will arrive in the morning with more than half a day until the ceremony begins. You needn't be troubled. Either of you. And especially you, my king. I know you will be curious but rest assured I know the girl, and I speak the truth when I say your mother, our blessed sharífa, as with all things, has shown herself ever wise and keen-eyed. You will be pleased by the bride she has chosen for you when she arrives. Ah, here we are. Your chambers."

Yassr indicated their rooms as the servants following behind entered ahead of them, carrying the rest of their things.

"I have prepared a place for your handmaids and attendants further along the way," Yassr said, gesturing loosely along the corridor. "They will be shown by the servants. For now, you need only rest. The banquet will be ready within the hour."

Yassr was good to his word. An hour later they were reclining at a long table in an even longer banquet room with other gathered heads and vassals of the Sovereignty. Zikram of Geled. Sufiya of Qareb. Uncle Játhon, prince of Caphás. His father, King Sulamar of Calapaar. Játhon's wife, Queen Satyana of Hikramesh along with her father, Jashar, the king of Harán. There were governors from the High Eastern cities of Tirash and Kaloom. A bejewelled, nose-ringed cohort from the great market city of Qalqaliman far to the south. Consuls from beyond the Black Mountains of Calapaar to the west and north. Everywhere Sidon looked the table brimmed with dignitaries from each corner of the Sovereignty. He hadn't seen so many of them in one place since his anointing the year before.

"They grow bolder by the day," Yassr was saying as they ate. "No, by the *hour*. Kivites, they are..." He flapped a pudgy hand, groping for an insult, then glanced at those present and muttered unintelligibly instead. "Tell them, Zikram," he said, nudging the ribs of the Geled's governor beside him. "Tell them what you told me."

Governor Zikram smiled sheepishly and cleared his throat to speak.

"Perhaps fifty of them," Yassr cut in again instead. "Fifty!" He gestured wide-eyed at the others reclining at the table, his palms out as though to entreat them. "Imagine, fifty of these... *barbarians*, crossing into our lands, gleaning from our fields. Bold. They grow much too bold."

"But is it boldness or despair, Yassr?" Játhon said. "Sometimes the two are easily confused."

"They incur on the Sovereignty. Their motives matter little."

"No, dear Yassr, their motives matter much. What do they intend? Invasion? Conquest?"

Some at the table sniggered. The Kivites were a mongrel people, a hundred tribes or more and as fractured and scattered as they were primitive, dwelling beyond the northernmost reach of Calapaar between the Twin Seas. "They entreat, perhaps," Játhon continued dryly. "They desire terms of trade." He was leaning back on one elbow by the table, his other hand turning lazily at the wrist as he spoke.

Prince Játhon, Mother's elder brother, had had this serene mocking way to him for as long as Sidon could remember. It was a manner Sidon had never liked.

"You see, motives *always* matter," Játhon said, addressing the table. "Often more so than whatever deeds follow them. It is winter; their granaries and storehouses, if they have such things, no doubt grow scarce. Their harvests are spent." He returned his attention to Yassr. "Their incursions are not of boldness, they are merely the nervous fidgetings of the scavenger. Despair, as I say."

"But what if they're not?" Zikram managed.

Geled was the northernmost city of Calapaar, nearest to the Reach and the scattered territories of Kiv beyond it. Although the city was one of the Sovereignty's strongest forts, it still made sense for Zikram, as its governor, to be nervous. Which was probably why Sidon found himself, unexpectedly, speaking up.

"Yes," he said. "What if Yassr is right?"

"Well," Játhon raised an eyebrow, glancing at Sidon. "If it proves to be so you will have me to do your bidding, with the armies of Tresán and Caphás at my back. Either way you'll need not trouble yourself with Yassr's wanton flights of imagination... my king."

More sniggers. More eating. Sidon let his gaze wander toward the drawings on the wall. The likenesses of the seven Sharífs who'd come before him were marked out in postures of repose or war along the pale span. Sidon examined each one as the chatter moved on to other things – the trouble with Hardenese seamstresses, why never to trust a butcher without sons, how stubborn were goatherds in Súnam, why would anyone *go* to Súnam. Sidon nodded at what seemed appropriate junctures until he noticed Yaron, one of the royal courtiers, crouching at his mother's shoulder, murmuring into her ear. His mother nodded once and rose from the table. Sidon looked at her, but her gaze, as she turned, passed straight through him as though he wasn't there.

He watched her turn and walk from the room. The familiar silent reproaches seemed to echo in her every step away from him. *Too young. When you're older.* They were there in the curt patient nods of Elias, the chamberlain. There in the scathing way his mother had woken him in bed the night before. There in the cool smiles and clever words of Uncle Játhon and the other governors and vassals at the table. There in all their obscure and useless, boring talk of shipping routes and gold, trade and spices. Sidon could suddenly feel the banality of it all, holding him at arm's length like an unruly child from the things that really mattered, all because he was *just too young.*

He rose to his feet.

The conversation at the table abruptly died.

"Sharíf?"

He ignored them and marched after his mother. Why shouldn't he know her counsels? Why should things be kept from him? He was nearly fifteen. Soon to be wed. He was the ruler of the Five Lands by right, the king of kings. If he wanted to know the counsels of his mother, he would know them.

He saw her huddled with Elias at the end of the corridor as he stepped out of the banquet room. She turned and spotted him as she glanced over the chamberlain's shoulder. Her gaze lingered, mildly annoyed, forehead crimping, and suddenly what seemed so clear as Sidon had sat in the banquet room watching her leave, just as quickly turned murky again.

Her gaze passed on as she conducted Elias around the corner, away from Sidon's prying and out of view.

"The chamberlain has been agitated since the herald arrived."

Sidon jerked around to find the slavegirl, Iani, standing behind him with a washcloth and a platter. Mother, still annoyed at the girl's being here, had ordered her to help with serving the banquet along with the other servants. The roasted flesh of a small pig's hindquarters sat on the wooden tray surrounded by an assortment of stew-drenched onions and chopped pieces of plum.

"I'm sorry. I didn't mean to startle–"

"You didn't," Sidon snapped.

The girl paused, bowed hesitantly, and turned to enter the banquet room.

"Wait. What herald?"

She stopped. "Oh... I do not know, Sharíf... It was not my place to ask."

Sidon turned back to the empty space where his mother and the chamberlain had been whispering together moments before. "Nor mine, it seems," he muttered.

He looked back around to find the slavegirl still standing there, nervously gripping the platter with both hands.

"What is it, Iani?"

Her eyes dropped to the floor. "Forgive me, my king, but... there is nothing that is not your place. You are sharíf."

When Sidon didn't answer she bowed apologetically and quickly shuffled into the banquet room with the pork.

Sidon thought about following her in, thought about returning to his seat at the table and the talk of cedar and trade roads and all the other things he was expected to quietly listen to and learn. Then he thought about the crowned drawings on the wall. Karel the Young. Arvan the Scribe. Theron the Great. Kaldan the Quiet. *There is nothing that is not your place. You are sharíf.* He stepped back from the doorway, tugged his tunic straight, and walked instead toward the corner his mother and Elias had moved around, his heart knocking gently in his ears with each step. He came around the corner.

"...and better now that the census has been passed."

"Even so. Something should be done now if there is to be..."

The chamberlain trailed off when he saw Sidon. The queen mother turned around.

"What are the two of you talking about?" Sidon said.

She blinked. "What did you say?"

"I... I just think it's time I was told of these things."

The sharífa stiffened, and then stepped forward and began to steer him by the shoulder back toward the banquet.

"I want to know."

"It does not concern you."

"Why not?"

"Not now, Sidon."

"If not now, then *when*?" He shrugged loose. "I am sharíf."

"You are a *boy*."

"I am the ruler of the Five Lands."

She sighed and turned away from him, back to the chamberlain, ready to usher him further down the corridor, away from Sidon.

"I ought to know."

"Not now."

Sidon grasped her arm. "It is my place to know what–"

"I said not *now*!" Her arm flailed out. The back of her hand struck Sidon hard across the cheek, snapping his face to the side with a loud flat slap.

Silence.

The chamberlain's eyes flicked rapidly between mother and son.

Sidon touched his jaw and looked at his mother.

Chalise's lips were quivering. The blood had drained from her face. "Oh... my son... I..." She reached her hands hesitantly to cup the reddened cheek.

Sidon stepped back, out of reach.

Chalise slowly drew her hand back.

"I am not your son," Sidon said finally. "I am *sharíf*, your high king... and when you speak to me you are to address me as such."

The queen mother hesitated, then, slowly, bowed her head. "Yes... I'm sorry... my king."

Sidon looked at the chamberlain. His voice came low and cold. "You will tell me what the two of you have been whispering about."

The chamberlain's gaze slid like a merchant's watching a scale. To the sharíf. To the sharífa. Before calmly fixing once more on Sidon as though nothing of note had happened or been asked. "It is thought the graverobbers, the rebel Shedaím, may be here, in the city."

"In Qadesh? You are certain?"

"Not certain, no. But..." His eyes again flicked momentarily to the queen. "The question of whether to close the city gates and shut them in... I thought perhaps we may stand a better chance of searching them out if they've no way of escape."

"But if we close them," Chalise added, "your betrothed

could be prevented from entering in the mob that will build outside the walls. It could ruin the wedding and..." She trailed off as Sidon's glare turned to her.

"Close the gates," the sharíf said. "And set some among the watchmen who will know my betrothed when they see her. Should she arrive, she will be let in, whilst the archers on the wall watch for any who try to follow without being bid."

The chamberlain bowed. "Very good, Sharíf," and moved quickly away down the hall.

Sidon spared his mother a final glance and then turned to return to the banquet room and continue his meal. When he came around the corner the slavegirl was standing there. She stepped back hurriedly, part fear, part excitement. For him, Sidon realized. She'd been listening to the whole thing.

He smiled and favoured her with a curt nod as he passed by, feeling almost grateful to her. *There is nothing that is not your place. You are sharíf.* The words echoed in his head as he strode through the door to return to the banquet room. For the first time, they actually felt true.

Thirty
K I N

Most of the scroll was covered in pictures, each one etched in charcoal and ink over the rough leathered page. Then, every so often, the occasional line of writing, unintelligible scriptures of dots, lines and glyphs that were mostly unfamiliar and yet every so often hinted – a shape here, a cursive scribble there – at something that would round into meaning, though never did. Neythan gazed at the drawings. They were sparse, with the odd smudge of colour, red or blue, inks that would've been costly even today. Blue dye was never an easy thing to find. Filani, the dye merchant, would say the same if she were here. A strange woman, that one. With stranger sayings. Perhaps she'd have been able to make sense of these scriptures. Maybe she'd have been able to read these words.

"What are you doing?"

Neythan snatched the roll to himself and began to quickly shuffle the page back along the thick wood pin.

"I was only asking."

He covered the rolled page with the tattered vellum wrap of the scrollcoat.

"I wasn't going to take it."

"I know. You just surprised me, is all."

Zahia stood by a jamb of the shack watching him. He was a strange creature to her, he could tell. Which was fine. In a

284

way, she was just as strange to him. She had long awkward limbs that, by habit, she hugged to herself; her knees against her chest when she sat, one hand around her elbow if she stood, as though trying to keep their corners and lengths out of the way. And her mouth, always poised in a querying half-smirk, like she was amused but unsure whether she was allowed to let it show, as though hearing a joke she wasn't sure she understood.

She stepped beneath the shelter and reached a hand to fiddle at the back of her scalp beneath her hair. It was nearly time to leave. The sharíf's wedding would soon begin. There'd been announcements and heralds that morning and Neythan could already hear crowds of people beginning to fill the streets. He planned to go along with the rest of them, a chance to observe the sharíf's bodyguard – especially the man who'd wounded him – before returning to Hanesda to find the brothel the blind elder had visited.

"Were you reading?" Zahia said.

"No, not really... just thinking."

"You do a lot of that."

Neythan looked up at her.

"I mean, you seem to. Off in your head all the time. Pa used to say I'm that way too. Too much and too often. One day I'll go off and not know how to get back. That's what he'd always tell me, but it was never true. You always come back."

"Yes... I suppose you do."

She took another step in and sat down a few feet from him in the dust by an empty grain pot, hunching her knees to herself as usual.

"Used to hide under here when I was a girl," she said. "Pa would do his work outside the door of the kitchen and I'd always want to see, and touch. I didn't know you had to wait till it was dried to do that."

"Must have been annoying for him."

"No," her lips curled to a slight smile, tugged by memory. "No. Not really. The clay's as easy to mend as harm when it's wet like that. He'd just tell me not to do it, but he'd be smiling when he said so. He was only warning me because Mother told him to. It was like a game we played…" She had large ears where she folded the black lank flop of her hair to keep it out of her eyes when she worked, she did so now with her fingers as she watched him. "You never speak of your family," she said.

Neythan glanced sidelong at her, then back toward the street in front of them. "No. I don't suppose I do."

"Are you an orphan?"

The question amused him somehow. "No… well… not really."

"I've said something funny?"

"No… Sorry… It's not something I'm used to being asked."

The thing Neythan had grown to like about Zahia was the way she could remain so politely incurious. Just like Gaana, her mother, with her quiet though generous fussing, checking his wound, serving him food, talking sometimes but from a tidy inward distance, an invisible arm's length that kept things mundane, maternal and neat. Unlike Yoani, Zahia's younger sister, who was always laughing and teasing, shyly with him at first but now with a certain cruel smiling abandon. A price of familiarity, Neythan supposed. No wonder she and Caleb were so fond of one another – they had the same sense of humour. Then there was Petur with his questions – "*Why is the sky blue?*" "*Why's your elbow scarred?*" Like an old man in a child's body. "Head too big for the rest of him," Yoani liked to say. Always wanting to know. Never shy to ask. Neythan had spent the morning with him, taking him out onto the water in the skiff for the first time, a small and dirty raft of mossy oak with gashes of chipped timber where the wood had split with wear. Hardly a boat at all really, not at all like the one Uncle Sol would use when taking Neythan as a child on their fishing trips back in Eram. He'd told the boy as much when he'd asked yet another question of where and how he'd learnt to fish.

"And I was about your age too," Neythan had told him. "But in Eram the water is not like this. Here it is still. But Eram is by the sea."

"What's so different about the sea?"

"The sea… it is its own thing. Like a creature, an animal, the way it moves… it has moods, you see. Every day she is different."

"She?"

"It's what my uncle would call it. Because of its moods, I think."

"Just like my sisters."

Which made Neythan laugh. He brought the boy back in time for lunch, Petur talking the whole way and continuing to talk whilst they all ate, telling of how he'd learnt to toss and pull in a net though he couldn't yet throw it as far as Neythan but one day would, isn't that right, Neythan. To which Neythan had smiled and nodded and ruffled the boy's hair the way Uncle Sol used to ruffle his. The boy was a lively soul, just like his sister, Yoani. But not Zahia, the eldest. Long and awkward, the quieter of her siblings, smart like her brother but coy like her mother. Her gaze often held questions her lips did not speak. Not today, though. Today she was different, curious, her gaze sticking to him, awaiting an answer.

"So you are not an orphan?" she said.

"I suppose you could say my family is a strange one," Neythan said.

She nodded thoughtfully. "What does your father do?"

"My father?" Neythan thought about it, turned to shuffle the scroll away to buy time. He tugged the tether over the scrollcoat to bind it shut.

"Is he… a potter, like me? Like my pa was? Or a mason, or a smith, or a tanner? Not a goatherd, I hope. Mama says you can never trust a goatherd."

"Why's that?"

"Because you can never trust a goat. She says the kind it takes to manage them must be as sly as they are or more so. She says a man always works with what he knows."

Neythan smiled. "Never thought of it that way."

"So what *does* he do, your father?"

"Maybe he is a goatherd."

Zahia smirked. "No. I'd know if you were a goatherd's son. I'd smell it on you."

"Only if I herded with him."

"What goatherd's son doesn't?"

"Maybe I ran away… Maybe I didn't want to be a goatherd anymore."

Zahia gave that a try in her head, then gave that wry uncertain smile of hers. "No… I don't believe you. What did he *really* do?"

Neythan just looked at her, smiling he realized. He let it fade and went back to watching the street.

The strangest thing about being here was it made him think of Ilysia; of Josef and Daneel squabbling at mealtimes by the dandelions whilst Arianna sat silently and ate, the only thing she would take seriously really, her eating, hardly talked when doing it. And then there'd be Yannick with those little wooden toys and ornaments of his that he'd spend hours carving and shaping to give to Yulaan, who'd smile and fuss, arms waving happily as though he'd brought a pearl or ruby and not a wooden toy. Yet Gaana was nothing like that, for her there'd be no more than a pursed smile or thoughtful touch of thanks on the shoulder. Like when Neythan fixed the table the day before last, or when he daubed shut the gap along the upper beam of the house's roof with pitch and some of Zahia's clay. And that's what was so strange, there was little here to resemble Ilysia, and yet being here he somehow couldn't help but think of it, and miss it, which in turn was beginning to make him miss being *here* too, even though he was yet to leave.

"It is because you've no family of your own," Caleb told him later that night on the way to the square. They let Gaana and the others walk on ahead of them. The dusk was coming in with a chill as the streets continued to fill with more people on their way to the ceremony.

"Think about it. You've known no kin but the Brotherhood," Caleb said. "They steal you away from your own whilst you are a child and–"

"We are *volunteered*, Caleb. Redeemed out of honour or by debt. You know this."

Caleb waved a hand. "Whatever. Thing is, you are taken from your own, so the Shedaím may make *themselves* your kin. But there is no kin like blood, Neythan. Whatever they may pretend. And now, your Brotherhood is... well, *broken*, has turned on itself, and so here you are, spending days with a *real* family. One that does not hunt and kill its own. One who would need you as you would them."

"They do not *need* me, or I them..."

"Oh come, Neythan. I've watched you all this week, I've been here. I've seen the way they all look at you. Gaana is a widow. You think there could be any greater comfort for one like her than to have a son who is grown? Or what of Petur, with no father? You think Gaana doesn't think of that when she sees you teaching him to fish, or to mend a table, or playing with him? You are as a prize to them, Neythan. You are their very need, and yet you cannot stay here with them. It is almost cruel if you think about it. May as well hold freshly baked bread before a starving beggar, let him ogle it, let him fill his nostrils with its warm comforting scent, then toss it away to the gutter."

"You told me to work for them."

"I'm not saying it's your fault. Just how it is. You cannot help but be blind to it. Your sha's as needy as they are, after all. It's the way of the Brotherhood. It is what they do. How else to make men slaves to their bidding if not by making them needy also? A man trains his beast the same way. Your fondness of Gaana and Zahia and the others is no crime. But it's better you know your own fictions, Neythan, the weaknesses of your sha, the better to keep from being deceived by them."

Neythan didn't answer. He looked away to the crowds as they roamed on ahead of them toward the square.

"You will ignore me, then?"

"There are better things to talk about," Neythan said. His voice was calm but distant. The same cold distance Caleb saw frost Neythan's gaze that first time he witnessed him kill, as though he was watching from some great height within himself, the way a man might watch an insect at his feet.

"Yes," Caleb said. "I suppose there are. Like this elder of yours for one."

They turned the corner onto the main thoroughfare. The crowds were even thicker here, almost filling the road.

"You still doubt me?" Neythan said.

"A harlot sees a blind woman in a brothel. A strange thing certainly, but hardly proof she's witnessed an elder."

"You didn't hear the way the harlot described it."

"I could well say the same of you for all the wine in your stomach when you were told the tale. And besides, why would she be there, this elder? To enjoy the view?"

"What better place to meet and not be seen?"

"A brothel? Hardly the height of discretion."

"But it is, especially for an elder. It'd be the last place

anyone would think for her to be."

Caleb paused. "*Anyone*, you say… But you can only mean the Brotherhood. It would be the last place the Brotherhood would think for her to…" And then it dawned on him. He smiled. "You think the elder hides her meeting from *them*. The Brotherhood."

Neythan just kept walking.

Caleb looked up at him. "Ho. You do, don't you? Now *that* is quite something. You're beginning to impress me, Neythan… An elder for a betrayer…"

"I didn't say that."

"But it is what you are thinking. Or as good as. An elder meeting someone secretly in a brothel. Without the Brotherhood's knowledge. Even seeking to conceal that meeting from them. How did I not think of that? Of course, the question then is, who was she there to meet?"

"None of this is certain. We're just speculating."

"You're right. We can come to that later. First things first… I admit I never thought I'd say this, Neythan, but I'm beginning to like the way you think. I mean this is really… what? What is it?"

Neythan had stopped walking. He stood stock-still in the street, staring.

"What is it?" Caleb asked again.

Neythan was looking past him. "Her… It's *her*."

Thirty-One
BRIDE

Truth be told, Sidon didn't much like the garment. It chafed at the neck and no matter how many times Iani tried to loosen the threading it still felt too snug around his torso and pressed against his chest, squeezing his midriff. The slavegirl tugged again, yanking at the thick lacing that fastened the back of the vesture. The garment had a stiff prim feel not unlike the tunic he'd worn at his anointing a year ago; the woven goat hair, the polished leather. They were the only fabrics tough enough to hold the multicoloured array of neatly cut amethysts and emeralds stitched into the breastpiece.

"May as well be wearing armour," Sidon said. "Although that would likely be more comfortable."

"But not as seemly, Sharíf," Iani said.

"Seemly be hanged. I'd rather be able to breathe. And walk without sweating, or breaking a rib."

He grunted as she yanked again, standing behind him, and pulled the lacing fast, tying it to his cincture.

"How's that?"

Sidon took a breath. "Better... I suppose. How does it look?"

The slavegirl walked around him, tracing her hand around his lower back to his stomach and waist to make sure of the fit. She stood square on and looked him over, then smiled.

"You look like what you are, Sharíf. A king of kings."

He allowed himself a wry smile back and turned to look for his crown, propped on a cushion in the corner by a woodstool. He was moving to collect it when a knock came at the door.

"Come," Sidon said.

Elias, the chamberlain. He entered and stood by the jamb decked in a long, ornately patterned tunic of scarlet-dyed wool. Fine whorls of white stitching marked the baggy sleeves, curling in extravagant arcs around the forearms like the traced shapes of sea waves. A style familiar to his High Eastern homelands. His rheumy gaze slid from Iani to Sidon. "Majesty. It is time."

Sidon nodded and followed the chamberlain out, fidgeting with the jewelled breastpiece and the silken robe draped over his shoulder as they walked along the passage. For months this night had been stalking him, the night he would meet his bride, see her face to face, learn her name and then, that same hour, be wed. Elias had said he didn't need to worry but Sidon couldn't help it. What would she be like? What would they talk of when they were alone? Sidon had never been with a woman before. And what if the girl didn't like *him*?

Childish thoughts, Elias had said when Sidon asked. *A sharíf does not trouble himself with the opinions of his lessers.* Leaving Sidon to be troubled by the opinion of the chamberlain instead. For that *did* trouble him. Sidon had noticed a sense of admiration from the other man when he'd witnessed him reproach his mother the night before. He had no wish to see the newfound regard exchanged for disappointment, and so kept his questions to himself.

"Nearly a year ago exact you were anointed sharíf, my king," Elias said as they moved along the corridor. The chamberlain had drawn near to him, walking shoulder to shoulder, voice lowered, confiding. "But tonight, in taking a wife to be your queen, your mother shall cease to be sharífa and you shall become ruler in truth, the one elder and head of the Sovereignty. All remnants of your father's throne will be past. From this night your words shall be as law. What *you* command shall be."

Sidon weighed the chamberlain's words as they continued to walk. The torches on the wall were placed too far apart, carving the corridor into blocks of shade, dark to light, dark to light, the pair moving through from one to the other like a rite of passage. "My father used to say a king is a sage with a throne," Sidon said.

"Your father was wise, Sharíf. Made more so by his willingness to bend his ear to counsel."

"It is not a habit I will neglect, Elias."

"Then this truly is the most joyous of days, my king, for wisdom's voice speaks from your lips as it did his."

It was kind of the chamberlain to say that, Sidon thought. He allowed his gaze to drift to the dim lit walls and the images of Talagmagon and Markúth that were painted there, forbidden gods from a forgotten time.

Elias saw him looking at them. "Sharíf Kaldan," he said. "He couldn't keep from growing fond of some of these stories. There used to be similar paintings on the walls outside before your father removed them."

One of the images depicted Markúth swimming in the Swift beside a whale, although in the image the god and the fish were the same size. "Why didn't Father also remove these ones?"

"Your father used to say, as Kaldan did, that there was a kind of truth to some of these tales."

"Truth? About false gods?"

"There are no men without gods, Sharíf. They are always among us, and we are always given to worshipping them, even if we now call them by other names – thrones, riches, wine, women. Your father always understood this, knew how to use it. I think, were he here now, he'd say the old faiths, for men, were merely a kind of childhood, and that it doesn't matter whether there were once gods or not. He used to say that perhaps there were, acting as guardians, departing only when they saw men had gained the power to guide themselves. You see, to your father, the throne was the greatest symbol of this power. He used to teach that to the people like a doctrine. An ingenious thought if you think about it. Because it makes the sharíf who sits that throne more than a man. In a way, a *new* kind of god. Just as you shall be. Tonight."

When they reached the end of the corridor and entered the vestibule the two Shedaím were waiting for them by the main door. The noise of the gathering city was louder here, leaking through the walls. Sidon felt his gut clench and chest constrict, as if the months of nervous anticipation had suddenly gusted in with the noise, adding weight to the tight fit of the vesture he was wearing.

"The sharífa waits in the carriage," Abda said, stepping forward as they neared the doorway.

"Very good," Elias said. He turned to Sidon and seemed about to say something more, to offer some counsel or affirmation, but paused.

"What?"

"Your crown, Sharíf."

Sidon lifted his hand to his head and felt its absence. "By my fathers..." he looked around. "I must have left it in the room..."

He looked at the guards and the chamberlain. Elias's face was unreadable.

Sidon cleared his throat and straightened, trying to affect calm. "Go on ahead. Mother will want to be sure to reach the square in good time and make certain everything is in order. I will follow in the next carriage."

The chamberlain seemed to hesitate, but then bowed and went. The din from outside spilled in through the main doors as they opened. Sidon blinked, glimpsing the crowd. People were heading toward the square in droves.

He turned and went back across the lobby, and then into the corridor to make his way to his chambers, walking briskly. It was good they hadn't got all the way to the carriage where Mother was waiting before they'd noticed. The mood she was in. Nothing but blank stares and brooding silence since last night and what happened outside the banquet room. And with all the fussing she'd done that morning with Elias, seeing to the arrival of the betrothed and her family, ensuring the servants had all the–

He stopped abruptly at the doorway to his chamber.

"Iani? What are you still doing here? You should be in the caravan on the way to the square."

The slavegirl was standing in the middle of the room with her back half-turned. She seemed to be fiddling with something, looking down at herself, her shoulders slightly hunched as though reading some tiny inscription pressed close to her chest. She grunted frustratedly and turned to face him.

"The hem has parted," she said, holding a stitching needle. "I thought I'd be able to mend it before the ceremony but now I'm not so sure because... Are you alright, Sharíf?"

"What? Yes... no." He tugged at his too-tight collar with a finger. "My crown. I left my crown."

She glanced around, saw it on the cushion in the corner and picked it up. She walked across the room to hand it to him in the doorway. Sidon took it and placed it on his head, then glanced distractedly at the corners of the chamber, tugging again at his collar.

"All will be well, Sharíf."

"Yes." He nodded, still looking around vaguely. "Yes. All

will go well." He glanced at the open seam near Iani's waist. "You can fix that?"

Iani looked down at the parting doubtfully. "I fear not very well, Sharíf."

"But you will still be there, at the ceremony. You will still come."

She heard the insistence in his voice and, smiling a little, decided. "Yes, Sharíf. I shall."

Strange how comforting it was to hear her say that, and how worrisome the fleeting notion that she wouldn't. He resisted smiling back nonetheless. The sharíf is like a cornerstone, Father always said. It wasn't a sharíf's place to appear too–

"Ah, my king. You have found it."

Sidon's gaze switched to the corridor to find Yassr approaching with Elias. He stepped back from the doorway. "Uh... yes." He pointed needlessly to his head. "I did."

Probably Mother had sent them back to find him and help him look, trying to hurry him along to the caravan. She was probably refusing to leave until he'd made his way back along the corridor and through the lobby's tall doorway to sit in his seat opposite her. He turned back to the bedchamber. Iani had stepped out of the doorway. He reached for the door to close it on her and keep the chamberlain from seeing. He took the handle and leaned in.

"Wait for us to go," he whispered. "And then join the caravan outside. You will sit by me at the ceremony." He shut the door and moved away, walking swiftly to meet Yassr and Elias in the corridor and continue on to the waiting procession.

It took an hour for the carriage to move through the din. The streets were thick with people, cheering, jeering, it was hard to tell which. Countless arms stretched out to the royal carriage from behind the rows of armed cityguards. Horsemen flanked the caravan as it pushed toward the square. The sky was darkening. Streaks of orange, red and magenta spread out from the sun's elliptic as it sank beneath the housetops. Sidon could just make out the shrill blare of the crier's horn trumping above the clamour to announce his arrival as beneath it all the hammered rhythm of a drumbeat thumped on like the advance of an army. Mother remained ominously still throughout. She'd spoken not a word since Sidon entered the carriage and announced Iani would be seated by him on the platform.

The caravan stopped at the head of the square on the east side by the stage to let Sidon and his mother out. The two Shedaím and several of the cityguard came alongside, surrounding them as they made their way up the shallow steps to the stone platform.

The governors were already seated in a row at the back. Sidon and Chalise took their seats at the centre. The footmen of the cityguard started to light the staves on the wall behind the rostrum and out along the side streets as the crowd continued to gather.

Sidon watched as Iani arrived with the rest of the attendants in the second carriage. She was led up the steps and across the platform as commanded and sat down after being ushered to a seat beside him. Meanwhile, Yassr, having moved to the front of the platform, was already beginning to address the crowd.

"...and our great forefather Karel who gave birth to this Sovereignty nearly three hundred years ago, conquering these lands of Sumeria and founding our crown city. He too was only a boy, as our beloved Sharíf Sidon now is, yet it was he who did away with the priesthoods, ending their wars and preserving our lands. And what of Arvan the Scribe, the great sharíf who himself established the First Laws. Or his son, Theron the Great, who took hold of Calapaar to the north. And then there is Sharíf Kaldan, who built the west wall of Calapaar, and Tsarúth who conquered the High East. And Kosyatin who..."

Sidon let the man drone on, waiting to see his future queen step out from the final carriage, draped in the traditional silk veil that would continue to cover her until they stood to speak the vows. He'd seen the girl once before, two years ago, but it was at a distance. He couldn't remember what she'd looked like. They'd never spoken. Never met.

"She will be more nervous than you are, Sharíf."

Sidon had been so lost in thought he almost flinched. He glanced at Iani beside him. "I doubt that."

Which seemed to amuse her. "Do you?" She smiled, wagged her head. "How long have you been thinking of this day?"

"A year. Maybe longer."

The slavegirl giggled.

Sidon looked at her. "This is not funny, Iani."

She gave an apologetic nod but she was still smiling.

Usually it would have made him angry, but something about it all, the crowd, his forgetting his crown, the months of waiting anxiously for what this hour would or wouldn't be, his mother's cool silences and now this slavegirl just sitting there beside him and smiling at him like that, like there were no cares in the world at all, it somehow felt like a relief. He found himself smiling back. "You mock your king on his wedding day?"

"Sharíf. A bride, any bride, has thought of her wedding day three times a day since she was a child. And that's just if she's not an excitable kind. She will have played with her dolls, pretending she was one and her husband-to-be the other. She will have spoken the vows she is to say on that day a thousand times in her head, or out loud, or even in her sleep. If she is too poor for dolls she will have taken stones, or lumps of clay, or sprigs torn from switchbushes and pretended *them* to be dolls. One for her, one for her husband-to-be. And those sprigs will have danced together, and walked together in the cool of the day touching as though linked hand in hand, and they will have laughed and cried and perhaps even kissed. And the tall sprig, the husband, will have sung songs of his undying devotion to the shorter sprig, the bride."

Sidon was looking at her dubiously, still smiling. "Perhaps not all girls are as given to imagination as you are, Iani."

"Perhaps when it comes to this they are, Sharíf."

"I can tell you now, my mother has never entertained these fictions. Neither when she was a child nor since."

Iani seemed to think about it. "No," she said. "I think you are wrong. I think even the sharífa will have thought on these things too."

"And what about you? Do *you* think on them?"

She looked at him then. A timid half-smile hovered around her lips.

Sidon found himself smiling back as he watched her; the bashful dip of her head, her shy and simple gaze, the tidy way she cupped her hands together as she rested them in her lap. He glanced at those hands and thought of the doting way she'd fussed over his garments as she helped him dress, her palms smoothing across his shoulders and back, pressing the creases out.

"I used to, Sharíf," she said eventually. "As a child I would think on such things often."

"But not anymore?"

"My mother would say that kind of thing is for idle minds, Sharíf... Perhaps that's why you had no time to think on weddings as a boy. Perhaps you were too busy thinking on other things."

"My father, when he was well, would tell me to think on my brother's ways. See how well Joram writes, he'd say. Or, look, see how Joram sits a horse, or how he holds a bow, or how he stands... My brother was always very able, you see. I'd try to think of how I could be as *he* was..." Sidon blinked. His gaze returned to her. "I've never told anyone that before," he said.

Iani just looked back at him, that same attentive and uncomplicated gaze.

Sidon noticed he liked the shape of her eyes, the open set to her face, the careful way she listened. And then, suddenly, he found his thoughts straying to other things, imagining her as other than herself, no more a slavegirl, a princess perhaps, or a wealthy merchant's daughter, draped in other clothes and with more jewels, and then imagining the ease he'd feel were she his betrothed in place of the veiled royal stranger who was to soon emerge from the carriage.

"Iani, I..."

But her smile had faded fractionally. She was looking away, staring out to the crowd.

"Iani?"

Her jaw danced as though to speak, but didn't, as if she'd forgotten what to say, as though her thoughts had suddenly locked or lost themselves as she continued to gaze out to the growing multitude.

"Iani?"

But she didn't move. Her eyes grew still. Then blinked. Staring.

Sidon frowned. "What is it, Iani?" He followed her gaze out to the square. "What are you looking at?"

Neythan didn't move. He just stared. Even from this distance he could tell. The way she sat, the way she tipped her head as she spoke.

"Neythan, what is it? What's the matter?"

Caleb's words bounced off him, seemed far away. And then

Neythan was moving, striding forward, pushing through the gaggles of others on the street as they filed into the square.

She rose from her seat, drifting slowly to her feet as though called. She could see him coming now, swatting, shoving and sidling through the crowd. She watched him toss aside his mantle as he started into the press. She was sure now. His gait, the way he moved.

He could see her standing – ornately dressed, dainty and jewelled. Bracelets around her arms. Bangles of gold in plaited hair beneath a scarf. And she was looking at him. Just standing there watching him come.

"By my fathers, Iani, what's wrong?"
   But she wasn't listening. Just staring. She walked forward, moving to the platform's edge, ignoring the cityguards telling her to step back, ignoring everything, transfixed by his approach.

And now he was certain, he could see her face, those eyes, her gaze, the flicker of recognition, the subtle shift in her stance, all of it so familiar. He could hear his chest hammering, Caleb's voice calling from behind, then everything dissolving away, the crowds, the surroundings, the questions, why she was here, why she was so dressed, all of it shrinking to the still, small fact of her presence, here, now, real, before him. There was no Caleb, no sharíf, no past or future or dimming evening sky. There was only this. Only her. Removing her scarf, taking off her bracelets, waiting, just her. Here. Finally. *Arianna.*

Thirty-Two
ARIANNA

They say there are moments, when they come, that you can expect to remember thereafter, moments that are made memory before they even arrive, through imagination, through daydreams, or what the elders call "foreshadows". They are the reason for the meditations – *they allow your sha to visit where you are yet to go*, Master Johann once said, *so that when you arrive, you are ready*. For those experienced in the discipline the practice allowed their sha to even *awaken* there, in some yet to be encountered moment, an imagined future, and *foresee*. The skill required years of practice, as it had for Elder Safít, and even Uncle Sol, until his visions were deemed false by the elders and he, when he refused to recant, was judged a heretic and exiled from the Brotherhood.

Since finding Yannick's hacked and bloody body Neythan had foreshadowed *this* moment almost every night, imagining over and over again what it would be like to finally find her. And now here she was, Arianna, a sibling of sorts, and yet an enemy, the two commingling in Neythan's mind as the spectral image of Yannick's corpse hung ghost-like over them both, vague as reflection, knitting sibling to enemy, friend to foe, like some crude and deranged seamstress.

She stood still at the edge of the rostrum above the gathering crowd and cordon of soldiers, watching Neythan approach. The sharíf had risen and was walking toward her, talking without being heard. Finally he placed a hand on her shoulder to try to get her attention, and it was then she moved, quick and sudden.

She shrugged the sharíf aside, bolted along the edge of the rostrum and leapt into the crowd, stumbling a little as she landed, and then scampered through the adjoining alley on the other side.

Neythan went after her, shoving his way through the scattered mob. Trying to keep sight of her over the bobbing heads as he worked his way through the crowded square. He could already hear the noise of alarm swelling in his wake as he pushed his way through. Soldiers shouting. People shrieking. Men and women jostled and panicked. Some of the cityguard starting to give chase.

He sprinted into the narrow passage on the other side and turned. Snap of scarlet dress beyond the corner, darting ahead through the throng. Neythan followed, flapping and ducking at the low-hanging laundry drooping from wall to wall along the gangway. Up ahead the passage was filled with more people. Baskets and bodies reeled as Arianna tugged them into his path.

He fought and stumbled his way out into the small market through a gap in the wall, nearly tripped over a goat, bleating its complaint as he pushed through.

Lighter here. More torches.

A dog on a rope barking.

The last vendors packing down their stalls.

Arianna's fast pumping limbs receding beyond the corner. Neythan weaved, slammed into a passerby, kept running.

He was nearing the passage on the other side, waving people out of the way. Gawping faces turning toward him and trying to hurl themselves out of his path as he–

Glint of metal. A shadow in his periphery. Neythan swayed

back from the swung blade before he'd had time to think. He turned on his attacker. Tall woman. Pale and sinewy. Shedaím. The bodyguard he'd spied when watching the sharíf back in Hanesda.

She swatted again with the shortsword, hampered by the crowd. Neythan pivoted into a flailing passerby, grabbed and thrust him into the Shedaím's path, turned and kept running.

Arianna had lengthened the distance by the time he rounded the bend, skidding into the next street and on toward the gateroad.

Busier here. Sellers. Shepherds. Sheep and bullocks for the wedding. And the fishermen still coming in from the lake with their skiffs carried overhead. Neythan elbowed one, tugged the arm of another, spilling them into the path of the chasing Shedaím as he continued to chase Arianna.

He caught sight of her in the distance, veering toward the houses. She hopped onto a mule cart then onto another parked load next to it and leapt up to clasp the ledge at the top of the wall behind, scrambling like a cat onto the rooftop.

Neythan ran across the road and did the same, hauling himself up in time to see her scampering heels as she jumped across the gap of an alley and onto the roof of the adjacent house.

The city sprawled out beneath him as he ran along the roofs after her. He could see the watchmen at the northern wall, scurrying along its ledge in the distance to shut the main gate. Arianna was heading the other way, east along the jagged steps of the city's roofs and gaps to the corner watchtower where the wall was lowest. She was looking for a way out.

Neythan gained as he cut across the staggered levels of the next house, striding ledge to ledge like bollards. He was less than two cart lengths behind when something hit her, thudding into her ribs in mid-air as she leapt over another alley.

She landed hard against the wall of the next house, holding on to the gable and roof ledge, trying to pull herself up, and then dropped and fell into the shadowed alleyway beneath.

Neythan skidded to the roof's edge and peered down from the overhang.

Arianna was on the ground. The sinewy bodyguard was standing over her, sling in hand.

There were shouts coming from the street, a pair of cityguards closing in.

When Neythan looked back, the two women were already fighting.

He glanced back across the rooftops to the city gate. The watchmen were at the pulleys now. He could see the tall wooden slabs of the doors starting to hinge shut. Below, the two guards had arrived at the alley and were stepping in one by one, moving along the slim passage toward the fighting women.

Neythan went to the roof's corner and hitched himself over the edge. He dropped down into the alley and landed with a roll to break his fall, bumping against the wall opposite.

The soldiers had joined the fight, attacking Arianna. Or at least trying to. They kept bouncing against the narrow walls and getting in the bodyguard's way as Arianna parried them into each other.

Neythan walked up behind. Stamped against the calf of the one nearest. The man yelped and went down on one knee. Neythan snagged a flailing arm, locked it. Grabbed chin and skull and twisted hard. Dull snap of bone as the man turned abruptly limp and slumped to the ground. Neythan took his sword as he went down.

The bodyguard was already turning toward him. Neythan stepped in while she was still off balance. Swung blade. Knee to the ribs. Limbs tangling as he shoved her back into the other soldier.

Arianna danced on the periphery as the soldier fell into her. The man grunted feebly as she grasped a limb and yanked.

The bodyguard's eyes locked with Neythan's as she lunged back at him. She feinted, grabbed his wrist, then slammed him face-first into the wall as his sword clattered to the ground.

Vision whited out, sparks at the edges.

Neythan was slumping to the floor when she hit him again. He grabbed at her knee blindly, trying to drag her down. Heard another scream and then the dull clang of metal as blades smacked.

He was on the ground.

Arianna and the bodyguard were fighting.

He flailed around, found the dropped sword just in time, came to as Arianna reeled back from the bodyguard and thudded against the opposite wall.

The pale woman was wheeling back around toward him with her blade raised, the metal skidding off the stone of the narrow alley as she swung down for the killing stroke right as Neythan, still on his knees, drove his shortsword hard into her hip and shoved it through to the hilt.

The woman froze mid-motion with her sword still overhead as she stared down at him. He watched a string of bloody saliva drop from the corner of her mouth, but it wasn't until she slumped to her knees and then face down in the dirt that Neythan saw the blade Arianna had thrown, lodged in the bodyguard's back.

"You're welcome," she said when Neythan looked up at her.

He snorted as he climbed to his feet.

Arianna stood there, sword clasped loose and low. Bloody mouthed and panting. "Alone at last," she said.

Neythan stared.

Arianna shrugged her chin at the fallen bodyguard and soldiers. "I thought you were with them," she said. "But you are not... which makes me wonder why you *are* here."

"Is that all you have to say?"

Arianna tipped her head, quizzical. "You were expecting some grander welcome?"

"You must have known this was coming, Ari. Must have known that *I'd* come. That I'd find you."

Arianna smiled. "I know better by now than to trust what I am told to know."

Neythan matched the smile with a sour one of his own. "Good. Then I shall tell you what *I* know." He began to walk slowly toward her. "I know you are a betrayer. I know you slaughtered Yannick like an animal. And I know that you are going to die, here, now, like an animal, for that sin."

But Arianna only looked at him, her smile now a confused one. "Is that what you think?"

Neythan, still holding the soldier's sword, bent to tug the dagger from the bodyguard's back. "A blade in the back," he said, looking at it. "Apt..." He rose with it in one hand and the sword in the other. "How right it will be for you to die by the same means."

"You think *I* am the betrayer?"

Neythan took another step forward. "Let's not play this game, Ari. I was there. I saw what you did."

But something didn't make sense, the way she was looking at him, like he was some puzzle. It wasn't what he'd expected.

He took another step. "You broke the covenant, betrayed your creed, betrayed the Brotherhood."

"It is they, and you, who have betrayed *me*, Neythan."

And now she wasn't making sense at all. She seemed to be measuring him with her gaze, as though truly puzzled.

"You're not part of it, are you?" she said wonderingly. "You do not know *why* I killed him?"

Neythan took another slow step. What was he missing? "In the beginning I asked myself, but now..." he shook his head.

"Riches? A bribe? The precious *'freedom'* you always hungered for? It doesn't matter now. What matters is I found you."

But she didn't seem to be listening. "So, you really do not know." Her attention was elsewhere, distracted. "Well, that is good."

"You mock me?"

"No..." and then she did something even stranger. She lowered her sword, let it slide loose from her fingers and turned her palms to him. Open.

Neythan didn't say anything, just watched her standing there, still and unarmed.

"*He* was trying to kill *me*, Neythan."

"Pick it up."

"Yannick... He tried to kill me as I slept."

"You're lying."

"Am I? Why did I not kill you too, then? If all I sought were riches and freedom, and there you were, asleep and unguarded..."

Neythan stood still. It had been his first question after Godswell, the one he remained unable to answer, the one that bothered him most.

"Why would I not spare myself..." She gestured at him, the bodies, the blood, everything, "...*this*, by simply taking your life as I did his?"

And now he was uncertain, awaiting the answer, or a trick; she'd always been good at tricks.

"Yannick said it was *his decree* to kill *me*, Neythan. He said it was the will of the *elders*."

Neythan took another step now. *The will of the elders.* He thought of Elder Safít in the brothel, in Hanesda, who she'd been meeting and why. "Why would the elders seek your life?"

"I don't know. That is why I am here. It's what I've been trying to find out. What I know is they would have taken it, *Yannick* would have, had it not been for the dream that woke me."

"Dream?"

"You will not believe me."

Neythan almost laughed but didn't. The things he'd seen. The things he was now hearing.

"I saw a Watcher," she said. "That night in the inn, in my dream. A Watcher. They are… *real*, Neythan."

Neythan just stood looking at her. They could hear more soldiers nearing, the noise of tumult from the city square growing louder.

"I know what you will say. I don't expect for you to believe me, it doesn't even matter anymore. Nothing matters."

"What did this Watcher tell you?"

And the way Arianna looked at him, that same querying look he'd known back in Ilysia by the Dry Lake those years before. A fragile, uncertain smile, part joy, part wonder.

Neythan wasn't sure if he believed her or not, but too much fit for him not to ask. There were too many questions. Why she hadn't killed him as she had Yannick. Why Elder Safít had been at that brothel if, as seemed likely, she somehow had. If the eldership had transgressed their own laws, if Safít had departed the temple she was sworn to abide, then what else might be true that he would have once called a lie? Less than three moons ago he thought Watchers no more than a myth. Now Arianna was claiming to have seen one, just as he had.

"We must leave here," was all Neythan said. "The city. We need to find a way out."

"You believe me?"

Neythan just stared at her. No way to answer. "We must leave," he said again.

Arianna was still smiling, but something else was there too, something he couldn't read. "Well," she said in the end. "After all these years we finally agree on something."

Thirty-Three
B E T R A Y E R

They escaped by the eastern watchtower, leaping and hopping along the rooftops to cross the city. They felled a pair of watchmen and lowered themselves partway down the twenty-foot drop with a cart rope before climbing the rest of the way, digging and clawing into the narrow sills of the stonework like apes and scampering away into the Bulapa Lake forest to wait and rest in silence, nothing to say, too much to say, their presences surreal to one another. Familiar strangers.

"You never liked Yannick," Neythan said eventually, breaking the lull. They were both lying on the grass, face up beside a clutch of shrubs and bracken, staring at the blue-green gloaming overhead. He said it as much to spoil the silence as anything. Nearly two months of wishing her dead, it made any shared quiet, at least for now, feel itchy.

"I didn't trust him." She said it calmly, as though the words were a discovery, floating up from some great distance within her she'd only just realized was there. "And with good reason it turns out," she added.

"So you say."

"Yes, so I say. But it's funny how quickly a blade at your throat can help you make your mind up about someone."

"And that's what you saw, Yannick with his dagger at your neck."

"Yes. That is what I saw."

Neythan didn't answer. They stared at the sky. The leaves of the forest shivered in the breeze like the sound of pouring rice. Part of him couldn't believe they were lying here like this, speaking, and not engaged in mortal combat. For weeks he'd foreseen nothing else.

"The strange thing," Arianna said, her words still floating, calm and deadpan, "was afterward I liked him more... I mean just sitting there like that at breakfast, the morning we left Ilysia, same as always, quiet as always, and all the while plotting how best to kill me... You think about that afterward, you know. You wonder, was he thinking of it then, killing me? When we ate? When he went to his bloodtree? When he greeted me?"

A long cloud was drawing slowly along the sky above them in the shape of a hare.

Arianna marked his silence. "You blame me," she said.

Neythan thought about it. "He is dead. You are alive."

"You'd rather it the other way around?"

"I didn't say that."

"You think me a liar."

"I think you could've been mistaken."

Arianna laughed. "You see, that's the problem with you, Neythan. You do not see things as they are, you see them as you'd *like* them to be. I tell you Yannick tried to kill me, you say I must be mistaken."

"He could have been confused."

"No, Neythan. He was not. It was his decree."

"He actually said that."

"Yes. The only time I hear him speak and it's so he can tell me that killing me is his decree. He told me as I tried to wrestle the blade from him. It was as though he was trying to convince me to let him do it – *it's my decree, it is the will of the elders.* As though that should make me willing to die... Well.

I am not willing."

"If that's true, then he was not at fault."

Arianna sat up and looked at him. "For trying to *kill* me?"

"He had no choice."

"There's *always* a choice, Neythan."

"What would you have done, had the decree been yours?"

"What would *you*?"

Neythan thought about it.

"See?" Arianna said. "You, Josef, Yannick – you're each the same that way. That's why I didn't wake you."

"Because you didn't trust me."

She didn't answer. He could hear her getting up, moving around. He kept watching the cloud. It was more the shape of a house now.

"You used to trust me," he said. And there it was, that thing they never spoke of, the thing that years ago had changed everything between them. He could feel its gravity opening to them in the silence.

Arianna's movements slowed.

Neythan sat up and looked at her. She was tearing at the hem of her dress; stale sweat steaming from her shiny thighs. It was getting cooler, and darker. She looked up and saw him watching, waiting for an answer.

"Your uncle used to trust you too," was all she said, and let the silence do the rest.

Neythan, to this day, could never fathom why Uncle Sol told him the things he did: his visions, his beliefs about the Brotherhood. Neythan had been just a boy. How could he know that telling, when asked, of the things his uncle shared would also mean his uncle's exile? How could he know that it would be his own divulgences that would banish his only remaining bloodkin?

"I loved Master Sol as a father," Arianna said. "He was the only one who understood me. You knew that. And then he was gone. Because of you."

"It wasn't my fault."

"Then whose fault was it?"

"He should never have told me the things he did."

"He told you because he *trusted* you. Like I *trusted* you. But you chose to betray him. You chose to tell the elders."

"*They* came to *me*. They demanded the truth. I was a child. What was I to do?"

"Lie, Neythan."

"It was forbidden."

"Just as it is forbidden to turn our swords on one another, and yet here we are. Yannick did not hesitate, and neither did the elders, to turn their swords on me."

She was right. Truth was he'd always known she was right. He'd known it when she changed toward him those years ago, making herself a stranger to him, breaking the furtive bond they'd known, that nameless thing forever marked by that one night of words unspoken by the Great Dry Lake. It was then Neythan discovered it was not just his uncle he'd unwittingly exiled, but also himself. The only two people able to dent the solitude he'd known since Father and Mother died were now gone from him, one by the Brotherhood's edict and the other by her disgust at his part in it. Everything changed from then. Afterward, sometimes, they would bicker, they would banter, but they would never talk, not like they had that night with their feet dangling above the Dry Lake, as though they were the last ones left in the world, as though possessors of some shared secret only they could understand.

"Look."

Arianna was brandishing her palm. She'd been using the rag she'd torn from her dress to wipe it.

"That's where I caught Yannick's blade," she said. "When he tried to slit my throat as I slept."

Neythan looked at the thin line of rouged, shiny flesh that

crossed her palm.

"It's healed well now, but it wasn't easy to hide. The apothecaries in Hanesda ask a fortune... Touch it."

Neythan did, and then looked up at her. She held his gaze.

"You see?" she said. "I am not lying. I was not mistaken." She sat back on her haunches, still watching him. "We've no kin but each other now." Her eyes were staring into his, waiting for him to acknowledge the truth she'd always wanted him to, the truth he'd always resisted. "The Shedaím are not our kin," she said. "They never were. The Brotherhood is not true."

Neythan, after a long pause, nodded.

Arianna continued to watch him, then rose from squatting beside him and stepped away, sitting down again by the bushes.

"I never blamed you, Neythan," she said quietly as she tied the rag around a wound on her calf. "For your uncle, I mean... It's just, I didn't trust you anymore. I couldn't."

"And what about now?"

She glanced at him, and then away through the forest trees, toward the city in the distance where the cityguard and watchmen were no doubt still seeking them. "Now?" She shrugged, wry smile. "The elders seek my life, and you're the only one who knows the truth of it. And you've chosen to hear my side, in spite of everything. What right have I to not trust you now?"

"I suppose that will have to do."

Their tacit covenant hung in the quiet between them for a moment before she paused and turned to look back at him again. "Why *have* you chosen to hear my side?"

The forest was beginning to chill further. The sun had receded toward the horizon, peeping out from behind the city watchtowers. Neythan let out a long sigh and decided. "The Watcher you spoke of... I have seen one too."

She stared at him, then smiled, then laughed. "Is that so?"

"Yes. It is... I need you to tell me what she said to you."

"*'She...'*" Arianna's smile faded. "You *have* seen her."

"Was she the reason you were in Hanesda?"

"Yes... Yes." She shuffled on her seat to face him now, newly fascinated, excited even. "She visited me, in my dreams... I thought I was going mad but when she spoke to me that night in Godswell, told me of what Yannick was going to do, that I needed to wake up... after seeing the truth of what she said I knew it wasn't madness... And so I went to the place she called me, to a waterfall. That's when she told me."

"Told you what?"

"That I'd find the answers in Hanesda. She told me what to do. She provided everything. The clothes. Silver. Everything. And then... took me there."

"*Took* you."

"Yes."

"To Hanesda."

"Yes."

"How?"

"I don't know. She showed me... it was like a door. When I stepped through to the other side I was by the main road, a mile from Hanesda. I could see the city before me..."

Neythan's head wagged slowly.

"She did not do the same for you?"

"No. She did not. She spoke riddles. I cannot remember half of them. She told me where to find you."

Arianna nodded thoughtfully to herself.

"What else did she say?" Neythan asked.

"That was all. When I came to the city I made it my aim to meet the sharíf, to try and discover his involvement, why my death had been ordered."

"And did you?"

"No... I don't know... I don't think he knows anything.

I tried befriending him, prompting him, seeing how he'd respond. But he is as he appears."

"What of those around him, his counsellors, his courtiers?"

"His chamberlain, Elias. He was different. He knew things. He was not like the sharíf. He is not as he appears at all. I'd catch him watching me sometimes. I think he knew I wasn't as I appeared too. So I began to watch him back, just little things, slipping into his bedchamber when he wasn't there, looking around. His letters and so forth. After a while I began to follow him, sometimes out of the palace. Sometimes I'd see him meeting people – judges, governors, vassals. Just him. A chamberlain. They'd come to the city, visit with the sharíf awhile, eat with him, then later, when I followed Elias, I'd find them meeting with him in a cornerhouse or grove, or often in the old man's vineyard or some other place. They'd meet so long I'd have to leave for fear of being missed from the palace."

Neythan's turn to nod and think.

Arianna looked at the grass again, trying to remember anything else. She laughed to herself.

"What?"

"Strangest thing was… well… one night I followed him. I'd thought he might meet a vassal from Hikramesh who'd visited with the sharíf the day before. So I follow him. He goes along toward the city baths where his cornerhouse is. I'm expecting him to stop there, as is his custom when meeting these people, but he doesn't. He continues on to the east quarter and stops at a brothel instead, a whorehouse… I mean, the man is *old*, Neythan. I was told he was once cupbearer to Sharíf Kosyatin. He must be at least ninety years. Maybe older. You'd not think him… well… *able*… What? I'm just being honest. At that age you don't think a man can–"

"No. It's not that. The elder."

"What elder?"

Neythan stared hard at the ground. "I was in Hanesda, during a new moon. I went to a brothel."

"You went to a *brothel*?"

"It wasn't like that. I was… Just listen. One of the harlots there told me she'd seen an elder once."

"What would a harlot know of elders?"

"No, I mean she saw a woman, but an old woman, well aged, frail, and blind, but like one who could see. The way she moved, the girl said, was like one who could see. She said that had she not seen the woman's eyes for herself she'd have not thought her blind."

Arianna understood. "*Elder Safít?*"

"She described her likeness, at least from what I can remember. I'd taken wine."

"You'd taken *wine*? What's happened to you? What else have you been up to?"

"I had no choice… I… Look. Never mind that. Think about what I am saying. For Safít to depart Ilysia is forbidden. She is Eye to the Brotherhood, sworn to abide the temple. To consort with anyone other than Shedaím would defile her visions. For her to be in Hanesda, and in a *brothel* of all places…"

"She'd never go to such a place. No Shedaím would. Apart from you, it seems."

"But that is what *any* Shedaím would know and say. What better place to keep yourself from being seen by those of the Brotherhood? What better place would there be to meet with someone you'd not want it known you'd met?"

"Elias. The chamberlain."

"Exactly. Elias."

"But why would they meet?"

"I don't know."

"So we take him? Question him?"

"We've stirred a hornets' nest now. He'll be at the sharíf's side, right at the heart of it."

"So, what then?"

"Ilysia," Neythan said. "We go to Ilysia."

"You've just said you think it likely Safít has met with a member of the sharíf's house, a forbidden act. And I've just told you Yannick's decree to kill me was *given* by the elders. And you want us to go to Ilysia? More peril lies there than here."

"No. The Shedaím hunt *us* now. There will be no Brothers there."

"What do you mean, *they hunt us*?"

Neythan paused. "Yannick is not the only Shedaím to have fallen. There have been others."

"What others? How many?"

"I don't know. Many, I think. Maybe six. Seven perhaps."

"*Seven*? How?"

"I don't know."

"And they think it is us? The Brotherhood. They think we could do that?"

"Yes... I thought *you* had done it."

"But I have been here."

"Yes, I know. I believe you. That's the problem."

"And now believing me is a problem?"

"Yes... No. You don't understand. All this time I'd thought it was *you*. I didn't have to think of how or by what means. I'd seen what you did to Yannick. It made sense to think you were somehow finding the others and doing the same. That you're not means there's some other who *is*. Some other hunting Shedaím, hunting *us*, slaying Brothers one by one."

Arianna sat there, taking it in. She stood again, pacing around the small clearing where they'd been sitting. And then, abruptly, she shrugged. "You know what? I don't care. The Shedaím have made themselves my enemy. If anything, this heretic is my friend."

Neythan shook his head. "That's just it. I'm not so certain

it *is* a heretic."

She stopped pacing and faced him. "There's none but a Brother who'd be able to do what you say has been done, Neythan. If there was, we'd know. The *Shedaím* would know."

"Perhaps they do."

"If that's true, then why hunt us?"

"I don't know. Why decree for Yannick to kill you?"

Arianna thought about it. None of it made sense.

Neythan looked at the sky. The house-shaped cloud had passed on. "It will be dark soon. We'll need a fire to sleep by."

"Sleep? Here?"

"We can't leave yet."

"Why not? They will soon discover we're not in the city. I'd rather not be here when they do."

"They will think us far away by then. They won't hunt us here in the forest."

"Why take the chance?"

"We need to wait for someone."

"Who?"

"A friend. He's still inside. We need to wait until they open the gates again. He'll know I'm waiting for him."

"You told him that?"

"No. But he'll know."

Arianna stared at him.

"We need to wait for him."

"Fine," she said finally. "One night."

"And then we go to Ilysia."

Arianna's look was dubious.

"There will be no fruit in seeking Elias," Neythan said. "He and the sharíf will be surrounded by an army after today, and there is no guarantee of answers with him even if he were not. Ilysia is where we will find the elders. It is where we will learn the truth."

"And you would enter the temple?"

"I will," Neythan said. He rose to his feet and went toward the fringes of the clearing and began to forage for firewood.

Arianna just looked at him. "You've changed." Which made Neythan stop and look back at her. "I think I like you better this way," she said.

Neythan gave a brief uncertain smile.

Arianna just stood there appraising him, and then turned to the thickets to gather more wood. Neythan did likewise.

Thirty-Four
GELED

Daneel shifted uneasily in the saddle.

"Bones, brother... A man ought never to be able to feel the bones in his own arse."

Josef said nothing.

"How long have we been riding for?"

Josef shrugged. "About two weeks."

"I have blisters there, you know. Several."

Josef glanced at him and then back to the road.

The terrain curled upwards to the east; dry sunbaked shale leaning against the horizon on one side. Daneel had spied wild goats standing amongst the loose footing and grazing on tough sprouts of whatever rare vegetation was able to survive these surroundings. He spat to the side and surveyed the distance to this latest crest in the highway, perhaps a mile or more. How long to the next village, he didn't know. They'd been five days in the open country since the last one. What he wouldn't give for roasted meat, but the goats were too far up the shaled slope, out of range of his bow, and he doubted his horse could find footing up there anyway. He glanced ahead to the other two Shedaím further up the road, Salidor sitting tall in his saddle with Jasinda riding beside him.

"We should never have come by this road, Josef, you know that as well as I do. Salidor keeps this up and I'll have nought but scabs and saddlesores for a seat. Hey, Salidor and saddlesore, they rhyme. Perhaps he's named after it."

"It's not that bad," Josef said.

"Not that bad? Tell it to my arse. We should have gone by the townships along the ivory pass, but no, Salidor says they'd delay us too long. Then through the hilltowns by the Calapaari Sea, but no, they're 'full of inbreds and...' What did he say again?"

"Fishmonkeys."

"*Fishmonkeys*. What under the sun is a fishmonkey?"

Josef only shrugged.

"That there'd be meat on them would be enough for me. Mouldy bread and locusts for three days now. I need a proper meal."

"The locusts weren't bad."

"I'm of a mind to cut the man and quarter his horse."

"That's not funny, Dan."

"You think I'm joking?"

"It's not funny."

Daneel muttered darkly and squinted at the horizon. Salidor and Jasinda had come to a stop by the crest ahead.

"Besides," Josef said, as they strode their horses up the sloping road to join them, "you'd be the same." He looked at his brother. "If you were in his place."

"I'd never be this blindly pigheaded."

"Really? If I was killed and it was given to you to hunt the one who did it, you'd be all peace and calm?"

"I didn't say that. But neither would I do this. We're weakening ourselves for no reason. Say we were to happen upon Neythan and Ari here, now, we'd be too weak to face them... and us going about like this, the four of us together like children, the whole thing is ridiculous. How can Gahíd mean for us to find them this way? Better to send us off in twos, cover more land."

"He fears to lose any more Shedaím."

"Yes, that he does. He fears it more than he seeks Neythan and Ari... I won't complain though."

"You just did."

"Well, I shan't any longer. After all, what will we do if we *do* find them?"

Josef didn't answer.

Jasinda was walking back toward them from the crest. Salidor had come to a stop ahead of them where the road fell away. It was beginning to rain.

"The two of you," she said as she approached, looking them over. "You're always whispering. Like handmaidens."

Josef ignored the barb and gestured to Salidor behind her with a jut of his chin. "Why has he stopped?"

"The path ahead is steep," she said. "There's a pond on the other side where we can water the horses. You'll need to steady them for the descent."

"The horses need to rest," Daneel said.

Jasinda appraised him lazily and leaned over and spat. "You should not think them as fragile as you. They will rest at the pond below, where they can drink."

"What's the delay?" Salidor had come trotting back to them from the bluff. He came to a stop beside Jasinda.

"The boy wants to rest," she said.

"Rest?" Salidor's large craggy head angled toward the twins. Stubbly grey scalp, his eyes bruised from lack of sleep. "Rest, you say?"

Daneel sighed heavily. "I simply suggested–"

"Suggest? Yes. As well you might, seeing it's not the blood of *your* kin that awaits justice."

"We seek the same justice, Salidor," Josef said. "But Daneel is right. The horses tire. And the way down is steep."

"You seek only comfort, seeing that Sha'id was neither your blood nor sharím."

"We are each of the Brotherhood. Let us not forget our–"

"*Forget*? Forget, you say? No. I have neither the comfort nor luxury of forgetting. The brother of my mother's womb is *dead*."

"You misunderstand me."

"No. No it is you who do not understand, though I wager you would, one of you at least, were you to learn the same grief I have. Perhaps I should acquaint you with it."

"What?"

But Salidor had already turned, walking his horse back up toward the bluff's edge.

Jasinda sniffed. "I think he means for us to go down now," she said. "Rest later." Then to Daneel, "Calm yourself." She nodded at his hand, clasping the hilt of his sword by his belt. "Salidor is only talk. It is the grief that speaks, not him."

They went down the bluff as the rain fell. The horses' hooves skated over the loose rocks, their hindquarters shuddering and their forehooves stabbing and pawing at the damp ground as they went down. In the end they stayed no more than half an hour at the pond as the rain hardened, flinging down fat heavy drops and turning the dirt soupy. They continued on. The rain hammered down until it got so Daneel was too wearied by it to complain about his rear.

"We're not far now," Salidor barked through the steady slapping applause of the downpour. "Just beyond this hill and we'll see the city. We'll of course bed for the night. We have a pigfarmer there, if you can believe such a thing."

"A pigfarmer?" Daneel asked. The normal practice of the Shedaím was to keep an innkeeper, very occasionally a smith, so their weaponry could be replaced or maintained alongside having bed and shelter.

"I know," Salidor shrugged, sharing Daneel's gripe. "Stinks of the beasts too." He turned, half-smiled, half-grimaced through the rain. "But the food will be good though."

Daneel smiled at that. "Meat?"

"That's right, and plenty of it."

Daneel decided he may be able to forgive the man his stubbornness after all. Shelter, a fire, and meat would be decent consolation for the sticky pinching chafe of his saddle. He decided to be civil. "You've stayed there often?"

"Some. I have a place near Çyriath, a small homestead. Rare I have a decree south of Parses, so I keep myself there. When I am to come further north, I stay here in Geled. Not a bad place. The Sovereignty's northernmost city, you know. They say when Theron the Great took it he did so expecting to launch campaigns from there into the Reach." Salidor laughed. "Wasn't enough for him to have taken these lands from the Kivites, he wanted to take the territories they were fleeing to as well. Anyway, not a bad place, as I say. Strong fort. And far enough away from the crown city to not be meddled with by Sovereign consuls too often." He glanced back at them over his shoulder. "It can be that way for some of us, you see. In the lands where the Shedaím find no trustworthy ranger they keep a Brother and have him stay instead, learn the place, know it. We can never be as rangers of course, our faces cannot be known, but we can play half the part of spy nonetheless. Brothers like me, we just watch. Like when you are to fulfil a decree, but longer."

"I didn't know there were any like that."

"There are few... since the crimes of your friends, even fewer. But the few of us there were, were mostly here in Calapaar. Likely there'd be one or two to the south too, near Súnam perhaps. You'll find no trustworthy ranger there either."

"Why not?"

"Well... everyone has a tale for that. Some say the Súnamite queen knows the Shedaím's business. That she's familiar with our ways, or if not, at least aware we are more than rumour."

"You think that's true?"

"Who's to say? I just do what I'm bid in my own quarter. And my quarter isn't Súnam. It's here in this cold and rain… Perhaps one day you'll know an answer for yourself. If they make you as I am, to abide in one place. If they do, the place they'll have you is the border of Súnam, or near it. Have no doubt of that."

"What's the furthest north you've been?"

Salidor pushed the air through his cheeks. "You may as well know sooner than later, a Brother's business doesn't know the same borders as a soldier's. I've seen more than a few Kivites in my years, shed the blood of more than a few too."

"They send you into the Wetlands, beyond the Reach?"

"They send wherever trouble's found. And plenty of it can be found in Kiv. They send me or some other to cut the weed before it sprouts. But the problem with a weed, is that it's a weed. You can cut all you want, but until you uproot it or burn the thing whole it'll keep coming up again. It keeps me busy enough, put it that way."

"Why? What trouble is there?"

"What trouble isn't? What trouble won't ever be? They think they have claim to land that's no longer theirs, and the lands they live in are scarce, and barren mostly. There'll not be a day come that they don't seek sovereign lands for as long as they remain. No. More chance telling a man not to seek food for his stomach. Theirs are ugly lands, and they raise a people who are the same, like nettles and ivy together, built to endure, and one way or the other they'll prick the hand of the one who says they can't. And that's the trouble. Because they've no head or root. No matter where you cut, in the same place, what was cut soon returns. Like I said, keeps me busy enough."

They carried on through the rain to the shallow hill's

edge, Salidor warming to his stories, as did Daneel and Josef
to listening to them. They were a comfort against the rain,
something else other than the relentless wet chill to think
about. After a while Salidor went on to telling jokes, the kind
Daneel found funny but Josef didn't. It was perhaps because
of this that Josef saw it first, then a beat later, the others, their
laughter halting abruptly and giving way to the loud silence
of the rain as they stood atop the hill overlooking what lay in
the broad lowland beneath.

In the distance below them the city smouldered, ash black
ruins and lingering clouds of greasy low-hung smoke, like
mist, but darker, settled about the broken rubbled walls of
what used to be Geled. The once-tall watchtower lay halfway
upended, like a snapped twig, collapsed in a heap of blackened
stone in front of the now missing city gates.

"What by my fathers…" Jasinda's voice trailed off.

The rest didn't speak at all.

From this vantage they could see how the east wall had
been smashed in, caving back on itself, and how it was the
only one of the city walls that even vaguely resembled what
it had once been. The others were piles of stone, mere humps
like giant graves, settled about the city's edges like long lumps
of charcoal.

It was Salidor who moved first, nudging his horse forward
and down the gentle slope into the muddy basin. The entire
sodden plain seemed to jump and ripple as meaty slaps of
rain pounded the drenched earth. The others followed, their
horses' hooves sliding in the mud as they went down toward
the destroyed city.

As they neared they could see the gates were still there,
but buried, their thick doors crumpled and sodden and slick
with ash, and the walls where their hinges had been, folded
inwards and half-collapsed. There was a gash through the
front wall beside it, disturbing for its neatness, as if a giant

shovel had been ploughed through to dig and clear the debris. Josef stared and pointed at it, a clean gaping wound amid the disarray. Salidor went toward it to take a closer look. He came to a stop and just stared, the others with him, and then slowly climbed down from his horse.

"Salidor."

Jasinda's voice seemed to startle him. He looked around at her and the others as though he'd forgotten they were there.

"We have been invaded," he said. "I know not by who or what..." he blinked, as though waking from sleep. "The sharíf must be told. And Gahíd. They must be told immediately. Whatever army did this will be marching south as we speak." He pointed at Jasinda. "You must go to Parses, find the captain of the guard there, have him marshal a defence and ready the citadel. We must hope what has been done here is recent." He pointed at Josef and Daneel. "You two. You will go to Hanesda, to the sharíf. Tell him of what has been done. Tell him Geled is fallen."

"Gahíd instructed that we stay together. So that–"

"What he said does not matter now! You must go, each of you. Now. The time is short."

"And what of you?" Jasinda said.

"I'll search this place out, see what can be learned of the enemy, how long since their departure. Then I'll return to Hanesda and tell whatever I find. We must know our enemy."

They stood there in the rain, watching him, waiting for what else he would say.

"War is upon us, Brothers. Go. Go now!"

Josef snapped at the reins of his horse and turned, nodding to Daneel. "Come, brother."

Daneel began to follow.

"And you," Salidor said, as they turned. Daneel looked back. "Do not think of rest on the way back."

Any other day Daneel would have rolled his eyes and answered; instead he glanced once more at the scorched and soaked rubble and just nodded. And with that they were on their way, galloping across the waterlogged earth with their horses' hooves kicking up grey mucky clumps of mud in their wake.

Jasinda watched them go, and then turned back to find Salidor already clambering his way through the gap beside the broken gates. She climbed down from her horse to follow him. "Salidor. Wait."

He glanced over his shoulder. "You should go too, Jasinda. The sooner you reach Parses, the better."

"And I shall. But wait."

He paused on the other side of a piled row of bricks, standing within the ruined city wall and gazing at the mess within. The embankments of the half-moat that barred what had once been the way to the tower were gone, submerged in water. The bridge across was still visible, just, lying beneath the surface. A vague boardwalk hovered in the grey murk of the newly risen waters. Salidor couldn't tell whether it was flooded from the rain or the mess. Probably both. The tower on the other side was mostly missing, no more than a short wall with jagged edges where bricks of stone met with empty space like missing teeth.

"Have you ever seen anything like this?" Jasinda came and stood beside him.

Salidor shook his head.

"Could it be Kivites?"

Salidor nearly laughed despite himself. "Kivites? They're naught but scattered tribes and beggars. What armies begin to rise from among them, what leaders lift their heads, I myself have gone and ended. Kivites could not have done this, nor any army I have known or heard of. But that is not my concern right now. Do you see what is?"

Jasinda looked around at the torn walls and collapsed tower and flattened ashy houses and smoke. "Yes. I think I do."

"No bodies. I can see not one. I can see nothing that even..." and then he stopped.

Jasinda looked up at him. "Nothing that even, what?"

"Look. Do you see that?"

"See what? What is it?"

"There. In the water... Do you see... something is moving... *there*... by my fathers, what *is* that?"

Thirty-Five
FUGITIVES

In the end they waited three days for the city gates to open again, eating berries mostly, and a fish Arianna managed to spear from the banks of the lake with a pike she'd made by sharpening the end of a bough with her sword. The worst thing had been the cold. It was more than half a day before she or Neythan were able to rid themselves of the lingering bone-deep chill from having remained in the open air and dew of the lakeside wood for two straight nights, huddled together with only fodder and a small fire for warmth.

When Caleb eventually emerged from the city he came out on a mule-drawn cart he'd traded for, exchanging the sword and cloak Neythan had left behind, and making up the rest of the price with a small golden trinket he'd taken from the tomb of Analatheia in Hanesda. Neythan only looked at him when he explained that part. Caleb, unconcerned, shrugged back. Neythan wondered what else he might have taken but was too grateful for the cart to ask.

Neythan and Arianna met him where the road turned by the forest, running up from behind and leaping into the trundling cart to cover themselves. They used the waiting blankets in the cartbed to hide and stay warm as Caleb drove along the road out. It wasn't until they were beyond sight of the city watchtower that Neythan told Caleb to turn them west, toward Ilysia, before going on to explain why the woman they'd been hunting for the last half year was now in the cart with them, along for the ride.

"So, I have fulfilled my end of the bargain then," Caleb said.

"You have."

"And you will not forget our covenant."

"You know that I cannot, Caleb."

All of which Arianna observed with interest, declining to ask for explanation as she lay down beneath the blankets in the cart and finally went to sleep.

It was late evening when they arrived at the township. A broad sprawl of houses, tents and sheds stretched out along a narrow grassy stream, a city in almost every way save the lack of a wall and watchtower and the untidy make-do way the houses clustered together. They tethered the mule against a mooring post nearby a wadi on the outskirts of the settlement, leaving it to lap at the water whilst they set a shelter by turning the cart on its side and fastening tent sheets between it and a young tree.

"I'm surprised you believed her so readily," Caleb said quietly when Arianna had wandered down to the water to bathe.

"I'm still not sure I do."

"Then why is she here?"

Neythan shrugged wearily. "The things she said… they make sense. They make sense of everything really. Why she killed Yannick. Where she'd been in the time since. Why she was with the sharíf… And then there is what she has said of Elias. It all points the same way."

"And what way is that?"

Neythan looked sidelong at him. "A heretic among the elders."

Caleb's eyebrows climbed.

Neythan waited. "You've nothing to say? I thought you'd be glad to hear me finally say it."

"I'm glad for you to heed the truth, however uncomfortable it may be.'

"Well. Be satisfied then. I've heeded."

Again Caleb didn't answer.

"Did you bring the book?"

Caleb raised a finger and turned to the sack of provisions to rummage. He pulled out the foot-long scroll and put it down in front of them.

"Thank you, Caleb."

Neythan uncovered the scroll and slowly unrolled the page, bringing it to the last place he'd examined.

"Thing must stretch thirty feet," Caleb said.

"Further, I think. The roll's an inch either side of the pin. Whatever story it tells is a long one."

"You're obsessed with it."

"I'm just interested."

"Why? What's so interesting?"

"You've seen the name that marks the cover, Caleb. Qoh'leth was father of the Brotherhood."

"What I see is that no matter how many times you look at the thing the words remain unreadable, whatever the name of the book."

Neythan just shifted the pin, lengthening the scroll to see more of the strange dots and glyphs. They seemed pressed into the page, lifting from it like scars, and there were patches of fabric and thin shards of bone, wood and metal threaded into parts of the vellum. "There must be a way to read it."

"If there is you'll not find it by ogling the thing every night."

"You've a better suggestion?"

Caleb shook his head and turned from sifting through the provisions to squat by the fire with his long palms outstretched. "You and your lust for meaning, Neythan," he said slowly. "And so now we go to Ilysia."

Neythan turned from the page and looked at him. "You're displeased."

Caleb rubbed his hands above the warmth and shrugged.

"All our aims meet there. You want to know who betrayed you all those years ago. And I want to know the truth of... of all this. Why they decreed for Yannick to kill Ari, if they did. Why the elder met with the sharíf's chamberlain in the brothel. I must know if she is a betrayer, and to what end. Or if some other truth lies at the heart of all this."

Caleb chuckled quietly into the fire, wagging his head.

"What's so funny?"

He straightened, standing over the short flames. "Some other *truth*, you say... and tell me, Neythan. What *is* truth?"

Neythan laid the scroll aside.

"After all you've witnessed. And still you do not consider yourself, Neythan."

"Consider myself?"

"You've seen your friends butchered at the hands of one another. You've journeyed half the length of the Sovereignty. You've even seen the countenance of a Watcher... and yet you're still seeking for the world to have an order to it."

"I'm seeking for answers to what was done."

"And what if there are none. Or only some."

"Then why do you seek *your* betrayers?"

"Vengeance, Neythan. Only vengeance. That is all this world is. There is no order. No great law to it all, no perfect and pleasing way from which things have fallen. There are only men and women, with their greed and their pain and their pleasures, and all they are, all they do, is to seek whatever ends those appetites determine." He squatted down again and took a stick and began turning the half-cut of log in the flames, watching the cinders spark as it rolled. "You'll not find answers in the hearts of men, Neythan. Only ever deepening fog, and a continuing desire for those things that are his own, whether kin or riches. Seek your meaning and answers a hundred years or more, whether in Ilysia or in that scroll. But you'll find none. There is no right. No law. Man is without reason, save for whatever reason serves his belly and that fog, and the desires that lie beneath it. Kin and riches, Neythan. There is nothing else."

"Then why are there Watchers? Why did you believe I'd witnessed one?"

"Why shouldn't I? I've seen a great many strange things I'd have not thought true of the world. But I do not assume their virtue. No. If there *is* a law that all living things hold to then it is this. Whether man, beast or Watcher, each holds to what is his own, and in this way each is a law unto himself."

"And so what then? You'd have me seek nothing?"

"I'd have you seek what can be found, Neythan. As I do."

"As you do what?" Arianna came stalking slowly up the damp grassy slope from the wadi, rubbing at her wetted hair with the ragged towels Caleb had brought from Qadesh. She came to a stop beside him and stood there in front of the fire, her face glowing with its colour. She looked at each of them. "Well, don't stop on my account." She prodded the towel into her ears to dry them and then tugged at the tunic she'd changed into, patting herself down. "It's a little baggy but I think it'll do. It's warmer than the dress." She glanced up at them again and gestured. "I've interrupted?"

"No," Neythan sighed. "No interruption." He began to roll up the book again. "It's getting late. We should get some sleep."

"Ah," Arianna said. "About that... it may be we'll have to leave a little sooner, or, well... soon."

"Why?"

She continued rubbing at her hair and turned, looking for a blanket. "When I was bathing, you see, a couple of men saw me and, well... I suppose they thought they'd come in and have their way... I don't think it'll be long before someone finds them."

"*Finds* them?"

Arianna turned to Neythan. She saw the look on his face. "Why always so dark-minded, Neythan? They're just... sleeping. I expect they'll wake by the morning. It's just I hadn't the energy to hide them very well. I've eaten no more than half a loaf and a few berries in three days. We need to do something about that, by the way."

Caleb shook his head, smiling. He glanced across the fire at Neythan. "You know, she's growing on me, I think."

"That's because you've already had a chance to wash."

Arianna shrugged and grimaced in commiseration. "Sorry?"

Neythan sighed. "Where are they?"

"Amongst the reeds by the water."

"Come, then. It's too dark for us to journey on anywhere else, and we need the rest besides. We'll hide the men together. And then set up camp elsewhere along the wadi."

"But I've only just got dry."

"*Come*, Ari."

Arianna sighed and looked at Caleb. "Have *you* put him in this mood?"

Caleb, still amused, brandished his palms in disavowal.

"*Arianna.*"

"Fine, fine. I'm coming."

Thirty-Six
DUMEAN

"Yasmin… maybe… perhaps it is best to let this thing lie, yes?"

"I'm just asking questions."

The old man, Yaram, just smiled and nodded, but there was no humour there. He glanced to the side, beyond the woollen blanket shelter where he and Yasmin were sat eating bean rice with their fingers from a shared dish, and watched two boys squatting by a stall in the sun. Their backs were turned to him, drawing on the ground together as the bazaar hummed around them.

"Zaqeem was a complicated man," Yaram said. "More than you know. He had friends, strange ones, in low places *and* high places… These questions you ask, were you to find those able to answer, you may also find them sharing what they've been asked, and who asked them, with others… you understand."

Yasmin wasn't sure she did. She wasn't sure she understood any of it. She and Hassan had argued again. *A mistake to go to Súnam,* he'd said, *a mistake to involve you in any of it.* All the while refusing to tell her what *it* actually was. Who were this "Fellowship of Truths" Zaqeem had apparently belonged to? Who *was* this brother she'd never known? And so she'd left Dumea that night by boatman, coming east along the River Crescent and then the Swift, halfway across the Sovereignty to arrive here, in Hanesda, to speak with the uncle who'd fostered Zaqeem as a boy and mentored him as a man.

Yaram scratched the side of his forehead beneath his turban. "Even now, I can still remember when Zaqeem was that age," he said, nodding at the boys in the street. "Always with a pen and tablet in his hands, always at study."

"My son, Noah, does not share the habit," Yasmin said.

"He doesn't? Well. You should bring him here. It will do him good. It's hard to set your hand to the plough when you've never known harvest. You should show him the city, the school, the sovereign courts, and leave off from these questions of yours. Nothing good will come of them. Not to you or anyone else."

"You already know I can't do that," Yasmin said. "You know why."

Yaram scratched at his beard and made a low displeased sound in his throat.

"If you could at least tell me who I might speak to about Zaqeem," she said. "Who in this city knew him. His habits. His ways."

"His habits and his ways... There are a great many habits of his you'd do well to never learn of, child. Your memories of him are few, I know that. Do not sully them."

"What do you mean?"

Yaram's pale eyes slid once more toward the boys. Apparently they weren't drawing on the ground, after all. A hawk lay dead between them, piled flesh, beak and bones, battered dusty feathers and wings sticking out at odd angles. The boys were poking at it with sticks. "What if I were to tell you that those who knew him best were gamblers, vagabonds and wastrels? What if I were to say to seek Zaqeem's ways is to seek the underside of a pretty rock, or the innards of a whitewashed tomb? All goodness and light without, decay and rot within."

Yasmin just looked across the table at the old man. Zaqeem

was dead. Tobiath had been missing for two months and it was becoming increasingly apparent that Hassan was hiding things from her, and had perhaps been doing so for some time. "I need to know the truth," she said.

Yaram sighed and looked back to the bazaar. "Will you not heed a man in his old age, Yasmin?"

"I can, and I do, uncle. But he was my brother. I need to know."

Yaram repeated his unhappy growl. He watched the bazaar, watched the wind ruffling the dead bird's feathers on the ground whilst the boys continued to prod. He sighed heavily.

"There are two I know of," he finally said. "They may provide a beginning... one in the clay street, by the pool near the watergate. His name is Barat. But you will need to be careful of him. Not a wholesome man. I was forced to have dealings with him when making guarantee for Zaqeem's debts. If you must meet him then do not do so alone."

Yasmin nodded.

Yaram looked at her to see she understood, then back to the bazaar.

"The second, she is an innkeeper. Rona, she is called. A Tresánite. She is on the straight street by the markets. Zaqeem stayed there most often when he came to the city. She will know what his comings and goings were."

Yasmin bowed her head. "Thank you, uncle. I owe you."

"No... The debt is mine for having told you, debt to your fathers." The old man stared hard at the dead hawk on the ground; he could see the shape of its eyeless skull. From this angle it seemed as though it was looking at him. He looked at Yasmin. "And you will pray to them for me, that they may forgive this debt of mine. If they can."

She went after sundown, quickstepping with Mulaam, the servant she'd had bring her here, through the narrow streets surrounding the market. There were people everywhere despite the hour, stallkeepers packing up their tables and wares and carrying them away in sacks. A shepherd went with an oil lamp, leading three ewes down the narrow road on one side and shielding the lamp with a curled hand like some precious jewel. Opposite, an old man tapped a feeble rhythm on his drum, croaking out an old and obscure song for coins from passersby whilst others leant against the walls, sipping from mugs of sourwine with bloodshot eyes. Yasmin and Mulaam hurried their way through with the hoods of their cloaks up over their heads, trying to avoid the passing glances of others on the street. With every step Yasmin found herself wondering if Zaqeem had walked here before them. Had he come by night? Did the dark narrow road with its departing vendors feel as fraught to him as it now did to her?

They reached the end of the road and turned into the alley Yaram had told her about. They found the door just where he said it would be, and then knocked and waited.

A woman opened, looked Yasmin up and down, and then glanced at Mulaam. "You are strangers," she said. "There are other inns by the market road."

"I was told this one is best," Yasmin said.

The woman acknowledged that with silence. She stared at Yasmin for a few moments, and then up at Mulaam, and then shut the door. Yasmin looked at Mulaam. They stood there in the alley. Yasmin was about to knock again when the door reopened. The woman's arm thrust through the gap, brandishing a purse. She held it out to Yasmin in her palm.

"I'll give no more to beggars or thieves," she said. "I've patrons I'd not have you disturb, but if you force me, I will. There's plenty a man in here."

It took Yasmin a moment to make sense of what the woman was saying. "Oh. No, no. That's not why we're here." But when she stepped forward to explain, the woman moved back. Yasmin decided to do the same, give her space, let her see they were no threat. The woman was small. Her face was narrow and hungry, a certain hardiness to her; as angry as she was afraid. "It's true we're not seeking a room," Yasmin said. She looked at the purse still clutched in the woman's hand. "But neither are we after your money."

"Then what do you want?"

"You are Rona?"

The woman's eyes narrowed. "What do you want?"

"I need your help."

Rona relaxed a little. "You've not the look of one in need of my help."

"We came to ask about a man you perhaps once knew," Yasmin said. "He came here often, I think. His name was Zaqeem?"

The woman's wariness returned. "You've no business here with me," she said. "And I've none with you. You find some other to trouble. Some other."

"I just need some answers."

"I've no answers for you."

"A question or two, and then we'll leave."

"Leave now."

"I will not," Yasmin spoke quietly. "I cannot. Not until you answer our questions." She glanced at Mulaam, who then reached into his cloak to fish out the purse. He bounced the small parcel of cloth in his palm. The silver jangled inside. "We will not be ungrateful for your help," Yasmin said.

The woman's eyes fixed on the parcel. It was a large purse. Mulaam pulled the drawstring and opened it. The silver inside glittered dully in the moonlight. "Just questions," she said.

Mulaam stepped forward and handed her the purse.

"Only questions," Yasmin said.

The woman took it quickly and opened it further to examine the contents.

Mulaam conjured a second purse from his pocket and jiggled it in his palm as he had the first.

"Should your answers prove helpful," Yasmin explained.

The woman looked at the second purse and then again at the one in her hand. "Alright," she said. "But this big one," she jutted a finger in Mulaam's direction. "He waits here."

The woman let Yasmin in and led her through a second doorway, and then down into a narrow passage flanked with string-draped doorways on either side. Yasmin could hear the lulled heavy breaths of others behind each one, and in some the muffled murmur of voices. The small chamber Rona eventually brought her to closed with a wooden door. The woman lit a lamp and gestured for her to step all the way in.

"Just sit over there," she said, pointing at a short upended stool between two tall clay pots and what looked like half a ladder tipped over.

Yasmin went over and righted the stool, brushing off the dust to sit. The woman locked the door and stood in the other corner. She turned and looked at Yasmin like what she was – a problem.

"I don't want trouble," she said.

"Why should there be any trouble?"

"I..." She took a deep breath. "What are you to Zaqeem anyway?"

"I want you to tell me why you'd think there'd be any trouble."

"You know why."

"No, I do not. I *wish* to know."

The woman smiled bitterly. "No. If you don't know, if you truly don't, then you shouldn't wish to."

"Why not?"

"Because there's no good from it. Once you know a thing, you can't unknow it. That's the way it is for everyone. I'll give you back your silver if you like, or maybe I'd ask to keep just a bit of it, for letting you in and all. But I'll tell you, what would be best is to keep from knowing any of it."

"I'm not here for what is best," Yasmin said. "I'm here to know the truth. Tell me what trouble you fear."

"What I fear?" The woman smiled again. "You think I don't know he's dead, what happened to him?"

"They say it was done by bandits."

The woman laughed then. She placed her hand to her forehead. "You'd not be here if you believed that."

"No, I wouldn't. So why don't you tell me how he *did* die?"

"I don't know how he died. I just know how he didn't. I know it wasn't the way it's said it was. It wasn't bandits."

"How do you know?"

"How can I not? He had debts... He had... He was a man of appetites, Zaqeem was. A nice man. A charmer. But he had appetites he never saw to taming."

"He gambled?"

"Oh, yes. He gambled plenty, and drank, and any and everything else a man with means might do. He'd be here every second month it seemed like. Especially around the new moon, or harvest. Whenever there were going to be men and women making merry, Zaqeem would be there and not shy about it."

"You knew him well?"

The woman shrugged, sadly. "Some. Never as well as I'd have liked. He came to me only sometimes, when he was drunk mostly, but even then he'd know how to charm, how to make you smile. And me, I... well..." she gestured feebly at the small cluttered space around them. "He was like summer to me, when he chose to be. So I'd never refuse him. Though I knew there'd be nothing to come of it. Zaqeem had many women. That was his problem."

"Was it?"

"Well, let's just say he wasn't picky about who they

belonged to, a husband, say. Sooner or later he was always going to come upon an angry husband."

"So Zaqeem had enemies, then."

"Oh. Zaqeem had as many enemies as he did friends, and of all kinds and for all kinds of reasons. I always feared over that for him. He wasn't a bad man. Just… he wasn't a wise one either. But that's not what I meant. What I meant was Zaqeem was never shy about what women he'd court, their station and so on."

"And he would bring these women here?"

"Sometimes. He didn't mean anything by it. Like I say, I don't think he really remembered those times when he came to me alone. He was drunk mostly on those times. So it's not like he was meaning anything by bringing them here. It was just his habit. And he knew I'd not tell. I wasn't like how I'm being now."

"Your not telling can neither help nor harm him now, Rona."

The sound of her name seemed to jolt her. She glanced up at Yasmin. "No… I don't suppose it can." She stepped in from the corner. Her face straightened abruptly, tautened, as though all the feeling and sadness of before had been wilfully pressed from it. "There's something I will tell you. Something I should tell you since we're speaking this way. My mothers and fathers forgive me for saying it. But should I not say, it would be the greater sin."

"What is it?"

Again she licked her lips. "Some of the women, when he brought them, I'd know their faces. Only sometimes. Rarely, really. Just one or two. I've an eye for faces, you see. They'd come in hoods and all what else but I'd still know them. There was one, when I looked I knew who she was straight away. Took all my strength to keep from showing that I knew her."

"Why? Who was she?"

"She..." The woman's lips quivered. She leaned forward and whispered. "I know what you see sometimes, it can't be certain. I know that. But if who I saw wasn't her it was the very likeness of her. A good likeness."

"Who?"

"I saw the sovereign queen mother," Rona said. "Chalise of Caphás... I saw the sharífa."

Thirty-Seven
HUNTER

Neythan blew on his broth. He puffed the steam from the lip of the wooden cup as he sat watching Caleb haggle with the gypsies from across the bonfire. It was close to midnight. They'd arrived here from the rivertowns along the Swift only an hour before. The town had been lively and busy as noon and remained so even now; local custom; people lingering around a blazing pyre into the small hours, eating and drinking to the sound of strings in the light and warmth cast by the flames.

Neythan turned to watch a troupe of older women opposite, stamping and strutting to the minstrel's tune as men clapped in time to their steps. The hot ashy smell of cooking spices drifted in from behind where others were roasting goatmeat atop barrelled cookfires as they all sat, hemmed in by the housing, facing the fire at the centre of the square. It was like Hanesda at new moon, that same sly festive hum, as though all had awaited the sun's turned back before venturing out to play.

"Do you remember this song?"

He glanced at Arianna beside him. They were sitting together on a little patch of grass that lined the square's south side. Others sat similarly within view of the bonfire, chatting idly, playing games, doing chores as though it was still daytime.

She was nodding at the minstrel away to their left, a small bird-boned man with narrow wrists and nimble fingers that danced over the strings like a scrambling crab. His eyes were closed. His mouth open. Neythan could see his throat trilling like a hungry chick's as he sang.

"*...and the moon said on to the stretching sky, if you'll be my home I'll be your eye, and the sky said back on to the glowing moon, I need but one and I have the sun...*"

"Yulaan used to sing it," Arianna said. "When we were children. Remember?"

"Seems you've a better memory than me."

Arianna shrugged. "Should be no surprise. I'm better than you at most things. Always was."

"Rich words."

"True ones." She lifted a fist, began to count them off with her fingers. "I'm better than you with the sword..."

"Debatable."

"Crossbow."

"Perhaps."

"Longbow."

"Definitely not. When we began maybe, but we were children. The tale has changed a fair way since then."

"I ride faster than you."

"You're *smaller* than me."

"So you'll take the aid it grants your longbow, but not the speed it grants my horse?"

Neythan smiled, shrugged concedingly. He looked back to the bonfire. "I'm still the better cook."

"Oh, speak *truth*, Neythan."

"I am. You have forgotten those flatcakes Yulaan had you make that time? With the spiced honey? The day after Josef returned from his witnessing–"

"It was my first time at the dish."

"Daneel was sick for a week, I think. Even now I cannot

lose the taste–"

"Yet your plate was clean."

"–Like turned milk."

Arianna laughed, incredulous.

"*Salty* turned milk."

She thumped his shoulder, smiling, and then sat back.

Neythan laughed and did the same, resting his elbows on the grass as they watched the bonfire and the minstrel. The man was standing now, stomping his foot as the older women danced and flounced like peacocks, fistfuls of skirt and elbows out, ankles flashing beneath the lifted hems as dust skidded up from their steps.

"*…and when the moon came offering jewels, the sky just laughed and called him fool, I dwell on high and need no keep, no food to live or bed to sleep…*"

"You miss it?" Neythan said. "Ilysia?"

Arianna shrugged and made a wry face; half-squint, half-pout. It was to be expected. Since they were children he could scarce recall a day she'd not hint at leaving. Whenever they were beyond earshot of the others she'd prod him with her theories – *They say Tirash is full of merchants. What would it be to see the snows of the Reach? Do you think it's true what's said of the Narrow Sea?* – her thoughts always trending waywards, like bees in summer, dancing busily from one thing to the next.

"Suppose I can't say I blame you," Neythan said. "Eleven years, just a handful of days away from the mount throughout… By the time we were to be sworn I doubted I'd miss it myself."

"And have you?"

He nodded. "Took less than a week for me to think of being back there."

Arianna glanced aside, weighed him with her gaze. "No," she decided, and turned back to the bonfire. "You do not think of being back there. You think of things being back the way they were."

Old habit, her speaking that way, recognizing his mind as though it were her own. He turned toward her as she stared into the flames, the down of her cheek bronzed by the firelight.

"Were he here, Master Johann would call it the beggar's mind, you know," she said. "An ill way to think. He said as much to me once."

"Why?"

"I'd asked him – halfway through our sharím – what a girl like me might be, were I not there, in Ilysia."

Neythan grimaced a little. "Bold thing to ask."

"Yes. Well. I don't suppose I thought so at the time."

"What did he say?"

"He said there was no fruit in thinking on it. He said…" She frowned, trying to recall the words, then enunciated them precisely. "He said each owes their shape to the road that's made them, and to wish for another road is to be brother to him who wishes for death. You cannot have one without the other."

"Well… He was never one for light words."

Arianna remained silent.

Neythan turned to look at her. She was still frowning as she eyed the flames. "You dislike the saying," he said.

Sour smile, like a dinner guest before food they've no taste for. "What does it matter if I do? In the end he's right, isn't he? We are what we are. You. Me. We've spent our lives being taught to be so. When I sleep I dream of blood. When I start from sleep a blade is ready in my hand. All that I am has been shaped for but *one* purpose. I cannot make it otherwise. Neither can you. So suppose there comes a day when the Brotherhood is no more, Neythan. Suppose we are the ones who *bring* that day to pass. What will that make *us*? What will we be without the Shedaím? What *can* we be?"

Neythan thought about it, looked back across the square. Caleb and the gypsies were laughing now. Neythan laughed a little himself.

"It amuses you?" Arianna said.

Neythan just smiled and shook his head. "I was just thinking... I seem to remember one telling me not to mind those teachings; that the creeds do not make us what we are. With all that's happened... well... Let's just say I'm starting to finally think she may have had a point. So, wouldn't that be a thing, for me to sit here and give to her the counsel she once gave to me. To say the Brotherhood has not made us, and that we can be whatever we want. Who'd have ever thought that I'd be the one to speak such things, and you'd be the one to doubt them?"

Arianna turned and looked at him. That same wondering look he remembered from the Dry Lake those years ago in Ilysia. The same look she'd given him in Qadesh when he'd believed her, as though there was some needful answer he'd given, without having even known there was a question.

Neythan just looked back, watching the silence in her eyes, the amber glint of the bonfire lodged in her gaze like a still spark.

"Neythan..." she paused, leaned in. "You and I... Perhaps we..."

He saw something on the periphery, beyond her shoulder, and glanced up. A man, hooded, watching them from by the bonfire. Something about the way he was standing. Something familiar.

"Neythan?"

Neythan's gaze returned to her – lying on her flank beside him, her smile uncertain now – then back to where he'd seen the watching man. The man was no longer there, a pair of giggling girls in his place, chasing each other, rolling damp rags in their fists as they tried to swat at each other's arms.

Neythan sat up, began to search the crowd.

Arianna turned, following his gaze. "What is it? What's the matter?"

"We need to go."

"Go?"

"I can't be certain but I think I just saw–"

There was a sudden crash from behind. The dancing women started screaming. When Neythan turned, several houses along the square's south side were suddenly ablaze, dirty black smog spilling up from the windows, flames glimmering from the doorways as those inside came running out. The crowd by the cookfires was standing there, stunned, watching, then shifting restlessly, starting to panic.

Neythan was about to rise when Arianna leapt at him and drove him to the ground. He landed hard, glared up at her, then saw the arrow buried by his shoulder, the shaft still shuddering from impact as it protruded from the dirt where he'd been sitting a moment before. Arianna scrambled to her feet quickly and yanked him up. Neythan stood and turned to scan the gathering by the pyre opposite. He saw the hooded man again, standing still amid the increasingly panicked multitude on the square's north side, his copper-skinned face lit by the hue of the bonfire, the curved length of a longbow in his hand and those familiar cold sleepy eyes staring back across the clearing. At Neythan.

"Jaleem."

Arianna turned. "What?"

Neythan nodded toward the pyre. "I said it's–"

Another crash. More screams. People were beginning to swarm the clearing; an old woman scooping up a child, two men wrestling with a halter-rope as the attached mule bucked and yanked. Others knocked over barrelled cookfires as they fled, bodies bumping in confusion as the crowd rushed to escape the growing blaze.

Arrows began to streak across the sky, quarrel tips aflame, flying from every direction like tiny comets as more houses were set alight.

"What *is* this?"

A man leapt at Arianna from the crowd before Neythan could answer.

Another came at Neythan from the side, blade swinging. Neythan dodged and rode the man's momentum as he yanked free his own shortsword, then turned and slashed at the man's back as he stepped aside.

The square was filling with more of them, men, haggard and armed, spilling in from the side streets and pushing their way through the panicked mob toward Neythan and Arianna in the middle as villagers scattered and ran.

Neythan swivelled around; Arianna was at his shoulder, hacking in short, sharp arcs as another pair lunged at her from the throng.

A tall, rangy man came shoving his way toward Neythan through the crowd, pushing aside a fleeing old woman as he swung a battleaxe at Neythan's chest.

Neythan felt the bump of villagers against his back as he danced out of the way, then watched the axe-wielder come at him again, jolting to an abrupt stop as Neythan's thrust sword sank in beneath his ribs. The man doubled over and coughed blood. Neythan twisted the blade, kicked him to the ground, and then turned, ready for the next oncomer.

Arianna stood a few paces away now, bodies sprawled by her feet. She'd claimed a bow and quiver and was spraying arrows across the clearing.

Neythan looked back to the square.

Jaleem was nowhere to be seen.

More fires along the eastern banks of housing, smoke billowing across the sky like a grimy fog.

Where was Caleb?

He glanced about for the gypsies and saw nothing but scrambling bodies. He shoved a few aside and went striding toward the spot where Caleb had been haggling moments before.

A large man stepped out from the crowd ahead in light furs. Wide gut. Wider shoulders. Face smeared with soot and the whites of his eyes shining. He held a longsword low in one hand. He saw Neythan and hefted the blade, patting the edge expectantly against his ample palm.

Neythan could see Jaleem beyond him by the banks of housing to the north, standing still as the crowd's tide spilled around him.

"Jaleem!"

But the hunter said nothing, didn't seem to hear, just stared out at Neythan from across the distance, solemn and silent

Neythan glanced around.

Arianna was still rapidly loosing arrows on the attackers in the street, marching forward, firing as she went.

Neythan turned and started to run toward Jaleem.

The giant began to move into his path, gripping the longsword with both hands.

Neythan sped, then hopped, long-strided, and swung his sword from the shoulder at full-pelt, tossing it blade over hilt and watching it whirl through the air across the square and hammer, blade first, through the big man's skull, lodging with a solid thud as it split the eye socket. The man grunted and toppled slowly back like a chopped tree.

Neythan kept sprinting as he went down.

Jaleem stood ahead of him by the banks of housing, not fleeing, not moving, just watching Neythan come as he neared and then passed the bonfire and sprinted up onto the green on the other side.

He was within a ship's length, could see the blacks of Jaleem's eyes. Could see him calmly step forward, clear of the crowd, and reach into his sleeve for what Neythan assumed would be a weapon but turned out to be no more than a closed fist.

Neythan pulled his dagger free from his waist.

Jaleem swung his fist overhand, throwing something.

Neythan watched the thing through the air as he ran, saw it arc slowly overhead, over the crowd, blurred by the night, then beyond his view as his gaze lowered to fix back on this man from Ilysia who'd come and hunted him all the way since–

Everything whited out. Sound like a thunderclap. Neythan abruptly weightless, pitching rapidly forward as the ground jolted violently and swung him through the air like a dashed stone. He slammed against something hard; bounced and skidded.

He blinked. Ears ringing. Night overhead, chunks of ash floating slowly down in pale flakes like dirty snow. Acrid smell on the air. He tried to rise. Couldn't. Just lay there awhile. Tried again, rolled onto his front and pushed up onto his elbows.

The air was clogged with dust. Rubble littered the dirt. Small fires shimmered here and there through the chalky smog. Neythan saw shadows wading through it, people staggering around, then figures approaching, nearing, standing over him, bearing down.

They reached down and rolled him over.

"Neythan... Can you hear me, Neythan?"

Blurred faces, heads and chests powdered by grit. They pulled him up. Arms draped over shoulders.

"Come on, Neythan." Arianna's voice. "Let's get out of here."

Thirty-Eight
DUST

"So they weren't trying to sack the town?"

Caleb, holding the reins, shook his head. They'd left the town almost immediately, once they were sure Jaleem wasn't among the bodies that littered the square following the blast. The explosion had gusted outward from the pyre, spraying shards of splintered timber beyond the clearing and showering the green that ringed it in ashen chunks of debris. In the end it had harmed relatively few; all the bodies, bar a pair of middle-aged men in linen shifts, were marked by the bloody puncture wounds of Neythan and Arianna's shortswords, and a number of others by arrows. A mother and several children had been hit by the scatter of stone and mortar where a muralled wall, now rendered rubble, had sat by the bonfire's west side.

"All a distraction, I think," Caleb said. "There were no more than, say, twenty men. They knew they'd a better chance of getting to you in the chaos of a blazing town than coming straight for you. Probably learned that lesson the last time, when they attacked us by that well. And with the two of you being together this time, well, it seems they, or this *Jaleem* at least, were wise enough to think better of engaging you both openly."

"And you're certain Jaleem wasn't among the dead."

"He wasn't there. The pair of you had felled most of the men with him. He probably only used the blast to be certain of getting away."

Neythan and Arianna sat in the bed of the cart beneath their blankets as Caleb drove them north along the dry scrubbed plain. The moon was dim. They'd need to sleep soon, and eat. They'd already been two days in open country before arriving at the township, but with the panic of the inhabitants and Jaleem still unaccounted for it made little sense to risk staying there.

"That blast," Arianna said. "I've never seen anything like that."

"Neither have I," Caleb said. "Although I may have read of it. Years ago, in the library at Dumea. There are parchments there that speak of something like what we witnessed. The writings name it *firedust*. I hadn't thought their witness true until now."

"You've been to Dumea?"

"I've been to many places, Neythan."

"Where is this firedust found?" Arianna said.

"It isn't. It is *made*. Sulphur. Cavestone. Copperwood. Cidlewood perhaps. The mixture is uncertain. The way the method is described differs from one writing to the next, and there are many writings in Dumea, believe me. Everything from the scripts of ancient tribesmen to the writings and letters of the old priesthoods speak of it. But what they say of its properties changes with each account. I could never succeed in making the stuff. As far as I knew, no one had. In Dumea the scribes think the tales of it no more than a fiction. It would seem this Jaleem has discovered otherwise. One thing is certain; that man is no more a carpenter – as you have called him – than I am a handmaid."

"It is what he was in Ilysia," Neythan said. "What he may have been before then only the elders would know. It is like that with every villager on the mount."

"Well, let that the elders chose to send him after you shape your notion of him. Twice he has found us. Twice he has caused problems. Whatever he was – or is – at the very least he knows how to make a nuisance of himself."

"So what do we do now?" Arianna said. "If *he* has been able to find us, others will do so too."

"Maybe," Neythan said. "Maybe not. Either way it changes little. The land is wide from here to Ilysia. We'll find high ground to rest for tonight. And then continue on tomorrow. If all is well, and the mule and cartwheels hold up, we will arrive in Ilysia before the week is out."

Thirty-Nine
MAMMON

"The old comely hag was besotted with him," Barat said.

Yasmin just looked at him. Even with Yaram's counsel it had taken more than a week to find this man, seven days of bribes and whispers and winks and waiting. Yet after no more than an hour in his presence she was already beginning to regret the meeting. *Not wholesome*, Yaram had called him. The old man could barely have spoken better truth. Barat sat there, loudly chewing aromatic leaves of some kind, plucking them from the stems and branches of a clipping he held loosely in one fat meaty paw. Yasmin noticed the odd white bud along the branches but felt no inclination to ask what flower it was. Fear she'd be offered one. Fear at being here.

They were sitting in a sort of shack, wood planks and fodder scattered loosely over the top for roofing, lying abreast of brick walls roughly a man's height. The shack cornered what Yasmin assumed, from the smell, to be a garden, where Barat had plucked the strangely fragrant branch. As for where that garden was, she had no idea. She and Mulaam had met Barat's man outside the city in a grove of pomegranates. They'd been blindfolded, led away, brought here, the blindfold only removed once she'd been taken to sit in this small narrow hut. When the rag over her eyes lifted, Yasmin found herself sitting opposite the bare-chested, shaven-headed, pot-bellied

Barat with Mulaam nowhere to be seen. Barat smilingly went on to introduce himself, counselled her not to be concerned with Mulaam's whereabouts, he was safe, he was fine, mere precautions, and then commenced answering her questions.

Yasmin watched as the man leant forward, letting his broad, hairy stomach hang between his thighs as he eyed her and smirked, half-smile, half-sneer, making the row of gold earrings in his chubby left lobe tip and jingle. His voice was a low, gentle growl. His sweaty lips sifted through a thick black beard as he spoke.

"Zaqeem was besotted with her too," he continued. "You try to warn a man in these things, but once he's heat in his loins there's no sense in him. Might as well reason with a bear over meat."

Yasmin tried not to let her revulsion show. "And you are sure it was her?" she said.

"Sure as the silver Zaqeem paid me to keep it secret. I saw her with my own two eyes. It is as I've said, the sovereign queen is a comely one. And I seldom forget a comely face."

The man sat back again, rubbed the bullish red girth of his neck and let his back rest with a gentle slap against the wall behind.

Yasmin cleared her throat and tried not to fidget. Her hand was trembling. They'd taken her purse already when they came upon them in the grove, pulling the wool rag over her eyes from behind before manhandling her all the way here.

She swallowed. Her throat was dry. She decided against asking for water. "How was it arranged?" she said instead.

"Zaqeem would bring the silver to my man. I'd set a place for them, different each time. I've many houses in the city, and many friends whose house I might borrow, sometimes by favour," he smiled. "Other times by force. After the place was set I'd bring her to it, then send word to him of where to go."

"Bring her to it?" Yasmin said. "How?"

"Ah, Dumean..." That was the other thing that made Yasmin nervous. It was rare for men this far east to know the accent, most here seldom travelled west of the Yellow River. That Barat evidently had, and had taken to nonchalantly addressing Yasmin accordingly, only served to discomfort her further. Which, from what Yasmin could tell, seemed to be precisely Barat's aim. "I told you at the start," he said. "Some questions I answer for silver, others for gold."

Yasmin swallowed dryly. She could almost feel the heat of the other man the shack was so small. "Perhaps you can tell me how long it went on for then," she said. "How it began?"

"Agh." Barat slapped his ample stomach and tossed a palm at the air; a Haránite gesture. "How it began? Who can tell? Zaqeem was given to banquets. His tastes always ran richer than his pockets. The best wine, the best food, the best dancing and music and all else. He often found himself in company humbler souls such as you or I never would. It was part of his charm. Some days I'd be tempted to cancel a debt of his here or there, just to hear another tale of his doings. I never did though – cancel a debt that is, I'm not that way minded – but if I was, Zaqeem would've been the one to draw it from me." The man smiled again, plucked another leaf from the stem and tossed it into his mouth and crunched.

"What of how long?"

"Hah. How long? Listen, he came to me when he'd found no other way around it, when he'd begun to feel the danger of his doings. He may have been at it a year or more before then for all I know. All I can say was I helped him this way for a year myself."

"A *year*? That long?"

Barat looked at Yasmin; it could almost have been pity if not for the grin. "Yes, Dumean. That long."

Yasmin breathed in the truths, forcing them down like bitterleaf. Bilyana's words together with Barat's not only placed the sovereign queen in Zaqeem's lap, it made her the most likely means by which he came upon his secret – a banished heir still living, and an ineligible one on the throne. It was enough to split the Sovereignty. So why would the sharífa have told Zaqeem? Why risk war? Stray words born of fondness? Or was there some other reason? "You say he began to feel the danger of his doings…"

Barat shrugged, tipped his big hairless skull and grimaced, cracking a bone in his neck. "Zaqeem was a reckless sort," he said. "Like me. But just because the moth likes the light of the flame does not mean he cannot feel its heat. That last week I could tell he felt it. It's why I set them a place away from here. Zaqeem insisted. Said people were following him. If any other man had told me that I'd have slit his throat ear to ear where he stood. The kinds of people who talk of being followed, they're either careless or sullied. Neither one is good for business. But like I said, I liked Zaqeem. He was the kind to bring out my forgiving side. And so I set him a place far away from here, just north of the Havilah." Barat took another leaf from the branch and folded it into his mouth. "It saddens me now, but then what choice did I have. The offer was good, a lot of gold. A man has to do what is best for himself."

"How much did he pay you?" Yasmin asked.

"No, Dumean, it was a she. Comely also."

"I don't understand. You said Zaqeem was the one who–"

"Listen to me, Dumean. There would be a banquet in the township where I sent him, a rich banquet. They have many in the townships there, by the Crescent. And so Zaqeem would be there too, at the banquet, and then leave to meet the sharífa in the place I set for him. But there would be no sharífa… Zaqeem would meet those who'd been sent for him instead."

"Sent? I don't understand what–"

"Too much gold you see, Dumean. A man like me, I must do what is best for myself. It saddens me, yes. Just like us, here, today. This saddens me too. But as I have said, a man must look to himself and his own."

It was then the men came in. They were not Barat's men. They wore the pale tunics and tan sashes of the cityguard. They pulled Yasmin to her feet roughly, yanking her up by the arms.

"I am sorry, Dumean," Barat said. But when Yasmin, being hauled from the shack by the armpits, turned to look back, Barat was smiling.

An hour later Yasmin was sitting in what felt like a small wicker chair in a corner chamber, underground somewhere, listening to the shuffled scrape of leather on stone behind her as unknown footsteps made their way down a stairway to where she sat, bound and alone. Again her eyes had been covered, a sack this time, tossed over her head as they dragged her, toes scraping, from Barat's presence to wherever she now was. The fabric was rough and tickled her nose, itching her nostrils. She kept wanting to sneeze.

"You're a curious one, aren't you?"

A man's voice, quiet and smooth. Very calm. Yasmin didn't recognize it.

"Yes, you are very curious, asking questions wherever you go. Many questions... But tell me, what is it you seek?"

"Who are you?"

"Me? No more than an onlooker. Curious, like you."

"The men who brought me here were soldiers of the cityguard. You are of the royal house."

"Am I? Well, if you say so. But then I am not the one sitting bound and masked. And I am not the mother to a young son who has come to a strange city to ask dangerous questions. And so, unlike you, who I am does not carry consequence..."

He is a handsome boy by the way, your son, I mean. Noah, isn't it? Isn't that his name?"

"You would harm a child?"

"Harm? Who spoke of harm? I merely make conversation and now you say such things. But then again, perhaps it is not so strange. It's said the heart of the guilty can weigh heavily; it can make one given to skittishness. Perhaps this is what ails you – guilt. But fear not. Confession is good for the soul. You ought to think of me as your remedy."

"*Remedy*? *Confession*? I am–"

Yasmin felt the fist strike her jaw and ear hard. The left side of her face exploded with numbness, then pain, her left ear ringing.

"Now that was rude, wasn't it? A little out of turn, speaking to me that way. Raised voice and so forth. You're a guest here, after all. I understand you are distressed but it doesn't do to insult your host now, does it?"

Yasmin almost choked on the shock. She could feel the pain blossoming across her face. "A guest? Your men dragged me here. I am a prisoner."

This time she was struck in the mouth. The blow hammered square on her lips and just below her nose. She could feel her face beginning to bruise and blood leaking along the inside of her lips and gums. Her tongue stung.

"And now you insult my hospitality too. I expected better than this. I hope you're not teaching such poor manners to your dear son."

Yasmin couldn't spit out the blood with the sack still over her head and so she swallowed it instead, coppery and sour, gulping it down along with the sob that had begun to swell in her throat. She coughed. Breathed deep. Her voice a croak. "What do you want?"

"Ah, now that is a little better. I'd have thought it impolite to ask but now you mention it there *is* something you could help me with. This Governor Zaqeem, you see, the one you are asking everyone of. What happened to him, it was a very tragic thing. You were his sister, yes?"

"Yes."

"Good, good, then you will appreciate better than most the anguish caused by the misfortune of his passing. When a loved one dies it is never an easy thing. More so when that death is premature. It compels feelings of... frustration, anger, confusion. It can all seem such a waste, yes? Especially when the departed is a soul so... *noble* as Zaqeem's was. It is only natural for his dearest to have questions. After all, what salve can ever better that of understanding? What other balm for suffering is there save an answer to that everlasting question – *why*? Far be it from me to deny the gropings of grief, I count it her unenviable prerogative to seek what comfort she can. Nonetheless... sometimes her hungry claws can grope too far, trample the healing wounds of others. Governor Zaqeem was an esteemed and well-loved man as you will know. The bringing up of these questions, well... it is unseemly, and for many, very painful. Sometimes it is the call of kindness and consideration that asks us to stay our impulses, however natural they may seem."

"You want me to stop asking questions."

"Ah, you see. I could tell you were of a generous spirit, Yasmin. Very generous. It will be my hope that your son lives long, free from harm, to learn the generosity of his mother. It would be a shame for such traits to perish in the one who has them, before she has had chance to confer them on her offspring... it would be a tragedy not unlike the one that befell good Zaqeem, wouldn't you agree?"

"I understand."

"Good. Good. I am happy. Is it not a wholesome thing when parties can come to agreement? Perhaps as a show of goodwill you will make your departure from the city by week's end. It is not that you're unwelcome, of course. It's just there are some for whom being reminded of these things has been too much to bear. I fear your continuing presence here would make them... uneasy."

"I will leave."

"Good. Very good." Yasmin flinched when she heard the man rise from his seat. "In that case I shall bid you farewell. And hope the next time we meet that we can do so in less discomforting circumstances."

Yasmin listened as he walked across the room and slowly past her toward the exit before stopping to mutter with another standing there. The man then walked up the steps from where he'd entered and through what sounded like a shackled door at the top.

They dumped her an hour later, sack on head, tossing her blindly to the hard soaked grit of a rain-drenched road. She pulled away the dull abrasive cloth, roughly puffing its hairs and threads from her nostrils and brushing them from her head to find she was in the straight street again, yards from Rona's inn, alone. No Mulaam. She climbed to her feet. There were few in the road: an old woman, with a black scarf wrapped tight to her small frail skull and blacker eyes, stared silently as Yasmin wandered through the waning late afternoon sun. Perched on the step of her house's doorway, she squinted at Yasmin as she passed, her mealy wrinkled jaw chewing. They'd dumped her here deliberately, Yasmin knew, to show how long they'd been watching her, to show they knew of her visit to Rona. Yasmin tried not to think of what might have become of her. Or might she have been the one who told them of her inquiries in the first place?

She walked through the city back to Yaram's house, hoping to find Mulaam there.

When she came in she found the old man sitting with

Noah, stooped over a scroll with a finger poised, pointing at the page. *What was the child doing here? When had he arrived?* Noah turned and stood when he saw her. The boy smiled only briefly, and then his face slackened, his eyes darting fearfully back to Yaram. Yasmin felt the swelling along her jaw and was trying to imagine how she looked and how long Noah had been here when Hassan came in from the kitchen.

She saw the colour drain from her husband's face as he looked her over; her rumpled shift and cloak, dirtied elbows, sweaty brow, bloodied lip, bruised and swollen mouth. "Gods... who did this to you?"

"You're here," Yasmin said, wonderingly.

"When I realized you had left Dumea, and that you had taken Mulaam with you..." He looked about her, in search of the servant. "Who *did* this to you, Yasmin?"

Yasmin saw the tears welling in her husband's eyes and choked up the sob she'd swallowed. Her shoulders heaved and shivered as he came across the room and held her. "We must..." she whispered as he squeezed her to him. "We must leave the city at once."

"*Leave*? No. Whoever has done this will pay and–"

"Hassan," Yaram said. Hassan turned to look at him. "You must listen to your wife. You must do what she asks. And you must do it quickly."

Forty
TIDINGS

"You shouldn't have spoken with her."

"I wanted to."

"This is not about what you want."

"No, Gahíd. It's about your failure to learn she was coming here."

"You should've left it to me. You're exposed now."

"Exposed?"

"She will know your *voice*, Játhon."

"So? When shall she again hear it? Even if she did, of what use would it be to her?"

"She'd know you were her interrogator."

"Good. Then my speech would be a reminder to her of our agreement and her need to keep it."

"You've no *idea*, have you?"

"Gahíd," Elias interrupted. "Let Játhon alone. What's done is done. And he's right; that he spoke with Hassan's wife is of no consequence. They will not meet again, and it wouldn't matter if they did. My concern is why *Hassan* is in the city, and why he's yet to leave."

"They will depart today by noon," Gahíd said.

"You are certain," Elias said.

"I am."

"As certain as he was Hassan would not come here in the

first place, no doubt," Játhon said. "Or that Tobiath would not be the threat he nearly became."

"Játhon!"

Játhon looked back to Elias and gestured apology. Unconvincingly.

Elias let out a long, tired breath through his nostrils then turned again to Gahíd. "You *have* been careless though, General."

"This says the man who, for how many weeks, daily set eyes on the woman the Brotherhood hunts and was none the wiser."

"Was it only I? Was not your own kind – the sharíf's bodyguard – deceived by her?"

"Only those belonging to her sharím could have known her face."

"Then what hope had I? The girl is cunning. She knew these things and used them well. That is all."

"But it's not all, is it?" Játhon cut in, turning again to Gahíd. "It was you, Gahíd, who promised they could be contained. Had we known this long would pass without their being caught we'd never have chosen this course."

"Is that so? And what course would you have chosen instead? What wonderful plan did the two of you put aside in order to come to me, begging for my help?"

"This bickering is getting us nowhere," Elias said. "The sharíf will be here soon. We need to think now. Where they are, where they will go."

"That's just it," Gahíd said. "We don't. The heretics do not matter now."

"They can hurt us, Gahíd."

"How?"

"Why do you suppose she saw fit to pose as a slave, make herself a companion to the sharíf? What does she seek?"

"Now *that*," Chalise said loudly as she strode through the

chamber's doors from across the other end of the broad throne room, "is precisely the question I've been asking myself the last few days."

The three men at the table froze. A courtier followed the sharífa in.

"You've not been waiting long, I hope," she said.

The men stood belatedly to their feet and bowed as the sharífa climbed the steps to the large bronze and ivory throne. She sat, settling her arms along the thick bone-carved rests, and looked down on them at the table. "Well?"

"No, my queen," Elias said. "We have not been waiting long. It is good to see you are well after the way the wedding was interrupted. What happened in Qadesh..."

"Need not be spoken of again here," Chalise said. "My son, as you will understand, has been somewhat distressed by the events. He'd grown to trust the girl. He has asked me to attend to the court in his stead, until he is well enough to resume."

"Of course, Sharífa."

"So. Why *am* I here? Phanuel here," Chalise turned her hand, gesturing to the courtier standing in the doorway, "said the matter was urgent."

"And it is, my queen," Elias said. "Phanuel. Bring in the general's men."

The courtier hurried out past the doorkeeper and then returned several moments later, leading Josef and Daneel into the throne room behind him. This time the doorkeeper reached out a long dark arm and stepped out, pulling the door shut behind him.

Chalise watched the two young men in as they came to stand before her. They faced the throne and then bowed – the one on the right doing so from the waist, the other from the neck only, and without dropping his gaze. Which Chalise didn't like. She glanced to Gahíd sitting at the counsellors' table behind them. The elder looked away.

"You've the look of field rats," she said to the pair.

The one on the right answered. "We rode without stop or rest from Geled, my queen. We've been near to twenty days and nights in open country."

Chalise cocked an eyebrow and looked at Phanuel. Phanuel bowed. "They refused to bathe or change their clothes until they had seen you, Sharífa."

Chalise sighed and nodded at them. "What is your name?" she said to the one who'd spoken.

"I am Josef, my queen."

"And you?" Chalise asked the other one. Their likenesses were uncannily similar. Brothers perhaps. Likely twins.

"My name is Daneel," he said. His brother beside him cleared his throat. "My queen," Daneel added.

Elias saw Chalise's jaw clench. "Tell the sharífa why you are here."

"Yes," Chalise said. "Do. Geled is a long way. What news do you bring from that good city?"

The one on the right, Josef, seemed about to answer, but hesitated. The room waited. In the end it was Daneel who spoke.

"Geled is no good city anymore," he said. "In fact, it's no city at all... my queen."

Chalise looked at him.

"The city is gone, Sharífa," Josef explained. "Destroyed."

"What do you mean, *destroyed*?"

"No less than what we've said. The walls are broken, its citadel in ruin, the buildings no more than rubble."

Chalise looked at them as though they'd just spat on her robes. She glanced at the others sitting at the counsellors' table. Their looks were sombre. Silent. She looked back to the messengers.

"You saw this yourself?"

"We stood as close to its ruins as we now do to you. We and

the others with us, Jasinda and Salidor."

"And where are they?"

"Jasinda rides to Parses to warn the citadel. Salidor stayed to search the ruins and see what might be learned of those who destroyed it."

Chalise stood. She came slowly down the steps of the throne, her eyes fixed on the messengers. "You are of the Shedaím, yes?"

"Yes, my queen," Josef answered. "We are."

"I seldom see your kind so young. Those of you who come here do so as my bodyguard. They're usually older." She stood there a moment just looking at them, and then passed by them to the counsellors' table. "Perhaps their youth swells their accounting of what they saw. Surely these tidings cannot be true?"

"They are the first to bring them," Gahíd said. "But they are true."

"How could there be no other word of this?"

"Geled is an outpost, only a few miles from the Reach. There are few villages close by. If there were no survivors, it would be possible to raid it without word reaching us."

"The general is right," Játhon added. "Before winter they receive barley and wheat from Çyriath. Farmers and merchants would be the only other way for word to be brought. There are few reasons for men to travel that way otherwise."

Chalise turned from the table and began to slowly pace the chamber. "Then the Kivites have gone too far this time. I want you to send men there, Gahíd. Destroy them, every man and boychild. I don't care how long it takes. Let them wither like a weed in the cold with none to carry on their lines. I will convene the council. Not even Fatya can deny–"

"Sharífa."

Chalise turned to find Daneel addressing her. The boy

bowed his head when he saw he had her attention, lowering his gaze this time.

"The city we saw was razed to the ground," he said. "It was nothing. No more than piles of stone and ash. Had I not seen it myself I'd think it the work of Kivites too. They are the only people nearby. But they are no more than scattered tribes. Raiders and bandits. What we witnessed was carnage. The work of an army. A *powerful* army."

"The boy is right," Gahíd said, before Chalise could answer. "The Kivites have done no more than rob. They overturn homesteads. They raid villages. They have never been able to do what has been done to this city. Josef and Daneel say the walls were *broken*, Sharífa. The citadel was destroyed."

"Then you say we are invaded?"

"Until we can know more, there is no other way to name it, my queen."

"By who? Súnam would scarcely dare it, and they are too far south to have marched an army all the way to Geled unseen."

"I agree, Sharífa. Perhaps when Salidor returns we will be better able to judge who this enemy is. Until then we must prepare, send word west and north. We will need Aryith to march on Parses to strengthen them, and Tirash will need to be fortified. Whatever army did this won't have come south of the Black Mountains yet."

"Then do it. Elias, I want you to convene the council."

"Of course, Sharífa."

"Phanuel, Játhon, you will come with me. I want word sent south to Qalqaliman and Hikramesh too. We may need them should this army prove larger than we'd like." Chalise strode quickly toward the door, the courtier hurrying behind and Játhon rising to follow, and then she stopped. She turned back and pointed at Josef and Daneel. "And someone get these two cleaned up."

The three of them departed, leaving Elias, Gahíd and the twins in the room.

Gahíd waited until the doorkeeper had closed the doors again and then beckoned to Josef and Daneel.

Elias leaned over toward the elder as the Brothers wandered across. "What are you doing, General?"

"You said it yourself, the Dumean is dangerous, and we have learned he consorts with Súnam. We lingered too long with both Zaqeem and Tobiath before doing what needed to be done. We should not make the same mistake a third time. If we are to be at war, we will no longer have the luxury of patience."

Elias hitched an eyebrow, and then nodded agreement.

Josef and Daneel came and stood before them.

"I hope your journey has not left you too weary," Gahíd said.

"It hasn't," Josef said.

"Very good... Do you remember the decree you were given at the first?"

"Yes, Elder Gahíd."

"Well. It so happens the steward of Dumea is in this city. He is to leave shortly, by noon. And so you see then how fortune smiles on us, bringing you here now, just as it is time for that decree to be fulfilled. So..." Gahid gestured to the chamberlain sitting next to him. "Elias here is going to show you where the man and those with him abide. But I want you to wait until he has left the city. You've had no time to watch him here. He will go west by the desert road to make his way back to Dumea. Few travel that way. He will be alone. It will be simpler. Follow him. Do what was to be done from the beginning. Leave none who may be with him alive. And then you will return here, to rest."

Forty-One
B L O O D

The sun was bright. The sky lay wide and cloudless. A daytime moon, a quarter full, lodged faded in the fresh spring blue like the chalky edge of a god's thumbprint.

"Good omen," Daneel said as they climbed onto their horses.

"So they say," Josef answered.

But that wasn't true. It wasn't what *they* say. It was only Mother's saying. Days like this once made him think of her. Days when the air's very stillness was busy, clogged by the salty sour smell of too much pollen and the omnipresent thrum of hustling insects. On days like this Mother would be pulverising cardamom on a flatstone by the door, the crushed pods' bitter scent kicking up off the rock as her slim tawny arms worked, forearms flexing, shoulders rowing, as she pounded and scraped, pounded and scraped, back and forth again as though to a song only she could hear.

She had always favoured him, Daneel knew. Father preferred Josef. Even now he could remember that whispering smile she'd smile that made him wonder what secret was in the offing, inviting his complicity, needing no words. She was so unlike Father.

In summer the old man would come lumbering in, heavy and breathy from the field. The wiry grey hairs of

375

his chest would be slick and black with sweat and the air around him moody and stale. He'd beckon Daneel out to the cropfields to help and learn but Daneel never liked to go – all that tall yellow grass, huge golden rods thrusting up from the dusty soil, sharp as Father's whiskers and like a forest. Daneel would plead not to go, over and over, until Mother intervened. "*He can stay with me,*" she'd say. "*He can help me cook,*" leaving Father to shake his head as he took keen, clever Josef instead.

Daneel could still remember the jokes she'd play, always with a wink in his direction; feathers under Father's nose as he slept, or flicking water on his face, or hiding his clothes. Father would wake and laugh, though not always. And less so after his fall one harvest in the field. That fall cracked and wrenched his ankle and turned his stride to a limping hobble that never went away. That limp was like a god, touching everywhere and everything, taking Father's strength, keeping him from the field, making him old, bringing them hunger.

Father never beat Mother before that limp but after a while it became a habit. And then one day he beat her so hard with a scouring pan by the stream that its narrow rocks and water turned copper red, just like when he cleaned his tools. He wept for an hour after that. Josef and Daneel watched him. And then he rose and took Mother beyond the crop fields and into the woods to bury her behind some tree he'd never tell them where. Funny how you never really believe in death until it happens. And then it's everywhere, at the edges of things, like Father's limp, waiting to come in.

After that, Father didn't talk about it and wouldn't let them talk about it either. Mother's gone away. Mother's sleeping. After a while he wouldn't even let them talk about *her*. A vow Josef kept but Daneel wouldn't, no matter how Father beat him. Daneel never forgave Josef for that; not speaking of her.

It was strange to think of it all now. So long ago. Before all this. Before Ilysia. And Father long since dead. But then Master Johann always said the sha is a funny thing. Like wind. You feel it, but cannot tell where it comes from, nor where it will lead.

They watched the boy climb up and into the cart and his father and mother come around from in the house with the provisions, handing them up to the child after him. The cart was hooded with dirt-coloured sheets, draped over on posts to keep the rain out. Which was good. It would make them easier to spot if there was a crowd on the road out.

In the end, there wasn't. And so they followed easily as the mother, father and child – father at the reins, mother and son in the cart – rolled along the city streets and into the main road and then eventually on along the broad peopled way toward the city gates to depart.

Daneel and Josef were several miles out from Hanesda and down the desert road before the horse and cart they were following began to speed up. Only a little. Which, they supposed, was to be expected. The road was as lonely as Gahíd had said. Hard not to notice two strangers following on the same way, especially when those strangers had been following on that same way without nearing for over an hour no matter how you slowed or stopped or whatever else. And Hassan was a smart man, Daneel and Josef knew as much from watching him all that time in Dumea. And so they knew, in the end, they would have to chase him.

They sped to a trot to match his pace. The Brothers didn't speak, didn't glance to one another, and yet both tugged the hoods of their cloaks over their heads and their scarves up to cover their mouths and faces as the hooves of their horses began to skip over the dry yellow dirt of the highway.

The land was without vegetation. The horizon was broad, birdless and silent. The land would roll on this way for another two days were they to go that far, nothing more than sloping pebbly desert riddled here and there with briars, weeds and scorpions and only the wide but shallow muddy river running along the road beside them.

The road lurched westwards into the sun as Daneel and Josef quickened their pace, the quiet rumble of the cartwheels and the light hollow clap of hooves on rock the only sounds for miles in any direction. Broad cloud shadows crept along the dry stony hills like drifting continents. The quiet was loud, the stillness felt big. And then it began.

The cart bolted into a sprint, the horse whinnying at the snap of the father's lash. No more pretence. Daneel and Josef dug their heels and sped after it. Dust from the road tossed up around them in sandy clouds as the horses' hooves hammered the dried dirt of the highway. Ahead, the cart's wheels danced as it raced, hopping small jittery leaps over the uneven road as if the ground beneath was hot to the touch. The road sloped upwards, air rushing as they chased, yanking and clawing at their clothes and buffeting their ears. They gained quickly; the cart was driven by a single horse, strong but tiring. The road came down again, turning north, the high sun working its way to their left, moving the cart out of shadow.

Daneel could see the boy in the back, his fright-grimaced face glimpsing out through the swinging drapes as he sat hunched, clutching his mother and the cart's sidewall as the whole cart hopped and rolled from side to side. Josef rode alongside as the road narrowed, moving up to where the father, Hassan, sat at the reins as Daneel backed up the rear. Daneel saw his brother draw his feet up to squat in the saddle and steady himself. And then watched as Josef jumped, leaping across the short rushing void and landing chest first as the cart bucked.

The corner of the driver's bench slammed up against his breastbone, knocking him backward. Josef scrambled to hold on, feet and legs dangling as the rocks and dirt raced dangerously beneath his heels. The father saw and kicked him in the face, snapping Josef's head back but not dislodging him. He leaned back to try again but Josef saw it coming and swung to one side. Hassan's thrust foot pushed at empty air as Josef slipped a dagger from his waist and plunged it handle-deep into his calf.

Hassan screamed and reeled back on his seat, leaning away and pulling the horse's bit as he did so. Her jaw and brow yanked, turning her, steering her off the road and into the escarpment. Hassan tried to correct it but it was too late. Her forelegs slid, her hooves scrambling into loose rocks and shale for purchase, and then the cart wheel following after her. The carriage tipped as the mare anxiously pawed and the road slipped away beyond her, as the car's full weight toppled onto the slope toward the water, yanking her down, screaming, tumbling, into the shallow river.

Daneel came to a skidding halt at the lip of the embankment and leapt down from his horse. He scrambled down the slope to the water's lip. The cart was already sinking. Ends of upended timber lurched slowly to the muddy surface as sacks and pots and bits of bread began to bob and spread out along the river's dirty pane in the cart's wake. Daneel waited and watched and saw no other movement save the mare's impotent kicks, thrashing weakly against the sticky muddy water as she tried to right herself, the tongues of leather from the bit still pulling her down.

He began to wade in, thigh deep, working his way toward the half-submerged mess, his steps mired in the soft silty riverbed beneath as the murky cold of the marsh wrapped around him.

"Josef!"

No answer. Just the horse's whinnies and whimpers as she tried to free herself. Daneel looked back to the shore, saw no change there either, his own horse loitering above the escarpment, facing the road, tail swishing at flies, apparently disinterested. The sudden thrashing of water brought his gaze back around. Josef and the other man had surfaced a few feet from the now almost sunken cart, wrestling. Frothy suds of black greasy river rode up around them as they twisted and writhed. Daneel began to make his way toward them, wide slow strides through the watery sludge. Hassan had somehow managed to wrap something around Josef's throat and was yanking, teeth gritted, jaw clenched, as Josef twisted to pull him beneath the water again. The mother was nowhere to be seen.

It was then Daneel heard the boy, his half-infant shout. He was on the opposite shore, had somehow freed himself from the wreck and stood there soggy and slick as a seal from the black grime of the river. The father heard the boy too and began shouting.

"Run, Noah! Run! Run!"

But the boy was standing there and not running, shivering and rigid and watching his father fight in the water. Josef was beginning to get on top of him now, his hand clutching the other man's chin, his other arm locked around the man's arm from behind.

"Run... Run!"

Daneel left them to it and began to swim and wade toward the shore where the boy stood, swiping at the heavy water in long steady strokes as he dragged himself to the other end. When he reached the bank the boy was crying, his voice broken by whimpers, looking for his mother, calling to his father. Daneel looked and saw that the other man had somehow wriggled free of his brother and was wading to shore, not far behind. The boy was bouncing on the balls of his feet, arms stiff against his side, his hands tight knotted fists of white worry, staring after his father as he swam toward him. Josef was nowhere to be seen. The father was getting closer. Daneel turned back toward the boy and dragged himself out.

"Father."

"Run!"

And the boy could see him now. Daneel. Black from the river, face muddied, a dark long demon come to invade his world. Father was coming to shore, running, water sliding from his back. The child's wide gaze switched back and forth between the two as they approached. He moved toward his father. Hassan's mouth opened to call to his son, but he didn't, he stopped, frozen, jaw locked, his throat panting and clicking. And then he flinched again, his arms jutting outward in a sharp brief spasm. He took a few clumsy steps forward, eyes locked with his son's, snatching at breath that wouldn't come, the air suddenly slippery.

"Run," he whispered again.

And then collapsed, face first, into the dirt and sand, Josef's two daggers sticking out from his back.

Josef came stalking slowly out of the river behind, his hair drenched and stringy. He looked at Daneel, who'd now come to stand by the frozen, shocked dull-eyed Noah. Josef gestured to his brother, apologetic shrug.

"My feet were caught in the horse's reins," he said. "Beast nearly pulled me under. Probably would have, had the father not been distracted by the boy here."

Josef was breathing heavily. Daneel nodded. He'd now caught the boy and held him with a fistful of his tunic by the shoulder. The boy wasn't struggling. His eyes were as dead as his father, staring at the prone body, at the blood. Daneel was staring at the body too. Josef followed his gaze and looked at the fallen man; perhaps he was still breathing. He saw that he wasn't and looked back to Daneel again, puzzled. He looked at the boy. He looked at his brother.

"The mother," Josef said, "have you seen her?"

Daneel shook his head.

"Well. Finish the boy and we'll go back in and look for her together."

Daneel looked down at the child, saw the paleness around his neck and the soft wet down of his cheeks, saw the many tiny spangled spots of water pimpling his face, saw his father's fate already sinking into him, like cold venom, and whoever he'd been or would be forever leaking away, giving way to some other shadow.

"Daneel. Kill him."

And then the boy looked up at him too, expressionless, his tear-mottled face and pallid baby flesh pinched pink at the ears and nostrils. And Daneel could somehow guess at what lay behind those dark flat eyes. The boy, all of a sudden, was so familiar, so transparent, so... *known*. Like seeing himself, what he'd felt and since forgotten, all those years ago by the stream where Mother lay prone.

"What do you wait for?" Josef said, walking toward them. "Kill him."

Daneel didn't move.

Josef stopped walking and waited. He watched his brother and the boy standing there. The clouds shifted in the silence, like spectators restless in their seats, letting the sun in. Daneel saw the white-gold light sweep over Josef, turning his drenched hair and sodden leather iridescent, as though clothed with a million tiny jewels. And then the clouds closed again, like shutting doors, the transfiguration reversed. And when his brother spoke his name again Daneel felt sure.

"Dan," Josef was both smiling and frowning now. "Come on. We have our orders. Kill the boy and be done with it."

"Orders."

"Yes. Orders."

"So precious, are they? So sacred?"

Josef's breath, heavy from the river, stilled. "What's wrong, Daneel?"

"We can't kill him."

"What?"

"I said, we cannot kill him."

Josef looked at the boy as though expecting him to answer, to explain his brother's words. The boy remained mute.

"Why not?"

"It's not right."

Josef squinted. "What's that supposed to mean?"

Daneel didn't answer. He didn't move. Neither of them did. They just stood there, ten feet apart, the cloud-veiled sun at Daneel's back.

Then Josef took another step forward. "Alright. Enough now, Daneel. We are not children anymore. You don't get to play this game and do whatever suits your whim. We have what we have been decreed. That is what we have. That is what we are to do."

Daneel just shook his head. His gaze drifted aside. "You know, I never understood it until now. You always do the right thing, brother, *always*... Ilysia. Here. Home... I never knew why it bothered me so much."

"Dan."

"I could never see why it troubled me... But now I do."

"We don't have time for this. We need to find the mother. The road is unoccupied but it shan't remain so. And our horses..."

"Why do you follow the orders, Josef?"

"*What?*"

"Why do you follow them?"

"We... We are sworn to... Why are we even *talking* about this?"

"You pretend, brother."

"If we lose the horses we'll not return before nightfall."

"You pretend it is for virtue that you follow. But it is not for virtue. You don't follow because it is the right thing. You follow because you don't *know* what the right thing is. You follow because you must be told. You follow because you're lost."

"Lost?"

"Yes. Lost... I see it now."

Josef stopped scanning the water and turned square to his brother. "Dan. Listen to me. Whatever this is we can speak of later. But right now we must do as we have been bid. Now. Kill the boy."

"No."

"*Daneel.*"

"I said no."

The boy's teeth chattered, shivering as he watched them talk.

Josef took another step. "We were commanded, Dan. You cannot just... *refuse.*"

"Why not?"

"Why *not*? You swore an *oath*."

"Then I'll swear a new one."

"You... You'd be... You want to be an oathbreaker? For him? For *this*?"

"We are not going to kill him. We mustn't. I feel it."

"You *feel* it? What is wrong with you? You're speaking like... like a fool."

"Fool?" Daneel thought about that. "No. Perhaps folly is to take commands without meaning, from men we do not know?"

"Our commands are of the Brotherhood, the ones who rescued us when we were still children, when we would have been slaves. Or have you forgotten that? Have you forgotten what we swore?"

"I'm not as given to forgetfulness as you are, brother, and

I never was as given as you to oaths either. That's why I still remember our mother."

Josef flinched as Daneel said the words. He stretched and worked his jaw as though he'd been slapped. "So that's what this is about?"

"What this is about is refusing a yoke of worthless vows. But you do not see that, do you? You cannot. Just as you couldn't with Mother."

"This has nothing to do with Mother."

"Doesn't it? Did you do then as you do now? Did you reject sense for the sake of following your precious orders?"

"Hold your tongue, Dan."

"As you did for Father? Is that what I should do? Be silent, like you? Follow orders, like you? Feel nothing, like you?"

Josef drew his sword, pointing it at him.

Daneel did the same. "Ah, so you *do* feel something."

Josef remained silent. His lips clamped thin and tight.

Daneel stared at him. He looked down at the boy at his side and then back to his brother, blade still outstretched.

Josef remained silent.

"I shall tell you what *I* feel then, Josef. I feel no oath, except to my own will, and to what my own mind decides... and I decide that the boy will live." The blade nodded in his hands as he spoke. "He. Will. Live."

The cloud's shade seemed to chill the air. They stood there, each watching the other, neither speaking until Josef gave a small careful nod.

"Very well," he said coldly. "We will make a bargain, then." He lowered his blade. "I will not lift my sword against you. Not now. But if this is to be the path you choose, to take the boy, know this: you will be like Neythan and Arianna now, and they will hunt you, the Shedaím shall hunt you... and after this day, I shall hunt you too. You are my blood. And for that I do not lift my blade now. But when we meet again,

if we should meet again, you will have no such guarantee…
brother."

Daneel's lips parted to speak but didn't. He just nodded
once, and then pulled at the boy's shoulder and stepped back,
watching his brother and then turning to walk the child up
along the low bluff above the riverside. He kept walking, his
back to his brother, tugging the orphaned, blank-faced child
along by the sleeve and feeling in himself, in his every step
away from his silent watching sibling behind, something
leaking out of him, like the child had watching his father die,
something like life, something like blood.

Forty-Two
TRUTHS

It was like that time as a child when her brother, Zaqeem, held her by the arms, grinning up as he tossed her high into the air. Yasmin had felt the world within her then, its deep heavy yaw rushing up from inside, pushing through her guts and stomach and into her throat as she swung up from his arms into the fresh summer breeze and hung there, for just a moment, before the inevitable fall into his waiting arms beneath. Part of her wanted to smile at that, because she thought she'd no memories of him. She'd tried before to think of him and couldn't. But here, now, as she sank into the cold, deep black and watched the sun's glow wink down through the water, she could feel that same slip in her guts she'd felt as a child, that same taut suspense, but this time drawn out, stretched across moments into dread as the river's chill swam around her.

And so then she thought of Noah. Smart, sulky Noah. The way he'd sit beyond the city walls, lingering in the lemon light of the lowering sun with his pigeons as the air cooled and the farmers and herdsmen came in from their roams. And Hassan, buried in his books, his endless quests for lost old things in obscure places he wanted to discover and bring back to the library. And she could see it all falling away, shrinking out like the blurred watery light of the sun above her, leaving her behind, swept away by the icy current. And beneath it all the intolerable certainty that this was her fault. Because it was, wasn't it? She'd done this, brought the fear they'd felt as they were chased from the road by the two horsemen. The terror on little Noah's face. Her beautiful Noah. It was all her fault. Why hadn't she listened to old Yaram? Why hadn't she left Zaqeem's secrets in the grave? Why had she persisted in digging and digging until those dangerous questions of hers had yanked the peril from her dead brother into the lives of her husband and son?

She didn't want to die. But she knew now that she would. She could feel the air in her lungs thinning as she sank deeper into the water, a blackness crowding the edges of her vision. It was all she could do not to sob as the last bubbles slipped from her mouth. And she knew then it didn't matter what she wanted. It had never mattered. She was small, and life was big, as big and broad as the current snatching her further from the shore and down into the river's murk and algae-green gloom. The rocks ran beneath her, isles of sharp stone prodding from the riverbed. Gusts of silt kicked up from around them as though tossed by the wind. Idly, Yasmin wondered which would take her first, the air she couldn't breathe, or the jagged granite lining the riverbed, or even the throbbing wound on her head where her skull had smacked against the bed of the cart as it crashed down from the road into the river's embankment. And then after a while it didn't seem to matter. None of it mattered. Not the questions. Not Zaqeem. Nothing. So she let go, stopped fighting. Let the cold in. Let it slip into her limbs and spine. Let it fill her nostrils, her throat, her chest, pressing its weight in on her until she couldn't feel her fingers, or arms, or even the blink of her eyelids. Until she couldn't see. Until the icy darkness began to sweep over and through her and suck away everything else, leaving only the cold and...

She felt hands on her. Aggressive fingers yanking at her shoulders, pulling her up and out. And then there was a new weight to everything, and hands pressing down on her. But she felt so cold. Like she herself had become the cold. Colder even than the time Hassan had taken her north to the Reach, where Calapaar's borders met the snowcapped mountain ranges beyond the Wetlands and tipped into the barren Kivite territories. The way Hassan's ears had reddened that day, as though the blood inside was suddenly aglow. And his hands too. Those hands. There were hands on her chest now, pushing down on her in an angry hard rhythm. But it didn't matter, she could hardly feel it, as though her body was some distant thing those hands were gently thumping. She would sleep now. Just for a little while. Just to rest. Until she felt better. She could feel it coming on, that gentle tipping into welcome slumber, and she felt sure she was about to finally let go, when another distant thump hammered on her breastbone and the icy cold that had become her began to swell up from inside until it was rushing up like vomit into her throat and mouth and nostrils and…

Yasmin coughed and spluttered. Then she heaved, vomiting up water on the gravelly embankment beneath her.

She was no longer in the river. She could feel the gritty dig of shale and pebbles and the cold sodden weight of her clothes. Her mouth was salty. The vague sound of one or two others nearby, the crunch of feet on grit. She tried to open her eyes but they were stinging, like her lids had been rubbed raw. She blinked through it and opened them anyway. Sunny blue sky. A slight breeze. The noise of water.

"No, little dove. You are not dead."

Yasmin recognized the voice. She blinked again and saw its owner, squatting in front of her. That same sleek dark skin. That same cool speculative gaze, looking at Yasmin as though she was a child, despite Yasmin being her elder by at least ten years.

"What..." Yasmin coughed again. "Imaru?"

The queen of Súnam's daughter inclined her head in acknowledgment. She was dressed in the pale hooded cloak of a nomad. Two tall Súnamites stood on either side, dressed similarly in hooded garb that hung down to their ankles.

"Where am I?" The barren pebbled plain of the West Road lay on one side, all pallid dirt and shallow slopes and the odd dry weed sprouting through the rocks and stones. Behind her the slow drift of the Crescent ambled on. It began to come back to her. The road out from Hanesda. The hooded horsemen. The river.

"Hassan. Noah... Where *are they*?" She started to get up. Imaru reached out and stopped her, resting a palm on her shoulder. The look on the Súnamite's face. Yasmin's gut went cold. She felt her insides clench. "No."

"I'm sorry, Yasmin."

Abruptly Yasmin retched, but nothing would come out. Nothing left to vomit. She was empty. So empty. "No," she whispered. "No."

"Listen to me, Yasmin."

But she couldn't. Her eyes were stinging again; the tears felt like sand. Imaru let her weep for a while before speaking again, softly. So softly.

"We found Hassan by the shore on the far side." Imaru leaned in, took hold of Yasmin's other shoulder. "But the boy... We have not found him. There are tracks. We think he is alive, Yasmin. We think he can be found. We can find him together. We can help you. We want to help you."

Yasmin pushed Imaru's hands away and shuffled back. "*Help me*?" Her husband was gone. Her son was gone. She could feel the floor of herself falling away, crumbling, tipping into some horror-filled void beyond grief, beyond pain. And now this woman was talking of help. This woman who'd met her but once, and mocked her with her gaze when doing so. *Help*? "What are you even *doing here*?" Yasmin said.

Imaru seemed about to answer, but then stopped. She glanced up at the two men with her, and then to the river. The current was slower here, not like how it was a quarter mile to the west where they'd spotted her being pulled along beneath the water and then dived in to fish her out. "I'm going to show you something, Yasmin. Something you need to see... Perhaps you will understand it, perhaps you will not. But the truth is we're here because of your brother, Zaqeem... I suppose you could say he has sent us here to you."

"What are you talking about? My brother is dead."

"Yes. He is." Imaru lifted both hands to remove her hood, then reached into her cloak. She withdrew a small flute of snowcane. "Here. Take it."

"What is it?"

Imaru didn't answer.

Yasmin glanced at the guard standing behind Imaru. Dark skinned, flecks of grey salting his coarse beard. He'd been scanning the horizon but instinctively looked back at Yasmin as she watched him. He stared at her for a moment, expressionless – his eyes a strange pearlescent grey – and then turned his gaze back to the landscape behind her. Yasmin brought her attention back to Imaru and took the snowcane. It had been sealed with her brother's signet, his full name and the emblem of her father's house – the familiar image of a balanced scale beside a sun half-submerged beneath the sea's horizon. Yasmin remembered asking her father about that emblem, whether the sun was rising or setting, and how he'd jokingly give her a different answer each time she asked. She tugged the lid free from the seal and tipped the flute, patting it against her palm. A small and tightly rolled scroll slipped out.

"What is this?"

"A gift your brother hoped he'd never have to give."

Yasmin frowned and unrolled the scroll to find there were multiple pages. She began with the first.

The witness of Zaqeem son of Tishbi, governor of Qadesh, for the one he has chosen to bear it. These words written in the second year of our king.

So then, sister, we finally say goodbye. It will be strange to you. But it is the custom of those I have come to belong to. Although even if it wasn't, it would still remain something I would want to do. Perhaps that will be strange to you too. You will think such a thing could not matter to me, that I have seldom thought of you. If you think on these things at all you will perhaps even believe I left our home in anger, or mystery, or whatever story Father gave to explain my not being there. I want you to understand these things could hardly be further from the truth. What is true is I have thought of you every day, sister. And whatever lie Father may have told to have you believe otherwise has come from fear. Fear of the future. But fear also of the past. It is for this fear I was sent away. And it is because of this I have left these words for you. So that you will know the truth. Truth Father kept from you. Truth I, in the end, also kept from you. In the hope you would not need to learn it. But now you must. That you are reading this letter will mean that you must. It will mean that your safety, perhaps even your very survival, will depend on you learning these long-hidden truths.

You will have perhaps been taught that I was exiled from our family, my home, for my interest in ancient practices. And perhaps this is almost true. But I shall now ask you to ponder where this interest began. What writings might have first stirred my appetite for these forbidden traditions? Where did they come from? Where did I find them? Think, sister.

Where is it you first came upon collections of texts? Before you were a wife, or mother. Before you migrated all that way to the west and that magnificent library in Dumea. Was it not our father's scribing table? Was it not among his histories and genealogies? Was it not by that table he taught you of the tales every well-born child learns, how the things now counted common came to be? The history of the Five Lands? The Battle of the Banners? The founding of the crown city? The line of the Sovereigns?

What if among those many genealogies of his I discovered a scroll he did not intend me to see? A scroll in which our own bloodline was recorded? What if I learned there a secret? A powerful and magnificent secret, that we – you and I – are descended not merely from a line of scribes and clerics, but belong to one of the few priestly bloodlines to survive the Cull? What if our forebears carried power in their blood we've never been told of? Perhaps even great power. And what if, dear sister, I discovered that these forebears covenanted with Sharíf Karel long ago for their survival, and vowed to abstain from practicing their arts as long as his line remained? These would be curious things to learn, no? Even more so when considered in light of my other great discovery – that the sovereign line has been broken, that there is illegitimacy on the throne. Perhaps the very kind of illegitimacy to free our line from the vows that have bound it.

You will think this all fanciful, of course. But you must understand, if I were to tell you all these things it would be because they are true, and that my death has been brought about because of them. You would say, of course, it is a lie, yes? Zaqeem, so terrible, even from his grave reaches out to torment our family with his deceits. I understand, sister. I do. I can imagine what Father has said of me. And in truth, I thought these revelations a lie too. But then I wondered why Father might call us scribes, why he might cover a lie with a

lie. I was confused, and desired answers from him he proved
unwilling to give. When he forbade me to ask for them, I
became all the more desirous to know what they were. So, he
exiled me. Banished me from my home.

Afterward, I was lost, sister. For a great many years I gave
myself to wine and harlots and whatever the silver Father
had sent me away with would buy. I gained for myself a
reputation, and vices I never saw how to free myself from.
But the questions would never leave me, sister. I could not
forget them, no matter how many skins of wine I emptied,
or women I lay with. The questions would not let me rest.
So I gave myself to study, to discovering their answers. With
the same vigour and urgency with which I'd delighted my
flesh I furnished my mind. I became a learned man, a cleric,
and then, eventually, even a governor. I was respected, sister.
I was admired. Having been exiled from my father's house,
I became one of the most learned and esteemed men in the
Sovereignty. But even then the questions did not leave me.
Were these ancient arts in my blood? What were they? How
to wield them? And so I continued to seek for the answers
and in my search came to know people. A certain group of
people who could help me find the things I was looking for.
The Fellowship of Truths, they called themselves. They were
able to bring to me hidden writings on the priesthoods, scrolls
they'd obtained from catacombs and ruins. They even brought
me copies of some of the writings from your library of Hophir
in Dumea. Through these many writings I learned unnatural
skills, sister. Rudimentary, but skills nonetheless. I came to see
that what Father's genealogies had claimed lay in our blood
is no lie. But I have arrived at this discovery too late to truly
exploit it. I was too old to further my learning in these arts
as one with our blood might if they were to begin as a child.
If they were to begin, perhaps, at Noah's age. Perhaps such
a one could master the practices I could be no more than a

novice in or only read of. Perhaps such a one, if they learned
to wield such arts, could change things.

Yes, sister. I know what you are thinking. Why should
Noah be brought into all this? Shouldn't I do as Father did,
and keep it from him? Protect him from these truths? But
these thoughts are an illusion, sister. The blood cannot be
denied, it is the thing that holds what has been, what is, and
what shall be. And what shall be cannot be denied, or hidden,
any more than the sun can be hidden from the sky. Even if the
seasons hide it, or the clouds, in the end it will show itself, and
what then? Should dawn be, for Noah, a thing that comes
upon him, that he seeks to escape but cannot? Shall men
learn of him? Hunt him? As they did our forebears? And he
be unable to defend himself, because he was not taught what
and who he is? Yes. You will think that ignorance is safety, as
Father did. But there is no safety. There is only what is. I have
learned that now.

So, what lies before you is a choice, sister. But if you are
reading this, then you will know there is no choice without
consequence, and there is no consequence without change, and
there is no change without loss. But you need not fear that,
just as Noah need not fear the dawn, if he is ready for it. If he
is made *ready for it.*

Yasmin put down the page. The pages behind it were rolled
one inside the other into a scroll almost an inch thick.

"Notations." It was the man's voice. The tall, dark guard
who'd been staring at the horizon beyond Yasmin. "The sum
of Zaqeem's studies. For your son to learn from."

"You know all this." Yasmin nodded at the page in her
hand, the letter Zaqeem had written her, looking at Imaru.
"You know what is written here."

"I can guess."

"Then you are one of them, this Fellowship of Truths."

"I am."

Yasmin shook her head. She looked down again at the roll of pages. So many.

"Your son is alive, Yasmin," the man said. "We can help you find him."

"And in return?"

"You will persuade him to study the pages, and learn the practices written in them."

Yasmin laughed bitterly. She'd never been able to persuade Noah to study. That had always been Hassan's job. "I want to see my husband. You said you found him... found his..."

Imaru placed her hand on Yasmin's and, for a moment, just gazed back at her without moving, perhaps allowing Yasmin time to change her mind. When Yasmin said nothing, Imaru, eventually, nodded. "Very well." The black woman rose to her feet. "Come."

Yasmin got up and followed as Imaru led her back along the embankment of the river, against its current, to a low sharp rise that sloped down toward a narrow, pebbled shoreline. She saw him from a short distance. Prone and face down in the dirt, still wearing the deep blue tunic she'd given him last year. The only extravagant thing he owned. That he was wearing it now had been a gesture to her, she knew. They'd argued before she left Dumea. It would be his way of letting her know it didn't matter. He'd come only to bring her home. Home. The word seemed like a mockery now, a tattered ruin of something that once was, just like the lifeless sodden body of her husband, lying there as the river's tide brushed against his arm.

"You did not bury him."

"We did not know whether you would have him burned, buried or cast to the waters."

Yasmin, trembling, hugged herself as she stared down on the body. Hassan's beautiful body. It took a while for her to notice how Imaru's guard had come to stand beside her now, at her shoulder, staring down at Hassan's body with her. He removed his hood, revealing a shaven scalp.

"It is likely Noah saw it happen," he said. "He will be different now. He will know already this world is not safe."

Yasmin looked at him. The man seemed clearly older than her yet his skin was glossy and smooth, like he'd been cut from some refined slab of black marble. And something about the way he stood there, still as a mountain, blocking out the sun...

"Who are you?" Yasmin said.

The man turned slowly, fixing that implacable grey-eyed gaze on her once more. "I am Imaru's master, Yasmin. My name is Sol."

Forty-Three
FAITH

He keeps trying to make the clay set but it won't keep. The grey lumpy suds squirm around his hands, slopping through his fingers, like a toddler not wanting to be cradled.

"You're pressing too hard. You must be gentler."

It's what his father always says, or used to say, back when he was still here, his uncle too. And so he pats the muddy soft brick like dough, coaxing it to shape. It'll need more sand before it's baked, he knows. He's done this before. This is all familiar.

When he turns to stand, the salty warm air that wafts into his nostrils is familiar too. He can see that everything is the same. The same broad hammer-shaped beachhead, sprawling far below where he stands on the promontory, the peninsula pointing out from the rocky cape like an arrow. The same cool grey horizon above it, meeting with the sea where he and Uncle would fish. But his uncle isn't here. No one is here. And it seems to be speaking to him, the sea, the soapy lispy wash of its waves as they lap and crash, calling out, beckoning. Be gentler. Be gentler. And so he turns back to the bricks to obey, but they are gone. His bloodtree stands in their place, its stark barren height taller than he remembers, and there, on the lowest bough, a giant white eagle sits perched, waiting, its long black talons patiently gripping the wood, the tough wrinkly skin of its feet a pale grey, and its pure white plumage glinting in the half-light like the silvery scales of a fish, as though the feathers are hiding the moon. He has never seen the eagle before, in truth he has never seen a creature like it, but when it turns and looks at him, Neythan recognizes who it is.

"You took too long to find her," it says, the same voice that was the sea's.

"I did not know where to look."

The eagle is twice the size it ought to be. Her eyes have the same amber-gold glint as before, faintly fluorescent, like distant flame. She stands on the bough facing to the north, but with her gaze turned to him.

"Why didn't you help me?" he says. "Why didn't you help me as you helped her?"

The eagle's bony brow arches over her stare. Her hooked narrow beak looks like ivory. "I could not help you, Neythan. It is as I told you. The heart receives no more than what it desires. And you had strayed from your path. You were unclean."

Neythan pauses. "I was unclean."

"Yes."

"I don't understand."

Her gaze lowers, eyeing the ground. "Do you see the earth beneath your feet?"

Neythan looks down at the soil. Dark and silty. Cool, clean and soft between his toes.

"In a king's palace," the eagle says, "or on the breast of his garment, the same is dirt. Here, it is only soil. A thing is not unclean because of what it is. It is unclean because of where it is." Her words seem to issue with the same slow surging weight of the sea. "You were where you ought not be. Your soul had strayed. You were out of place. I could not help you. Arianna was quicker to hear, quicker to heed. You are not as she is. You refuse to see what you cannot understand." She nods behind him to the waiting coastline. "You are as a vessel that thinks it holds the sea. You believe whatever you can hold is all there is. She is not like this. This is why I could help her. I could not help you."

The eagle continues to watch the waters behind him. Neythan

turns to see too, but when he looks the sea and coastline are gone. Replaced by desert, blank and empty, stretching out toward the horizon. Neythan stares over the arid, pale ground. The eagle is standing beside him now, nearly as tall as he is, watching the cracked, barren land.

"The time is short," she says.

He can feel the ground vibrating. The dust atop it shivers. And then he can hear the sound of voices. Like the voices of men but lower. Deeper, mournful, groaning, thousands of them, swelling louder and louder and coming on from some unfathomable distance or depth too far or near to tell.

Neythan turns to the eagle.

"They are songs," she says. "Though not the songs of men. They are songs of blood. Of the blood shed by the hands of men."

The rumbling is growing. The ground is quivering like an earthquake, making it hard for Neythan to keep his balance. He lifts his arms to steady himself but beside him the eagle remains still. And then he sees the dust before them begin to lift, rising into the air in slow curlicues, like tongues of incense smoke, like limbs taking form, coming to life, all across the horizon.

"What's happening?"

They're beginning to lean toward him, reach for him, slow, swaying arms made of dust. He sees they are red, as red as blood.

"I must go now," the eagle says.

"Go? Where?"

The eagle's wings lift and stretch, their span as wide as a barn. The feathers flicker against a silent wind as she rises into the air. "They are unclean."

Neythan looks back to the desert. The mournful voices are growing louder as the dust continues to coalesce, rising up above them, a forest of slim bloody vines stretching skywards, as a shadow in the distance behind it all begins to pierce the horizon like the sun at dawn. He shouts to her.

"You must stop this."

"I cannot," she says. "Just as I could not help you." The eagle is suspended against the sky, hanging calmly as her gaze shifts to the horizon of red tendrils sprouting from the desert as the low groaning chorus continues to grow. "The songs too are unclean. They are the work of man, and they are what brings them." She looks down on him again. "Only a son of man can prevent the sins of man. That is why we call to you. There are laws between you and me."

Neythan tries to run but the ground jerks and upends him. The dust continues to rise, the shadow rolling across the sky, lengthening out from the horizon as these living red pillars reach toward him like swaying serpents, singing sad and deep as he tries to scramble away on the ground. They're trying to touch him. One lays hold of his ankle.

Neythan jolted awake in the cartbed, sweating. He could feel the slow dip and rise of the wheels beneath him as they trundled along the uneven road.

Arianna roused from beneath her blanket on the other side of the cart. She peered out drowsily. "What... What is it?"

It was early evening, the sky still brooding between day and night, like it had in his dream. Neythan stared out at the lengthening road in their wake. The shallow tracks of the wheels lined the dust along the darkening plain like snake trails.

"The Watcher," he said.

Arianna slowly sat up. "What did she say?"

But Neythan just stared at the twilit trail behind them.

"You're awake," Caleb said from the driver's seat, glancing over his shoulder. "Good. And just in time." He looked at Neythan in the cartbed and then pointed ahead.

Neythan pushed himself upright and turned. He saw it. The familiar hulking shape ahead of them, looming high and black against the dim sky, its dark peak touching the moon. Finally. They had arrived. The Mount of Ilysia.

"Good... Evil... Why be distracted by such things? They are the creations of men. As are the gods. But perhaps these are a noble fiction. All the blood men spill, for vengeance, for conquest, for power... Amongst the animals there is no need to right such acts. For them, to slay or devour is a part of life. But our nature does not allow us to think this way. For us there must be a reason. And that reason must have a name."

ARVAN THE SCRIBE, KING OF SUMERIA AND SECOND SHARÍF OF THE SOVEREIGNTY, AT THE COUNCIL OF THE FIRST LAWS

BOOK I OF *THE WRITINGS OF YOAZ SON OF ABIRAM, FIRST SCRIBE OF HANESDA, IN THE TWELFTH YEAR OF OUR KING*

Forty-Four
HOME

Neythan remembered the feather shadows of the trees as they dappled his face, caging the sun beyond gnarled boughs and greenery as his uncle bore him on the long journey north to Ilysia. He remembered how strange it felt, the journey, his mind so numb and empty, a still and quiet weightlessness to it all somehow as if captured snug in the buoyancy of a breezeless lake, being carried along without thought as the wheels of the cart shuddered over the root-knotted soil, and then later, as they passed clear of the forests and into the plains, the rubbly bumps of an open featureless terrain stretching mile after dusty mile beneath the sharp white glare of a naked sun.

But what he remembered most were the words of his uncle, his voice hoarse and thin, a taut whisper meandering over his shoulder as he sat at the reins and floating back to Neythan in the cart behind like drifting smoke. All the way there, day after day, murmuring quietly and tensely like there would be nothing more important he would ever say. He told Neythan of Ilysia and the Shedaím, and of how Neythan was born to be one of them and how Ilysia was his real home. He said the Brotherhood had dwelt there for centuries, abiding secretly in the mount and separated beyond reach of the world by its great height and its thick wooded roosts of pine, oak and rock and the welcome fact of its being so unfeasible and pointless to scale.

"That's why they chose it," Sol had said. *"The peak's so tall and difficult, unreachable to all but a few... as is the way of the Shedaím."*

He said it was there Neythan would come to truly know himself, and without going there be estranged from *ever* knowing himself and instead be lost. He said there in Ilysia he would surrender his life and will to a way that was ancient, and that men often resisted surrendering themselves in this way, because they lust for freedom, but that this lust is a deceit. He said there is no such thing as a free man and that each has his own master of one kind or another, and that a man who finds a good master comes to know rest and he who doesn't knows little, but a man with no master at all is as chaff driven by the wind and finds no rest though he thinks himself free. But no one is free. Neythan knew that now.

He sat in a trench downwind from the settlement, watching the villagers of Ilysia ready for sleep in the distance through the trees. Their quiet and tiny shadowed shapes wandered around tidying and putting out evening fires. Just like usual. Routine waits for none. Arianna sat beside him with her back to the village, leaning against the dirt wall of the trench, eyes to the sky, staring at the silver black night, the moon one-third full and the stars as multitudinous as dust, the whole thing like a deep wide sea of glittering mica above them. No clouds.

"I used to think they were eyes, you know," Arianna said quietly, as Neythan watched another extinguished flame smoulder in the distance. "Millions of eyes. Far away. All watching."

Neythan glanced first at her and then up into the tinselled blackness. "The eyes of who?"

"I don't know. The night. The gods maybe."

"There are no gods."

"You still believe that?" She said it casually, as though the idea was quaint, or mildly amusing.

Neythan thought about it, returned his gaze to the village. He thought about the Watcher. He shrugged.

"I never believed it," Arianna said. "Even before I saw the Watcher."

"Why not?"

"There's too much of everything. The sky. Thunder. The way the rain is sometimes, when the wind is up. And the sun, these stars... all of it is too much. Whenever Master Johann would tell of the old faiths and say why they were no more, I'd never see why... No one ever says where all this came from. No one explains."

"Why must it come from somewhere?"

"Everything comes from somewhere. Things don't just pop out of thin air unbidden, do they?"

Neythan shrugged.

"At Hanesda, they told me in Súnam they believe the stars are firelamps. They say the gods flung them across the heavens to mark the seasons as you or I would mark a road or field. Like boundary stones. That's what the Súnamites believe. They don't renounce the faiths there, in Súnam. Did you know that?"

Neythan nodded.

"Because I didn't. I didn't think there were any who defied the First Laws."

"Súnam does not belong to the Sovereignty, and even if it did it would be too distant to be ruled by sovereign law. A sharíf's arm can only stretch so far."

"And since when did you become so expert?"

"I met one – a Súnamite."

Arianna looked at him. "Is that so?"

"An old woman... a priestess perhaps."

"What did she tell you?"

"Not much. She didn't want me to think her a priestess."

Arianna seemed to find the thought pleasing, amusing even. She sat back again. "I think I'd like Súnam," she said. "I think I'd like to go there one day."

Neythan glanced sideways and then back to the settlement. He watched the last fire go out in the distance, saw the ashy smoke merge with the night. "There. That was the last one. We should wait an hour or more, until we can be sure they're all asleep. That way we'll walk through unseen. Who knows, perhaps the elders will be asleep too when we reach the temple."

"*If* they sleep," Arianna said, as she dropped her gaze and turned her attention to the village.

"Everyone sleeps," Neythan said.

"Just as everyone dies," Caleb added. He was sitting away from them, deeper in the trench.

Arianna looked at him, and then Neythan, nudging her chin in the little man's direction. Neythan just shook his head, *don't ask,* and continued to watch the village. Caleb had been that way the last day or so, his mood growing grumpier and more sullen the closer they drew to Ilysia. Hunger, most likely. The hardest thing about the journey here had been finding food. They'd expected to make do with whatever game could be found in the open country – hares, field rats, perhaps the odd jackal – but in the end had to feed mostly on crop scraps, swiping the not yet whitened heads of unripe wheat stalks along the fringes of fields belonging to villages they'd not risk entering in case the Shedaím kept spies there or they came, again, upon Jaleem. They ate the kernels dry mostly, raw and chewy, chomping as they walked and using what remained by day's end to roast over the fire. The one day they managed to happen upon meat was when they found a diseased ewe alone in a field. Probably left there by some hired hand to whom the flock didn't belong. They ate the meat sparingly, tugging out the healthy remaining flesh and leaving most of the carcass. Couldn't chance getting sick now. It gave them strength enough to finish the journey and make it here, at least.

And so here they now sat, less than two hundred feet downslope of Ilysia. Three weeks from Qadesh to the mount, another day to scale it and make their way to this grassy trench, squatting with empty stomachs and watching the village like waiting thieves.

They waited a while more, and then rose from the ditch and began to stalk up the shallow incline toward the settlement. The houses were no more than dreary blunt shapes against the gloom, draped by the moon's half-light. Here and there they listened for the slow murmuring sighs of sleep, cringing with every pace as they sought to pad lightly through.

The settlement was a crescent-shaped commune. Stone-cut houses and wood shacks leant against the slope and barred the way through to the Forest of Silences; a mile-deep stretch of trees and neat greenery that led up toward the mount's zenith, where the Tree of Qoh'leth and the Temple of Elders awaited. Neythan guessed it would take them about an hour to reach it. He'd seen the peak only three times, counting the swearing-in. The first time as a child, Daneel goading him into scrambling up the hill beyond his bloodtree to take a look. In the end they'd gone together, and together received a beating when Tutor Maresh found them hiding in the rushes staring at Qoh'leth's tree. They'd never seen a tree like it. They'd never seen anything so big.

The second time was the day Uncle Sol was sent away, but even then Neythan didn't see the temple, forced to wait outside the giant willow's drooping canopy as they led Sol through the curtain of boughs and sprigs to the temple within to be judged. Father gone. Mother gone. Uncle exiled. That was when Neythan first felt the shadow inside himself, that soul-deep weariness. Heavy, cold and creeping, like a kind of grief, making him want to cease everything and everyone, even himself, like that cool night when he held the blade and watched the stars and if not for Yannick would have taken the blade and...

He pushed the thought away, burying it, the way he'd been taught, the way Master Johann said he must.

They carried on through the village to the stream on the other side that marked where it ended and the Forest began. They crossed over, stepping on the wide flat stones just beneath the surface.

Neythan had always loved the Forest but he'd seldom visited by night. It was never the same at this hour. The stillness, so comforting by day, became something different, inverted somehow, cloaked by a quiet sense of menace that made him think of tombs. The tall trees blocked out the moon, casting long sepulchral shadows that marked the slope as the steep grassy rise disappeared into further darkness.

They slowed as they passed Yannick's tree. It was leafless now, the trunk gaping open with a deep wide crack down the middle and the dead boughs leaning out to either side of the wound so that the branches touched the ground. Pockets of empty bark riddled the ashy grey wood as though the whole thing were being eaten from the inside. Neythan almost slowed to a halt it was so unrecognizable. Arianna too, allowing Caleb to guess at whose it was. He lit the small claypot lamp he'd brought with him to take a closer look.

Neythan knew in another month or so the tree would be gone altogether, no more than dust and ash, feeding the soil that had once fed it. He'd seen it before. They'd all seen it before.

"The lamp will give no more than an hour of light," Caleb said as they stood looking at the dry, brittle wood. "We cannot tarry long."

They moved deeper into the forest, past Josef's familiar tall straight oak, and then Daneel's bloodtree too, which seemed different somehow, the boughs slightly wider and the leaves, where the moonlight touched, a deeper shade of red, almost crimson, bloody even, or was it just the darkness?

"So many dead," Arianna whispered.

Neythan glanced at her beside him and then around the gaping grassy slope. She was right. As many as seven or eight other trees, flourishing and strong when they were last here, now as decrepit as Yannick's, collapsing in on themselves. Dead Brothers. But by whose hand? Perhaps tonight they'd finally learn the truth. Or perhaps they'd learn nothing at all. Perhaps they'd all die here on this mountain as betrayers and heretics, their own bloodtrees crumbling into ashy hollows, just like Yannick's.

They eventually came upon Arianna's bloodtree, the tiny leaves, small as petals, hanging still against the dark and the strange ever-changing blossoms now, as they drew near with the lamp, coloured black and white, bowing from feathery branches like drooping out-held hands. Neythan had never seen the blossoms that way, alternately pale and bruised. Judging from the way Arianna continued to stare at them as they passed, neither had she.

After another quarter hour they came upon Neythan's, though it took a moment to realize it was his. The tree had doubled in height, now twice the size of a man. The size it had been in his dream. The bark was paler. The branches spread in every direction so that the tree's bloom was almost spherical, like the feathered head of a hawksbeard flower. Neythan had to duck beneath the slim, silver boughs to touch the trunk, staring at the blossoms that littered every branch as he did so. They were white mostly, but pink toward the stems, like orchids, as though only having recently grown into the colour they now were. *Each tree has its own season,*

Master Johann had said. Until now Neythan had never really believed the words. He wished he could ask Master Johann what it meant, why now, why blossoms, why that colour.

"Come, Neythan," Caleb said. "We haven't all night."

They carried on for another quarter of an hour before reaching the long, broad crest of the mountain top. The grassy slope levelled off into a wide plateau. The thick canopy of trees that had shrouded out the moonlight thinned, giving way to a large clearing not unlike a garden, filled with bushes and shrubs mostly, and pocked with the odd boulder and rock here and there. And then they saw it, waiting at the garden's centre, the dark, dominating presence of the Tree of Qoh'leth. The first bloodtree.

"The temple sits somewhere within the canopy," Neythan said.

They crouched, resting their legs from the long hike and staring at the tree, more than seven times the height of the others they'd passed. Although it was not truly a willow it was obvious why it had often been called one. Its many limbs bent under their own considerable weight, arcing out and down from its fantastic height and forking into innumerable branches and sprigs that came to rest against the ground, creating a huge dome-like canopy, just like a willow, but as wide as a cropfield. It was a wonder the thing couldn't be seen from the village below.

Caleb put out the lamp and checked the oil. "We must move quickly."

They rose from the rushes and began walking across the clearing toward the tree. The clearing was cold, naked to the sky, uncovered by the wood they'd climbed through. They reached the edge of the vast canopy. The thick wall of knotty, tangled sprigs was as dense as briars. There was no way to push through.

"Must be an opening along it somewhere," Caleb said.

"Or we could perhaps cut a way through," Arianna said.

"No. We'll make too much noise, and we don't know what's on the other side. Best to find an opening, somewhere we can look in first."

Arianna glanced both ways along the breadth of it. "Could be a long walk. It's not as if we'll be able to see anything in there anyway until you light the lamp again. Neythan, what do you think?"

Neythan grunted. "We'll walk awhile, look for an opening..." He reached into his satchel to fetch out a moondial, glad for the cloudless night, and looked at the faint angled shadow by its blade. "We'll search for no more than half an hour. If we find none after that we cut a way through. Whatever we discover or not, I'd rather we were able to leave before dawn than be here when the village wakes."

They walked toward the east around the dome's compass, away from the tree's vast shadow and toward the moon, feeling along the tangled wall of branches for an opening as they went. They found no doorway, but came upon a short and narrow hollow they could crawl and burrow through. They went in on their bellies, one by one, squirming and wriggling forward with their elbows until they'd crawled clear of the canopy into the space that waited within. Inside was pitch darkness. They waited, squatting, listening for any sounds. Eventually Caleb reached into his cloak for the lamp and nudged Neythan beside him.

"Light?" he whispered.

"Yes."

"Hold this."

Caleb brought out his flints and snapped the small stones together over the wick spout until it kindled. The light, as small as it was, was probably as good for being seen as it was seeing, but they had little choice. They turned and viewed the opening they'd come through and the grassless damp earth beneath. Beyond that they could see little else, the space extending well beyond the brink of the little flame into a wide chasm of blackness.

"One of us will need to stay here," Neythan said. "We've found no other way in or out. Whatever we discover, it's likely we'll need to leave in a hurry. We'll not want to be searching for a door when that happens."

The words hung in the silence. Arianna looked at Caleb. He looked back at her. He then looked at Neythan and saw he was staring at him too.

Caleb smiled thinly, and sighed, shaking his head. "I see."

"You're the reasonable choice," Arianna said.

"Am I? And why's that?"

"Well, because you can't–"

"You are smaller than us," Neythan interrupted. "You can wait here in the hole and remain unseen, the better to keep watch. We will go with the lamp. The temple is somewhere out there. When you see this light disappear you will know we have found it and entered. When it reappears you will see we've made our way out again. Call to us then, and we will find you, and this door, and make our escape."

"And in the meantime I just sit here?"

"There are five hours until sunrise. If you begin to see the light of day through these branches, consider us dead. Leave. Go back down the mount to the mule and cart and make your way without us."

Caleb looked them over. He made a grumbling sound in his throat and handed over the lamp. Neythan took it. Arianna held out her palm.

"The flints," she said.

Caleb reached in his pocket and gave them to her. He pointed at Neythan. "And do not speak of dying in there," he said. "You are not to die. You still have a bargain to keep. Remember?"

Neythan smiled and nodded.

Caleb's gaze lingered on him, then he shooed them away. "Go on then. Find the temple, and return with our answers."

Neythan rose and drew his shortsword. Arianna did the same, and the pair of them stalked into the blackness.

They went slowly. The ground hardened until they eventually came upon buried flagstones that turned into a path. They followed it through the dark to a clump of giant sinewy tree roots: huge webbed cords of wood snaking over and under one another and turning the path lumpy. The roots thickened as they continued further, and then reared up over stone walls. Neythan lifted the lamp. They were at the base of the huge tree's trunk, its impressive girth spreading wide in both directions and mingled with slabs of stone walling that seemed to be a part of it, as though the tree had grown out of and over a large building, now sunken, swallowed by the tree's incredible size and labyrinthine roots.

Neythan shook his head and gazed. "Of course... The tree *is* the temple."

They followed the path as it curved left along the trunk's vast breadth and came to a stop at a long and narrow opening. What looked to have once been a door was now swallowed by the pale clustered ligaments and nubs of more roots. The jambs were entirely covered. Arianna took the lamp and examined the opening, leaning in with the light to see the corridor that opened and stretched beyond it before turning to look back at Neythan.

"Well," she said. "I suppose we'd better go in."

Forty-Five
TEMPLE

The narrow walls of the short, dirty passage flickered in the lamp's dingy glow before widening into a small enclosure upheld by several pillars, each one marked with glyphs and scribbles like the ones in Neythan's scroll. He whispered this to Arianna, who glanced briefly at the writings and, finding nothing intelligible, quickly dismissed them, turning her attention to the rest of the low-ceilinged chamber.

The room was lit by a small lamp in each corner, a wickless flame on a shallow sink of sooty oil. Another two passages, narrow and unlit, lay on either side from where they'd entered.

Arianna sniffed the sweet incense-laden air and asked the obvious question. "Which way?"

Footsteps echoed from one of the tunnels before Neythan could answer. He doused the lamp. They each rushed to a pillar, standing sideways behind it with their daggers cocked. The slow, scuffed steps grew nearer. Two hooded figures robed in linen emerged from one of the passages and passed into the next, moving one behind the other, heads bowed like tired ghosts. Neythan and Arianna hid behind their pillars for several moments after they'd gone before daring to move again.

"We should follow," Arianna whispered.

"Follow? We sit in a hive seeking one hornet. I'd rather we

didn't disturb the whole nest."

"We'll have no choice over that, Neythan. We're here now, and who knows where the blind elder might be? She could've been one of the two who just passed by. We should split up."

"What?"

"Yes. I follow the pair who just passed. You search out the other passage. We'll return here to swap stories."

"I don't like it."

"There will be no liking of anything here, Neythan. We knew that before we came. But this place could be a mile wide for all we know. You saw how big the tree is. If we remain together we could be searching until dawn and there'll be more than a pair of vigil-keepers to contend with if we're still here by then."

"If we part now we've no way to find each other again."

"I'll follow them," Arianna said. "You search the other passage. If I discover anything I'll come and find you. If you do, you come find me."

"Ari…"

But she was already moving, skipping away into the other passage where the figures had disappeared.

Neythan said nothing, bit down, clenched jaw, running his tongue over his gums. Long sigh through his nostrils. *Should've brought Caleb.*

He let Arianna go and went to the tunnel opposite. He listened to make sure no others were coming before he stooped to enter. The passage was blackness. Neythan felt his way, palms gliding out ahead over the narrow walls. The tunnel's mild bend eventually became faintly visible. Light was coming in from somewhere up ahead. He continued on and came to another room far larger than the first, tall and cavernous and bathed in light by tens of tiny flame-lit wells like the ones in the first room, this time lying in long tidy rows along steps that led down from where Neythan stood to a dusty circular floor beneath. The steps compassed the entire chamber, ringing it like an arena. Each wall was graven with a giant image of a man standing and pointing with a drawn sword to the adjacent corner – to other doors, Neythan realized, each one just like the one where he stood atop the ring of steps.

The graven men were simple and bald and little more than outlines. But they were not identical. Each was marked on their outstretched arm. The symbols were like the ones on the pillars of the first chamber, like the ones in Neythan's scroll. How could that be? And then he saw it – what looked like his scroll, propped against the bottom step, wrapped in its familiar dark vellum. There was nothing else in the room.

He paused, just staring at it, and then looked at the other doors. Finally he entered, going slowly down the steps for a closer look. He reached the bottom and stepped down onto a solid timber floor. It wasn't his scroll. It was slimmer, although it was clear it had been made by the same hand as the one he'd taken from the tomb. He walked across the canvas to read what name titled it. He crouched and craned his neck. *Qoh'leth*? Again? But how could that be? He looked at the emblem beneath the name and found the same elongated jaguar that marked the coat of the scroll he'd retrieved from the tomb, but this time the emblem was set around what appeared to be an image of a small flame.

"So it is true then."

Neythan recognized the voice instantly. He turned to find Master Johann coming down the steps behind him from another doorway. He was wearing a thigh-length smock and the thin leather breastplate he'd always use when training them.

"The betrayer returns," he said. "And counts his covenant of so little worth that he even enters here, transgressing the sanctity of this temple?"

"Master."

"And yet he still calls me by that name."

Neythan bowed. "I shall always call you by that name."

Johann's descent slowed; he frowned. "But with false lips. If I were your master, you would not be here now. You'd have not broken covenant, nor turned your hand against your own."

"I did not. I can explain."

"The time for explanations," came another voice from behind, "is past."

Neythan turned again and found the old blind elder walking slowly down the steps on the other side, clothed in the same hooded linen garb Neythan and Arianna had seen worn by the earlier figures. Some sort of ceremonial clothing. Neythan wondered what ritual he'd interrupted.

"There is but one penalty for those who betray the creeds entrusted to them," the old woman said. "As you well know, Neythan. I was there when your own mouth spoke the words and swore the oath."

Johann walked along the step's long curve, around Neythan, to meet the elder. He stepped down in front of her to join him on the wooden floor in what was beginning to feel increasingly like an arena.

The woman remained on the steps behind Master Johann. The glazed whites of her eyes were as blank and unseeing as Neythan remembered, despite the deftness with which she moved.

"We were expecting you, Neythan," she said. "*Waiting* for you actually, and Arianna too. Actually, she is already being seen to. She is very strong-willed, but even strong things must break."

Neythan drew his blade.

Johann stepped forward and drew a shortsword from a sleeve on his back. "Arianna has sinned as you have,

Neythan," he said. "Did you think we would not know it, or that we would not foresee your coming here?"

"My quarrel is not with you, master." He pointed to the elder behind. "It is with *her*."

"Already you speak as a betrayer then, and cannot see it. How can your quarrel be with Elder Safit and *not* be with me? There was a time you understood these things. How did you fall so quickly from the way I set before you?"

"She is a betrayer, master. She has deceived you. She has deceived us all."

Johann was moving before the last words left Neythan's mouth. He lunged forward. Neythan braced. Their swords met in the middle.

The master feinted, thrust his blade at Neythan's gut.

Neythan smothered the blow and stepped in, grabbing a forearm, trying to hook the other man's ankle out from beneath him.

Johann knew the move, of course, and twisted instead, let Neythan's weight carry forward over his hip as he flicked a heel and slashed again with his blade, sending Neythan reeling into the lower steps on the other side.

The master sighed, turning his back as he prowled the arena. "And now you blaspheme an elder in this hallowed chamber?"

Neythan pressed a couple of fingers to his flank as he climbed to his feet. They came away bloody. "I do not blaspheme, master. You must listen to me. The decrees, our edicts, they were false. Yannick was *commanded* to kill Arianna. That was his decree. She slew him to defend herself."

"You speak ill of sacred things, Neythan."

"I speak the truth, master."

Johann turned to face him. "Then what of Qerat? Or Nassím, and Sha'id? And all the others who are slain?"

"They were not by Arianna's hand, nor by mine."

"Coincidence, then? That seven of our kin should die in the same season Yannick fell, more than has ever been lost through an entire sharím?"

"I don't know. I don't know who killed them." Neythan pointed at the blind elder with his sword. "She is the one who knows."

Johann smiled sadly then charged forward again.

Their blades clanged like smith's tools. The older man hacked down two-handed as Neythan blocked and staggered back. Lamps splashed off the step as Neythan bumped the arena's edge with his heels. Oil spilled and greased the floor.

He stepped in as Johann slipped. Grabbed an elbow and yanked.

The master shrugged it off, reversing the grip. Smacked a forearm across Neythan's jaw and followed with a kick as he stumbled back.

"The sorrows of sin belong first to the liar, Neythan."

Neythan ran his tongue around the gash in his mouth. He spat a gob of blood to the side. "I do not lie, master. I know how this seems. I'd thought the same. I pursued Arianna, thought her the guilty one until I learned the truth."

"Truth? What truth, Neythan? All I hear are half-answers and fables. If it was as you say then why did you not return here, as you were taught, and show it? It is sinners who run, Neythan. Just as it is sinners who lie."

This time Johann came in low, sliding feet first, blade swinging. Neythan leapt and flicked his heels up as Johann skidded by, landing with a roll to take him out of reach.

"Master, please. You must listen to me."

"Ah, listen. Is that what I must do? What *we* must do?" Johann gestured up to the steps. Others had now entered the chamber. Four figures, all dressed in the same ceremonial linen, and hooded, their faces shrouded from view. "Tell us, what other lies do you require us to heed here in this sacred place? What other blasphemies? I suppose you will deny that Abda, the sharíf's bodyguard, fell by your hand too?"

"We slew her only to defend ourselves. Only to escape."

"He admits to the blood of our kin," the blind elder announced to the others. "First he says he has slain none of ours, now he says he has. You see, Neythan. You barely know who you have slain and who you have not. So cheap have the lives of your fellow Brothers become. Your very mind is bent away from truth."

This time Neythan rushed forward, sprinting toward the elder. He leapt high, swinging down from overhead with his blade as the blind elder stood there waiting to be met by the savage cleave of his–

Johann came in from the side and cut him off. Their swords locked together as he came down. They staggered sideways, embracing clumsily as Johann tried for a trip. Neythan saw it coming, locked his arm instead, twisted, wrenched the sword loose. Followed up with a knee to the ribs. The other man flipped, shrugged loose and kicked out again as Neythan danced back out of reach.

"Better, Neythan," the master said, smiling wryly as he rubbed his elbow and flexed his now swordless hand. "You have not forgotten *everything*."

Neythan spat another gob of blood. His teeth and tongue were red with it. He glanced to the blind elder standing serenely on the steps. "I know it was you, Safít," he said, breathing hard. "I know you met the sharíf's chamberlain in the harlot house. I know you are not what you pretend."

But the elder was unmoved, almost sympathetic. "Your sins and madness will perish with you, Neythan, and be purged from this order. As will Arianna's."

Neythan felt at the bloody wound on his flank and watched the man who'd taught him all he knew circling opposite, measuring him like prey.

"I am not your enemy, master."

"Your uncle told me the same thing when he was exiled. I'd hoped his blood in you would not render the same rebellion. We *all* hoped, Neythan." He stopped circling and began to approach, edging carefully across the floor, hands loose and open. "You do not need to be *my* enemy. You are an enemy of the *Shedaím*. But I see now, like your uncle, you never understood these ways. A man cannot understand what he is not."

He sprang at Neythan, fists flurrying. Neythan avoided the swordless strikes with ease. He blocked with the shortsword as he leaned back, slicing Johann's forearms and cutting him off as he tried to retrieve the dropped blade.

Johann veered and ducked, stepped inside Neythan's chopping arc and stamped at his ankle, trying to take the fight to the ground. Neythan was still trying to counter when Johann leapt up head first.

Neythan's vision whited out, eyes rolling as Johann's skull smashed into his chin. He reeled, felt his legs kicked out from beneath him, blurrily saw Master Johann already in the air as he began to fall, leaping up to come down on him knee first before his back had hit the wood canvas beneath.

Neythan shifted, letting Johann's shin land on his shoulder instead of his chest as he lifted the shortsword in his other hand.

They hit the ground together and rolled. Then remained there, unmoving.

Neythan groaned. His shoulder throbbed. He eventually rolled to face Johann. He saw the blood first, seeping from where his blade had sunk deep into the other man's gut. It was already pooling. He looked at Johann's face. Saliva drooled lazily from the the old man's mouth. His black eyes fixed on him.

"Neythan…" One long wheezed breath and then he grew

still, eyes staring but no longer seeing.

Neythan stayed like that, looking into Master Johann's sad, frozen gaze, his stomach turning cold as he stared.

He heard the elder step down to the arena floor. "It seems you have done your work well," she said.

Neythan rolled away from his master's prone body and slowly lifted himself, holding his shoulder. He looked at the elder, now standing across from him on the wooden floor. He could feel a cold black rage rising through him like a song. "I've not finished my work yet."

She smiled thinly and gestured to the other four elders on the steps. They were standing in pairs. Neythan expected them to come down, join him on the floor, attack him, but they didn't. Instead he watched as one elder from each pair drew a small knife and calmly slit the throat of the elder next to them. Blood spurted from the cut elders' open necks as they gagged and gurgled. And then they fell, rolling down the steps to a dead stop at the arena's edge opposite him in a bloody heap.

And silence.

Neythan looked at the two bodies, tangled limbs soaked red, and then back to the blind woman, stunned.

"I expect you are a little surprised," she said.

Neythan said nothing.

She took a pace toward him.

The two remaining knife-wielding elders, their pale linen garments smudged and speckled with bloodspray, turned and began to ascend the steps to leave.

"I've been waiting some time for this, Neythan," the blind woman said.

Neythan began to kneel and reach to Johann's body for the sword but what came next surprised him even more than what he'd just seen. The blind old woman rushed toward him, impossibly quick. She grasped and held his arm before he could retrieve the blade. She pulled him back, slamming him to the ground, and then came down on top of him, driving her knee into his injured shoulder and pinning it there. Sharp pangs shot through the joint. She grabbed and locked his other arm as he reached up, and then shoved it down, snatching the shortsword and driving the blade hard into his hand, *through* it and into the wood canvas beneath. Neythan screamed. The blind elder stayed there, leaning over him, letting him feel her strength, her blank sightless eyes staring into his.

"Finally," she said. "We at last have a little privacy. To speak freely, without pretence."

Neythan couldn't breathe, his chest shallow, from her weight, from fear, from the pain. And then he suddenly knew, the answer he'd come all this way for was now looming over him. His words came out tight and whispered. "It was you."

The elder laughed quietly and inhaled, breathing in his scent, savouring it like perfume. "You were always my favourite, you know," she said. "How long I watched you. So keenly I watched you. It's how we chose you."

"You killed them."

"You'll have many questions, Neythan, I know. And I shall answer them. I shall. We owe you that much."

Neythan struggled and twisted, trying to free himself. She pushed him down again and pressed the heel of her palm against the pommel of the blade in his hand, leaning on it. He screamed again, louder this time, and stopped struggling. She lifted her palm but let it hover above the pommel until he became completely still. Then her face lowered to his and hung there; a cold moon of pale, papery skin, almost translucent, as though showing through to the bone beneath.

"I will explain everything, Neythan, but you must calm yourself. You must behave. There are things I must tell. Do you understand? It's important you understand. That you see what was done. Why you are here."

"I know why I am here."

She smiled. "No. You do not."

"I came here to kill you."

"You came here because I willed it."

Neythan stared up at her, panting, hate and fear like bile in his throat.

She reached down. Her cool, bony fingers took hold of his jaw and held it. "You were chosen, Neythan," she said. "Most are redeemed to this Brotherhood by payment. Most every disciple is bought from some impoverished family weighed down by too many debts, destined for slavery, under a yoke that will never lift. And so when we come, the Brotherhood, with gold and silver enough to spare them, to free them, asking to take but one child in return – the choice is easy. *Easy*, Neythan. So desperate are they, you see. And desperation is the thing. The strength of the soul. It allows us to do what would otherwise remain undone. And it is this *desperation* that is your great gift, your greatest talent."

"You know nothing about me."

But she only smiled. "How can you say that, Neythan? After everything. Of course I know you. I have always known you. I watched over you. You were not like these others who came before: the offspring of mere debt and poverty. You were an orphan, and remain so, as do those of your sharím, each of them fatherless or motherless or both. That is what makes you all so special, but none more so than you, Neythan. You were the only one to *witness* your loss, *see* them die, and though you do not remember, your sha does. The sha forgets nothing, keeps it all, uses it all, as it has with you. As I knew it would…"

Neythan wanted to struggle but didn't. Her hand continued to hover above the blade in his palm. She leaned in further, whispering now, as though conferring a secret, as though confiding. "You feel it, don't you, the loss of your parents. A deep loss within yourself, like a worm in the gut, ever hungry, never sated. It's how you've felt your entire life. It's what's made you as you are, able to do great and terrible things, to others... to yourself... that same worm, gnawing within." Her fingers crept from his jaw to his face, gripping his cheeks, pressing in hungrily. "Do you see?" she said. "Do you see your own perfect and beautiful predictability? We *knew* you would not return when Arianna slew Yannick. We knew how relentless your pursuit of her would be, how unceasing, just as with every other task given you. And so we knew you, with her, would provide the perfect distraction. And so you have."

"Distraction?"

And she smiled again. "From what is coming. From what the Watcher sought to warn you of. Yes, that's right, I know of her visitation too. I feared for you then, Neythan, when you met her. I thought you would be lost to us, but you remained true to the way we set for you. It's why we are telling you these things, telling you the truth, because we are grateful, and because you can bear it. You can hear our side. So many play at such things, you see. They pretend to want to know, to seek truth, but underneath it is a fiction. Men do not truly want truth, they reject her. She is a demand, you see, Neythan, a demand on every soul that would receive her. And that's why so few do, until they come before Death's lonely door only to find her there, loitering at his elbow, ready to tell all, ready as she has always been, awaiting a willing ear... Are you that ear, Neythan?"

Neythan just stared at her, her white birdlike skull, her quick crinkled lips, the slim silvery capillaries marking her forehead and temples. Every detail of her newly alien, looming over him like some decrepit vulture, waiting to pluck his flesh. "What do you want with me?"

"I only want for you to hear our side, Neythan. That's all. From the beginning, our side."

"I don't understand."

"Then listen to me now, Neythan. Listen to the truth that has always been. Sharíf Karel did not do away with the old faiths because he deemed them folly and lies. He did so because he knew they were true, and that their gods were true, and he wanted their power. He killed the priests so he could take their place." She pointed across the floor to the scroll still leaning by the step, the book that had first drawn him into the room. "And steal their books, learn their ways. Do you understand, Neythan? The ways of the Magi are not dead, they continued through Karel on to this very day. I know. I am one of them. I serve those old gods."

Neythan's brow hitched, refusing to believe.

"Yes, Neythan. The old gods. It is they who wrote the words on these walls, as they did the words in that scroll, and the words in *your* scroll too. Yes... we saw when you took it. We were glad when you did. It is such a precious thing, and a gift we did not expect, that you would take it from Karel's dead queen and bring it here, to us. It is why we are so grateful, why we are telling you these things."

"We?"

She grinned then. Her face contorted, shifting somehow, like it was no longer her own. "Yes..." she stretched the word, relishing it. "That's right... How else would a woman, aged as I am, be able to best you?" Her voice lowered abruptly. Like the voice of a man, or the voice of several men speaking as one. Neythan stiffened. "You cannot have believed these feeble bones, this aged flesh, to be... alone. We are here together. We have always been. It is how we watch." And Neythan could suddenly feel it, a new weight to the air, like shadow on skin, an unseen gaze. "Imagine, Neythan. Imagine what it would be for us to abide with *you*. How strong we would be together. How powerful. All you need to do is understand, see our side." The woman's knuckles were stroking him now, softly skimming his cheek, like a mother to a child. "We can show you, we can show you such beautiful things, Neythan. We can heal you, all your sorrow, all your *pain*."

And Neythan could feel the words, the strangely blurred deep voices, like the thrum of music, tugging him, *touching* him, like warm rain, like a gentle breeze, and he was drifting, as though to slumber, lifting from himself, the words becoming his own, their thoughts becoming his own and the weight of everything slipping away, his pain, his rage, his fear, his need, to some other place, to stillness.

"See our side," they said. And suddenly he could, he could feel their words and power and…

The arrow came suddenly, tearing through their throat. No. Through *her* throat, its pointed tip and shaft abruptly there, protruding from the woman's neck, and the shining, the light, everything, suddenly shrinking away. He was back to the arena floor and the old blind woman kneeling over him. But now she was thrashing, gagging, clutching at her split neck as blood sprayed.

"Neythan!"

And he was coming to, groggy, looking up.

Caleb on the steps, bow in hand.

Another arrow loosed. The blind elder fell from him, a quarrel in her back. She was screaming, twisting, jerking, voice more beast than man.

Neythan pulled the blade out from his pinned hand and rolled sluggishly to one side, tried to climb to his feet. The room lurched. Caleb was shouting something.

Neythan looked up and saw Master Johann's shortsword. He turned as Caleb loosed another arrow to the elder's chest. The old woman had been coming to her feet. She collapsed again, choking, trembling, howling.

Neythan scrambled toward the sword and took it.

Caleb fishing for more arrows.

Neythan rising.

The woman standing again. She was staggering toward him, Caleb screaming, her face all sorrow, pain, coming closer, pleading. A few paces away. Caleb was shouting but his words were blurred, just noise. The woman reached out, clutched Neythan's shoulder. She was speaking but he couldn't hear. He wanted to hear. Wanted to know that warm relief she'd shown him. And then her face, suddenly, was somehow no longer her face but something else, abruptly hollow, enraged, eyeless, shrieking, reaching for him.

Neythan recoiled and shoved the sword through her chest. The woman's spine stiffened and quaked, she staggered back, eyes rolling, and then looked at him, her eyes suddenly clear, no longer glazed blind whites but instead cloudy black irises almost socket-wide staring at him, into him, through him. And then she smiled.

"This is only the beginning," she whispered. "You are too late. We are coming."

Neythan yanked the blade from her chest and then swung full-bore at her neck. The sword went through. Her head lopped off like a snapped twig and rolled. Her body stood there, headless and still, and then finally slumped slowly sideways and collapsed to the ground.

Neythan didn't move. He just stood watching, panting, continuing to stare down at the decapitated body, waiting to feel sure she was dead.

He flinched when Caleb came up to pat his arm. They stood there together and watched the body. It didn't move.

"That's the thing with some people," Caleb said, looking down at it. "They just can't help but talk too much."

Forty-Six
HERETICS

Caleb bandaged Neythan's hand with a torn strip of cloth from his cloak as they sat on the steps. Neythan stared without expression at the still headless corpse of the elder and the crumpled body of Master Johann as Caleb worked and mopped. He couldn't get the blood to stop; it kept oozing from Neythan's hand and running down his trembling fingers, dripping from the tips.

"Where's Arianna?"

Neythan continued to stare at the dark pool puddling around Master Johann.

"Neythan."

Neythan blinked.

"Where's Arianna?"

"I don't know."

"Right... well, we'll find her."

Caleb helped Neythan up and had him lean on him as they went up the steps to the door they'd entered.

"What did the elder do to you? What was she doing?"

But Neythan didn't answer. They followed the long and dark passageway back to the first chamber and then waited there awhile, listening for others, resting. It was more than half a day since either of them had eaten. Neythan looked at his hand and held it as it continued to bleed steadily, soaking

through the loose wrapped rags and dripping on the floor. He
felt weak, groggy, drained by the elder somehow. He leaned
against the wall and forced himself to his feet.

"Come on. She went this way."

He led Caleb into the next tunnel, leaning as he went,
letting his shoulder slide and scrape along the wall to steady
himself. They passed several empty rooms; living quarters,
one that looked like a kitchen, another with nothing in it
save more scribbled markings, each one doorless and lit by
small oil wells whose quiet lights leaked out into the slim
corridor to illuminate their way.

They continued further in and slowed as they began
to hear the sound of voices up ahead, low and rhythmic.
Neythan couldn't make out the words. Too dizzy. He readied
his blade as they crept on along the tunnel to the lit doorway.
They leaned around the jamb's corner. Two figures in white
linen. They were kneeling with their backs to the door, facing
a large altar on the far side. Neythan could see Arianna lying
on a stone gurney against the wall. She was tied down at the
wrists and ankles. Her eyes were closed. The chamber was
filled by the ashy sweet scent of incense, silver-blue wreaths
of smoke hanging in languid curls, clogging the air and
making shapes like… Neythan blinked. The smog seemed to
suddenly shift, coalesce, shaping into a face, a skull, looking
at him. Then it was gone again. He glanced at Caleb to see if
he'd seen it too but he was just looking at the men. Neythan
looked back to the room. Nothing. He shook his head.

Caleb was looking up at him now, beginning to motion
instructions. He pointed at his bow and then the elder on the
left, and then at Neythan's sword and the elder on the right.

Neythan nodded agreement. He crept slowly into the
chamber, blinking through the smoke. Still woozy. The chants
grew louder, the elders' stooped hooded heads bowed and
nodded. Their hushed words seemed to be echoing around

the room, stirring the air, a thousand mad whispers tugging Neythan's attention this way and that like a band of invisible bats. He stumbled, distracted, dizzy, knocking over a pot and toppling against the wall.

The hooded men flinched and turned. They were rising to their feet quicker than Neythan could steady himself. The one furthest away slumped almost as soon as he stood as Caleb's arrow plunged through him, puncturing his chest with a thud. He slid down to the floor, blood blossoming around the wound.

The other came up snarling. Reached for Neythan, teeth bared, hands clawed. Neythan stumbled back. He let himself fall as the man came on, then shoved his blade into the oncomer's groin as they went down. The man grunted and hissed through his teeth. He grabbed at Neythan's throat, bony calloused hands squeezing around his neck and trembling with fury.

"You are cursed," the old man wheezed, his wide bloodshot eyes staring into Neythan's. "There is a shadow on your soul."

The man's head jolted as another arrow burst through his face, locking his jaw open and jutting out on the other side near his eye. His hands loosened from around Neythan's throat as he slowly sank to the floor.

Neythan climbed to his feet. He stood with hands on knees, breathing hard, then rubbed his neck. He turned at the choked spit sound of Arianna coughing. She lay half-conscious on the bed covered in sweat.

Neythan let Caleb take his sword and cut her loose, then helped pull her up from the stone gurney and walk her out of the room and back through the tunnel as she murmured and babbled and limped.

When they eventually made their way out it was still night but lighter. The dim sky was visible through the giant tree's canopy. Dawn on the way. They followed the path to

a shrouded opening out and then lumbered back down the
hill and through the Forest of Silences, stopping frequently to
rest. Although the air seemed to do them good, Arianna and
Neythan were growing increasingly weak. The sun was rising
by the time they eventually passed on through the village and
came to the trench they'd hidden in to spy on the settlement.

"You're shivering," Caleb said. "Both of you."

Neythan looked down at his hands, and then across to
Arianna. He felt hot. He was sweating. So was Arianna. She
lay on her side with her knees curled to her chest, her whole
body trembling.

"What did they do to you?"

"I don't know… We cannot stay here."

"No. We cannot. Come."

It took them until the following day to make their way
down the mountain. Neythan, weak as he was, walked with
Arianna's arm slung across his neck as he dragged her down
the craggy slopes to the mount's foot. When they finally
reached the bottom and Caleb saw the mule and cart still there
where they'd tied them, he laughed with relief. They loosed
the animal and climbed into the cartbed. Caleb snapped on
the reins and let the mule walk them into the plain. Neythan
and Arianna drank water and then slept, covered in blankets
and still shivering as Caleb drove them forward.

Neythan's sleep was fitful and bitty, filled with whispers
and a dark falling space and a vague recurring notion of
oncoming grief. Someone dying that he didn't want to die. It
was a familiar dream. He awoke thinking of Master Johann's
dead gaze but when he opened his eyes he was lying face up
in a large tabernacle with the sun pressing through the goat
hair of the tent sheets. The tabernacle was high and open on
one side. An empty sunbaked plain sat beyond his blanketed
and outstretched feet.

"Awake at last."

A woman's voice. Deep, slow, vaguely familiar. Neythan rolled his head toward the sound and found the old Súnamite woman, Filani, sitting on the ground beside him in a black baggy smock with a shawl over her head.

"I was beginning to think you'd never wake," she said. She lifted a cup of water and put it to his lips. Neythan sipped.

"Filani…"

The old woman smiled.

"Where am I?"

"We are halfway across the Salt Plains. A few days from the Gihon. We will continue south through the Havilah to Súnam. I know a way through the sands, and this way no one will follow."

Neythan just looked at her, confused. His throat felt parched and salty. His whole body ached, his head worst of all. He could feel the thud of his own heartbeat pulsing through his skull. And fatigue, extreme fatigue, trying to pull him back to sleep. He resisted.

"We found you," she explained. "We'd been looking for you a long time."

"Who is 'we'?"

"My niece and I… the one I entered the village to find the day I left you and Caleb by the well to wait. You remember?"

"Yes. I remember. We did wait… We were chased."

"Yes. We saw. It was then I was sure of who you are." Her eyes narrowed against the light breeze skipping in from the plain as she looked out to the dry dusty horizon. "I must ask you to forgive me, Neythan," she said. "There were things… things I could not tell you before, not until I was certain. It's why I sought to bring you to my niece. She is good at seeing these things."

"What things?"

"She'd be able to tell if you were what I thought you were, and who I think you are."

Neythan didn't understand. The effort of making sense of the words and everything else seemed to press in on his fatigue like added weight. He closed his eyes and let sleep roll in like a wave.

This time he dreamt of motion, the slow, buoyant yaw of an ocean over and around him, dark and hefty and vast. Dim aqueous gleams glinted about the gloom like luminous ghosts and whispered to him, just as the temple's air had seemed to, quick sibilant murmurs, words just beyond hearing. And then it came to him. He was drowning. The glints were not lights at all but eyes, staring and winking and watching him die.

He awoke with a start to find Caleb dabbing his forehead with a damp kerchief.

"Ah, welcome back to the land of the living."

Neythan felt hot but he was shivering.

Caleb swiped again at his brow with the kerchief. "You have some kind of fever," he said. "From the elder somehow, I think. It is getting better, though…" He gathered a steaming pot from behind Neythan's head. "Here."

Neythan sniffed the pot doubtfully. He felt sickly and dazed.

"You must eat," Caleb said. "You've been asleep four days."

"What?"

Caleb nodded, setting the pot down and dipping a spoon into it, stirring.

"Four days?"

"Yes. I thought you were going to die. We all did."

"What happened?"

"I rode us about a day's worth from the mount, just to put distance between us and it. I rode until I could no longer stay awake, but when I tried to wake you to take over, you wouldn't, and neither would Arianna. We were in the middle of nowhere without food and little water and neither of you would wake to take us on to shelter. I knew something was wrong but I could not stay awake. I was exhausted. So, well,

I slept. If Filani hadn't found us when she did... Here, eat."
He lifted the spoon to Neythan's lips. Neythan nibbled and
sipped. Hot. Brothy. "She came with her niece. Nyomi, she
is called. Though I had to learn that from Filani's lips. The
woman herself will hardly speak. A lesser soul would count it
rude, Neythan... here, good... Anyway, they'd been seeking
us for weeks, hunting us, ever since we parted from her at
that village. Though she will not say why. Says she'll tell *you*
only, and only when you are strong enough to hear it. But,
well, when she saw that scroll of yours... no, it's fine, it's safe.
The scroll is safe. Just eat. Here, eat... But listen, when she
saw it... you should've seen her, Neythan. Any would think
she'd happened upon a tomb of gold. And then the niece,
Nyomi, she smiles for what must be her first time since the
womb, bows to it even, the scroll I mean, and even smiles at
me, all friendly all of a sudden... That's when she insisted we
go to Súnam. That's where we're going, by the way, where
we're on our way to."

"Why?"

"She says the scroll can be read. That there are those who
know how to read it."

"Who?"

"How would I know? Mystics, probably. Like her. You've
heard the way she speaks. Could be there's a whole clan just
like her."

Neythan pushed the spoon away and tried to lift himself,
pushing himself up. He flinched when he pressed his hand to
the ground.

"You'll have to be careful with that. Nyomi redressed it
only an hour ago."

Neythan held his bandaged palm to himself. The wrappings
were thick and dry. The wound had forgotten to ache when
he woke but was now remembering. He turned and saw
Arianna lying on another bedmat beside him.

"She is fine," Caleb said. "She's recovering more quickly than you, actually."

"She has woken?"

"Yes. A few times. She is fine."

"Good... that is good."

"There's something I wanted to ask you," Caleb said. He waited for Neythan to turn back to face him. "About when we were back in the temple... when I came in... do you... *remember* any of it?"

"Any of what?"

"What the elder... Do you know what she was... *doing*, to you? What she was trying to do?"

Neythan just looked at him. His head still ached. His pulse seemed to be tapping a rhythm through his eyes.

"It was like you were... floating, you see... when I came in, I mean... above the ground."

"Floating."

"Yes." Caleb was watching him closely. "And you were speaking. You were saying whatever she said. You were each speaking the same thing at the same time. Strange words."

"What words?"

"I don't know. I've not heard words like them."

"I don't remember any of it," Neythan said.

"Did she tell you anything? Did you learn anything?"

"I learned she was the one who killed the other Brothers."

"I see... and did you learn why?"

Neythan thought about it. "She said she was Magi. Said she'd always known what I would do, and that Arianna and I were just a distraction. She told me the scroll I took from the tomb was written by gods."

"Then it is true," Filani said as she entered the tent. She hobbled in slowly, stooping a little under the awning as she passed beneath the shade and lowered onto a mat.

"What is?"

"I told you once that the world is a veil, Neythan, with secrets, things hidden, as is the sun or moon on a cloudy day. Do you remember?"

"Yes. I remember."

"My people, for centuries, have known of your kind as one does a rumour. *Many* in the Summerlands do. In Súnam we say rumours are as the vultures that circle a carcass – they are there for a reason... I suspected you to be what I now know you are the first hour I saw you, Neythan. I suspected other things of you too. Do you remember what I asked you then, after we first met?"

"You said I was troubled. You asked me why."

Filani smiled. "And do you know *why* I asked?"

"No."

"I think you do, Neythan. I think you knew even then... No man abides by fire without carrying the odour with him. So it is with unseen things, each leave an aroma, a mark that lingers. I could smell it on you, Neythan. You know of what I speak."

"The Watcher."

"Yes. Such a one *did* visit you... tell me: what did the Watcher say?"

Neythan hesitated.

"I am not your enemy, Neythan. If I was, I'd have left you to die where I found you, out on the plains baking in the sun. But instead you are here. Our paths did not cross without reason. Not then. Not now. You know this within yourself. I am here to help you."

"Why?"

"Because you are here to help us all. But only if you tell what was said."

"I cannot remember the whole of what was said. In truth, I remember little of it."

"Tell me what you *do* remember?"

"I remember... she spoke of darkness... coming darkness."

Filani's face changed. She nodded slowly. "Then its coming is sure," she said, almost to herself. She locked eyes with Neythan. "It has begun by destroying those things that would withstand it. Like your Brotherhood. And the Fellowship."

"Fellowship?"

"The Fellowship of Truths. They are an order of men and women committed to the overturning of the Sovereignty."

"You are part of this Fellowship?"

"No..." Filani, for the first time since Neythan had met her, became genuinely melancholy then. The lines on her face seemed to deepen, become drawn. "I was, many years ago," she said. "But the Fellowship is made up of many, some of them even officials on the Sovereign council, like Zaqeem son of Tishbi, the governor of Qadesh. Or Tobiath son of Abner, the chief scribe of Dumea."

Neythan took that in slowly. The names were like weights thudding on a floor. "I watched Zaqeem die by sovereign decree, and Tobiath is husband to the decree I received when I took my covenant and became a Brother."

Filani gave a single slow nod. "Then it is as I thought. They sought to use the Brotherhood to destroy both itself and the Fellowship."

"Then you know of what is coming?"

"No, Neythan. It is *you* who knows. I have seen only the shadows, you, the things that cast them. It is with *you* the Watcher visited. It is *you* who carry one of their books." She pointed at the scroll in the corner. "There are others like it, but what is written in them cannot be read by anyone."

"Then how are they read?"

"In Súnam, the priests and elders will explain everything. They will answer your questions."

"But you won't?"

"It is forbidden for me to speak to you of these things

without their consent. It is the vow I took, the law that was given me. In Súnam, you will understand."

"In Súnam…"

"That is where we must go. And will do so once Nyomi has prepared the wagon."

It was then the niece, a Súnamite, middle-aged, stepped in from around the side of the tent where she'd been working. She was much lighter than Filani, bronzed, as though of mixed blood like Neythan. She stood by the door of the tabernacle and glanced at them all before turning to address her aunt. "It is ready now," was all she said.

And with that Filani rose. "Good. Let us tarry no longer." She looked at Caleb and Neythan. "In a few weeks we will be in the Summerlands. It is there you will find your answers."

Outside, Nyomi had fixed a canopy over Caleb's cart using staffs tied with scrim, just high enough to lie beneath, a shelter for the feverish Neythan and Arianna. They climbed into the cartbed and covered themselves in the blankets beneath its shade as the others packed up the tabernacle.

An hour later they were journeying on toward the south. Nyomi and Filani resumed on camelback whilst Caleb held the reins of the cart, driving the mule as the wheels slid and sifted over the grit of the sloping plain as it stretched out beneath the hot white meridian.

Epilogue
DARKNESS

Curious thing, the night. Especially how people respond to it. The simple absence of light, and yet see how it turns the bold hesitant, the strong weak. He'd seen it a thousand times, was fascinated by it. How it would change people. For what, when all's said, is darkness? Not seeing, not knowing what's there. No more than mere uncertainty, a kind of void. Strange, amusing even, to see the way men's imaginations were prone to fill it, making every stray sound an enemy, the slightest noise some malevolent foe. Such a funny thing, the mind; never so lively as when separated from what it knows.

He'd not known the habit in himself until now, until this very night in fact, hanging, bowed over, on the neck of his horse. He could feel her fear too, warm against his cheek, surging through her rapid pulse, heaving through her haggard snorts as she plodded on through the rain. How he hated the rain. Every drop stung; drumming against the wound on his head where lobes of flimsy flesh flapped in the wind like a tossed sail. He could feel the cold knifing into him through the gash there, down his neck and chest like the blood he'd bled. The blood he'd seen. All that blood. More than he'd ever forget, there when he closed his eyes, there when he opened them too, stained to his thoughts.

He fumbled by the throatlash for his skin of water.

Remembered he'd dropped it hours before. His fingers weak and clumsy now. Hard to stay awake. He tried to lift his head to see which way his mare was carrying him. Too dark to tell. Nothing but blue fog lifting against the night as the moors steamed in the downpour. He willed her to keep going. Could feel she wanted to stop, the sag and halt of her steps, the way her hooves scraped with each pace as though too heavy for her to lift.

He bowed his head, too tired, then twitched awake. There was a muffled voice on the wind. Someone close by. He strained to lift himself, saw the flicker of light in the distance. Campfire. Maybe shelter. He leant on the reins and let her carry him on toward it until the voice grew louder, the firelight brighter. Moments later the voice was near, and then shouting. Then he was being dragged from his horse, his weight borne up and carried. He heard himself groan as his broken thigh was handled, his slashed hip, his cracked ribs pressed as he was brought to rest, wheezing, on his back, staring up into the night sky watching bolts of rain shoot down like tiny falling stars, each one glinting in the campfire as they dropped from the cold black emptiness above.

"Quickly, quickly... Bring the water."

And so it came, running over his lips and down the sides of his mouth. He gawped like a fish, nearly a day since he'd drunk. He heard someone speaking but couldn't make sense of the words. He felt so tired. Felt like sleeping.

"Salidor?" The voice hovered above, owner just out of view.

He blinked at the sound of his name, stared up from the ground to the voice that had spoken it. Two faces stared down at him through the downpour. One man. One boy. The man was familiar. He fumbled for a name. "Josef?"

"No... No, it is Daneel."

Salidor looked up at him, wondered vaguely at what he

was doing here, why he wasn't in Hanesda. Then wondered who the boy was at his side.

"What happened to you, Salidor?"

Salidor blinked again, slowly, his thoughts sluggish;, his breaths felt heavy. He was so tired. "Jasinda is gone," he said, weaker than a whisper. "It took her. It…" He winced at the memory, the words alone enough to bring it all back, her screaming, her blood, so much blood. "It is gone," he said. "It is all gone… they are coming."

Daneel knelt, examining Salidor's swollen face. The flesh was broken, half-torn away on one side. Gore hung from his jaw and neck. He'd lost an eye. Daneel could see shards of cheekbone prodding through the red seeping viscera. There was another deep gash in Salidor's shoulder, opened threads of sinew showing down to the bone.

"Salidor. Who did this to you?"

But the man's remaining eye had closed. His breaths were slowing. Daneel stretched out an arm to ward Noah back, keep him from crowding the broken man on the ground. The boy obeyed quickly and stepped away to watch from the campfire, one part curious, two parts afraid. They'd journeyed this way from the Swift after leaving Josef, going north through the Salt Lands to avoid whatever pursuit might come. No point returning the boy to Dumea and what remained of his kin. The Brotherhood would be waiting for them there, likely squatting in the city's watchtower with a longbow. Josef had always been good with the longbow.

And so Daneel came north instead, planned to go up to the Ivory Pass by the Calapaari Sea, maybe find a boatman to take them across and beyond the Sovereignty, out of reach of the Brotherhood, if that could ever be so. But that was before staring down into the ripped, battered face of the man before him; wounds unlike any he'd ever heard of or seen before.

"You must tell me who did this to you, Salidor."

"They are coming…"

"Who? Who are coming?"

"Gone," Salidor said, his words barely more than a faint breath. "The city is gone… all dead… they are coming."

"Who, Salidor? Tell me."

The man blinked, his mouth gaped as though trying to imbibe the air.

"Beasts," he said finally. "Strange beasts… Dark beasts." And then he closed his remaining eye, and said nothing more at all.

Next —

PALE KINGS

ACKNOWLEDGMENTS

"Writing is not a career for those who are easily discouraged."
So said someone famous and wise whose name now escapes
me...

But for my part, to have gone from the tiniest kernel of
an idea to writing a novel and eventually seeing it published
has been both a surreal experience and a long, often bruising
journey. It's one I couldn't have made alone, which means I
have a few people to whom I owe both what remains of my
sanity, and a debt of gratitude.

So, to Elizabeth. Your encouragement was in many ways a
catalyst to my beginning this journey. Thank you for always
being excited to read my writing. I'll always celebrate and
appreciate the part you played in this story. Always.

I am so thankful too for the love and beauty of my family.
My mother, Shimeer, whose strength, courage and dignity
I will never be able to fathom or measure. My brother, and
hero, Daniel. My sisters: Iveren, Iember and Hannah; whose
personalities and colour continue to shape and build me –
thank you for being the beautiful and dynamic women that
you are. And special thanks to Iveren in particular for your
reading of those earlier drafts – your care, patience and
encouragement were invaluable. Each of you are, and always
will be, a profound treasure.

Burt Ronald... Dude, I'm so thankful for your friendship

these last couple of years in particular - your insight, your empathy, and of course the banter. Love you, brother.

To Rachael Kearney, for seeing both this journey and its destination, and cheering me on toward it. You are a precious gift. Thank you.

Thanks to Chris Dabbs and the rest of the Unlimited Potential gang for teaching me to take my passion and dreams seriously.

To my brothers from other mothers: Eniola Foloranmi, Michael Nnadede, Mikey and Ian Fennell, Adrian Ekechukwu, Michael Carolan, Lance and Damien Salmon, Leigh O'Neill and the rest, for being what you are and keeping me company on this crazy ride called life. All love.

Special thanks to John Wordsworth for your diligence, enthusiasm and guidance and for being the literary equivalent of Jerry Maguire. And to my agent, Robert Dinsdale, for your keen insight as a reader, and for the belief and, quite frankly, inhuman levels of perseverance and passion you showed in helping to bring this project to fruition. I am unspeakably grateful.

Thanks too to the editing savant otherwise known as Phil Jourdan. You have a dark and mysterious gift, my friend. To Marc Gascoigne, for being an all-round publishing don and a dude seemingly incapable of anything less than deeply fascinating conversation. And last, but the opposite of least, my deepest thanks to God for all of the above, you make each day that much more fun and beautiful.